BITTER
PASSAGE

BITTER PASSAGE

A NOVEL

COLIN MILLS

LAKE UNION
PUBLISHING

Published by Lake Union Publishing, Seattle

www.apub.com

Amazon, the Amazon logo, and Lake Union Publishing are trademarks of Amazon.com, Inc., or its affiliates.

ISBN-13: 9781662520600 (paperback)
ISBN-13: 9781662520594 (digital)

Cover design by Faceout Studio, Spencer Fuller
Cover image: © duncan1890 / Getty

Printed in the United States of America

For Annelie, Sky, and Ainsley

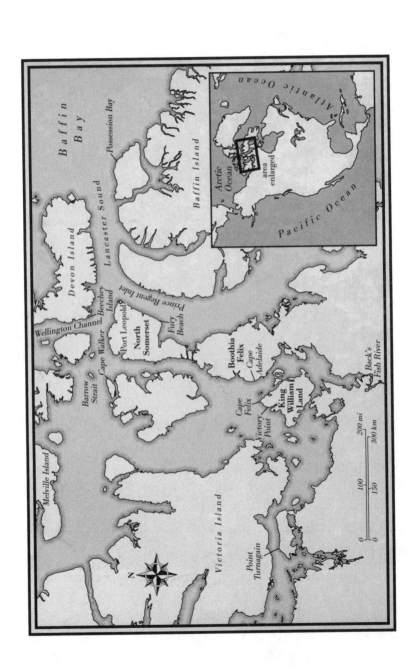

In May 1845, Sir John Franklin left the Thames in command of two Royal Navy ships—HMS *Erebus* and HMS *Terror*—to seek a navigable sea route across the top of the Americas. Having searched for the Northwest Passage for nearly three decades, the Admiralty was optimistic. Franklin's ships featured canned provisions, steam locomotives, and screw propellers. He told a passing whaling captain he could make his provisions "spin out seven years" by supplementing his stores with game. One hundred and twenty-nine men sailed north across Baffin Bay, bound for Lancaster Sound.

Three years later, they had not returned.

HMS *Enterprise*, commanded by Captain Sir James Clark Ross, and HMS *Investigator*, under Captain Edward Bird, left England in 1848 to search for Franklin. Stopped by the ice that winter at Port Leopold, sledge teams did not leave the ships to search for Franklin until the spring of 1849.

Four years had passed since Franklin's expedition was last seen.

CHAPTER ONE

The sun had not set for three weeks, but snow still covered much of the land. Seven men walked south along a barren coastline.

The wind was a bayonet at Adams' throat. He adjusted his goggles and pulled his cap lower. Licks of pain curled up his legs, the flesh ropy and sore on his bones. The search party had left the ships at Port Leopold only a day before, but nine months' confinement aboard ship by the winter snows—and four months at sea before that—had left his muscles spongy from inactivity. His pulse flickered in his throat. Under his thick hose and stockings, his toes were a dull ache in his boots. His scarf reeked of stale tobacco. He eased it down from over his nose to hawk and spit on the snow. The wind carried the taste of salt off the bergs in the inlet to the east.

Adams glanced back at the five men marching over the hard-packed snow behind him. Three seamen dragged the heavier four-hundred-pound sledge—the pock-scarred baker Porter; Worthington of the piratical red beard; and the wiry, terrier-like Payne. Two others—the tall, hulking Billings and Humphreys, a corporal in *Investigator*'s marine detachment—hauled the other. Grunting and puffing, they bent into the cold wind, leaning into their harnesses with scarves tight across their noses and gloved hands thrust into coat pockets. Their beards were flecked with ice, their eyes rimmed with red. Humphreys was limping.

Adams thought of his sore feet and knew that the men, forced to pull such weight across the frozen ground like yoked beasts, would be in a worse state than he. In weeks of training on the frozen surface of the bay at Port Leopold, the skin of their hands and feet had torn like tissue, scabbing over and tearing again with little time to callus. They had come to him in the sick bay, peeling bloody stockings from stinking feet like so much dead skin.

Lieutenant Robinson strode thirty yards ahead, straight-backed, his shotgun strapped across his shoulders. He gripped a telescope in his gloved hand. Robinson had picked the men for their endurance and would demand that they march without complaint. He would look to Adams to treat them. Adams had added extra linen bandages to his medical bag before departure but now feared his supplies would not last.

Adams wondered if *Investigator*'s other sledge teams were faring any better. His friend, Lieutenant John Barnard, had led a party north across Barrow Strait while Lieutenant Willy Browne had gone east across Prince Regent Inlet. Mission commander Captain Sir James Clark Ross had taken his own team from *Enterprise* west across the northern coastline of North Somerset. Captain Bird had ordered Adams to join Robinson's party for a trek eighty miles southward, to the twenty-five-year-old wreck site at Fury Beach.

"Sir John knew Parry off-loaded provisions there in '25, when *Fury* sank," Bird said. "It's a place he might go if his ships were frozen in."

Snow fell in tiny flakes, spinning in the wind. Adams scanned the treeless landscape as he walked, blinking in the grey light. The sledge runners hissed over the snow. The brown outline of thousand-foot hills rose in the west. He watched for a plume of smoke or a waving arm as they picked their way over patches of bare gravel. To the east, ice floes jostled in Prince Regent Inlet, buffeted by the currents like slow-moving boats on the surface of a pond. Great broken chunks of ice scraped on the shallow floor of the inlet, snapping with loud reports like gunfire.

The snow stopped, and the sun emerged. Adams thought the air was so clear it might shatter like glass if only he extended a finger. The cold left a smooth, stony sensation on his tongue. Far above, the first ivory gull of the season paused at the apex of a steep ascent, its wings spread and its head pointed to the heavens, a tiny angel in rapture. Adams bowed his head, put his hand on his coat pocket, and moved his gloved fingertips over his Bible.

He again counted the days until Sunday. It was Thursday, an eternity since the ship's company had last gathered for divine service on *Investigator*'s upper deck. Sunday services had anchored him in the year since their departure from the Thames, drawing him back to God after endless mundane days treating blisters and sprained wrists. Even after the ship was frozen in the ice at Port Leopold and the black hand of winter closed around them, Adams bowed his head daily to pray with men crushed by melancholy. Now, out on the empty, snow-covered expanse, without the opportunity to commune with the men in worship, he felt unmoored. Robinson had rejected his request to stop for even a brief prayer after six hours of walking.

"There can be no stopping," the lieutenant had said. "You wanted them kept warm. Walking keeps them warm."

———

Lieutenant Robinson paused to wait for Adams and the sledge team to close the two-hundred-yard gap that had opened between them. He bent to fill his canteen from a thin stream that trickled out of the bare hills to the west. The clouds dissolved, and the sky was bright and hollow.

He watched Adams approach across the gravel. Would this be another request for a prayer? He was suspicious of the man's righteousness, mistrustful of anyone so convinced that his achievements hinged on some heavenly edict. A man's ingenuity and courage determined his fate, of that Robinson was certain. Absolute faith unsettled him. He thought it lazy for a man to submit so utterly to an invisible power, especially one so capricious. It was too easy to blame one's failures on the Almighty. Too easy to make excuses. He decided he would permit Adams a brief prayer only on Sundays. They had no time to waste.

Robinson led the searchers down from the cliffs and onto the shingle. Sheets of frost-shattered limestone disintegrated under their boots and sliced chunks from their soles. At times the beach disappeared, catching them between cliffs and floes thrust up from the sea by wind and tide. They passed the sledges over their heads and clambered over twenty-foot hummocks of ice. The wind cut through Robinson's sweater and heavy coat. Sweat ran down his face and froze in his beard. Snow fell again, specks of powder twirling around them in clouds. The men brushed the particles from their coats and caps and trudged through the drift to the summit of a small hill. To the west was a deserted landscape pitted with ravines.

Robinson called a halt as a commotion erupted in the water near the shore. Amid a great blowing and splashing, half a dozen long narwhal tusks emerged like javelins from among the chunks of ice floating in the inlet. They clattered against each other before the round, speckled heads of the whales appeared, chasing baitfish through the rippling water. The seven men stood and watched as the narwhals butted each other, jostling and urgent in their hunt. A moment later, the small fish dispersed, and the whales vanished beneath the surface as suddenly as they had appeared. As the search party walked on along the shore, the only sound was the crunch of boots on the stones.

At five o'clock in the morning, Robinson ordered a halt on a narrow beach. The wind died, and the air was still. Without the ceaseless, numbing wind in his face, his cheeks glowed with warmth. The men dropped their harnesses and sank to their haunches. They drank from their canteens and urinated in the snow with long sighs. Steam rose from scalps matted with sweat as they removed their scalskin caps. Men coughed and spat. Five-hundred-foot cliffs towered above their heads.

Wisps of clouds shrouded the broken cliff-tops, stoles around the shoulders of giants. As Adams approached him, Robinson craned his neck to gaze up at the parapets.

"God creates such beauty," said Adams. "Does He not?"

Robinson grunted. "I see little but ice and rock, and rather too much of both."

"The sunsets. The shape of the clouds. Unearthly."

"You will see sunsets and clouds daily in England, too, if you look."

"Look at the colours in the ice. Green, like emeralds mounted in glass."

Robinson tipped up his canteen and drank. He wiped his mouth with the back of his glove. Ripples rose on the surface of the inlet.

"Look at that," Adams said. "The wind over the water is like the breath of God. Do you know your Psalms? Oh, to 'dwell in the house of the Lord all the days of my life, to behold the beauty of the Lord.'"

Robinson eyed him. There was something almost laudable in the man's tenacious cheer. "That wind will cut you in two when it picks up."

The ripples on the water disappeared. Silence fell. The sun was a bronze lamp above a mirrored sea, reflecting off puddles of molten copper in the ice.

"I have never seen a sun like that," said Adams.

"It will only last a minute." Robinson hitched his knapsack higher on his shoulder. "I am sure God made this land with a purpose in mind, but I cannot imagine what it is."

The big seaman, Billings, stopped, his head thrust forward like a foxhound's. He raised a hand and pointed. "There! I see something in the water!"

The faces of the other six men turned as one to peer through slitted eyes into the white haze to the south. Robinson's heart knocked in his chest. He removed his goggles and shielded his face with a gloved hand, but he saw nothing.

"Where, Billings?"

"In the water!" Billings began to jump up and down. "I saw it moving."

"Is it men?" Robinson scanned the landscape in vain. "Is it men, Billings?" He unslung his telescope and raised it. The rest of the party stood in silence, awaiting his verdict.

"Something moves there, near the shore." He spoke with the telescope still held to his eye. "Perhaps an upturned boat, but I cannot make it out."

He and Adams hurried along the shingle, leaving the men to drag the sledges in their wake. A mile down the beach, they halted. Fifty yards from them in the inlet, a flock of petrels attacked a whale carcass rolling in the shallows. The screeching birds fell like harpies from the air to rip and tear at the carcass, tossing their heads back to swallow bits of blubber. Spreading their wings for balance, they climbed atop each other, their beaks snapping and stabbing and slashing at the quivering flesh.

Robinson sighed. He chewed his lip and kicked at the stones. Of course it would have been too convenient to find Franklin and his men so soon. *Adams will say God has decided to make us work for it,* he thought. *That great rewards are not so easily won. On this at least, I would agree.*

Billings and Humphreys arrived and shrugged off their harnesses. Billings stood at Adams' shoulder, staring wide-eyed at the dead whale. Robinson studied the big man. When the other men tired after hours of walking, Billings showed no sign of fatigue. He patted Billings once on the shoulder.

"Well done, Billings. Speak up if you see anything else."

The four other seamen arrived, gawping at the carcass trembling in the cold grey water. They slapped Billings on the back and tousled the big man's hair.

"How did you see this from so far, Jimmy?" Payne asked.

Humphreys clapped Billings on the shoulder. "Jimmy, you'll never want for work once you're paid off. Every picklock in London will want you on the street corner, watching for the sheriff while he goes to work."

Billings drew himself up, grinning. "I can see real good."

———

They made camp in the lee of an enormous block of ice thrust onto the shore by the tide. Adams instructed Worthington to fetch fuel from the sledge and warm their salt pork on the little stove. The smell of tobacco and unwashed bodies was sour in the tent. The stove hissed as the sailcloth shuddered and flapped. Robinson sent two seamen to scour the shoreline for driftwood, but they returned empty-handed.

The men smoked in silence, their expressions distant, faces like masonry. The fatty smell of the pork rose from the pot, the heavy odour slick in Adams' nostrils and thick at the back of his throat. He leant over the stove and sniffed. The pork had not gone bad.

Thank you, Lord, he thought. *We have so little and need so much.*

Worthington distributed each man's biscuit ration. The hungry men plucked their pork from the water before it heated through. Billings wolfed his portion down in three bites and sat looking around, forlorn. The others ignored him, staring straight ahead and chewing without comment. Their exhalations and the stove's heat rose and condensed on the canvas ceiling. Within minutes, freezing water droplets fell, prompting curses as they burst on noses and trickled down necks.

Adams ate mechanically, working his jaws carefully before tearing off another strip of the hard flesh. He paused to pick scraps of fat from between his teeth with the tip of his knife. His biscuit had frozen solid under the sledge cover and had yet to thaw. He cupped his ration in his hands and breathed on it, tapping it on his knees until it was soft enough to gnaw. The broken fragments were like sand in his mouth. He sipped from his canteen between bites to force the biscuit down.

Stiff with cold, the men unrolled the waterproof floorcloth, laid out the buffalo robes, and took out their blanket bags. Facing away from the men, Robinson sat in silence, writing in his journal. Before letting them sleep, Adams examined the men's blisters and wind-swollen faces. He rubbed and blew on half-frozen fingers more marble than flesh. Billings' huge shoulders bore angry red welts from the track rope.

"You're a good fellow, Jimmy," said Adams, "but you do too much alone. Share the load."

Billings bobbed his head like a puppy and looked at the ground. "Yes, sir."

Payne and Worthington complained of sore feet. The eyes of the fourth man, Porter, were bloodred from the glare off the snow.

"Use the green crape I gave you," said Adams. "And wear your goggles. Or you won't see what pies you're making when you get home."

Porter pressed his palms to his eyes and sucked air through his teeth. "I think there might be an easier way than this to earn the money for my shop. I'll have to sell them at tuppence each to make it worth the effort."

Payne grunted. "Tuppence for a bloody meat pie? Would you pay that, Jimmy?"

Billings swung his shaggy head around, a vacant grin on his face. He nodded. "I like pies."

"You silly bugger, you gave all your wages to your ma."

Billings touched an index finger to his lip, then nodded again, smiling. "But I promised I'd buy a pie at his shop."

"Get him to make you one when we reach Fury Beach," said Payne. "Should be flour and sugar there."

Billings looked baffled. "Why?"

"I told you, Jimmy," Porter said. "Captain Parry left barrels of stuff there when *Fury* was wrecked: flour, peas, sugar."

"Bloody Esquimaux would've eaten the lot by now," said Payne. "Or the bears."

"It ain't what they eat. Why d'you think we're goin' there? To see if Sir John's there."

Worthington sighed. "When I get home, there's only one thing I want to do, and it don't involve eating a pie."

"Your wife will charge you for it," Payne shot back.

The men spluttered with laughter. Billings' cheeks reddened. He smiled and turned his face into his shoulder like an abashed child. Robinson lay down in his blanket bag and rolled onto his side, facing the tent wall.

Adams knelt next to Humphreys, who sat with his head bowed, his eyes shut in pain.

"Your feet?" Adams asked.

Humphreys nodded.

"Show me."

The marine's hands went to his boots but then fell away. He shook his head, huffing through his beard. "Can't get 'em off."

"We must look after your feet. Your Alice will want you to go dancing."

Humphreys grunted. "Aye, that she will. There's a blind fiddler—Welsh fella—comes by the public house in Axbridge most weeks. They'll let you dance for a penny."

Adams grasped one of Humphreys' boots and eased it off, then rolled the man's stocking down and removed it. He recoiled, wincing at the acrid, vinegary odour. The corporal groaned and fell back on his elbows, grunting through clenched teeth. Adams pulled his scarf over his nose and inspected the man's foot. A long blister ran along the ball of the foot, crowned with a sac of loose white skin. Adams pricked it gently with the tip of his knife. Pinkish fluid ran down the blade. He pressed a scrap of linen on the blister to absorb it. The flesh of the foot was bone white, but the toes appeared scalded, the colour of claret, and grotesquely swollen. Adams took each toe between his thumb and forefinger, inspecting it carefully. Detecting no sign of decay, he bound Humphreys' toes with a strip of linen.

"Put your dry socks on," he said. "I will have Payne make the cocoa."

Adams remembered what Tatham, *Investigator*'s ice master, had told him on their way north through Davis Strait the year before. A former whaling captain, Tatham made a living piloting merchantmen and supply ships through the ice to the Hudson Bay outposts and fishing stations on the Labrador coast.

"They don't know what's comin'," the ice master had said as the men danced to the fiddle on the lower deck after supper. "They're still on fresh rations. Wait till they've been on salt junk and biscuit for a whole winter and haven't had a woman in a year. And haulin' sledges is no easy toil. It can break a man."

———

Adams and the sledge team followed Robinson along the shore to a small bay fed by a river that stole into the canyons to the west, then walked inland until they reached a point shallow enough to wade across. Adams and Robinson strode ahead up the opposite slope while the men followed a hundred yards behind. Robinson swept the hills to the west with his telescope, then scanned the inlet to the east. The two officers pulled their scarves over their noses as the men hauled the sledges up the gravel hillside.

Adams thrust his hands into his pockets. "Humphreys' feet are bad," he said. "He got them wet, and there is no chance to dry them."

"Are the others afflicted?"

"They will be. One pound of salt pork per day, a pound of biscuit. A bit of sugar and tea and chocolate. It is not much, given what you ask of them."

"It is all they will get." Robinson's tone was flat. "You should not be so familiar with them."

Adams frowned. "Familiar?"

"You rub their sore feet, make them tea."

"You require them to haul. Their welfare is my concern."

"Do not imagine that these men are your friends."

No, not friends, Adams thought, *but after a year together in the belly of a ship, one cannot help but know a man.* Billings, the heavily muscled man-child, who whittled toy boats and hoped to become a ship's carpenter—strong, obedient, incapable of independent thought, and oddly untouched by the brutality of his Mancunian upbringing. Payne, whose ribald jokes and lurid tales were so popular on the lower deck that the illiterate seaman had once asked Adams to write them down so Payne might have them published upon his return to England. Porter, the would-be piemaker, who claimed he once broke a man's leg with a shovel in a brawl. Worthington, who boasted that his wife was a housemaid in a large manor and cheerfully admitted, when challenged, that she was also occasionally a whore.

"I am only civil to them," Adams told Robinson. "A dog that has known only ill treatment turns mean."

Robinson regarded Adams with a sceptical eye. "For a man confined with them for a year, you understand nothing about them. Do not afford them ideas above their station."

"We are all united in our purpose."

Robinson grimaced and slapped his thigh. "You could not be more wrong. These men care nothing for Franklin. They are shoemakers and farmhands. Their allegiance is to whoever gives them a full belly. Were you in command, we would have a song before bedtime, or a story and a cup of tea when they tire and put down their track ropes. They must haul and lift and pull when ordered, and you must not let them forget it."

———

Adams lay in his blanket. Robinson meant to drive the men like livestock, then. Adams knew better than to contradict him, but the lieutenant was wrong. He wanted to tell him that stories do not lead to weakness. They fire passion in a man, drive him to great discoveries.

"Unknown Parts," he whispered.

"What's that, Mister Adams?" Billings lay awake beside him. "What's Unknown Parts?"

Adams smiled. "Just something I remember from when I was a boy, Jimmy. When I was five, my father would unroll great maps on the table. I remember him tapping a place on the paper. 'Look,' he would say. 'Look at Africa. What does it say there?' I used to stand on a chair and stretch my neck to see. There was a large blank section between Abyssinia and Guinea."

"And what did it say there?"

Humphreys spoke from across the tent. "I can guess. Unknown Parts."

"Exactly," said Adams. He remembered his father saying the words, uttering each syllable like a jewel to hold up and admire. "Then he would point to Greenland, just a lump near the top of the world. Then Baffin Bay to the west. Between Baffin Bay and Behrings Strait, the map was blank. 'Somewhere in there is the North-West Passage,' he would say. 'The greatest prize of all. Imagine being the first to find it!'" Adams could still see his father, sitting back in his chair, a faraway look on his face. "'What might we discover there?' he'd say. 'Mountain ranges? Great lakes?'" Adams made a face for Billings, his eyes wide and staring. "'Mysterious creatures?'"

Billings giggled and hid his face in his blanket. Silence in the tent. All the men were listening now. Adams thought of his father pulling him close, placing him on his knee.

"He used to tell me there is no greater calling than discovering uncharted lands. Every Christian man must spread civilisation and the word of God to the poor, ignorant masses. And he said it takes a special man to venture into those blank spaces, the Unknown Parts. Dangerous work. One must face disease, dreadful storms, savage natives."

Payne grunted. "And ice and snow enough to freeze yer arse."

Adams smiled. "That too. Once upon a time, the empire needed fighting men like Nelson and Wellington. Now it needs men like Cook and Clapperton. Empires are made through exploration now, not conquest." He propped himself on his elbow and looked Billings in the eye. "Make no mistake. It is God's work."

He lay back and stared at the tent's ceiling, remembering how his hand had shaken one night as he held up a book and asked his father to read it. His father's eyebrows had risen in mock surprise as the flames in the fireplace cast a glow across his whiskered face, tiny shadows deepening the wrinkles around his eyes.

"Read?" he had asked. "Read what? Let me see that." He reached for the book and peered at the cover as if for the first time. He read aloud, his voice precise and stentorian: *Narrative of a Journey to the Shores of the Polar Sea, in the Years 1819–1822*. Good heavens," he said, looking gravely down his nose. "Who wrote this?"

It was part of their game. "Captain Franklin!"

"Ah, Captain John Franklin." His father had smiled and nodded. Adams had held his breath as his father sipped from a pewter mug. In the fire's light, tiny droplets of ale had sparkled on his beard. "A very fine man. He is brave. He is gallant." He lifted the book and winked at his son. "Shall we find out just how brave he is?"

"Yes!"

"Well, then. Where were we?" His father had opened the book and flicked through the pages with his fingertip. "Ah, yes. When we last left the stalwart Captain Franklin, he and his men were retreating from Point Turnagain through the barren lands to Fort Enterprise, were they not? And what were they doing?"

"Starving!"

"Indeed. They were starving." He raised the book to catch more of the reflected light of the fire, and read aloud. "'The carcass of a deer was discovered in the cleft of a rock, into which it had fallen in the spring. It was putrid, but little less acceptable to us on that account in our present circumstances; and a fire being kindled, a large portion was devoured on the spot, affording us an unexpected breakfast, for in order to husband our small remaining portion of meat, we had agreed to make only one scanty meal a day.'"

The five-year-old Edward had stared into the flames, entranced, imagining he was at Franklin's side, his telescope in one hand, Bible in the other. He could see the two of them summiting a mountain, silhouetted against the halo of a rising sun, the Passage stretching out before them in the distance. Franklin's hand was on his shoulder.

Billings' voice tugged Adams from his reverie. "Mister Adams, why does the Admiralty want to find the North-West Passage?"

"'Cos they've fuck all else to do," Porter said, his voice muffled by his blanket.

Adams nodded. "Jimmy, it is thirty years since Napoleon was beaten. What is a navy to do when there is nobody left to fight? I shall tell you: it can find new territories, for England and for God. A passage through the ice across the top of America will make getting from England to China much quicker. Empires are built that way."

He chuckled at Billings' blank expression.

"You see, Jimmy," he continued, "man covets that which he lacks. He seeks to learn that of which he is ignorant. Much of the ocean north of the Americas has never been explored. Nobody knows what is there. Once the unknown is known, it may lose its allure, but until then, it shines very, very brightly."

CHAPTER TWO

Robinson woke the men in the evening. Their blanket bags were crusted with frost from their breath. They drank cocoa and ate biscuit, and then he led them south along the broken shore. A faint halo ringed the sun. Icebergs in the inlet were turquoise at their jagged tips, but a deep blue lay trapped within. Birds jostled on ledges hundreds of feet above them.

Robinson led them across a patch of gravel coated with a carapace of hard ice. For a time, the sledge slid smoothly over the ice, and their pace quickened. Then, without warning, the snow was knee deep. They walked hunched over, their faces averted from a wind that picked up long tendrils of drift and bore down on them like an army of phantoms over the ridges and depressions.

They came to a ragged circle of stones that might once have been a tent ring, but blooms of orange and green lichen suggested they had sat unmoved for centuries. Whale bones lay scattered. Nearby they discovered a pit in the earth where Esquimaux had once cached meat or blubber before concealing it with driftwood and moss. The walls of the hole were lined with flat stones, several of which had toppled into the bottom. Robinson ordered Billings and Payne to search the pit. They found nothing, and the party walked on. The raw wind swept over them. Lightning crackled far to the south, bony fingers reaching down from the heavens to rake the earth.

Porter was snow-blind. Adams bound his eyes, tied a rope around his waist, and tethered it to the sledge. Porter stumbled along behind Payne and Worthington, kicking stones across the gravel. Billings pulled the smaller sledge alone without complaint. Humphreys hobbled behind the others, leaning on a staff cut from a tentpole. He fell back, disappearing whenever the party descended a hill or turned into a bay. Robinson strode on ahead.

They pitched the tent on a flat expanse of gravel. Adams unwrapped the strips of crape from Porter's head. The man swore and recoiled at the dim light of the candle.

"It's like bits of glass in my eyes," he said. Tears left pale tracks on his grimy face. "It burns inside, but you don't feel it till it's too late."

"It is why we walk at night," said Adams. "It would be worse during the day."

Porter sighed. "I hated the winter when we were frozen in at Port Leopold. Dark all the day. Stuck below deck all the time, nowhere to go, nothin' to do. But I miss it now, that darkness."

"And when winter returns, you will want the light," said Adams. "You will darn socks for your mates just for a piece of candle. You will be atop the mainmast in March, watching the horizon for the sun."

Porter nodded. "I cried when I saw it."

Adams bound Porter's head with clean crape and told him to lie down.

"I don't think we're gonna find 'em." Porter's voice was a whisper. He turned on his side, facing away from Adams.

"What did you say?" Adams asked.

"Can't see how we're meant to." The blanket muffled Porter's voice. "What's the point of watching every hill and beach for Franklin's men? If you look at this bloody place for too long, it burns out your fuckin' eyes."

As the men slept, Adams listened to their breathing. He opened the tiny locket Frances had given him when he told her he would ask her father, the rector, for her hand upon his return from the Arctic. Her father was a genial man with a keen interest in science and discovery that his daughter had inherited. He had made no attempt to hide his affection for Adams but cautioned him to be patient.

"I am not a wealthy man," he had said, "but I would sooner have a good man for her husband than a rich one. You have my permission to write to Frances, but even a good man must acquire some means if he is to take a wife. I ask you to do that. She is still young, only eighteen."

Adams touched his fingertip to the lock of hair she had enclosed in the locket. He imagined her praying for him at St Mary's Church and doing embroidery for the charity bazaar. How many times in the year since they parted had she consulted the fortune teller at the market about his fate? Crystal gazing had become her guilty pleasure. He knew she repented each Sunday but would not begrudge her a harmless amusement.

Dearest Frances, he wrote. *Lieutenant Robinson dismisses the men's motives as merely pecuniary, and I fear greatly he is correct. This, I believe, is a greater risk to our mission than the cold or weather. Strength arises from belief, from faith. I see now I must tend more to the men's spirits than to their physical ailments, but we have few opportunities to commune in worship. Can one man make another brave? Surely our chances of success are better if the men embrace the higher purpose of their task. Humphreys' feet are frozen, and Porter is blind, but I feel certain they will better endure their trials if only they acknowledge that sore feet and burning eyes are but paltry concerns when rescuing the man who would find the Passage for England. I do what I can to inspire them. I would be their lantern in the mist if only Mister Robinson would allow it.*

———

"I always wanted to be Sir John," Adams said.

"*Be* him?" Billings appeared bewildered.

"When I was a boy, Jimmy. I was five years old. My father made me a little wooden cutlass I fancied a crusader might wield as he entered Jerusalem. I used to play at explorers with my brother, Richard."

"A toy sword." Billings smiled.

"Exactly. A toy. I used to wave it about when I stood on the low stone wall snaking along the boundary between my father's estate and the neighbouring farm. I would shout, 'I, Captain John Franklin, hereby claim this North-West Passage for King George!'"

Adams remembered standing on a low hill two hundred yards from the main house. He could make out its sandstone walls and slate tiles. The tower of the parish church in Great Barton rose above the trees in the distance.

"My brother wouldn't always let me be Franklin, though. He had a wooden sword too. And a paper helmet. And he was three years my senior. Every time he would say I got to be Franklin last time, so it was his turn this time. I had to be someone else."

Billings looked confused. "Who else could you be, sir?"

Adams winked at him. "Richard wanted me to be John Ross, but I refused. He hadn't found anything at the time. He'd even missed the entrance to Lancaster Sound. But that was before his expedition to the bottom of Prince Regent Inlet in '29."

Adams recalled the tousled grey sky that day, the stiff breeze that had ruffled the long grass on the hill. He had wondered if the prospect of bad weather would prompt their father to return home early from London. The boys' governess had excused them from their lessons an hour early to mark the occasion. Desperate for peace, their pregnant mother shooed them from the house. She lay, white faced and sweating, on her bed, her enormous belly slung beside her.

"Richard insisted I be Lieutenant Back or Captain Parry," Adams continued. "Or poor Lieutenant Hood—he died on Franklin's journey down the Coppermine. But we both always wanted to be Franklin. One day we could not agree and had to use our wooden swords to settle the matter. As we were about to have at each other, the gander waddled up the hill from the house with three geese in tow. He was in a bad mood too."

Billings spoke in a hushed voice. "What did you do?"

"I pointed the tip of my wooden cutlass at the gander and shouted, "We ate our shoes and we are very brave!" I gave him a whack on the neck with the flat of the sword. That soon sent him packing."

Billings nodded, sombre now. "That *was* brave. I got bit by a gander once."

Adams fell quiet. He would not tell Billings the rest. He would not tell him that a shout from the house startled him and Richard as they duelled. He remembered their father emerging from the garden and starting up the hill. There was an urgency in his movements, something sharp and unfamiliar. He waved with both hands at once, his voice snatched away by the breeze. Unbuttoned at the collar, his white shirt billowed like a sail. Laughing, the boys ran toward him down the slope, scattering the geese. William Adams was not smiling when they approached. Edward's wooden cutlass fell forgotten from his hand.

"Richard!" their father shouted. "Richard, be quick!" His eyes were round, his cheeks flushed. As the boys reached him, their father knelt and placed one hand on Richard's shoulder, breathless from his run up the hill.

"Richard!" he panted. "Run to the town for the midwife. Your mother needs her. Now! Run! As fast as you can."

———

Robinson put down his pen and closed his journal. He put both in his knapsack and placed it under his head. His sleep had been dreamless of late, but when he closed his eyes, he would imagine the future, and it would help him drift off. They would stride across the snow, and Sir John would be there, a wolfskin around his shoulders. Crozier and Fitzjames would be beside him, grinning and doffing their threadbare caps. Franklin's men would all gather behind him, cheering.

Robinson would extend his hand long before they came together, his arm outstretched like a bowsprit. They would shake hands for a long time, Franklin clamping his left hand over their shared grip.

The captain would ask, "What is your name, sir? For it shall be known throughout the empire!"

They would pretend the water in their canteens was brandy and toast the queen. The men would cheer again, and the job would be done.

The news would reach England before they returned to the Thames, carried back by whalers they would meet in Davis Strait. After visiting Whitehall for a private meeting with the First Lord, Robinson would return to Burslem. While his brothers' wives sat blank faced, his own wife, Elizabeth, would smile and wink at him over the dinner table, and afterward his father would regard him with a wholly unfamiliar display of pride.

"You have done well, Frederick," his father would say. "I must confess, you have exceeded my expectations."

Robinson rehearsed the scene in his mind, polishing the finer points like the facets of a gemstone. His father would dismiss the women and invite him to stay for port and cigars. Like distant uncles, his two brothers would blink at him curiously, stiff in their dinner jackets, their whiskers curled in the same style as their father's. But for once, Robinson would not be required to sit in silence and listen to his father and brothers discuss the performance of their cotton mills. Instead, they would toast to his health and lie about how certain they had always been that he would bring great honour to the family. He would decline to linger, and the astonishment on his father's face would be worth a thousand years of indifference and humiliation.

Later, when it was over, he would relay it all to Elizabeth. Recovered from her illness, she would lie beside him in bed, her head on his chest.

"My face betrayed no malice, darling," he would say. "I made sure of that."

She would smile. "You are not a vengeful man."

"I put down my glass and pushed my shoulders back, and I told him, 'I shall not stay this evening because, for the first time, I am invited, not commanded, and because, for the first time, I can refuse you.'"

She would kiss him and tell him how proud she was of him, and for a time it would almost be enough to compensate for his father's disdain.

———

In the early evening, Adams took his shotgun and returned two hours later with five ptarmigan. Payne cleaned the birds and put them in the pot with a can of soup. The men woke to eat. Adams said grace, and they sat silently in a circle, bent over their pannikins. The soup had a pungent, loamy flavour, but Adams, grateful for the fresh food, crushed each piece of flesh between his teeth and held it on his tongue before swallowing.

"Corporal." Robinson looked at Humphreys and gave a curt nod. "The flask, if you will."

Humphreys' beard split in a wide grin. "Yes, sir! Thank you, sir!" He knuckled his forehead and limped from the tent, returning a minute later with the rum flask. A cheer went up from the four seamen.

"Bless you, sir!"

"You're a fine fellow, sir, thank you kindly!"

Humphreys poured each man a gill, then one for himself. They passed around the kettle of water and mixed the grog. Lifting their cups, they toasted the lieutenant's health, then did the same for Adams.

When the men were asleep in their blankets, Adams stepped out of the tent. The sun was a blurry smear on a grey sky. There was no wind, and Adams found he was not shivering. He removed his cap and gloves and flexed his fingers. The morning air was coolly pleasant on his skin.

He took out his sketchbook and sat on a rock overlooking the inlet. He imagined he was out on the ice, looking back at the shore, and drew a broad band of sunlight stretching away across the ice to the base of the cliffs above him. The great rock walls reached into the sky. As he outlined them with his pencil, they became Sir John's epaulets, then his shoulders. The captain's jaw emerged from a bank of clouds lit from behind by a bright, bursting sun. His cocked hat rose proudly. When the image was complete, Sir John was a giant gazing serenely out over the Passage. Adams put down his pencil and sat staring at his creation. He took his Bible from his coat pocket and laid it on the rock before him, then knelt and bowed his head in prayer.

Adams turned his sketchbook to a fresh page and began a new drawing. The image was as clear in his memory as on the day of their departure eighteen months earlier. His pencil moved swiftly and confidently across the page, outlining the masts and hulls along the Thames. He recalled the jolt underfoot as *Investigator* slipped her moorings and began to move. The ratlines thrummed and the boats creaked in their davits as the band played on the pier. The heavy-bellied ship was slow in the water, every last crevice and shelf stuffed with barrels and crates and sacks of food, equipment, and coal. Kites fluttered in the air above the water. Other navy vessels at anchor along the Thames saluted with cannon fire and hoisted signal flags. Men lined the gunwales, flapping their hats and shouting as the crew waved back and sang along to the band. Drawn by the steam tugs, *Enterprise* and *Investigator* slid slowly through the water and made their way out of the river mouth. The crowds on the bank grew smaller, until they were tiny patches of colour on the shore, their fluttering handkerchiefs no more than white dots. Adams remembered thinking, *They will want to tell their friends they saw Franklin's rescuers leave. They will all want to say they were there.*

They woke in the evening. Adams ordered the men to pack the tent as Robinson stood far off on the crest of a distant rise, his telescope raised. They walked through the grey night, their boots in rhythm on the stones. Ducks flew northward and kittiwakes wheeled high above, their white bodies and yellow beaks shiny against their grey wing feathers. At midnight, the sun hovered at its nadir. The clouds fell away, and the sky was a polished bronze cuirass. They trudged on. The sun whitened as it climbed, and the light was sharp in Adams' eyes.

At eight o'clock in the morning, Robinson called a halt. The men dropped to their knees and pressed the palms of their gloved hands to their inflamed eyes. Robinson ordered them to pitch the tent. As Billings and Worthington prepared the supper, Payne and Robinson took inventory of their provisions.

Humphreys limped into camp twenty minutes later. Adams removed the man's boots, and again the tart stench of rotting wood rose. The tips of Humphreys' toes were black. Adams flinched at the smell. The corporal sat staring dully at his feet.

"They offered me three quid to sign," Humphreys said.

"What?"

"When I joined up. I was a weaver back in Middleton. The recruiters said they'd give me three quid to sign my name. Never thought I'd get paid that much to sign my name. The buggers didn't think I could write, but I did it."

He leaned forward, took one of his blackened toes between his thumb and forefinger, and gently moved it back and forth, then sighed and lay back in the tent's gloom. The wiry silhouette of his beard moved when he spoke.

"Only gave me two shillings, sixpence up front, though. Had to wait for the rest. But the wife was happy."

Adams bound Humphreys' toes with fresh linen. He found his own spare pair of dry stockings and put them on the marine's feet.

"Keep them dry," Adams said. "If we must cross a river, get one of the others to carry you on his back."

Humphreys' beard moved again. "I told Alice I'd just be away for the one voyage, y'know. Then they was offering double pay to come and find Sir John." He shook his head and gave a low whistle. "Well, that was quite somethin', wasn't it? How could a man say no to that?"

———

Robinson watched a mass of iron-grey clouds stretch across the southern horizon like a dark gate to another world. He was anxious to make a start. The men ate their biscuit and drank their cocoa; then Robinson ordered them to march. With the inlet to the east, they continued down the coast over large patches of snow-covered ground and sweeping pebble-strewn beaches.

The storm clouds swelled, pushing toward them. Flecks of snow fell. The water in the channel turned black. The clouds bunched and darkened, turning the colour of old copper in the late-evening sun. Robinson crouched on the shale, rubbing dirt between his fingertips. The terrain to the south and west was flat and featureless. He eyed the tumescent sky and spoke to the men.

"Fetch the largest stones you can find—so large each wants two men to lift it. Take one of the sledges. Bring the stones here and fasten the tent ropes to them with your stoutest knots. Do it quickly."

The wind freshened. Robinson and Adams worked with the men to haul the stones to the campsite. The snow stung their faces. The ice in the inlet a hundred yards to the east was no longer visible. They brought the sledges into the tent and looped ropes around the runners to secure them. The gale howled down over the white earth. They lay in their blanket bags with their hands over their ears as the wind tore at the tent, and each man said his own kind of prayer.

———

The gale trapped them in the tent for a day and a half. Robinson lit a single tallow candle and took out his journal and writing implements. Adams puffed on his pipe in the shadows. A soft chorus of snores emanated from the row of seamen.

"To whom do you write?" Adams asked Robinson.

Robinson frowned at him, his pen poised above his ink bottle. The man's clumsy attempts at familiarity vexed him.

Adams looked away. "I did not mean to intrude. I was merely curious."

"Do not be." Robinson returned his attention to his writing. He dipped the nib into his ink bottle. The scratch of the pen across the paper was like a whisper in the tent.

Adams was undeterred. "I write to my sweetheart, Frances. We knew each other as children in Great Barton. One day we hope to marry."

Robinson did not reply or look up. If he ignored the man, Adams might be silent. His pen scribbled. The wind blew. The canvas walls convulsed. The stitched tent seams squeaked and groaned.

"I had not seen her since she was a little girl," Adams continued, "but we were reunited when I visited my brother in Great Barton after my time at Haslar Hospital with Captain Parry."

At this, Robinson put down his pen. "You were at Haslar?"

"I was. For three months, before I transferred to Devonport."

Robinson stroked his whiskers. The man might be of more use than he first imagined. "Tell me, did you treat men at Haslar for scurvy?"

"Mild cases, yes," said Adams. "Many men on the voyage home from the East Indies would eat only salt pork and biscuit. They would not even take their lemon juice."

Robinson grunted. "In the Arctic, scurvy is rarely mild. Franklin's men may be sorely afflicted."

"Fresh food is of the utmost importance. Preferably fresh meat."

"I suspect they will have little of that with them," said Robinson.

"If nothing else is available," said Adams, "I would suggest adopting the Esquimaux diet: reindeer, geese . . . or we could hunt seals."

The man's ignorance rankled him now. "Have you ever shot a seal?" asked Robinson.

"No."

"You cannot even get close to them. They are far too shy."

Robinson lay down in his blanket bag and gazed at the tent's ceiling. He tried to imagine an Esquimaux taking a seal, crouched for hours beside the animal's breathing hole, spear raised. Parry, John Ross—they had shot plenty of game: bears, ducks, foxes. Would there be reindeer? He wondered if a narwhal or beluga could be taken with a shotgun. He extinguished his candle and lay in the gloomy light. The wind plucked and shook the tent walls.

If he found Franklin and his men, how would he feed them?

CHAPTER THREE

When he woke, Adams was shocked at the cold. They lay like dead men, loath to move lest tiny pockets of warmth be lost. Worthington's beard was frozen to his blanket bag. Adams and the other men lit their pipes and puffed until the contents glowed. They held them beside Worthington's chin.

"Don't set me beard alight, you bastards," Worthington muttered.

Worthington coughed until his frozen whiskers parted reluctantly from the wool. He sat up, rubbing his chin. Robinson watched silently from the shadows.

They waited for evening before breaking camp. Adams wrote by candlelight. He squeezed his ink bottle in his armpit to keep it from freezing, shifting uncomfortably on the stones beneath the floorcloth.

Dear Frances, he wrote. *For months I wished only to get off* Investigator. *But now I remember her population of stinking, wasted men as a rich city of souls from which I fear to be torn. When shivering on the ground in my blanket, I recall my damp horsehair mattress as the softest of beds, and the company in the gun room as the wittiest and noblest of men.*

Frances was the only person he had ever told about the day his father returned early from London, the day Edward and Richard had duelled with the gander. When his father ran up the hill in his shirt-sleeves, he had spun Richard around and shoved him in the back.

"Get the midwife! Now!"

William Adams had turned and run back down the slope to the house. Edward stared after him. When he looked around at his brother, the sun was in his eyes. He lifted his arm to shield his face from the glare. Richard was a jerky silhouette disappearing over the top of the hill into a ball of light, his elbows and knees pumping. Edward stood alone on the slope. He looked at the gander. It stared back at him. The wind strengthened, cooling the sweat on his face and arms. White clouds bunched on the horizon to the north. Edward picked up his sword and ran down the hill toward the house.

The midwife had taken two hours to arrive. With her husband's horse lame and unable to pull the box cart, she sent Richard half a mile down the road to the neighbour's cottage to request the use of his two oxen. When she arrived with Richard behind her in the cart, Edward was waiting at the front door, his finger filthy from drawing shapes in the gravel. Richard climbed down from the cart. Edward grabbed his brother's hand tightly and would not release it. The midwife hurried through the door. The boys waited on the front step as the sun sank. Richard put his arm around Edward's shoulder. Both boys were cold now, but neither was brave enough to enter the house to retrieve their coats. The western sky caught fire.

Both boys started as a drawn-out scream split the air, echoing from inside the house and ending in a series of racking sobs. Edward began to cry. The boys' father sent them down the lane to the cottage of a farmer whose children Richard and Edward often played with. But on this night there were no games, nor even conversation. The farmer and his wife spoke in whispers, their faces changing shape in the shifting candlelight. The brothers remained with the farmer's family for the night and the following day. The farmer pulled on his boots every few hours and disappeared, only to return soon after. He shook his head at his wife but said nothing. The farmer returned them to the main house as the sun sank on the third evening.

In their parents' bedroom, William Adams lay on rumpled sheets, his arms around his wife. His red-rimmed eyes were open, seeing nothing. Edward walked over and stood by the bed. His father's chest rose and fell, but he gave no sign he was aware of the boys' presence. Edward looked at his mother. Her eyes were closed. Her arms were by her side, and her white face had been washed. She was dressed in a fresh nightgown. Edward looked in the crib but did not see the baby.

Years later, when they were grown, Richard would say their father left them the day their mother and newborn sister died. In the months after the funeral, William Adams crumpled into himself. The house was silent after supper. There were no more stories of explorers or Vikings, none of the exploits of Nelson or Wellington. The boys' father sat alone near the fire, sipping brandy and staring into the flames. One evening, when Edward approached hopefully with a book cradled in his arms, minutes passed before his father noticed his presence. Blinking, William looked down at the book and touched his son's hair.

"Not tonight, my lad," he said. "Perhaps you could ask Richard to read it to you."

Their father absented himself from their lives gently, melting into the shadows like an actor stepping off a darkened stage. The boys learned from schoolyard whispers that he was spending more time in the public houses. He allowed the boys to roam the hills after their lessons or shoot grouse with their old flintlocks until dusk. Edward could take down a bird from ninety yards in a matter of weeks. William's trips to London became longer and more frequent. The boys spent weeks with only the housekeeper and governess for company.

After his mother's death, the enigma of the Passage was a safe mooring in a current to Edward. He grasped at whatever he still remembered. Richard told him it would not help, that their father was irrevocably changed.

"Father said it was God's work," Edward replied. "The work is still not done. The Passage is not found. I will find it when I am grown."

Richard looked sad. "You are not brave enough."

"I will be. I will be brave. Like Franklin. And Father will be happy again."

Edward was eight when his father boarded the packet from Ipswich to London. The governess called the brothers in before dinner. Tears glistened on her cheeks. The corners of her mouth were turned down. She spread her hands, groping for words.

"'Tis a lot for a man, to look after two little boys," she said.

Edward looked at her and then at Richard, who shrugged. The woman cast her eyes up at the ceiling, desperate, then back at Edward again. Her face was grey in the twilight.

"Some men can fight battles or wild animals, but to raise two boys on their own—that's too frightening for some."

Later, the boat's captain told the boys he did not see their father go over the gunwale.

———

Grey and purple tinged the sky. The outcroppings were alive with guillemots standing like sentries, their heads turning one way, then the other. Eider ducks cruised in formation, diving low over the water. The sea to the east was calm and free of broken ice. Three large icebergs were grounded near the shore.

Robinson and Adams led the men along a stony beach. Whale bones lay strewn along the shore. The two officers eyed the ducks and checked their shotguns. They quickened their pace. The seamen dragged the sledges over the stones a hundred yards behind them.

There was movement in the sky overhead. Robinson threw his shotgun to his shoulder and fired at a flock of ducks. The shot sprayed out into the air, but not a bird fell. The birds shrank to specks and disappeared. Robinson spat on the ground.

A shout went up, and Adams wheeled around. Four seamen had dropped their harnesses and were running directly at the two officers, their faces twisted and red. Their mouths worked, but the wind snatched away their words.

Adams frowned. "Mister Robinson."

Robinson looked up from his gun.

Far down the beach, Worthington stood alone next to the sledges. He faced away from them, staring. Adams scanned the low hills that rose steeply into cliffs above the gravel beach but saw only scattered patches of dirty ice and snow. Then the air shimmered and bent, as on a hot day. The bear materialised like a cloud of fog rising from the earth, its ragged yellow-white coat difficult to discern against the snow-flecked hills.

Adams broke into a run, his shotgun heavy in his hands. Robinson was beside him, his boots slamming on the gravel. Worthington sank to his knees and bowed his head. The bear was so close to him that the man could have reached out and touched its snout. Adams shouted. The bear raised its massive head and sniffed the air. Worthington was between the two officers and the animal.

"Get down, man!" Robinson shouted. His shotgun was at his shoulder, arcing back and forth, seeking a clear shot.

Worthington slumped to the earth and lay still. The bear hesitated, then approached the prostrate man with an odd, stiff-legged gait. It looked at the two officers, who had closed to within forty yards, and growled, a low guttural noise that ended in a hiss. The bear's coat hung off its bony frame, its long tongue uncoiling like a reptile's.

Robinson stood beside Adams with his finger curled around the trigger of his shotgun. Adams thought to cry a warning—*No, not with bird shot!*—but his voice failed, and before Robinson's gun discharged, he knew it was too late. The detonation clubbed Adams across the back of the head, and in that instant the world was snatched away. He fell to his knees with his hands over his ears.

Bells rang in Adams' skull, high and shrill. The volley had caught the bear on the side of its broad head, and the animal wheeled away, pawing at a lacerated ear. The bear's incisors flashed in its long black mouth. Adams thought Robinson must be shouting but heard nothing through the hum in his head. The bear swung around to glare at

Robinson. One enormous paw fell on Worthington's outstretched hand, lifted again; then the bear came at Robinson.

Robinson dropped his shotgun, turned, and ran.

Adams thrust his hand into his shot bag, scrabbling for a heavy ball. He swore, his voice loud in his head, as one brushed his fingertips but rolled from his grasp. He glanced up. The bear was almost on Robinson. The animal stopped, its jaws wide. The droning in Adams' head faded, and he could hear the huffing of the bear, woolly and indistinct, as if his ears were stuffed with cloth. Robinson tripped and fell headlong on the gravel. Three feet from the bear's jaws, he drew his knees to his chest and covered his head with his mittened hands.

Adams upended his shot bag on the ground, blood roaring in his ears. His face glowed hot. He heard the clink of stones shifting under his boots, and then shouting, but whether it was his own voice or Robinson's, he could not tell. He plucked a heavy ball from the gravel, then grabbed his ramrod and shoved it down the muzzle. When he looked up again, the bear had the heel of Robinson's boot in its jaws and was shaking it. The lieutenant lay motionless.

Adams exhaled and lifted the shotgun. He took aim at a point behind the bear's shoulder. The gun trembled in his hands. He clenched his teeth and fired. The shotgun boomed and bucked, and the bear swung around as the ball struck it with a wet slap like raw meat thrown on stone.

The bear turned to escape, but Adams had found the lung. The animal staggered and hung its head, then swayed like a drunkard. Blood spurted from behind its foreleg, the crimson stain bright on its yellow-white fur. A foreleg buckled, then the other. The bear's hind-quarters remained poised for a moment before it toppled onto its side, its breathing rapid, splashes of bright red pooling between the stones.

Robinson uncurled himself. He sat up on the gravel, his chest heaving. Staring at the fallen beast with wide eyes, he crawled backward from it, his bootheels scattering pebbles. The bear coughed up a bloody froth and lay still.

The ringing in Adams' head receded. He looked at the sky and marvelled at the silence. He could feel the flesh of his cheek twitching, the contents of his bowels moving, his heart slashing in his chest.

Robinson stood and brushed himself off. Each movement slow and deliberate, he loaded his gun with a heavy ball from his shot bag and approached the bear. He studied the creature, then raised his shotgun and held the muzzle against its skull for a long moment. Robinson pulled the trigger, his shoulders jerking as the gun erupted and the bear's blood and pink brains splashed his boots.

Adams went to Worthington. As the seaman stirred, Adams bent down and rolled him onto his back. The man was uninjured, but from the stink, he knew Worthington had soiled himself. He gagged, the stench caustic in his throat. He stumbled away to stand upwind.

An unfamiliar Robinson approached Adams. The lieutenant seemed full of words he could not say, eyes wet and hands shaking, possessed of a shame he wished unacknowledged. Adams thought to make light of it, shake his head, clap Robinson around the shoulders and laugh, but neither of them was that kind of man.

The four other seamen gathered at the sledge. Humphreys pulled Worthington to his feet. The men stood staring at the dead bear, kicking it with their boots.

Adams could still smell Worthington's shit. His head swam, and he staggered. Something slithered in his stomach.

Robinson stood before Adams. "Captain Bird told me you could shoot. I did not know how well."

Adams placed his hand squarely on Robinson's chest and roughly shoved him away. The lieutenant stumbled back, his eyes wide in astonishment. Adams dropped to his knees and vomited on the stones in a hot rush.

———

Robinson walked slowly with Adams through a light breeze, the shingle loose under their boots. When the distance between them and the men had increased to half a mile, they stopped to wait. The atmosphere between the two men had shifted. Since the bear, something had thawed in Robinson, even as ice and snow remained stubborn and heavy on the land. As much as Adams' piety irked him, the man had saved his life. Robinson wanted to believe himself a fair man. Perhaps he needed to revise his opinion of Adams. Unfamiliar emotions of gratitude and obligation stirred in him, leaving him befuddled. Camaraderie was as alien to him as a foreign tongue. He would require time to become proficient.

"I once saw a portrait of Sir James Clark Ross," said Robinson. He pulled his scarf down from his face. There was a civility in his tone with which even he was unacquainted. "It was a fine painting, done when he was a young man. Do you know it?"

Adams nodded. "It was painted in '33 or '34," he said, "after *Isabella* rescued the crew of *Victory* in Lancaster Sound."

"Yes, yes. That one." Robinson's gaze was drawn to the west, where the midnight sun yellowed a trio of small bergs. Their shadows trembled on the water. The moon was full and fat. With a halo studded by three mock moons—one above and one on either side—it was like a gaudy piece of jewellery, an enclosed crucifix in the heavens, something a princess might wear.

"He looked like a god in that painting," said Robinson. His tone was wistful. "Staring out into the Arctic wilderness, bearskin over his shoulder, hand on his sword. I remember his hair, so thick and black against the dark background that his face seemed to float on the canvas."

"The most handsome man in the navy, they called him."

Robinson grunted. "Not anymore."

"All men age," said Adams. "There is nothing strange in it."

"Nobody painted a grand portrait of his uncle, though, did they? After four years on the ice, John Ross brought back most of his men alive. Was *he* not the hero?"

"Perhaps he made fewer enemies in the Admiralty than his uncle."

Robinson smiled and clapped his gloved hands. "Ah, so one needs to know the right people! This man should be honoured; that man should not. It seems odd to me. John Ross survived four Arctic winters, but they disdain him. If Franklin's ships are lost, they seem likely as not to put his statue on a plinth in Westminster Abbey. It's simple to ennoble a man once he is dead."

Adams stopped. He glanced back to ensure the men were out of earshot, then turned to face Robinson. "If you have such low regard for Sir John, why sail to his aid?"

Indignation flickered on Robinson's face. He had tried his best to engage Adams, but the man always seemed quick with a riposte Robinson found difficult to parry. Adams followed the lieutenant's gaze out to the bergs in the sea. Backed by the late-evening sun, they glowed red around the edges, sea smoke rising off their jagged tips. Out of range of their shotguns, walruses rolled, scarred and bristling, like toothed logs in the water.

Robinson looked sideways at Adams. "Because Franklin has something I want."

CHAPTER FOUR

"Darling Edward," Frances had pleaded, "either Sir John will find a way through the ice or he'll turn around and sail home. Why must you go?"

Adams had sat with her in the parlour and patted her hand. He was grateful to her father for encouraging his daughter's studies of the sciences. Her acuity of mind had drawn him to her, but she was now so familiar with the perils of discovery service that he struggled to allay her fears for his safety. He had written her but once of his fascination with the Passage before she had devoured the works of the most prominent writers on the subject. Parry, Lyon, Franklin, Scoresby—she could quote them all.

He smiled into her eyes. "Sometimes, God asks much of us. He is showing me a path to salvation."

She frowned. "By rescuing Franklin?"

"Do you not hear the word of God?"

She gave a mock pout and shook her auburn curls. "Do not tease me. You know I do."

"But you have not turned your entire mind to Him."

"Have I not? I rather think I have." She squeezed his hand. "But surely the Arctic is a wilderness. There are no paths there. None that wind back to England, at least."

Adams regarded her with gentle reproach. "It is there, as yet undiscovered. What is any path but bare earth before the first boots tread upon it?" He lifted his teacup and drank, then returned it to the table.

"Courage and trust in God are indivisible. Franklin is a worthy man. My father taught me that."

"Worthy of what? I would not disparage Sir John, but Father says the only people who care a whit about him are the Admiralty and a few newspaper editors in London."

"No," said Adams. "Her Majesty's benevolent hand will span the north if there are brave men of Christian virtue to find the Passage. Sir John ate his boots to survive but returned to the Arctic a second time, then a third. He will not be denied."

"One hundred and thirty men will have eaten their boots by now," she said. "What else is there for them to eat?"

Adams frowned. "Franklin is a warrior of our faith. He took it upon himself to carry the English Church to new lands. As the empire expands, so do our obligations."

"So what is it? You wish to be a hero? A warrior?"

"Neither."

"God's instrument, then?"

Adams considered this. "If He deems me worthy."

"If there is a North-West Passage, ice blocks it much of the time, does it not?"

Adams leaned forward, his face earnest. "Great prizes are not easily achieved. Franklin knew it. The North-West Passage is the quickest way to China. What if the Russians find it first?"

She sighed and gazed out the window at the oaks in the rectory garden. "Then I shall be sure to send them my commiserations." She whispered, even though they were alone. "Your father is gone. It won't matter to him now. You cannot change it."

"I do it in his name. So that he might be absolved." He looked away.

"It was not your fault, Edward."

The couple sat in silence for a long time. The clock ticked in the hallway.

"Dear Edward," she said at last, "I do not question your motives, for I know them to be noble. I speak only out of concern for you. If you are determined to look for Franklin, I wish only that you return safely to me."

Adams smiled. "Do not ennoble me too soon, my dear. Have you never thought the choices we make are not our own? That the Almighty plots a path for each of us? I am drawn onward like a slave shackled at the wrists." He leaned closer to her, his elbows on the table. He clasped his hands together, interlocking his fingers. "For the first time in my life, I know what my purpose is. I am meant to find Franklin. I know this is my calling."

———

"Because he has something I want."

As soon as he had spoken, Robinson wished he had not. Irritated at his garrulity, he thrust his hands into his pockets and turned his back on Adams to watch the men drag the sledges out of earshot.

Adams walked around and stood before him, staring into his face. "What could Sir John possibly have that should be yours?"

Robinson sighed. He studied Adams with an air of resignation. He had let his guard down, and he knew Adams would not let the matter drop. "Do you know what I did before I joined *Investigator*?"

"I do not." Adams shivered in the wind.

"I was on surveying service. Off the coast of Ireland, then on *Bonetta* in the Mediterranean. Five years of it." His face wore a look of disgust. "I met an old fellow a few months before we sailed, a retired commander. Sixty years old if he was a day. He'd been a lieutenant on half pay for twenty years. The Admiralty agreed to promote him to commander if he retired."

"Your point escapes me," said Adams, frowning. "I am cold. I wish you would speak plainly."

"My point is this: The navy has many lieutenants but no wars to fight. I have no patron to recommend me, no relative in the Admiralty. If I am to move up, I must distinguish myself. I cannot do so in battle. Discovery service is my last hope, or I will be on half pay and darning my socks when my teeth fall out."

"Surely finding Sir John will bring us all to Whitehall's attention."

Robinson shook his head, his jaw set. A vein pulsed in his temple. Now that he had begun to speak, he needed to make Adams understand. The man must be in no doubt of his convictions.

"If I am one of many, they will not see me. I must be the *only* one they see. The only one they hear from. If I find Franklin, they will make me a captain before we even dock in England. I will be forgotten if I am merely one of a dozen officers who found nothing."

Adams drew his jacket tighter around him. "Then Sir John is merely a body to be stepped over."

Robinson attempted an earnest expression. "Truly, I bear the man no malice. I hope he lives." He paused and looked sad. "But is history not a procession of the living over the bodies of the fallen? I merely hope not to trip over Sir John as I go."

———

At midnight, Robinson led the sledge team along the sweeping brown shingle toward Fury Beach. Thick chunks of broken ice drifted in Prince Regent Inlet to the east. Smaller pieces littered the wide beach, which ended abruptly at the sheer walls of brown cliffs scarred by aeons of ice and wind. Below the cliffs were huge mounds of moraine clumped like piles of debris from endless detonations.

"Look," Billings said, "there's something built there." He gestured at the cliffs. "It's not like the rest of this. There's straight lines, like timbers."

Robinson stared into the distance, seeing nothing but curtains of brown rock and carpets of grey shale in the haze. He swept the site ahead with his telescope. The second team of men arrived and stopped beside them, shivering and exhausted, heads hanging like penitent sinners under the overcast sky. As they continued along the stony shore, the remains of a simple rectangular wooden structure appeared in the low foothills above the water. A cold blue light bathed the frame of the ancient shelter, its smooth geometric shapes as incongruous in the emptiness as a cathedral on the moon.

Porter, the snow-blind seaman, pulled at his blindfold.

"Leave it, man," said Robinson. "There is nothing to see."

"I want to see," said Porter. Adams untied the blindfold from around his head. The man grunted in pain at the sudden light, squeezing his eyes shut and covering them with his hands. Worthington unhitched the rope tethering him to the sledge. Porter dropped his hands and took a few steps unaided, squinting through eyes like glowing brick-red holes.

Robinson approached to inspect the ruin. Adams and the men followed. The wind murmured over the shingle, and a lone distant seabird cried out from the cliffs above. The structure was a bleached skeleton thirty-one feet long by sixteen feet wide. Ragged scraps of canvas once used for walls and roof remained fixed by thick iron nails to weathered beams fashioned years ago from spars.

Billings touched one of the upright spars with his fingertips. "What is it, sir?"

"It was called Somerset House," said Robinson. "Sir John Ross' men built it in '32. They spent the winter here after their ship got stuck in the ice."

Billings nodded, comprehending none of it. "Sir John didn't build it, then?"

Robinson rubbed his beard and sighed. "No. Not Franklin."

Robinson joined Adams and the seamen in a search of the vicinity. They found ancient casks of dried peas and preserved carrots behind a collection of boulders. Barrels of flour and bags of sugar were concealed under sheets of canvas streaked with grime. Robinson broached a cask and brought out a pickle. He sniffed it cautiously, then held the tip between his teeth before crushing it slowly. It was soft, like a piece of old fruit. He savoured the briny taste on his tongue, then ate the rest of the pickle in two bites.

Rusted iron barrel hoops lay scattered on the ground like the ribs of some long-dead metallic creature. A box of nails lay in a snow-filled depression. The men returned and stood before him, steam rising from their collars. Robinson had them dig up the floor of the ruined structure and look for message cylinders deposited in the earth, then left to explore the beach below the campsite. As the men's shovels rang on the hard earth, he wandered among lumps of hard-packed snow scattered like cannonballs on the limestone, perhaps once part of the snow walls erected by John Ross' men to insulate their tiny house against the cold. He imagined Ross' men huddled by their tiny stove, plastering the cracks in the walls with wet snow as the winter crushed them in its grip.

The seamen found nothing in the earth. They leaned on their shovels, lit their pipes, and watched the smoke rise into the air. Adams sat on a boulder and rubbed his stiff limbs. Robinson came up from the shore and looked up at the cliffs. He took out his pipe and shook his head.

"Nothing," he said. "No footprints. No detritus."

Adams spoke. "Perhaps they might have—"

"No." Robinson cut him off. "They were not here." He had known it even as they approached Somerset House along the beach. Why pretend they had missed a boot print preserved in the frozen mud, or an abandoned glove or tool? Franklin and his men would hardly have hidden their presence. They would have swarmed the sledge team before Robinson's men even saw them. There would have been tent rings on the beach, broken barrels. Robinson turned his back on Adams and strode off, his unlit pipe in his hand. A great weariness fell upon him, a heavy weight he thought might press him down into the frozen earth and pin him there forever. Franklin's saviour was to be another man. He thought of Lieutenants Barnard and Browne leading their teams east and north, hoping with all his heart they would find nothing. Would

Captain Ross' team find Franklin in the west? He imagined Elizabeth sitting in her wicker chair on a warm afternoon, waiting for the carriage to arrive with news of his return. He squatted and put his head in his hands.

Adams watched Robinson walk away. Was their search to stretch into a second year? If none of the other sledge teams found Franklin by summer's end, he knew Sir James Clark Ross would try to sail farther west into Barrow Strait, to overwinter before launching new sledge teams the following year. The thought of caring for the men through another dark winter made his stomach churn. The last one had cost the lives of two men on *Investigator*, two more on *Enterprise*. The dying had begun early, only a week after Trafalgar Day, when *Investigator*'s carpenter, William Coombe, babbled like a lunatic and breathed his last as Adams held his hand, helpless. Numbed by boredom, the men's faces had grown wan. Their eyes sank into their heads as the ice shifted against the hull timbers, and the mercury froze, and a blizzard blew for weeks. The snow had been three feet thick on top of the main hatch, hard enough to cut into bricks with a sword. As the officers counted the remaining sacks of coal, the men counted the days until their next grog. Adams counted the sick. *Investigator*'s captain of the hold, Cundy, died only two weeks before Adams and Robinson departed Port Leopold. Adams had told the captain it was scurvy and nostalgia, but he didn't really know what made a man collapse into himself and die.

Captain Bird had just shrugged and nodded. "I have seen it before," he said.

To last another winter required faith. Adams knew that few of the men had it. *I have it, Lord,* he thought. *I do. But can we not finish the job now?*

Robinson ordered the men to pitch the tent inside the four empty walls of the abandoned shelter. They lay in their blankets, each man huddled against the next for warmth. His hips and knees ached. He could not feel his feet. His tea was cold the moment it left the stove. He chewed his pork and biscuit, then checked his shotgun and lifted the tent flap. The desolate shore outside was a tapestry of white and grey. The sun was rising in the sky. Nothing moved, land and sea frozen alike.

Robinson curled up in his blanket and cursed himself for a fool. Since before their departure from Port Leopold, he had known Franklin might not be here, but he had allowed himself to hope, and now disappointment was a heavy stone on his heart. The missing captain had not passed this way.

"Poor bastards."

It was a whisper from one of the men, but in the tent's gloom, Robinson could not tell who had spoken. He found himself thinking that how a man dies can determine how he is remembered, far more than how he lived. He had seen it himself, another lesson of his father's. A man had died on the railway when he was twelve. Robinson's father had taken him to Parkside to see Stephenson's Rocket pass on its inaugural journey from Liverpool to Manchester. The atmosphere was that of a carnival. His father and brothers strolled like lords in their top hats, tailcoats, and silk cravats among the shoeblacks and fruit sellers. His father, rarely one to display emotion, had been excited.

"It is remarkable, Frederick," he said, his eyes shining. "It will bring the cotton from Liverpool and take the cloth back there from Manchester, far quicker than on the canal. And it will carry people. All without horses."

When the trains stopped to take on water, Robinson had craned his neck to glimpse the Duke of Wellington in his carriage. The great black barrel of the locomotive rolled on, the chimney steaming. He did not see the man, Huskisson, fall onto the tracks, but screams cut through the babble of the crowd when the locomotive went over the man's leg. The faces of the men who carried him up were sprayed with blood. He saw the man's torn trousers, soaked red to the ankle. Later that evening, he heard the man had died. His eldest brother told him Huskisson had been a member of Parliament. His father seemed oddly unconcerned.

"Old Huskisson has made himself a martyr. Unfortunate, of course, but people shall know of the railway now. They shall think of him more for this than for anything he said in the Commons."

———

Robinson gave up trying to sleep and walked into the hills above Fury Beach. The tent stood within the ruins of Somerset House far below him. Something hard cracked beneath his heel. At his feet were fragments of a shattered wine bottle, crimson against the snow. At once he was reminded of the blood on Elizabeth's white handkerchief when she removed it from her lips.

"You are unhappy with your posting?" his wife had asked him.

Frail since the miscarriage, she lay in bed in a white nightdress. He leaned over her to pull the coverlet up. Her illness was advancing. The subtle jasmine scent she wore failed to mask the sickly odour of her breath, like stale beer. He sat on the edge of her bed, gazing out the window. The pond at the bottom of the garden glittered in the late-afternoon sun.

He sighed and caressed the back of her hand, gently rotating the wedding ring on her finger. So snug when he had first slipped it on her hand that he considered having it enlarged, it seemed enormous now, threatening to slip over her thin, bony knuckle and disappear in the bedclothes. He folded her fingers into her palm and closed his hand over hers.

"No, I am not unhappy with the posting."

"Just unhappy with how you got it?"

He pressed his lips together. "Something like that. Father insists I go on discovery service. He says it is for the best."

"Is he right?"

"He usually is."

He smiled down at her, remembering the early months of their courtship. Her father, a mercer, had permitted him to write to her only because the man was solicitous of Robinson's father. He had assumed his daughter would entertain no interest in a junior naval officer stationed aboard an old paddle steamer surveying the Irish coast. Both risking and expecting naught, he assumed Robinson was but a harmless distraction for his daughter until more satisfactory suitors appeared.

Written in the hours alone in his cabin at the end of his watch, Robinson's letters to Elizabeth were candid and guileless. At first, they were an amusement for him, a way to relieve his boredom and solitude. He corresponded with some phantasm, someone not quite real. Had she terminated their exchanges, he would have persuaded himself he had dreamed her missives, that it had been merely a game. That she had never been there at all.

But reply she did. He wrote of his fondness for Walter Scott. She professed her regard for *Ivanhoe*. Expressing his admiration for Wordsworth, she sent him pages of "Tintern Abbey" copied in her own hand. Their correspondence continued. He was a different man with pen in hand, someone no one aboard his ship would have recognised. Imagining the brown of her eyes and the curl of her locks, he wrote words he would never have had the courage to speak to her face. She came to know a person he barely knew himself, one without rank or uniform, stripped of affectation and doubt. An honest man. When he returned to England on leave, she had given him a lock of her hair. On his fourth visit, he had asked to marry her. She had not hesitated.

Bemused at his success in attracting a woman, Robinson's father would not easily permit him his triumph. "Her family is far from enthused about the match," he had said, his tone dry. "You are but a lieutenant, and Britain is not at war. Her father fails to see how you will move up. Frankly, so do I." He paused to sigh theatrically. "But the dowry is satisfactory, so I have resolved the matter with him." He tugged down on his lapels and sniffed. Turning away, he said, "I wouldn't have fancied your chances with her if it were not for me."

He tried to push thoughts of his father's acerbity from his mind as Elizabeth smiled up at him from her pillow. "Your father wants the best for you."

"He wants what is best for him."

She put her other hand over his. It seemed to require all her strength.

"You think he secured your position for you?"

He shrugged. "I could hardly have secured it for myself, as he does not fail to remind me. I have never met Sir John Franklin. Nor Sir James Clark Ross."

"Surely there is no shame in acquiescing this time," she said. "It is a wonderful opportunity."

The sun sank. The shadows on the lawn lengthened, and the bedroom light took on a coppery hue. Paler even than the pillow upon which she rested, Elizabeth's white face glowed brighter. She was the only person to whom he could ever reveal himself, and yet so many truths remained unspoken between them. The pair of them were like swordsmen dancing around in a mock bout, each anxious not to injure the other with their sharp blades. Determined not to dissuade him from embarking on his voyage, she refused to speak of her infirmity. To decline his mission and remain at her bedside would wound her more deeply than any sabre thrust. And so they spoke instead of his duty, casting it like a cloak over their fear and guilt.

"What if we do not find Franklin?" Robinson whispered. "I may go all that way and Father will say, "I gave you the perfect opportunity, and you did nothing with it." It will be my fault."

"You should not doubt yourself so."

I should not, he thought. *But I do.* He smiled and squeezed her hand. "I shall make you proud of me."

"Promise me you will control your temper. You do yourself no favours when you are overly impassioned."

He glanced down at her. She had closed her eyes. She murmured something, her voice inaudible, the effort of speaking too great. As she fell asleep, he whispered, so as not to wake her.

"You shall be proud. I care not what Father thinks."

He sat by her bed for a long time, her hand in his. *Pretending to ignore the lies you tell yourself,* he thought, *is like trying to pick cobwebs from your jacket. No matter what you do, they stick to your fingers, your hair, your stockings. There is simply no getting rid of them.*

Adams and Robinson stood atop the cliffs at Creswell Bay and turned up their collars against a pitiless wind. Belugas swam in the shallows seven hundred feet below. The floes breaking up in the bay spun like enormous chunks of meringue in the water.

They had left Humphreys at Fury Beach with Porter. Worthington, Payne, and Billings had carried driftwood up from the beach and made a fire on the cliff top. Now they roasted a fox Adams had shot an hour earlier. The three seamen capered like children around the flames, turning the meat as its rich odour rose on the air.

Adams followed Robinson along the cliff top, away from the men. Robinson's manner was conspiratorial, his cap pulled down and his shoulders hunched. He glanced back at the men, then turned to face Adams. "You and I will push on to the southwest," he said.

"What?" Adams stopped, frowning. "Humphreys must go no further. If his condition deteriorates, the others will need to carry him. It will be hard for them. And Porter's eyes are still bad."

Robinson's face was impassive, his tone flat. "Not them. Just the two of us. We will send the men back to Port Leopold."

Adams gaped at him, sure he had misunderstood. "But . . . we are expected at Port Leopold."

Robinson shook his head. "Captain Bird ordered us to proceed as far south as practicable. We would be *following* orders, not disobeying them."

"How can you know—"

Robinson spoke over him. "Two of us can move more quickly than seven. We can shoot enough game to feed two, but not seven. We could cover fifteen miles a day, perhaps twenty if the thaw is late and we walk along the shore ice."

"But—"

Robinson scowled. He grasped Adams' shoulder and shook it. "Be silent, and listen to me. We risk *more* if we go back now. Wherever Franklin is, we are closer to him than at any point thus far. I wager Captain Bird would gladly sanction an extended foray. To him, it would hardly be a risk."

Adams held his gaze for a long moment. This was not an order. Robinson was requesting his assent, not demanding it. "We do not have enough provisions for us and the men."

"We can do it," said Robinson.

Adams realised he had rehearsed his proposal.

The lieutenant counted on his fingers. "We have just over half the provisions with which we left Port Leopold. If we send the men back on two-thirds rations, we keep the rest. We cache half here and take two weeks' worth of food—mostly meat, bread, and cocoa. We'll leave the rum, tea, and sugar. We shall take the smaller tent and floorcloth, and one sledge. We can share one buffalo robe. We will have the spirit lamp and fuel. Give Humphreys the axe and the seine net; we shall take the shovel. With our spare clothing, guns, and bedding, we can reduce the sledge's weight to under three hundred pounds. Two of us together can haul it. We can abandon certain items along the way or return for them later."

Adams shook his head. "Seventy pounds of food cached here may keep the two of us alive, but it will not last long if we have survivors in tow."

At this, Robinson stepped back and nodded. He put his pipe in his mouth and tasted the stem. "True, we cannot plan for survivors. We are but scouts, but the other sledge parties are no different. I will ask Captain Bird to send the steam launch with emergency provisions."

"Over seventy miles?"

"Why not? By the time we return, it will be midsummer. The ice in Prince Regent Inlet will have melted enough for lanes of open water to be passable—perhaps not for the ships, but probably for the launch."

Adams turned his back and walked away, thinking. He stared at the ground, his hands in his pockets. His disappointment faded. Was this the way, then? Hope swelled in his chest. God was offering him a different path when he had expected naught. He felt like a pauper fruitlessly ploughing barren ground at the end of a long day, only to stumble upon a gold coin glinting in the mud. If he and Robinson were successful, it would spare the men of *Investigator* and *Enterprise* a second winter that not all would survive. They would save not only the lives of Franklin and his men but also those of their shipmates.

Robinson approached from behind him. "All we need is a fox or a ptarmigan every day or two. We can shoot enough game to stretch this out."

Adams drew the back of his hand across his mouth and touched his dry lips with his fingertips.

"You are a better shot than I," Robinson went on. "After the bear, I have no doubts. I will lead, you will shoot, and we will find them together."

Long serrated clouds scattered like bones across the heavens. The wind whispered over the ground. Adams looked down at pockets of snow accumulated in the cliff's crevices.

"Are you certain Captain Bird would order this?"

"You can walk eighty miles back to Port Leopold and ask him, or you can join me and find your man."

"The Lord has always been my guide." Adams took his Bible from his pocket.

"What does He say now?"

Adams opened his Bible and silently read the verse on the page before him. He looked up. "And I say unto you, Ask, and it shall be given you; seek, and ye shall find; knock, and it shall be opened unto you." He replaced the Bible carefully in his coat pocket.

"We have little time," said the lieutenant.

Adams stared at him. "They will be in poor condition."

"They will be dying."

"You have such little faith in Sir John."

"And you should not place him atop such a high pedestal. He is just a man." Robinson attempted a smile, but the effort twisted his face into a smirk. "Perhaps between us we shall strike the right balance."

Adams looked across at the cliffs on the southwestern rim of the bay. At their base, the crumbling floes glowed blue around the edges. The wind dropped away abruptly, as if capped by a thumb over a pipe.

"Three hundred pounds on the sledge, you say?" Adams turned back to face Robinson, his voice suddenly loud in the stillness. "How far do you think two of us will get, dragging that much?"

For the first time, he saw uncertainty in Robinson's eyes. The lieutenant squared his shoulders and looked down his nose. "You are not injured, are you?" he asked. "And are our legs not accustomed now to walking?"

"We would need another man." Adams nodded toward the three men squatting by the fire, each gnawing on a piece of roasted meat. "We should bring Billings. He can haul the sledge."

Robinson grimaced. "This is no task for a simpleton."

"You know he is stronger than any two of the others. If we are to cover any meaningful distance, we need such a man."

"He is an idiot."

"He follows orders," said Adams. "And he is the most keen-sighted of all of them. He sees what you or I require a telescope to detect, and he is curiously untroubled by the glare."

Robinson glanced back again at the men. He removed a glove and rubbed his beard.

Adams pressed his advantage. "He will do as he is told. If I am to go, he must be part of it."

Robinson gritted his teeth and sighed. "Very well. But you must be the one to look after him." He jabbed a finger at Adams, scowling. "I tell you now, I shall not be wiping his backside."

Adams huddled into his coat. "We are very different men, you and I."

Robinson's eyes narrowed. His gaze lingered longer than usual. Eventually Robinson nodded. "There are so many different kinds of men."

Far below in the bay, tiny plumes of white erupted as hunting seabirds dropped into the water.

Robinson stared at him. "They are waiting for us."

Adams held his gaze, making Robinson wait. He opened his Bible again, then closed it without glancing at the page. "Can we take at least some of the tea?"

It was the first time he had seen Robinson smile.

CHAPTER FIVE

Dearest Frances, Adams wrote, *I had a dream in which I wandered across the ice but was not cold. The wind whipped my hair into my eyes. In the distance I saw a man dressed in a Royal Navy captain's uniform. As I approached, the man faced away from me, his features concealed by the brim of his cocked hat. But I knew it was Franklin from the curve of his paunch and the curl of his black muttonchops. I reached out to touch the man's shoulder, and in that moment he grew taller and slimmer. As he turned to look at me, his features were those of my father when I last saw him twenty years ago. He had not aged a day. And Father said to me, "The story is unfinished, my lad. Write the ending."*

———

Robinson thought it a good evening for walking. The sun ebbed in a pearly evening sky strewn with distant pink clouds.

"You," he told Humphreys, "are to be in command. Do not delay. Get them back to Port Leopold, and the surgeon will look at your feet. You should be there in four days."

"Yes, sir." Humphreys nodded. "And how long should I say you will be, sir?"

Robinson exchanged a glance with Adams. "Ask Captain Bird to send the steam launch if we have not returned by mid-July."

"Yes, sir." Humphreys hesitated, then leaned in to whisper to the two officers, "Pardon me for askin', sir, but how will Jimmy fare? Sometimes he needs a bit of help, if you take my meaning."

"Mister Adams will look after him," said Robinson. "You just see to your own men."

Doubt clouded Humphreys' features. "Very good, sir." He knuckled his forehead, stepped back, and addressed the men in a loud voice. "Come on, then, lads—three cheers for the lieutenant and Mister Adams. They're going on with Jimmy for a bit. Let's give 'em a lively send-off!"

The men assembled and stood in a line. Billings grinned at the others. "I get to pull the sledge." Humphreys led the men in a subdued cheer.

"Lieutenant," said Adams, "if I may, a prayer?"

Robinson squinted up at the sky, then cast him a sour glance. "They should be on their way." He sighed, then threw up a hand. "Very well. Quickly, then."

The five members of the sledge party pulled off their caps and Welsh wigs and shuffled forward to stand around Adams in a circle. Adams took his Bible from his pocket, clasped it in front of his chest, then bowed his head. The men surrounding him did the same. Robinson stood ten feet away with his back turned and arms folded.

"O Lord," said Adams, "bless our journey so we might find our lost companions safe and well. Protect and deliver us from peril, and guide us home again with your light. We ask this in the name of Jesus Christ, our Redeemer. Amen."

Before the men had finished muttering their amens, Robinson turned on his heel and marched back to where they stood with Adams.

"There is no time to waste," he said. "Get your harnesses on."

He watched with hands on hips as they picked up the track ropes and looped them over their shoulders. Humphreys looked from Robinson to Adams, then glanced at the officers' sledge. He cleared his throat.

"Will you be taking the rum, sir?"

"The rum stays here," said Robinson.

Humphreys nodded, his expression stony. "Very good, sir."

———

Robinson watched the men until they vanished from sight over a distant rise. The snow on the low hills to the west glinted like wet silver. Flecks of drift fell out of an empty grey sky. Already harnessed, Billings stood by the sledge in silence, framed in the cold evening light.

Robinson went to the sledge, picked up the two flasks of rum, and poured the thick brown fluid onto the earth. He caught Adams' eye as the dark liquid pooled in the gravel.

"You think me churlish? Denying them their rum?" Robinson asked.

Adams looked away. "It could help keep them warm on their return. I thought you might let them have it."

Robinson's temper again flared at the man's naivete. "Are you really so unfamiliar with the seaman's fondness for liquor? They would guzzle it all at once as soon as we were gone. Then they would be drunk and dead in a snowdrift." He threw the empty flask on the ground. When he glanced up, Adams was holding out his Bible, an expression of calm on his face.

"You are welcome to borrow my Bible." Adams' voice was quiet. "If you choose not to pray with me, perhaps you would like to select your own prayer."

Robinson had refused many proffered Bibles in his life, but this time, for no reason he could comprehend, he found his hand extending to accept the small leather-bound volume. His rancour dissipated, and he stood weighing it in his palm. Its magic had never worked on him. He coveted the comfort the pious found in their prayers, but heard no voice in his head, felt no sense of awe. He gave the Bible back to Adams, then turned away so the other man would not see the colour in his cheeks. He picked up his knapsack, put his arm through the loop of the sledge harness, and studied the sky.

"We must make a start. In a few days, the weather will warm up. The sledge will be more difficult to haul when the snow turns to slush."

Walking abreast, they continued over the cracked and scarred land. Robinson yawned and felt the skin of his face growing tight and leathery in the glare off the snow. Now that his decision was made and their search had recommenced, his spirits were high. The temperature dropped as the sun rolled lower in the sky. The sledge runners hissed through snow that had melted during the day and refrozen, then scraped over patches of icy gravel. The sky was empty of birds. He looked across at Billings. The weight of the sledge pulled the harness straps tight against the seaman's coat as the track ropes stretched taut behind him. His energy unbounded, the young giant marched in long strides, his breath coming in deep gusts, his face a mask of concentration.

"Slacken your pace, man," Robinson told him. "The days will be long."

He observed Billings with a mixture of relief and disquiet. True, the man was compliant, but as with a powerful wild beast, Robinson sensed an intransigence beneath his docile exterior, a latent implacability he feared might surface if the young man were pushed beyond his limits. Robinson had heard tales from India of elephants obediently hauling great burdens one moment and trampling their handlers in a rage the next. What would he do if Billings decided he no longer wanted to haul the sledge, if he wanted to go home? Adams, he knew, could obey an order. He was less sure about Billings. But he knew Adams was right: having Billings haul the sledge would extend their search range, and for now he was glad to have the big fellow dragging it in his place.

Robinson pictured Captain Bird's expression when Humphreys and the men arrived at Port Leopold without him and Adams. Robinson suspected the captain, a practical man not given to fits of temper, would shrug and retreat to his cabin to await their return, aware he could do nothing to retrieve them from such a distance. If he and Adams were successful, the Admiralty would hardly court-martial the man who rescued Sir John. And if they failed, well . . . it would merely hasten the end of an otherwise inconsequential naval career. He had increased the stakes of his wager and was content with it.

———

In the morning, they stopped in a steel-grey light. Adams and Billings prepared to pitch the tent.

As Adams took his knapsack from his shoulder, his journal fell to the ground. The pages parted, and a piece of paper folded between them was blown across the snow-covered stones, flapping and tumbling like a small bird before catching on Robinson's boot. Robinson stooped to retrieve it.

Adams felt a brief stab of alarm. "I would thank you not to—"

But Robinson had already opened the paper. It was Adams' sketch of Franklin looking out over the ice pack. Robinson held the drawing in both hands, carefully studying each line. Adams felt his face grow hot. He waved a gloved hand casually.

"It is only something I did to pass the time. Just throw it away," he said, hoping Robinson would not. He had not intended Robinson to see the sketch but was annoyed now to find himself anxious for the man's approval. He turned away and joined Billings in lifting the tent-poles from the sledge. Robinson silently examined the picture while Billings unrolled the tent on the ground. Adams stood waiting, with a tentpole held in one hand like a spear.

"Your technique is sound," said Robinson, tracing the image on the page with his fingertip, "but you flatter him with this strong chin and overly confident gaze. It is exaggerated, a caricature. The kind of picture one finds in a child's storybook." He held the paper out to Adams.

Adams took the sketch, hoping the nonchalance in his tone did not appear feigned. He shrugged. "It is precisely that. I have drawn him this way since I was a boy." He folded the piece of paper and replaced it in the pages of his journal. He spoke quietly, as though to himself: "It is how I imagine him. All of them."

"Them?"

"All those who went north to seek the Passage. I was five years old when my father began reading to me and my brother about Henry Hudson and William Baffin. When he put the lamps out at night, I read by candlelight: Samuel Hearne's journey down the Coppermine, Mackenzie's canoe voyage from Fort Chipewyan to the ocean. Then Franklin and Parry." He cast a sideways glance at Robinson, gauging his reaction. Robinson inserted a tentpole, then pulled down on the guy to hoist the tent. He seemed absorbed in the task, barely listening.

The man's indifference chafed Adams. Robinson seemed empty of all passion. Adams failed to resist an urge to explain himself further. "Even then, I could see their bearded faces and hear their voices," he said. "The sound of the ship's bell. The thump of the pack ice against the hull. I could even smell the galley stove. I built models of their ships, just deck and masts, and made my own little fleet of discovery ships. I put them on a shelf over my bed."

"You have a vivid imagination," Robinson grunted as he stooped to tie off the last of the guys. He turned to Billings: "Get the floorcloth."

"My father instilled in me both a love of God and an admiration for those who do His work," said Adams.

"Mine fostered no such emotions in me." Robinson pointed into the tent as Billings returned from the sledge with the floorcloth over his shoulder. "Unroll it."

"God requires only devotion," said Adams. "My father once told me there is a path to righteousness for each of us, but we must strive for it, search for it, demonstrate our virtue."

"Pretty words."

"No. Guidance, like arrows on a map. Directions to Paradise, if only you will follow them."

At this, Robinson straightened and frowned. Adams had his full attention now. "Is that how it works, then? Follow instructions to win a prize? It seems less a demonstration of piety than a transaction."

"I will see the Passage found for my father," said Adams. "To atone not only for my sins but for his."

"That must be a great deal of sin."

"We are all sinners." An image came to him of his schoolmates hissing at him: *Son of a suicide!* He pushed it away.

Together they brought the stove, provisions, and bedding from the sledge into the tent.

"You are enamoured of stories." Robinson jabbed the stem of his pipe at Adams. "So I shall tell you one." Robinson ignited a quantity of spirits of wine in the lamp, threw a handful of snow into the kettle, and began warming their salt pork. The thick fatty smell filled the tent. Billings sat over the pot, staring into its depths, his eyelids drooping. He opened his mouth to try to catch the rising steam on his tongue.

"Once, when I was a midshipman," Robinson said, "I witnessed a fight on the lower deck. One man stood on the toes of another; then there was a shout and the swing of a fist, and in a moment the rest of the men circled the two pugilists and were placing bets on the outcome. Then the lieutenant appeared. He was . . . imposing. Almost regal, I should say. I remember how loudly his boots rang on the floor timbers. The men fell silent and stepped back and dropped their heads, and the two brawlers looked up from the floor." Robinson paused to check the meat, then took his chronometer from his pocket and began winding it.

Adams broke a slab of biscuit into three pieces and handed a piece each to Robinson and Billings.

Robinson went on. "I waited for him to bellow a reprimand, but he stepped in between them without saying a word. He held a belaying pin in his hand but did not raise it, carrying it down by his knee instead. His voice was so soft when he spoke that I could barely hear it. 'I would happily break your legs with this and dump you at the nearest port,' he said, 'and will do so if this happens again. You will each cook meals for the other's mess for a month.' In a second, the men dispersed. None said a word." He looked up at Adams. "And he would have done it. They all knew it. It was the *threat* the men respected, you see? In that moment, God held no authority over those men—a man held it all."

"God's is the last judgment," said Adams.

"Perhaps. But while we live, we answer to other men. I concern myself with only one judgment at a time."

They walked west at a steady pace over the snowy cliffs north of the ice-choked waters of Creswell Bay. A few miles on, they arrived at a large ice-encrusted lake and walked fifteen miles around its southern shore before striking out across an empty plain. Wiry yellow grass poked up through the snow. The icy wind stung their cheeks. Shallow rocky pools gleamed red in the late-evening sun. They waded across freezing streams, their knapsacks and spare socks brandished above their heads. At midnight, the sky was a deep blue overhead but a buttery yellow along the horizon. Their bodies cast long shadows on the snow. The sun lurked among tousled grey clouds tugged at the edges by far-off winds.

They pitched the tent at five in the morning and laid out the floor-cloth. To conserve fuel, they ate their meat cold. They pulled on their fur sleeping boots and crawled into their blanket bags, their shotguns loaded and primed by their sides.

Billings lay on his back, staring up. "Will we find Sir John tomorrow, Mister Adams?"

"We might, Jimmy, we might. Watch for smoke."

He and Robinson lit their pipes and wrote in their journals, then slept as the sun rose higher.

Robinson woke in the early evening. As Adams and Billings slept, he left the tent and stood looking out at a moon twinned in the mirrored surface of a meltwater lake.

Elizabeth had been with him while he slept. He wondered how Franklin had done it, leaving his dying wife, Eleanor, to go on discovery service in '25. *If I find him,* he thought, *it will be my first question.* He imagined Franklin sitting by his wife's bedside before leaving on his second expedition to the Arctic. Eleanor, cursed with consumption just like Elizabeth, was dead a week after he left for the Mackenzie Delta. When he finally received word, did Franklin feel relief that her ordeal was over? Or was it guilt that he had not waited?

Robinson felt no affinity for the man, save for this one shared sorrow. *Can it be I am like him?* Elizabeth's illness was like the onset of the long Arctic night—a gradual fading of the light, followed by an interminable darkness. And he with no means of stopping it. He wondered if Franklin's thoughts had mirrored his own: *I will be nothing if I do not go. She will soon be nothing if I do.* Elizabeth had sensed his hesitation and spurned his remorse. It was a burden she refused to carry.

"You have a chance to achieve something great," she said. "To be someone great. Whether you go or not, my fate will be the same."

What had Eleanor said to Sir John? Had she asked him to stay? Did he hold her hand?

Robinson wished now that he had not signed on to *Investigator.* He thought there was too much time to reflect in the Arctic and not enough distraction from one's darker thoughts, which fattened into malignant obsessions one had no hope of overcoming. *Cold and darkness feed repentance in a man, as wood feeds a fire.*

———

Adams walked at an even, mechanical pace, inured now to ten hours of daily trekking. Tempered by the endless repetition of movement, his legs were stronger, the sinews supple and muscles pliant. His feet were rough and unfeeling, the skin of his face and hands coarse. Billings hauled the sledge each evening without complaint, head thrust forward into the wind. But by the early-morning hours, Adams noticed the young seaman begin to tire and joined him in the harness.

"You must adopt a steadier pace, Jimmy. Do not use all your strength at once."

The big man bobbed his head. "Yes, Mister Adams."

Fury Beach was four days behind them when they halted, hunched against the cold atop low cliffs running north to south. A rocky shoreline was visible through the haze twenty miles distant, across a wide channel of water clogged with ice. Sun-splashed clouds teased licks of purple across the sky. Billings sat on the ground and stared into his lap, humming a tune to himself.

Adams knelt beside Robinson as the lieutenant unrolled his map on the ground and ran his finger over it, tracing their route down the eastern coast of North Somerset to Fury Beach. He moved his finger to a point across the map where neither the channel to their west nor the shoreline upon which they stood appeared.

"We are somewhere near here," he said.

Adams examined the map. A vast blank space stretched for seven hundred miles from the east coast of North Somerset westward to Cape Bathurst on the American mainland. For a moment, the wind dropped, and Adams experienced an utter absence of sound, as though suddenly swept up and cupped in God's hands. Below him, cliffs of myriad colours fell to the sea, their edges worn by wind and ice. Glaciers slashed through ravines and gorges like great knives.

So there it is, then, he thought. *This is the edge of the world. This is where we fall off.*

———

Adams lay down, but sleep eluded him. He listened to the wind buffeting the tent and the ice cracking and groaning in the pack. He thought of the winter they had all just spent aboard *Investigator* at Port Leopold. Boots squeaking, pots rattling in the galley, and backgammon pieces clicking in the gun room. Pipe smoke and the wet smell of salt pork. The walls and ceiling of the lower deck dripping with condensation. The men playing rounders on the ice or flying paper kites or whittling little boats from lumps of cork after supper. Others learning their letters at the clerk's school on the lower deck while the officers cleaned their shotguns and used empty brandy bottles on the gunwale for target practice.

Franklin would have spent precisely such a winter four years earlier, after leaving the whalers in Davis Strait. Adams imagined Franklin in his cabin aboard *Erebus*, dressed in his finest uniform, stiff and brushed to a sheen, buttons and boots lustrous. Cocked hat lending him a regal air, telescope twirling in his hands. His face would have been round, his skin clear, bushy black muttonchops standing out from his cheeks, paunch pushing against his belt. Had he worried then that they would come to grief?

He looked across the tent. Robinson took out his pipe.

"They say some of the younger officers were hoping to spend at least one winter in the ice," said Adams.

Robinson grunted. "And now they've had four. I suspect their enthusiasm has waned."

"Sir John said his provisions could last seven years. Do you think that is possible?"

Robinson shook his head. "Hubris. But I suppose it depends how much game they could shoot."

Adams remembered Frances' scepticism at the suggestion the crews could subsist on caribou and fox and musk oxen. How could Franklin and his men believe it possible? "It seems odd to me now that he arranged no rendezvous points if he got frozen in, no supply depots in case of misadventure."

"I suppose he thought he wouldn't need them."

Adams gasped at a burning sensation on his cheek. He sat up in the gloom, rubbing his face. A freezing drop of water had fallen from the tent ceiling and struck him, scoring his skin like the tip of a hot knife.

"And he left no message canisters," he said. "Nothing at Parry's cairn at Possession Bay. Nothing in Lancaster Sound."

Robinson drew on his pipe and exhaled blue smoke. "I have also been troubled by that. I can only think he was in a hurry. When do circumstances allow you to hurry in the Arctic?"

Adams considered the question. "When there is no ice."

"Precisely." Robinson pointed his pipestem at Adams. "He thought there was no time to stop and build cairns. It occurs to me he may have found Lancaster Sound free of ice once he got across the North Water. Open water in the Arctic is tempting. If you encounter it, you want to keep going. You saw the ice in Baffin Bay. It moves like a living thing, like a giant hand that closes around a vessel. Once caught up in it, you could be stuck for months and carried a thousand miles. Then, if you are lucky, the ship will rise up and sit on the ice until it starts to break up. But if you hesitate and do not take your opportunities, if fortune deserts you and your ships are nipped in the ice?" He drew in his breath and shook his head, imagining it. "Have you ever crushed a boiled egg in your fist with all your strength? Imagine the eggshell is your ship's hull."

"I think he is taunting us," said Adams. "Perhaps he is almost through to the west. He might be in Behrings Strait before we can rendezvous with him. Then we shall have to turn around and go back to England, or follow him through and sail round the Horn to get home."

Robinson made no reply. He gathered his blanket around him and lay down.

"If Sir John could see us now," asked Adams, "what do you think he would say? 'Go back, we are already through the Passage'? Or 'What the devil is taking you so long?'"

CHAPTER SIX

On the beach, Robinson searched for footprints and cairns and discarded boots but found only bear and fox tracks and an ancient walrus skull. He kicked it in frustration, and it exploded into powder. Bending into the cold wind, the three men clambered back up a steep gravel slope to the cliff top and pitched the tent on the snow-covered ground. Robinson ordered Billings to use the last of their fuel to prepare a meal of salt pork and cocoa. After eating, they left the stove on the stones outside the tent and slept.

In the evening, the ice was thick in the channel, encroaching upon the beach below. Plentiful the day before, the lanes between the floes narrowed and vanished as the pack fused into an interminable white desert. As Robinson and Adams pulled on their stockings and boots, Billings remained curled in his blanket. Robinson scowled down at him.

"Billings, get up," Robinson said.

The man did not stir.

Robinson felt a surge of irritation. "Get up, I said!" He drew back a booted foot and made ready to kick the seaman.

"No," said Adams, putting his hand on Robinson's arm. He knelt beside Billings and gently shook his shoulder. "Come on now, Jimmy. Time to go."

The young seaman sighed and sat up, bleary-eyed. "I'm tired, Mister Adams," he said.

"I know, Jimmy," said Adams. "But we have to go. We might find Sir John today."

Billings rubbed his face and yawned. "Unknown Parts."

"Yes, Jimmy. We are in Unknown Parts. But they shall be unknown no longer. Sir John is here too. Let us go and find him."

Billings nodded and pulled on his boots. They walked along the edge of the cliff until they found a scattered collection of stones. Removing their provisions from the sledge, they dragged it over the snow. They gathered the largest stones they could lift, then moved them back to a site close to the edge of the cliff and began building a cairn. They placed the largest stones at the base and piled more atop each other until sweat soaked their undershirts and their breath rose like smoke. When the cairn stood five feet high, they stood back with their hands on their hips. Robinson reached into his knapsack and produced an iron message cylinder. He sat on a boulder, brought out his ink bottle, and wrote on a piece of paper.

"I shall tell them Captain Ross has cached provisions at Port Leopold," he told Adams. "And that *Investigator* and *Enterprise* will sail west to Cape Walker when the ice in Barrow Strait clears." He rolled up the message and put it into the cylinder, then searched in the cairn with his gloved hand until he found a niche from which it could not easily be dislodged. He placed another stone over the cylinder and straightened. "We are one hundred miles south of Cape Walker. If Franklin is there, Captain Ross will find him. So we must go south."

"Sir John could have gone west from Cape Walker and become stuck in the heavy pack off Melville Island," said Adams.

"I'm hungry," said Billings.

Robinson looked at Adams. "I doubt Franklin went to Melville Island. Parry said that route was impassable, that the ice was too thick. Permanent ice, he said it was, not seasonal. Had not melted for decades."

"It would be folly to discount Sir John's courage."

Robinson felt his temper bubble again. "You embroider the man too prettily." Did Adams think Franklin's courage alone could conquer the elements? Perhaps Sir John could batter his way through the ice with the sheer force of his character.

"I'm hungry," Billings said again. He wheedled like an exhausted child. "Mister Adams, I'm hungry."

Robinson glared at Adams. "For God's sake, give him something to do. Make him be quiet."

"Jimmy," said Adams, "go and keep watch for bears, will you? Shout if you see one. I will give you some biscuit soon."

Without a word, Billings stood and lumbered away.

Robinson watched him leave, his jaw clenched. *I am marooned in the wilderness with a romantic and a fool,* he thought.

"I see nothing odd in holding a man like Franklin in high esteem," said Adams. "Sir John's accomplishments are admirable. A man would do well to emulate them."

Robinson did not attempt to conceal his disdain. "Which of his feats are so admirable? Losing half his men on the way back from Point Turnagain? Eating his boots to stay alive? Getting lost in the ice?" He lifted his knapsack onto his shoulder. "Let us hope you do not emulate him on this mission."

———

The sound of barking dogs woke them.

Robinson sat up under his blanket. Alarmed, he seized his shotgun, furious with himself for not hearing the animals approach. Then it dawned on him. Where there are dogs, there are . . .

"Esquimaux!"

They pulled on their hose and boots and looked out from the tent. Twenty yards away, a man stood beside a small sledge, to which six dogs were hitched. Short in stature and bronze of skin, he was clad in a reindeer-skin parka and breeches and held a long spear in his mitten. He wore a pair of snow goggles fashioned from a strip of sinew and two round pieces of timber with a slit cut in each. He pushed his goggles up to his forehead and stared at the tent with wide black eyes.

Shotguns in hand, Adams and Robinson slowly emerged from the tent. The dogs began barking again as Billings followed, straightening to his full height. The Esquimaux shouted angrily and crouched, ready to attack or flee. He raised his spear as if to hurl it.

"No, no!" Robinson placed his shotgun on the ground and stood to face the man with both palms raised open.

"We are white men! *Kabloona*, we are *kabloona*!"

"*Kabloona?*" The man looked at Robinson's raised hands and down at the shotgun, then at Adams. He shouted again and brandished his spear. Adams, too, laid down his gun and opened his arms. He forced a smile.

"We will not harm you," he said in an amiable tone. "Friends. We are friends." He glanced at Billings and spoke softly. "Jimmy, I think he is frightened of you. Sit down on the ground, will you? And be quiet for a while—there's a good fellow."

Billings sank to the earth. The Esquimaux slowly lowered his spear and fell silent. He continued to glare at them but did not attempt to approach. Robinson took off his cap to reveal his sun-browned features and pulled down the collar of his jacket to show the white skin of his neck. The Esquimaux took a step toward him, then another. He removed a mitten and slowly reached out to touch the exposed skin. He uttered a low sound in his throat and placed his finger gingerly on Robinson's neck. He looked at his fingertip, then reached out again and rubbed the same area of skin.

"No, my friend," said Robinson. "It will not come off."

The man then turned and leaned in to look at Adams, staring intently at his blue eyes. Robinson felt the excitement build within him. Here was a better solution than scouring hundreds of square miles of frozen mud for a footprint. He cast a glance at Adams.

"This is an opportunity," he said. "They will sledge a thousand miles in the summer when they go sealing. He may have seen them or knows someone who has." He took off his glove and snapped his fingers at the Esquimaux. "Look here. Have you seen white men?" He pointed at Adams and drew a circle in the air around his own face. Then he pointed two fingers at his eyes and those of the man. "Have you seen *kabloona*, like us? With faces like this?"

The man looked from Robinson to Adams and back again but said nothing.

"Come now!" Robinson's tone was impatient. He turned and made a wide sweep with his arm, pointing both north and south. "Have you seen *kabloona*?"

"Perhaps we should give him a present," said Adams.

"Yes, a present. Good." Robinson slid the knapsack from his shoulder and swung it around before him.

The man retreated a step, alarm on his face.

"No, no." Robinson raised his hands again. "You are quite safe." He reached into the knapsack and brought out a packet of needles. He opened the packet, held a needle in his fingers, and displayed it to the man. "For you."

The man frowned. He took a step closer and examined the needles from a distance. He made a sound of approval and uttered something in his tongue, a succession of clicks and hawking sounds in his throat.

Robinson again held out the needles. "Take them. They are yours." He mimed the act of sewing. "Much better than bone needles."

The man took another step closer, curious now. He reached out and took the small box from Robinson's hand. They watched the man shake the packet of needles in his hand, then stow it away on his sledge.

Robinson pointed at the man and made a sweeping gesture with his arm. "Where have you come from? From which direction?"

The man pointed to the southeast. Robinson's stooped to look into the man's face. "From Iwillik? Iwillik?"

The man became excited and beamed at Robinson. He beat his chest once. "Iwillik!" He nodded.

"He is from Repulse Bay, then," said Robinson.

"What about ships?" Adams knelt, brushed aside some small stones, and smoothed out a flat area of earth. With his gloved finger, he drew a crude diagram of a ship in the dust, outlining a large hull with three masts rising from it. The man bent forward and carefully inspected the diagram.

Robinson pointed out to the ice-choked channel. "Like this. A big ship. *Umiak. Kabloona umiak!*" Robinson spread his arms wide to indicate something of great size, then raised two fingers. "Two big ships!"

The man stared at them, then shook his head. He gestured at the ice pack with another stream of guttural sounds and clicks and grunts. He looked from Robinson to Adams and back again.

"I think he says there could be no ships in that ice," Adams said.

Robinson addressed the man again. "Where might we look, then? For *kabloona*?" He held both hands out to his sides, palms up. "*Kabloona*, which way?"

The man cocked his head and muttered to himself. He shrugged and pointed to the southwest. Robinson conferred with Adams. "Do you think he means they *are* to be found that way? Or that they *might* be?"

Adams tried again. He pointed to the southeast in the direction of Repulse Bay. "*Kabloona?* That way?"

The man shook his head vigorously and pointed again to the southwest.

Robinson sighed. "Should we believe him? He is but one man."

"He has no reason to lie about coming from Repulse Bay. And if he did, there is every chance he would have encountered Franklin if Sir John had gone that way."

Robinson pointed to the south and asked him about reindeer. "*Tuktu?*"

The man frowned and waved his hand dismissively. He pointed at the seal meat on his sledge and then at the ice-filled channel to the west, making an undulating motion with one hand.

"No reindeer, then," said Adams. "He is only fishing and sealing." He whispered to Robinson. "Do you think he would agree to travel with us? He could show us the best route, hunt for us."

Robinson looked doubtful. "He knows we have no dogs. We cannot match his pace. At least, not while there is still snow on the ground."

"We could offer him payment."

Robinson considered this. He wished he had learned more than a few words of the Esquimaux tongue. He looked into the man's face, then pointed at himself and Adams and made a beckoning motion.

"Will you join us? Show us the way? Hunt for us?"

The man stared at him, uncomprehending. He looked at Adams, then back at Robinson.

Robinson suppressed an urge to seize the man by the throat and throttle him. He took a deep breath and tried again, pointing to himself, to Adams, and then back at the man. "You. Come with us." He held out his shotgun. "What if I gave you this? If you help us find *kabloona*?"

The man blinked at the shotgun, then silently regarded the two men. Robinson held out a bag of shot, but the man showed no sign of understanding. He took the bag and peered inside, then pulled the drawstring and bounced the bag in his hand, the lead balls clacking against each other.

Then Robinson decided to try a different tack. "Do you have food?" He pointed to his throat, lowered his hand, and patted his stomach. He moved his hand around his belly, then pointed at the man's sledge. The man nodded and made an enthusiastic sound. He looked curiously at the two men's sledge and spoke again.

"He expects an exchange," said Adams.

"Of course he does. It is what they do. Let us trade."

Robinson again inspected the contents of his knapsack. This time he brought forth a knife, which he displayed between his thumb and forefinger. He gestured at the man's sledge.

"For some food. A trade."

Nodding vigorously, the man stepped forward with a smile and took the knife from Robinson. He clapped him on the arm and beckoned them to approach his sledge. The three men knelt beside it. The frame and crossbars of the sledge were made of bones lashed together with sinew. The runners were rolls of frozen animal skin. The man unfastened the sledge cover and lifted it to reveal a dozen char, frozen like small logs. Beside the fish was a large chunk of dark-red meat. A thick layer of blubber was attached along one side. With his new knife, he chiselled at the frozen mass until half a dozen of the fish came away in a solid block; then he sliced away a five-pound hunk of the meat. He lifted them from the sledge and handed them happily to Adams.

"Splendid," said Robinson. He smiled. "Thank you."

The man laughed and nodded. He pointed to his dogs and then at their sledge and spoke again.

"He wants to know where our dogs are," said Adams.

Robinson shook his head at the man. "No dogs. We pull." He went to the sledge, put the track rope over his shoulder, and mimed hauling it over the ground. The man stared open-mouthed for a moment, then erupted in laughter.

———

Inside the tent, the stench of seal blood and ordure rising from the Esquimaux made Robinson cough. His hands black with grime, the man produced a sealskin bag, from which he took a shallow oval-shaped stone. On this he placed a quantity of seal blubber and a wick rolled from a handful of dried moss. Striking two lumps of pyrite together, he lit the lamp and sat back as the three men cooked their fish over the tiny flames.

Robinson offered the man a piece of salt pork. He sniffed it cautiously, nibbled it, then grimaced and spat the morsel out. He cut several long strips from the chunk of seal meat on his sledge. Throwing his head back, he crammed as much as possible into his mouth before taking his knife and slicing the strip of meat off at his lips.

Robinson searched their bags for a gift that might buy the man's allegiance. He brought out his sextant. The man held it upside down, peering closely at it, then tossed it on the floorcloth. Uninvited, he seized Adams' knapsack and began rummaging through it. He curiously examined Adams' Bible and sniffed at his ink bottle before dropping both items. He reached across and seized Robinson's telescope, running his fingertips over the milled edge of its brass ring.

"Like this," Robinson said. He stood and opened the tent flap. Light streamed in. Robinson held the eyepiece to the man's eye. In astonishment, he pulled his head away and made a low noise in his throat. He clasped the telescope to his chest. Robinson took it from him gently.

"I'm sorry, my friend," said Robinson, "that was only a demonstration. You may look at it, but this is one item I cannot spare."

The man sat back, his face empty of expression. He stood to leave.

"Wait!" Robinson called.

The man ignored him. He left the tent, went to his sledge, stowed his lamp and sealskin bag, and threw several handfuls of seal blubber at his dogs. The starving animals snarled and fell upon it, snapping at each other in desperation. In seconds the blubber had vanished. The dogs stood on the snow, licking their snouts and staring at the man.

"He cares greatly for his dogs," said Adams. "And they for him, it seems. I have rarely seen such a bond between a man and his animals."

"I like dogs," said Billings. "I like it when they lick my hand."

Robinson frowned at him. "Never try to touch one of these. It will *take* your hand."

Billings looked down, a wounded expression on his face.

"They will not hesitate to eat their dogs when they are starving," Robinson said. "Or they will cut the throat of one dog, slice the carcass into pieces, and feed it to the others."

The man checked the dogs' harnesses and boarded the sledge. Without a glance at the three Royal Navy men, he unrolled a sealskin whip and made a sound in his throat. The dogs responded as one, bounding away to the north with the sledge in tow. The three remaining men shivered in the cold breeze as the sledge vanished into the white light, its runners hissing on the thinning snow. The man on the sledge did not look back.

"And if a family member is old or sick," Robinson said, "they will take them out into the wilderness and leave them there." He shook his head and turned to walk back to the tent. "Savages."

He sat on the ground near the cliff's edge and watched the ice pack move beneath high clouds crowned with halos of light. He was reduced to trusting the word of an ignorant native. The wandering sealer had said there were no reindeer here and no white men to the southeast. *If Franklin had gone east, there surely would have been signs of him at Fury Beach. We are blocked by water to the west; Captain Ross searches to the north. There is only the southwest. It is the only possibility left. Adams thinks we are being taunted. I am not sure he is wrong.*

The wind freshened. The light behind the clouds dimmed, turning them grey at the edges. Soon they would swell and darken. They were running out of time.

CHAPTER SEVEN

Robinson walked with his eyes on the shingle, watching for debris from the missing vessels. Split and broken by the cold, stones clacked under his boots. Slow-moving ice choked the channel to the west. Billings found hauling the sledge easier where they discovered areas of smooth sea ice near the shore, and then they covered twenty miles in a day.

Robinson ordered a halt. They made camp. A wolf howled somewhere on the flatland to the east. Clouds gathered overhead, and the translucent air became thick with vapour. When they woke in the evenings, they forced their swollen feet back into iron-stiff boots. Billings rolled up their blankets, packed the tent, and placed it on the sledge. The route south took them over jagged stones and marsh and clay pans. Snow flurries wrapped them in swirling powder.

The coastline was bare of vegetation. Robinson looked for footprints in the little snow that remained. He peered at the sky for signs of smoke and scanned the ice pack to the west for masts. Where the land shelf dropped off sharply, the sea ice reached to the shore. It crammed the small inlets and bays, determined to rise and swallow the land. Hummocks pocked the surface of the ice like blisters on the sea, their sides patterned with whorls. They climbed hills of scree, their boots sliding backward one pace for every two steps forward, then collapsed on all fours at the top and gasped for breath.

One morning they stopped on a low headland. Two glacial streams snaked across the plain below, bleeding into the ocean. A pair of eider ducks flew overhead. Adams shot one, the sound of the gunshot like a stone through a glass pane. The bird exploded on the earth in a cloud of feathers. Rivulets of blood threaded across the gravel, sparkling in the sunlight. Adams and Billings pitched the tent as Robinson walked the ground around the campsite. They collected driftwood, bleached white as bone and carried high on the shore by the ice, and cooked the bird on an open fire.

Billings ate his fill and sat near the flames, ineffable contentment on his face. Weary and sullen before the meal, his disposition was now unabashedly cheerful. Robinson watched him, awed at the man's lack of artifice. Billings could not feign stoicism or courage or bluster, would never deceive or beguile. His mood remained on permanent display. When he was happy, his face shone with light. When he was tired or melancholy, he sulked or wept. *But perhaps I have it backward,* Robinson thought. *Perhaps the true marvel is that other men can feign so much. Guile and deceit must be learned. Perhaps it is only natural that a man without the capacity to learn has not acquired them.*

Billings looked across at Adams, grinning. "Will we find Sir John tomorrow, Mister Adams?"

"We might, Jimmy."

Robinson and Adams filled their pipes as Billings flung handfuls of feathers into the air and watched them whirl away on the wind.

———

When Robinson slept, Adams pulled on his boots and heavy coat. He took his pencil and journal and sat on a boulder. The wind dropped, and the sun scoured the sky of clouds. Long sweeps of his pencil failed to soften the lines of the crenellated bluff south of their campsite. Despite the imminent arrival of summer, the hills were still dusted with snow, square and wrinkled like the head of a sperm whale. He shaded, then shaded again, but could not properly reproduce the iron grey of the sky.

The faintest of halos circled the moon, but the one on his page was too stark, too well defined.

There is too much life in this picture, he thought. *I cannot reproduce the deadness.*

He drew the birds fluttering near the bluffs—merely a collection of dots and specks—then erased them when, even as indistinct flecks on the paper, they lent too much animation to the scene. When he looked up from the page, the landscape before him seemed even more inert than the one on the paper. He wondered how he had done it. Somehow his sketch suggested life, but if one stood here and looked, one would swear there was none.

He tried to write a letter to Frances but found it difficult to describe what he saw. It was easier to name what was absent: people, dwellings, trees, colour. Just grey clouds and grey sea and the ice. He sat with pen poised over the page until he began to shiver, and then he wrote.

Dearest Frances, it is tempting to call this the last place God made, but I think He ran out of elements before He could finish it. There are not even shadows here, for there is nothing to cast them. I see now there is great comfort to be had in shadows—they are the shapes of those things we find familiar. Their absence makes this place so much vaster and more frightening. Will there ever be an end to it? There are times when I am overwhelmed by the beauty of this place, and others when all around me is ugly and harsh. Perhaps God does not reside here; perhaps He pays only the occasional visit. I think the Arctic is like a slow-acting poison. It is intoxicating. It can induce euphoria. But too much will kill a man.

Robinson led them south over vast gravel plains where tufts of olive grass had begun to poke up through large patches of snow unwilling to relinquish their grip on the land. The wind was a veil of whispers. Clouds so dark and heavy and full of rain, he thought they must surely crash to the earth. They passed a small bay. The sea between the beach and the ice pack was as still as water standing in a bowl. Billings knelt and scooped up a handful of snow, thrusting it into his mouth.

Robinson's jaw tightened. "Billings! I told you before: do not eat snow." He sighed and waved a gloved hand at Adams. "Make him understand, will you?"

"Mister Robinson is correct, Jimmy," he said patiently. "It will make you cold and burn your mouth, likely as not."

Billings hung his head. "But I'm thirsty, Mister Adams. My canteen is empty. We ain't crossed a stream in hours."

A fox scampered out from behind a low rise. Robinson dropped to one knee and shot it. With a whoop, Billings ran out across the plain to retrieve it. Robinson drew his knife, cut out the entrails, and tossed them on the ground, then licked the blood from his fingers and threw the carcass on the sledge.

In the morning they stopped and pitched the tent where mist lingered over the ground like gun smoke after a battle. Adams and Robinson agreed to conserve their meagre supply of candles. The tent's interior was dim, but the canvas wall glowed as the sun climbed in the sky. Robinson tied a strip of black cloth across his eyes and lay down in his blanket.

"I think time stops here," he said. "There is nothing to measure its passage. The seasons change, but each year is the same as the one before. If I stood on this spot a thousand years ago, I daresay it would have looked just as it does today: rock, ice, and wind. In England, one can watch time passing. Timber rots, colours fade, and people die. There is nothing like that here."

"Will we find Sir John tomorrow, Mister Adams?" Billings' voice was that of an exhausted child on the verge of sleep.

———

The heavy ice in the channel to the west did not break up. Adams stared at crags and hummocks studding the floes like nuts on a cake.

The shoreline was featureless, sweeping brown ridges of shingle thrust upon the land over millennia by the shifting ice. Patches of brown earth had begun to appear, but a thin crust of snow still covered much of the ground inland from the beach.

Adams' shoulders ached from the sledge harness, and his empty belly throbbed. His feet were sore, and a freezing wind numbed his face. It sucked his energy, dried him out, made his head ache. The sun was like the flash of a shotgun muzzle through the fabric of the grey sky. His eyes burned as if lined with pepper. He removed the strip of green crape from his snow goggles and retied it, folding it over itself. He gingerly touched his blistered cheeks with his fingertips.

They pitched their tent in the early morning. Robinson searched for driftwood but returned with empty hands held high in surrender. Adams sat Billings on the ground and unbuttoned his shirt. He sat back, eyes brimming, as the rank odour of the man's unwashed body rose and clawed at his throat.

Robinson approached, his shadow falling across them.

"My God," he whispered. "We might as well have flogged him."

The track ropes had left angry red weals in the flesh of Billings' shoulders. The skin was broken and turning purple in several places along the edges of the welts. Blood had oozed into the fabric of Billings' linen shirt and dried in rivulets down his back. Adams sighed and shook his head. An infected wound could kill a man in such a remote place.

"Oh, Jimmy," he said, "we shall have to lighten your load."

Billings looked up. "Cat's paw," he said. He pointed into the sky. "That cloud looks like a big cat's paw." He lifted his hand, fingers curled into the palm, and rocked it forward like a cat batting a toy.

"It would be a very big cat, wouldn't it, Jimmy?"

Billings nodded solemnly. "Maybe a lion." No longer shivering, he stared into the heavens with eyes that saw nothing.

"Have you ever seen a lion, Jimmy?"

Billings did not appear to hear him. Adams watched his face. This was how the man sank into himself, walling himself off from his hunger, fear, and pain. He merely made the decision to go. Adams felt a spark of envy.

"Come now, Jimmy," whispered Adams. "We must get you to bed."

Billings blinked and dropped his head. He groaned, misery creasing his face. Adams saw it now. Returning from that far-off place hurt Billings. He could take himself away, but returning was like bursting forth from beneath the calm, silent water only to find the air full of smoke and knives.

Adams rolled Billings into his blanket bag and wrapped his torn shoulders in strips of clean linen before removing his own boots. The stink of his own feet made Adams gag. He bathed them in meltwater, hissing at the pain of the icy water on his skin, then rubbed them dry with a scrap of linen and pulled on his dry bed socks. He and Robinson stretched out inside their blanket bags. The wind whistled and flicked at the corners of the tent. As they lay shivering, their breath rose in clouds, and moisture dripped from the tent's ceiling. Adams touched the Bible in his coat pocket.

I would like to read a prayer, he thought. *I should read a prayer.*

He slept.

The next day they arrived at the edge of a large frozen bay and walked eight miles over the ice before making camp on the opposite shore. The snow on the ground was melting, and it was harder to pull the sledge through the thick slush, but there was less glare, and the burning in their eyes began to abate. Adams removed his wet boots and lay down in his blanket bag. Billings snored beside him.

"It has been ten days," said Adams.

Robinson sat unmoving, his eyes glazed.

"A few ducks, a couple of foxes," Adams continued. "It has allowed us to stretch our supplies but is not enough to sustain us much longer."

Robinson blinked, reanimated. "The reindeer will migrate north." He began filling his pipe.

Adams pulled off a mitten and scratched his beard. "They follow certain routes. We may not be on one."

Robinson grunted. He massaged his leg. "My knees are very sore. And my feet are swollen."

"Jimmy's shoulders are bad. They will not soon heal up," said Adams. "I taste blood on my tongue. I have a couple of loose teeth, and my gums are putty." He sighed. "Strange that it should come on so soon. Scurvy, I think, is like a sin returned to haunt a man. An injury long healed opens and bleeds for the first time in years. A sore knee, an injured back, is again painful. A reminder that your past can return to visit you and make you lament it all over again."

Robinson pulled his shotgun onto his lap. He replaced the wadding and wiped the nipple and barrel dry. There was a stiffness to his movements. He turned away to scribble in his journal. After a while he put down his pencil and lay in his blankets. His breathing slowed, but Adams knew he was awake. Eventually, the lieutenant spoke, resignation in his voice.

"Very well. There is nothing for it. We shall hunt this evening. Then we shall turn around."

Adams took Billings and went hunting along the coast to the south. Robinson ventured inland with his shotgun, promising to meet them after midnight. With no sledge to haul, Billings trudged behind Adams without complaint, but Adams worried the light in the man had dimmed, leaving a hollowness he knew not how to fill.

The two men made their way along a brown stony beach to a spit of shingle that twisted away around a low bluff. The sky was dusted with low grey clouds. They shivered in the shadows of the cliffs rising overhead. The stones shifted and muttered under their boots, and a northerly breeze chilled their backs. The shingle beach narrowed, and the earth sloped sharply up to the east. Adams stopped where a small stream of meltwater gushed from a crevice, spouting over a jagged boulder like a tiny waterfall.

"Are you thirsty, Jimmy?" He shrugged his knapsack from his shoulder and laid his shotgun on the stones. "Let's fill our canteens."

He looked at Billings. The young seaman stared up at the slope above them, his mouth agape and his eyes wide in astonishment. From somewhere on the hillside behind him, Adams heard broken shards of rock slide and click under the weight of something large.

Bear.

Dread was a heavy stone in his belly. He swung around, his head full of images of yawning jaws and soulless black eyes and claws like obsidian blades. Something heavy struck him between the eyes. He fell backward, his nose crushed, eyes welling with tears. Panting, a large dark shape moved above him, indistinct in the gloom. He could not see Billings. His forehead burned, and liquid ran into his eyes. He shook his head to clear it. Flecks of blood spattered his gloves. He tried to sit up. The stock of his shotgun was smooth and familiar in his fingers. He dragged the weapon up, heavy against his shoulder, and aimed at the centre of the grunting mass above him. Only then did his vision begin to clear. The creature coalesced from a collection of blurry shadows, its edges suddenly sharper. Adams lowered the gun.

Crouched on the slope above him was a man.

CHAPTER EIGHT

The intruder's face was black with filth, his eyes rimmed with red. His cheekbones protruded above a scraggly beard shot through with grey. He wore a heavy overcoat and dirty box cloth trousers that flapped around stick-thin legs. Tendons stood out like ropes in his neck. Veins laced the backs of his hands like black worms.

Adams sat on the rocky earth, staring up at the man with his shotgun across his lap. In one black-fingered hand, the man grasped a stone. His other hand gripped a knife, its blade encrusted with dirt. The stockinged heel of his foot was visible through a gaping hole in his boot. His back hunched like a nocturnal beast captured suddenly in lamplight. Adams held his tongue, unsure whether a salutation would frighten or mollify. The man's wild stare flicked from one point on the ground to another before locking on Adams' knapsack. He launched himself across Adams at the knapsack, scrabbling at the buckles. Adams bent his knees, planted a boot squarely on the man's chest, and shoved him backward. The dishevelled figure staggered back but appeared possessed of desperate strength. He snarled and raised the knife, slashing at the air between them.

Adams found his voice. "Stop, man!"

The man came at him again. Adams raised the shotgun barrel, but the man's boot swung around and knocked the weapon from his hand. The gun discharged as it struck the earth, the echo of the explosion reverberating along the cliffs. Adams fell back again, and the man stabbed downward, the point of the knife ripping a gash in his trousers.

"Jimmy!" Adams shouted.

The man reared above Adams and raised his knife again. He seemed to grow larger in the grey light, like a balloon filling with air. Adams glimpsed a face assembled of bony brows and deep sockets, eyes pale blue, skin flaking from the lips. The man's mouth opened as if to scream, but he made no sound. Adams swung his arm at the man's wrist, and the knife spun across the stones.

"Jimmy! I need you!"

At last he saw Billings. The big man was crouched on his haunches twenty feet away. He stared at the earth, his hands clamped over his ears.

"Jimmy!"

The intruder's knee was on Adams' chest. The stink of his unwashed body was in his nostrils. Hands locked on his throat. Panic churned in him. His body demanded air. Through blood-misted eyes, he looked up at the face of the feral man. Lips, purple like week-old meat, drawn back in a snarl. The world darkened.

Then the man was gone from him. Adams sucked a long, ragged breath. He coughed and spat the stink of the man from his mouth. Billings held the thrashing man from behind, one huge arm circling his neck, the other clinched around his waist. Billings bent one knee, trying to wrestle the man to the ground. The intruder's ravaged face bulged from the crook of Billings' arm. He kicked out in panic, arching his back. Adams heard something crack, and then the man was limp in Billings' hands, like a marionette with its strings suddenly severed. Billings cried out in alarm and released the man as though burned by the touch of his skin. The man's chin fell to his breast and he slumped, boneless, to the ground.

———

"What in God's name have you done?"

Robinson stood trembling fifty yards away, his shotgun in his hands. His breathing was heavy in his skull, sweat freezing on his forehead. Tears streaming down his face, Billings wrung his hands and hopped from one foot to the other.

"I didn't mean to. I didn't mean to."

Adams sat on the ground near the corpse. Blood ran down his face from a gash between his eyes. He coughed again and put a hand to his throat, feeling for damage.

"Not his fault," he said to Robinson.

"Then it is yours!" Robinson felt a wave of fury crash over him as he ran to where Adams lay. "He could have taken us to Franklin!"

It was close to midnight. The gashes in the grey clouds had closed up, dimming the light like a veil thrown over a lamp. The cold northerly wind blew stronger. Billings knelt on the ground. He squeezed his eyes shut and pressed his hands to both sides of his head.

"The man was addled," said Adams. "Starving, I think. He wanted the knapsack."

"Then why not give it to him?" Robinson demanded.

"He had a knife. He tried to throttle me. If it were not for Jimmy . . ."

Robinson marched to where Billings knelt, thinking about how far he had travelled, how correct he had been in his prediction, and how this fool had snatched away his prize.

"Damn you!" he cried, "Can you not restrain a man without killing him?"

Hunched over, Billings howled like a gutshot dog.

If it were not for Jimmy.

Robinson felt the fury take hold of him, the blood hot in his cheeks, his fists clenching. Had the simpleton done it on purpose so they would turn back? Rage boiled up within him, swallowing him, spilling as a wave over a dam.

If it were not for Jimmy. It seemed to Robinson that the hands raising the shotgun were not his own. He did not feel the weapon's weight or his finger curl on the trigger. He wanted only to hear the explosion, see the idiot's blood and brains splashed on the stones. The muzzle trembled in the cold air, inches from the top of Billings' head. Oblivious, the seaman remained on his knees, bawling. The ocean to the east was as black as old blood.

Elizabeth's voice was in his head. *You do yourself no favours when you are overly impassioned.*

His heart tolled in his chest. He closed his eyes, dropped his chin, and exhaled, a long, slow release of breath. He took his finger from the trigger and lowered the shotgun. He put the weapon on the ground, then slowly removed his gloves and put his face in his hands. Allowing Adams to bring the simpleton along had been a gamble. But Robinson needed only one gamble to pay off. An image of his father was in his head, watching him with arms folded, malicious glee on his face. He knew what he would say.

Now what will you do, boy?

———

Billings had stopped crying. He looked up at Adams with red-rimmed eyes.

"I'm sorry, Mister Adams," he whispered. "I didn't mean to."

"I know, Jimmy." Adams patted his shoulder. "It's not your fault." Nor was it. It was his own. He had thought only to use Billings' great strength, and the young giant had merely done as he was told.

"I want my ma." Billings hung his head. "I want a pie."

"I know, Jimmy."

Adams felt a wave of helplessness. He had never been adept at easing pain that was not physical. He could tell Billings all would be well, and the young man would believe him. He could tell him they would find Franklin tomorrow.

"Pray with me, Jimmy." He knelt beside Billings and touched his forehead to the stones. Billings copied him. "Help us, Lord. We have now taken a life. How can this be part of it?"

Adams rolled the dead man onto his back. The stink of urine made him turn his head. Robinson stood behind him, saying nothing. Billings stood with his back to them, staring at the ice pack.

With the tip of his pocketknife, Adams lifted the corpse's lip. But for two molars on either side, all the man's teeth were missing. His blue eyes were half-open, the eyelashes filmed with ice. He was clad in a mismatched selection of Royal Navy–issue slops. Beneath his tattered coat, he wore a dirty sweater and two flannel shirts. They found an iron water flask in one pocket but no identifying papers.

"My God, there is no flesh on him at all," said Adams. "If we piled up his clothes, they would weigh more than he does." He pulled off the dead man's boots and tapped his frost-blackened toes. They did not yield as flesh should. "Like wood. I would have had to amputate."

He and Robinson turned and looked down the coast of Boothia Felix, snaking away to the south. A bank of mist clung to a small promontory a few miles farther down the beach. The haze obscured their view beyond the bluff. Adams raised the telescope and scanned the horizon for a wisp of smoke from a signal fire, a lonely flagstaff planted on a barren headland, a glint of sunlight off a telescope lens.

"You were correct, then," Adams said. "They went south."

Robinson chewed his lip and stared off at the distant haze. They buried the man in a shallow depression Billings scraped out of the iron-hard ground. Flecks of snow appeared in the air as they covered the grave with flat rocks. They stood over it as the sky took on the colour of lead. Robinson tossed a handful of gravel into the grave. The pebbles bounced out and skittered away across the ground. Adams said a prayer as Billings bowed his head. Robinson watched in silence.

"I heard a story once," said Adams, "from a whaler who saw a grave opened at Upernavik. A shipmate of his had died there the year before. The grave was only three feet deep. They couldn't dig any further down. The dead man was frozen solid, he said. Looked the same as the day he was buried. Skin, eyes—everything the same, like a man asleep. He said if you thawed him out, he would sit up and ask for his supper."

Robinson stared at the ground.

"This place permits us nothing," said Adams. "No food. No shelter. No warmth." He looked at the sky. "Should you die here, it even begrudges you a grave."

The dead man's sledge lay half a mile down the beach, with a blanket and a filthy piece of rolled-up canvas. One of the wooden sledge runners was missing. Adams found a small bag of musket balls wrapped in the blanket, but no gun.

Adams bent down and collected two pieces of fabric pinned within the canvas. One was a pair of linen drawers, once white but now grey with dirt, slit at the knee and hip with long gashes, along which the fabric was stained dark brown. The other was a shirt. One sleeve had been torn off at the shoulder. The same brown stains were visible along the edge of the cloth.

Something dropped from the sledge. Adams bent down to investigate and stood again, holding a tattered boot. The other, its sole flapping, was wrapped in the blanket.

"It seems he may have had a companion for at least part of his journey."

He watched the ice move in the ocean to the west, the broken pieces colliding in the current.

They broke up the man's sledge and made a fire. Frost smoke rose from the water. The moving floes chittered in the channel. Adams rummaged in the knapsack and lifted out six lumps of salt pork and a few pieces of biscuit, then put all but three pieces of pork and a single piece of biscuit back in the bag.

"Enough for one more day," said Adams. "Perhaps two."

He broke the biscuit into three pieces and gave one each to Robinson and Billings, then placed the pork on a stone at the fire's edge until it began to steam. Chewing his biscuit, Billings sat transfixed, staring at the lumps of salt meat.

Robinson sighed. "I wish we had brought more tea." It was the first time he had spoken since the visitor was buried.

Adams studied him across the fire. Robinson's features bent and flickered in the flames, as if he were two men locked in an argument. If Adams and Billings had managed to subdue the intruder, would they now be leading Franklin's man home with news of the lost explorer's location? The path had once seemed so clear. Now it seemed to wind away and disappear into the fog drifting in from the ice pack to the south.

Robinson tossed a pebble into the fire. "I tell you now, I shall not go back with nothing. I will not return to Captain Ross and say, 'Beg your pardon, sir, we found one of Franklin's men but broke his neck, then turned around and came home.'"

Adams sat with his Bible in his lap. He stuck the tip of his knife into a piece of pork and blew on it. "But if we find more like *him*?" He pointed with his chin at the grave.

"Deserters?"

"If that is what he was," said Adams.

"This is your doing," said Robinson. "And his." He jerked his thumb at Billings. "You wanted him along. I will have you accept the consequences. We must go on."

Adams was quiet. He passed the salt pork skewered on his knife to Billings. "Be careful, Jimmy. It's hot." Billings sat blowing on his meat and gazing into the flames.

"Do you waver?" Robinson asked.

God forgive me, I do, Adams thought, but shook his head. "This is the path the Lord has put me on. I must follow it."

"You volunteered for this mission, did you not?"

"I did."

91

"Then it is your choice to be here, not God's."

Adams stared into the dying fire, watching the glowing red coals fade to black. "Everything is as God wills it. If He did not choose me, He would have chosen a different man, and that man would be here. I know this: if we are to proceed, we must find more meat."

"Then we agree." Robinson stood, his shotgun in his hand. "Before we search further, we must finish our hunt. Bring the telescope, would you?"

⸺

They left Billings with the sledge and tent and took their shotguns, shot bags, and canteens, walking east across an ice-scarred plain. The sun was a fiery badge emblazoned on the sky. They stepped carefully over ground free of snow. Patches of red and orange lichen were splashed over the earth. Bear tracks in a patch of dried mud could have been an hour old or a thousand years, preserved by the cold like a fossil.

After two hours of walking, Robinson sank to his knees beside a cluster of small boulders and waved Adams down with his hand. He raised his telescope and looked up a sweeping slope at a collection of six brown shapes ambling along the ridge above them. The reindeer dropped their heads and nuzzled the lichen. When they raised their gaze and scanned the surrounding land, their antlers were silhouetted against the sky like misshapen candlesticks. The two men dropped flat and crawled slowly up the slope toward the herd. When they approached within sixty yards, Robinson put his mouth to Adams' ear and whispered, "The big one."

Adams nodded.

A large male picked its way along the ridge. A pouch of skin hung from its throat. Patches of white adorned its chest. Adams rose to his knees and aimed. For an instant, the reindeer stared at the odd creature that had risen from the earth, then turned to flee and, for the briefest moment, stood in profile.

The two men fired their weapons, and the small herd scattered. Both balls struck the large male. The animal lurched, and Robinson and Adams leaped to their feet, prepared to give chase, but the reindeer staggered once and fell.

When they reached it, the reindeer was not moving. The animal was sprawled awkwardly, its legs unbending and black eyes dull. One ball had destroyed its foreleg joint, attached now only by a piece of sinew. The other had struck the reindeer in the neck. Shiny blood coated its shoulder and ran onto the ground, pooling in the stony earth.

The two men sat on boulders under a darkening sky and sharpened their knives on stones.

———

Adams ran his knife down the backbone and peeled off the skin. He cut out the stomach and threw it on the ground. They took the haunches and shoulders and ribs and put them into the canvas bags that had held their salt pork. Robinson stood behind the dead creature's head with a leg on either side of the carcass. He grasped the antlers and twisted with all his strength. The spine snapped, and the head broke off. He cracked the spine and leg bones across a boulder and pulled out the marrow. Adams cut out the dark-red liver and wrapped the dripping organ in a piece of linen.

The two men sat with their backs to a boulder and ate with blood running down their chins. It was salty and metallic in their throats as they sighed and lay back on the gravel, their bellies rising and falling. They put as much meat as they could carry into their knapsacks and walked away, leaving the remains of the reindeer. The antlers stood up from the earth like a pair of skeletal hands cupped in worship. They walked west to the coast, where Billings waited with the sledge and tent. At the sight of the bags of meat, Billings clapped his hands in delight for the first time in days.

Fragments of fog drifted around them like wraiths. Ancient whale bones, pitted with holes, crumbled to ash beneath their boots. They approached a small glacier uncurling like a smooth white tongue down a ravine. Minutes later they trudged across it, finding it pitted with dirt-streaked holes and riven with fissures.

They descended from the hills to the beach and travelled south along the shingle. Two days later they approached a sandy promontory. Beyond it lay a frozen bay three miles across. The bay ice was solid and smooth, so they hauled the sledge across and walked to the far shore. A cluster of enormous boulders huddled halfway up a long, low slope above the beach.

Adams discovered an ancient piece of driftwood pressed flat into the earth. He prised it out of the soil with his knife, lit a fire, and cooked the reindeer flesh. They dug a hole at the foot of the largest boulder and deposited fifty pounds of meat wrapped in canvas. They covered the cache with a layer of sand, smoothed the earth over with the shovel, then stood and continued down the beach.

———

"We must cross the ice to King William Land," said Robinson. "There is nowhere else they could be."

They stood on the beach at Cape Adelaide and looked out across the strait. The ice was closely packed, the ocean sealed beneath it. Broken chunks of ice were thrust up against each other, fresh snow in the depressions between them despite the lateness of the season. Hummocks rising from the pack seemed afire, and the clouds glowed red at midnight. Robinson pointed to the southwest.

"Our visitor can only have walked across the ice from the west. There is nothing to the east but Prince Regent Inlet, and Sir John Ross proved there is no Passage there. Cape Felix is thirty-five miles that way, Victory Point only twenty miles beyond."

He stood close to Adams, his manner convivial. He moved to clap Adams on the shoulder but let his arm drop. For a moment, there was silence between them.

"Victory Point is just over two hundred miles to Point Turnagain," he added, "and Franklin had been there in '21. If the ships sailed south from Cape Walker, that is where he would have headed." Robinson fell silent as the significance of his own words dawned upon him. "He would have assumed that was the North-West Passage."

The fog thickened. The silhouettes of bergs shifted in the mist. Shapes loomed within them, like the shadows of unknown creatures entombed in the ice. They struck southwest toward King William Land, hauling enough reindeer meat for nine days. Free of cracks, the surface of the ice grunted and squeaked beneath their boots. The sun crackled in the sky, painting ribbons on the pack. They filled their canteens from meltwater puddles. A wolf followed them for two days, lingering out of range of their guns as if it knew how far their balls would carry. It watched them, its long snout dipping to the ice.

The three men threaded their way through the hummocks and ice crags, traversing leads that wound along the floes like veins across skin. Pools of water were few, and little more than ankle deep. Robinson felt no warmth on his palm when he held it up to the midnight sun. They suffered much from the glare and marched with scarves wrapped high on their faces.

Shoulders raw from the sledge harness, they stopped and pitched the tent on the ice. They rubbed their frozen feet and rolled out the floorcloth and blankets. The canvas tent shuddered as if gossamer. Robinson lay down and eased himself into his blanket, groaning. Gnawing on pieces of reindeer meat, he rolled onto his side and tucked his legs, nursing tiny pockets of body heat. The wind was like icy fingers stroking his bones.

In the evening, they walked on. With no visible landmarks, they were unsure of their location; each mile was indistinguishable from the last. Bludgeoned by the unrelenting sun, Robinson brushed rime from his eyebrows and squeezed the bridge of his nose between his fingers, but the white shapes around him remained blurred and ghostly. The horizon was a white line beneath an iron sky. Hummocks of ice reared up in places like misshapen sea monsters. Carried on the wind, long fingers of vapour ran across the ice and curled around their ankles.

The cold drove them on.

"There," said Robinson, pointing. "That is the coast of King William Land, I am sure of it."

Adams squinted through his goggles. The sky was blotchy with clouds. Curtains of light ran across their feet as clouds shuffled in front of the sun. Nearly blind from the glare, he could just make out a thin brown line atop the ice on the horizon. It seemed a long way off, but he realised the shoreline barely rose above the level of the sea ice and was probably no more than a mile away. Nothing lay beyond it; no cliffs rose above the water, no glaciers wound their way down ravines. The land had been flattened by the ice of aeons past, squashed by massive glaciers that had scoured all features from it.

We walk into oblivion, Adams thought. *Never have I seen so much of nothing.*

As he journeyed north the past year, Adams had imagined an invisible thread tethering him to England. Each time he reached a place more remote than the last—Disko Bay, Upernavik, Possession Bay—he thought, surely there could be nothing beyond this, surely the spool cannot pay out any more line. When *Enterprise* and *Investigator* were trapped in the ice at Port Leopold, the thread binding him to England seemed to have stretched as far as possible. The little bay at the tip of North Somerset seemed like the most isolated place in the world, the final citadel beyond which all was wilderness.

But then at Fury Beach, the thread unspooled even farther, and Port Leopold suddenly seemed a metropolis in his memory: two ships, years of provisions, warming stoves, mattresses, double bulkheads, a fully stocked medicine chest, the company of a hundred men. Now, here on the frozen sea, the Fury Beach campsite, the weathered timbers of Somerset House, its casks and barrels of twenty-five-year-old vegetables and soup, represented the height of civilisation.

Wherever they went next, Franklin would surely be waiting, a smile on his lips.

Just keep going into the nothingness, Adams thought. *We whittle down our existence a little more with each step away from what we know. Perhaps if we keep walking, we will simply wink out and disappear. And there he will be.*

He stared at the beach ahead, not looking where he put his feet. He felt the surface of the ice through the sole of his boot, just as he had thousands of times, and then his foot lurched downward as the ice gave way. Panic thrust a fist up from beneath his ribs, and suddenly he was waist deep in freezing water. The cold gripped him and pulled him lower. His legs would not move. The water was up to his armpits now. He tried to kick, but there was nothing beneath his feet to push against. In another moment the water was at his neck. The cold water stabbed at his throat, found its way beneath his clothes, scraped his back, curled around his ribs. The pain was like a burn, sucking the air from his lungs.

O blessed Lord, he thought, *forgive me my sins. Bestow Thy mercy upon me.*

He arched his back. Soaked, his heavy clothes weighed upon his limbs like armour. He stared up at the ice from the level of the water. It was only four feet thick but looked like the side of an iceberg, a hundred feet high. Blood roared in his ears. He forgot why he was there, could not imagine what he was doing. Then a tranquillity settled upon him, and his terror left him. He accepted it, this sense of astonishment. Before the water closed over his head, he thought, *How odd, this is how a seal must see the world.*

CHAPTER NINE

Adams was warm. He lay on his side beneath a blanket. Something large and hot pressed against his naked back. The ice pack moaned and creaked somewhere far away as the black ocean moved beneath him. He imagined the pressure ridges rising, great alabaster slabs forced against each other by the currents and wind with a sound like the breaking of bones. He tried to remember, to understand how he came to be here. The memory danced out of reach, hovering in the shadows of his mind like an apparition just outside the pool of light thrown by a lamp in a dark room. The wind whined across the ice outside the tent. He remembered dropping through a trapdoor into a dark cellar. He could not recall being wet or cold. His body felt light, and he thought he might float into the air, if only he wished.

O Lord, have I done Thy bidding?

He summoned his strength and opened one eye, squinting in the dim light. Robinson sat a few feet away, writing in his journal. It was Billings, then, lying against him beneath the blanket. The young seaman's bare chest pressed against Adams' back, his breathing a soft, steady cadence. His arm curled around the assistant surgeon's chest. His knee was nestled against the back of Adams' own. Adams tried to move his fingers but had no sensation in his hands.

I wish only to stay here, just like this, he thought, *never to move again. If he wakes and pulls away, I shall burst into tears.*

"We needed to warm you quickly," Robinson said. "You were quite senseless. Wet and freezing. We had to get your clothes off. The heat of his body was all we had."

Adams tried to speak. All that emerged was a dry, strangled sound in his throat.

Robinson studied him. "It is nine o'clock in the morning. Rest for the remainder of the day. We shall resume our march in the evening, if you can."

Adams swallowed, cleared his throat. A hoarse whisper rose from somewhere outside his head, the sound of his own voice unrecognisable. "Where are we?"

Robinson rubbed his eyes and yawned. "About ten miles south of Cape Felix. I would make you a fire, but we have no fuel."

Adams closed his eyes. Billings slept on.

"He nearly went under himself, you know," said Robinson. "He was drenched to the waist, upside down in the hole in the ice. You were sinking just as he reached you. Another moment and he would not have grasped your collar."

"He is a good man," Adams whispered.

Robinson lit his pipe and sat, smoking quietly. Finally, he nodded. "Yes. He is a good man."

"I dreamed of him. Of Sir John."

"Tell me."

"I saw the ships," said Adams. "I was floating like a gull, aloft on the freezing air. *Erebus* and *Terror* were in the ice, housed over with awnings."

The dream returned so clearly. He had seen their topmasts down, the sails wrapped and stored away. The ships' boats had been buried in the snow, for the sun had been gone a month, and no amount of prayer would coax it back before February. He looked away to the sky's edge, but the sun was cloaked, a mere glow below the southern horizon for an hour on either side of noon, a torch burned down to a smouldering nub.

"Then I was inside one of them. *Erebus*, I think. Sir John stood at the window of his cabin. He was staring out into a winter gloom that rose like a prison wall."

Adams fell silent, spent by the effort of speech. *Later,* he thought, *I shall write it down for Frances.* He would tell her he saw Franklin clasp his hands behind his back to hide the tremors from his men. The captain had stood just outside the small puddles of light spilled by two candles on the table behind him, watching his reflection fracture on the grimy pane. He listened to the deck timbers creaking and popping as the ice that trapped them shifted against the hull. Franklin's face was lined and his hair untrimmed. Grey stubble roughened his cheeks, and dark stains spotted his rumpled uniform. He wore his scuffed old grey shoes, not his best boots. His steward had not polished those for many weeks. Franklin had forgotten to remind him, and the man had grown too ill to fulfil his duties. The winter sky was a thick blue-grey veil that he went to push on with his shaky white hand before withdrawing it, cowed, lest his fingertips be seared on the freezing glass.

"And what of Crozier?" Robinson asked intently. "Did you see him also?" He seemed absorbed in Adams' tale, as if pressing for details from the witness to a crime.

"He was there. Beside Franklin at the window." Even in his dream, Adams could smell the brandy on Crozier. His eyes were sunk in his skull. He reported twelve sick this morning on *Erebus*, fourteen on *Terror*. "It is melancholy and boredom that does it," Crozier advised Franklin, "for when confined belowdecks, they have nothing to do but darn socks and wipe down the walls. It is too dark for hunting or skating on the ice, and too cold. If we let them out, we shall not see half of them again."

"Make sure the men get extra rations over Christmas," Franklin told him.

"I shall order an extra gill of rum for each man and a gallon of beer for each mess." Franklin looked pained, but Crozier added, "You know it will go better for them if they are drunk."

Franklin sighed and gazed out into the murk. "Four winters. I pray this shall be the last." Then he whispered so that no one, not even Crozier, could hear.

"Do you suppose they are coming?"

Adams closed his eyes. He would not tell Robinson the end of his dream. The ships were gone. Franklin's men shuffled across the dead land like ghosts, their gums blackening, teeth dropping onto their boots from gaping mouths. Purple scars ran with blood. Yellow skin stretched over rib cages and concave bellies. Eyeless sockets stared at the barren shingle, and fingers turned to bone inside their gloves. As they walked, the lichen-encrusted stones and bare ice became ugly, stunted forests where they encountered Esquimaux hunters, who lowered their weapons, stared at the apparitions, and asked, "Where did you come from?" Crozier waved at the north. "From there," he said, and then turned to his remaining men. "Perhaps they will think we descend from the sky. We may yet know what it is like to be gods."

Robinson puffed on his pipe. When he finally spoke, his voice was so soft, Adams thought he was talking only to himself.

"I think I have begun to envy Franklin."

Adams opened his eyes. "You?"

Robinson spoke slowly, groping for the words. "I can issue an order or follow one. I can have a man's obedience. But to earn his devotion . . . I do not know how to do that. Franklin endears himself to people who have never met him. They worry for him and pray for his safe return. They write poems and songs for him." He stopped and puffed once more on his pipe. "I find that extraordinary. How on earth does he get them to do that?"

Adams was unsure whether he was asleep or awake. The words were in his mind, on his tongue. Perhaps he said them aloud. It might have been only a whisper, or merely a thought.

"He is doing God's work."

Robinson led them ashore ten miles southeast of the northernmost tip of King William Land. The sea ice vanished from beneath his boots, and he stepped onto an empty beach of gravelly brown shingle stretching away to the west. Adams limped up behind him, still weak from his dunking in the sea. He bent over and coughed for an entire minute. Billings knelt and put his arm across his shoulders. Adams took Billings' arm, and the pair followed Robinson along the shore.

They walked north until the shoreline turned abruptly to the southwest. Robinson stopped and stared at the ice rearing up along the western side of the cape.

My God, he thought.

Thirty feet high in places, the pack extended for miles like a glacier peeled from a valley and unrolled across the surface of the sea, blocking the ocean passage from the north. It formed a huge barrier, ruptured and torn and built up into jagged clumps. Robinson imagined crazed demons gone berserk beneath the ice, trying to burst forth from some undersea prison. The mottled ice was ancient, with none of the translucence or trapped colour he had seen in the young bergs in Baffin Bay. Robinson stood in silence for a long time, gazing at the pack. Eventually, Adams spoke in a whisper.

"Have you . . . have you ever seen it like this?"

"Never." Robinson shook his head. "Not like this."

None of it made sense. No sooner was he convinced he had solved the riddle of the Passage than new evidence appeared to prove him wrong. The lost crewman they encountered could only have come from here, but how could any ship have sailed through ice like this? *I was so sure,* Robinson thought.

Robinson squatted on his haunches and hung his head. He picked up a stone and bounced it on the palm of his gloved hand, then tossed it back to the earth. Adams drank from his canteen and tightened the straps of his knapsack. He pulled Robinson to his feet, and they walked on.

Cape Felix was a low, stony beach shrouded in a heavy fog restricting visibility to fifty yards. Fox tracks speckled a patch of snow above the tidemark. The ice pack cracked and groaned out at sea, the sound like a distant battle underway somewhere in the fog. The land was utterly flat. No cliffs rose into the mist, no glaciers slunk through valleys. The shore was bare of driftwood.

Robinson's nose and throat were raw in the cold air. He wished for blue lights to burn, or a signal cannon. He shouted into the emptiness, but the mist snuffed out his voice.

"If the wreck of *Erebus* lay here," he said, "I might set the thing afire just to warm my hands."

Blind in the fog, they walked slowly. After midnight, the wind shifted to the northwest, and the fog disappeared, blown away like a cloak whisked back by a magician. Billings cried out in fear. Fifty yards to their left, a large shape seemed to step forward out of the dissipating mist. It was an enormous cairn of stones. The marker was immense in the flat, treeless landscape, a giant awaiting them on the barren shore. Thick chunks of stone had been carefully piled atop each other, arranged in layers between broader, thinner pieces. Longer segments jutted out beyond the column of the cairn with the appearance of truncated arms. Clumps of saxifrage hugged the earth around the base, their tiny white petals shuddering in the cold air. The cairn stood eight feet high and at least as wide. Robinson touched one of the stones.

"There is no old lichen or moss on these, and they do not look weathered." He knelt to examine the largest stones at the base of the cairn. "These are too heavy for a single man to lift." He looked around. "I see none this size in this vicinity."

"They brought them here on sledges," said Adams. "It is the work of at least half a dozen men."

The remains of a campsite were visible through the partially melted snow: pieces of canvas, the fragments of a broken bottle. The site appeared to have been ground into the earth by a gigantic heel. The three men explored, walking in opposite directions around the edge of a circle sixty feet across. They made out the outlines of three collapsed tents beneath a covering of snow. All lacked their centre poles. Robinson lifted the sailcloth of one tent and peered beneath. Three pairs of box cloth jackets and trousers and a pair of old mittens. Dirt and stones were scattered across blankets and a bearskin. Robinson frowned.

"Odd," he said. "They did not take their bedding."

Torn pieces of blue fabric and three empty food cans lay on the ground near the jawbone of a fox and a few feathers. A pike head sat next to a small box of needles and a pair of dirty blue trousers. He noticed a crude fireplace: blackened stones and pieces of charcoal and burnt wood.

"They burned their tentpoles to cook their last meal here," said Robinson. "Whoever it was had no intention of returning."

"The fellow we met carried bedding on his sledge," said Adams. "These blankets belong to other men."

Robinson walked among the debris, nudging various items with his boot.

"Only three tents," said Adams. "A handful of empty cans. A few bits of cloth. The entire company of two ships did not camp here."

Robinson nodded his agreement. "It was a staging point for a sledging expedition."

Adams gestured at the bones and feathers in the fireplace. "Or a hunting party's campsite. Or an observatory."

"I see no instruments," said Robinson. "I cannot imagine they would have carried their dip circles with them if they were retreating for their lives." He stepped over scattered knives, tin cups, and nails. Other objects—forks, spoons, bullet cartridges—poked out from pockets of ice and snow. A boot lay on its side on the open gravel. Ten feet beyond it, he noticed a bayonet scabbard and a comb. Something cracked like a bird's bone beneath his heel. He raised it to find a shattered clay pipestem in the mud.

Robinson ordered Adams to rest while he and Billings began dismantling the cairn. They removed each stone and carried it away, depositing it in a fresh pile. The work was slow. Their breath billowed in the cold air. Each time he removed a stone, Robinson knelt on the ground until he felt strong enough to stand again. He grasped his wrist and felt his pulse gallop. Even Billings bent over after putting down each stone, his hands on his knees.

"I see something," Robinson said. "There." He pointed into the cairn. A small iron tube, nine inches in length, was wedged within the cairn. He drew his knife and reached in. Ice had formed around the tube, bonding it to the surrounding stones. He reversed his grip and stabbed downward, chipping at the ice until the tube was free.

He and Adams exchanged glances. Both recognised the Royal Navy message cylinder as standard Admiralty issue. Robinson removed the top of the cylinder. He pulled off a mitten and withdrew a piece of paper from the tube, gripping it in the calloused tips of fingers showing the first signs of frostbite. Adams peered over Robinson's shoulder. Robinson squinted at the page for a long time before Adams could contain himself no longer. At first, his voice was trapped in his throat. When he spoke, it was a rasp.

"Can you read it? What does it say? Is it from Franklin?"

Robinson shook his head. He passed the paper to Adams and stood staring out over the campsite.

Adams held up the message. Scrawled in a shaky hand, the letters on the page swam in his vision. He read the words aloud.

> *My Deare Wyfe,*
> *We shall not escape the ice now. We are weak and hungry and cannot hope for rescue only redemshun in the hear-after. Remember me kyndly to your sister may God bless you and priserve you for He has shurely abandoned us. I look forward to asking Him what I did to diserve this. I ask of you not Him please forgive me my sins.*
> *Your husband, Phillip*

"Phillip," said Robinson, frowning. "Do you remember a Phillip on either ship?"

Adams heaved a sigh. He rubbed his temples. "I could once recite the names of all the officers. Now I can barely remember my own."

"An officer did not write this."

"And yet a seaman would likely be incapable of it."

Robinson grunted. "I have known some who knew their letters."

The sky was full of low grey clouds. Thunder rumbled in the cold air. Snow began to fall. Robinson massaged his sore legs. The picture in his head was shifting, breaking into fragments he could not reassemble into a recognisable image. He had once imagined Sir John and his men patiently awaiting rescue in a comfortable village of tents and snow huts, living off canned provisions or shooting game. But the evidence demanded a reappraisal. Franklin's men, it seemed, wandered the landscape, scattering boots, combs, and pipestems. He read the message again, then rolled up the paper and began tapping it on the palm of his hand.

"This is a man who thinks he will die. And he is apologising."

CHAPTER TEN

Adams scoured the campsite, but there was nothing. He wondered how there could be no messages, no documents. A handful of men had camped here. They hunted, cooked a meal. They slept. And now they were gone.

Robinson pointed to the north. "Perhaps they were caught in the ice near here but got free and sailed north again."

"And left that poor mad fellow?"

Robinson shook his head slowly. "There may have been a mutiny."

Adams was unconvinced. "But we have seen the ice north of here. How could any vessel sail through that?"

"Perhaps the opposite is true. If the men who camped here were returning to the ships, perhaps the ice cleared sufficiently to allow them to sail to the southwest, to Point Turnagain." He stared at Adams. "They may have already completed the Passage."

Adams pointed out at the ice pack. "That ice does not appear to have broken up anytime recently. If they are beset out there, I wager they have not moved."

Both men stared to the southwest.

Robinson gritted his teeth. "They vanish, they leave us clues, but none that make any sense." He spread his arms. "There is nowhere to hide, yet they are nowhere to be found."

"What is that?" Adams pointed at some pieces of red fabric lying in the gravel. He picked them up and turned them over in his hands. He noticed the familiar naval markings.

"It is part of an ensign, I think," said Robinson.

He took the fragments of cloth from him and studied them. "I can think of only one reason for an ensign out here."

Adams nodded. "To place on a coffin."

"They must have had a sledge to move the stones for the cairn, so they could have moved a coffin."

Adams looked around again at the deserted campsite. "Perhaps a burial party camped here."

They went looking for graves, walking in ever-widening circles around the campsite. They scanned the rocky ground for anything resembling a tombstone or grave marker but saw nothing.

Robinson sighed. "Could they have buried them in the ice, then?"

Adams gazed out at the pack. A white haze had descended, blurring the almost indistinguishable line between the ice and the sky. He thought of how far they had walked from Fury Beach. None of their shipmates knew their location. If they met with misadventure, nobody would ever find them.

"I'm hungry," said Billings.

Adams sighed. "I miss a hot cup of tea," he said. "A freshly baked loaf of bread. Tell me something you miss, Jimmy."

"No, do not." Robinson wore a strained expression, as if struggling to keep in check something coiled within him. "Do not. Please." He shook his head. "It does me no good to be reminded of what I cannot have."

———

Twenty miles on, they arrived at Victory Point. A large cairn stood amid the remains of a vast campsite on a wide gravel beach. They stood in the cold air, transfixed. Adams forgot the pain in his legs, the hollow in his stomach. The land rose gradually from the sea, a low, flat beach of crushed stone. Four tents stood around the cairn in a semicircle. Secured to rocks, their guys trembled in the breeze. Two collapsed tents lay in rumpled piles on the ground. The sun melted the ocean to gold. The floes to the west were blotchy with shadows, lined up one hundred yards from the shore like misshapen beasts eager to crawl upon the land.

Heavy winter clothing was heaped in untidy mounds four feet high on the gravel. Tiny icicles hung from the edges of folded overcoats and box cloth trousers. Debris was scattered over a wide area: pieces of rope and canvas, lengths of copper, broken pickaxes, splintered chunks of oar. Adams stumbled to the cairn, limbs stiff and tremulous. A small metal message cylinder was lodged in the stones clustered at the top. He seized the cylinder in a gloved hand, toppling several stones to the ground in his haste. He removed the cap from the cylinder and pulled the glove from his trembling right hand with his teeth and withdrew a sheet of rolled paper. Robinson's footsteps approached from behind.

"Give it to me," he demanded.

Robinson took the paper and unrolled it. Adams recognised the standard Royal Navy tide paper, crisp and nearly new. The upper half of the page displayed a series of lines for a commander to note the name of his vessel, the date, and his coordinates. The lower half of the document comprised a preprinted message written in six languages, requesting the discoverer of the note to forward it to the Admiralty.

Occupying most of the upper half of the page was a message written in an unhurried, confident hand.

28 of May, 1847 H.M. Ships Erebus and Terror Wintered in the Ice in Lat. 70°5′N Long. 98°23′W Having wintered in 1846-7 at Beechey Island in Lat. 74°43′28″N Long. 91°39′.15″W after having ascended Wellington Channel to Lat. 77° and returning by the west side of Cornwallis Island.

Sir John Franklin commanding the Expedition. All well.

At the bottom of the page, in the same large bold lettering, was an addendum:

Party consisting of 2 officers and 6 men left the ships on Monday 24th May 1847.

Gm. Core, Lieut.

Chas. F. DesVoeux, Mate

Robinson frowned. "It says they wintered at Beechey Island in 1846–7. That cannot be more than sixty miles across Barrow Strait from Port Leopold. It would not have taken them two years to get there from the Thames. The date must be wrong. Do they mean 1845–6?"

Adams pointed at the paper. "There is more."

Another message was written in the margin. The writing was a cramped scrawl, the lettering small and hastily scribbled. Robinson read it aloud, squinting at some indistinct letters.

"April 25th, 1848. H.M.'s ships Terror and Erebus were deserted on 22nd April, 5 leagues N.N.W. of this, having been beset since 12th September 1846. The Officers and crews, consisting of 105 souls, under the command of Captain F.R.M. Crozier, landed here in Lat. 69-37'-42"N., long. 98-41' W.

"This paper was found by Lt. Irving under the cairn supposed to have been built by Sir James Ross in 1831, 4 miles to the northward, where it had been deposited by the late Commander Gore in June 1847. Sir James Ross' pillar has not however been found and the paper has been transferred to this position which is that in which Sir J. Ross' pillar was erected."

"What does that last paragraph mean?" Adams asked. "It sounds as if whoever wrote it was drunk."

Robinson shook his head. "I do not understand it." He pointed out at the ice. "They were frozen in five leagues in that direction. And they came ashore a year ago."

He returned his attention to the message. As Adams watched, the profile of Robinson's face changed, the jaw slackening, the flesh turning pale.

"What is it?" Adams asked.

"Look here." Robinson pointed a trembling finger at the document.

Adams peered at the message. The final sentence began in the right-hand margin of the page, tracing up the page before turning left, the words upside down across the top.

Robinson read it aloud: "'Sir John Franklin died on 11th June 1847; the total loss by deaths in the Expedition has been to this date nine officers and fifteen men.'"

Adams took the paper in shaking hands. He tried to read the line again, but his eyes blurred with tears. He did not feel the strength in his legs go until his knees struck the gravel. Nausea churned beneath his ribs. He crumpled in on himself, his mind scrabbling for a support suddenly withdrawn. The moment stretched out until his chest hurt, and he drew a long, desperate breath that raked his throat. He would never grasp Franklin's hand or stand beside him. He would not pray with him.

"He was dead a year before we even left the Thames," Adams whispered. He could not comprehend it. Why had the Lord led him here if not to bring Franklin home?

Billings approached, concerned. "What is it, Mister Adams? Will we find Sir John today?"

A gust of wind ruffled the dark water near the shore. Shadows flickered on the gravel as a thin band of cloud passed before the sun. Adams shook his head and wiped his tears with his hand.

"No. We will not find him today, Jimmy."

Billings smiled. "Bear up, sir." He appeared to sense Adams' anguish and was anxious to console him. "Perhaps we will find him tomorrow, then."

The broken ice out at sea, the torn clouds above, and the desolate earth were all unchanged from a moment before, yet nothing was the same. The new moon hovered above the horizon, a distant grey crack in the sky through which one might escape, if only it were possible.

———

Robinson left Adams hunched and shuddering on the stones, Billings stooping over him with a hand on his shoulder.

He strode off a dozen steps and stood looking at the sky. Lightheaded, he thought how pleasant it would be to lay flat on the earth, but he was not certain he could stand again. The wind dropped, and the air was still. A bird fluttered somewhere, but he did not think to reach for his gun.

Sir John Franklin was dead. And the mortality: nine officers and fifteen men. More than a year had passed since then. The weight of his failure was like iron shackles on his body, threatening to take his breath, stop his heart. Anger at Franklin began to boil in him. The damn fool had not only gotten lost; he'd had the temerity to die.

The irony was not lost on Robinson. Of all *Investigator*'s officers, only he had taken the right trail while all other sledge teams had gone in the wrong direction. It had led only to the lip of a precipice, with nothing but a cryptic note telling of dead men. He imagined his father standing on the Thames dock, arms folded, glaring at *Investigator* as she tied up, a sneer curling his lip: *Well? Did you find him?*

What would Elizabeth say? He pushed away all thought of his father, groping instead for a memory of his wife like a drowning man flailing for a piece of flotsam in a heavy sea. The one that came to him was from years ago, when they had ridden out across his father's estate soon after their marriage, and barely a year since Franklin's expedition had departed the Thames.

They made their way past the orchard and the dairy and walked the horses along the canal, where their hooves kicked up puffs of dust on the narrow lane. Elizabeth was still hearty then, the illness within her darkly coiled and unseen. As he helped her from the saddle, her eyes were bright, her gloved fingertips soft against his chest. As the horses nickered, he spread a blanket on the grass beside an old oak's thick, knotted trunk. Sunlight flecked the leaves, scattering golden fragments.

It was her habit to read to him. She withdrew a book from the basket he had set down and sat close to him, giggling. Her breath was sweet against his cheek.

"Do not tell Father I am reading *Frankenstein*." Her tone was conspiratorial. "He would hardly think it appropriate reading for a young lady."

Unlike himself, she was adored by her parents but bored of their suffocating attentions. In the earliest days of their correspondence, he had suspected her interest in him was merely to cause her father chagrin, but he had decided he did not care if it was.

He laughed. "On that point alone, I might agree with him."

She widened her eyes in mock gravity. "But you are my Victor. And I am your Elizabeth."

"I should hope not! Frankenstein's Elizabeth was killed by his Creature, was she not? I would not see you suffer such a fate."

"It is too late, you shall not stop me. I am already near the end." She held the book up and read aloud: "'Seek happiness in tranquillity, and avoid ambition, even if it be only the apparently innocent one of distinguishing yourself in science and discoveries.'"

"Frankenstein's last words to Walton, I believe?" He smiled. "Then I cannot be Victor, as I shall not promise to eschew ambition. And discovery may be the only field where I might achieve mine, unless we soon find ourselves a war."

At once demure, Elizabeth had taken his hand and held it. "I am glad of it. I would not have you go off to battle and leave me. It would please me if you devote yourself to discoveries rather than war."

He sighed. "I'm afraid Sir John Franklin will make the last great discovery when he finds the North-West Passage. There will be little left for me."

Her lips were at his ear. She whispered, as if imparting a great secret, "There will always be more to find. More to know."

—

Robinson considered his options. If he could not retrieve Franklin alive, he would have the next best thing. Prove to the Admiralty that Franklin was dead, and he may yet be hailed as the man who learned the lost captain's fate. Perhaps he and Adams could find Sir John's grave. That might be enough for promotion.

There will always be more to know.

Robinson spat a gob of phlegm on the ground. He walked back to join Adams, looking around at the scattered debris of the campsite.

"Graves." His voice quivered. He coughed to steady it. "With that many casualties, there should be graves here."

Adams stood and scraped a muddy boot on a stone. He nodded wearily.

"An outbreak of disease?" Robinson folded his hands into his armpits and walked in a slow circle.

"Or an explosion. An accident with gunpowder, perhaps, or a fire aboard ship?"

Robinson grimaced. "Nine officers dead in a year?"

"Crozier may not have been drunk when he wrote this," said Adams. "Perhaps he was ill."

"What is that last little bit there, under Crozier's signature?"

The new commander of the expedition had left them a final line: *And start on tomorrow 26th for Back's Fish River.*

Adams shook his head. "Crozier knew there were provisions at Fury Beach. Why would he go to Back's River?"

"It is closer than Fury Beach, I suppose, but not by much."

"But there is nothing there," said Adams. "At least from Fury Beach he might reach a whaler in Lancaster Sound."

"I can only think he took them south to find game." Robinson began to see it now. "He needed fresh meat to hold off the scurvy. Twenty-five-year-old biscuit and pickles would not do the job."

"So he went to shoot a few reindeer. Then what? Seek help from the Esquimaux at Repulse Bay? That must be a further two hundred and fifty miles."

Robinson shrugged. He looked out across the flat, stony landscape to the south. He imagined a hundred sick and weary men limping across the shingle, leaning into their harnesses. He could hear the sledge runners scraping on the gravel and the groans of the sick, malnourished men hauling on the track ropes, their tattered boots slipping on the stones. The terrain stretched out into the distance, pocked and scarred.

Nothing made sense.

How on earth, he thought, *could you march a hundred men across two hundred miles of that?*

The three men explored the abandoned campsite, stooping and straightening like cranes. Adams retrieved pannikins and canteens, examining them for messages scratched into the metal. He collected a gimlet and a clothes brush. A pair of snow goggles protruded from the gravel near a sextant and a surgeon's tourniquet.

A shovel stood upright, its blade embedded in the earth. Billings grasped the handle with all his strength and pulled it like a knight tugging on Excalibur, but the shovel would not budge from the frozen ground. Adams joined him and ran his hand over the handle, imagining he might somehow commune with the man who had last used it. There was so much detritus strewn across the ground, he thought surely there must be men here. At any moment he expected Franklin's crew to come running across the shingle, shouting and laughing at their prank, but there was only the wind. Perhaps Franklin and his men had stumbled across some hidden pit, concealed by the spirits inhabiting this place, and simply dropped into the earth.

Adams inspected a small wooden box. He opened it with trembling hands to find a dip circle, complete with magnets and needles. A medicine chest sat abandoned on the gravel. He opened it and lifted out several vials and bottles: a two-ounce bottle of olive oil, others of ipecac and peppermint oil. He examined bottles containing tinctures and pulvered roots of jalap and bindweed and ginger, most less than one-quarter full. Bandages and sticking plaster and test tubes. A pair of woollen gloves lay on a flat rock a few feet away, as if placed there to dry only minutes earlier. He looked around, but the area was deserted.

Frances was right. They had both known it. She told him Franklin had too many men, and she was right. He imagined her now, wandering with her father through the gardens of the ruined monastery in Bury St Edmunds, where the two of them had walked before his departure. He pictured her among the crumbled thousand-year-old walls and tombstones shrouded in long grass, worrying for him as her father attempted to calm her fears.

"So many men," she would say, shaking her head. "Such big ships. Thirty years ago, Mister Scoresby recommended ships no larger than 150 tons. Larger vessels are susceptible to damage from impact with ice or rock. Why must the Admiralty send a vessel more than twice that size?"

How might her father answer? Perhaps he would attempt to disarm her with nonchalance. "The Admiralty is disinclined to lend weight to the opinions of a whaler."

She would not be mollified. "Scoresby is no ordinary whaler. He is a scientist, a fellow of the Royal Society. He has been at sea for forty years. Why will Their Lordships not listen to such a learned man?"

"I agree, my dear. But they are disinclined to heed a man without a cocked hat and epaulets."

"And they give them rum, Father. Mister Scoresby thinks it most injurious. He says men should drink only warm tea in the Arctic."

"No doubt, my dear, but a sailor and his rum are not easily separated. Even at double pay, I think the Admiralty would find few volunteers for discovery service if there were no rum."

Adams imagined her becoming agitated, her face reddening. "And most important of all, he said the only way from east to west is likely to be overland across the northern coast of America, not via a sea passage!"

He pictured her in tears.

"Why, Father? Why must they do everything wrong?"

CHAPTER ELEVEN

Adams sat up in the dim light. Robinson lay motionless under the blanket. Billings whimpered in his sleep like a puppy. The canvas tent wall muttered in the wind.

Adams looked out through the tent flap at the dead land. He did not recall laying out the blankets. His boots sat by his head. He found his ink bottle frozen beside him and his quill lost in the folds of his blanket. His journal lay open, but there was nothing written on the page. He thought again of the handwriting on the note from the cairn, how the atmosphere at the moment of its creation was revealed on the paper. The lettering of the first message was large and bold, perhaps penned while Franklin was in casual conversation with Fitzjames, sharing a brandy, discussing which route to take when the summer thaw freed them. He could imagine Franklin smiling, speaking the words aloud and signing off in fat black strokes with a happy flourish:

Sir John Franklin commanding the Expedition. All well.

But the second part of the message was entirely alien. It seemed to Adams that two disparate people—the first calm, the second agitated and desperate—were confined together and given only a single piece of paper to write on. The lettering was thin and panicked, scratched quickly on the document. Something had gone awry. Men were dead. The tale had to be told, but there was no time. The first message was a casual salutation, the second a cry of anguish.

And start on tomorrow 26th for Back's Fish River.

———

They sat outside the tent in a yellow light, surveying the remains of Franklin's last campsite. An easterly wind carried the faint earthy smell of new lichen over the gravel. Adams rummaged in the bag of provisions.

"The cocoa is all gone," he said. "And the tea is long finished. It shall have to be water with breakfast." He handed two strips of reindeer meat to Billings.

"We cannot go after them," Robinson said. "The note says they left a year ago. Back's River is five hundred miles from Port Leopold. Even if we got that far and found Crozier, we could not get back to Port Leopold before the ice melts and Captain Ross sails off. I do not fancy being left here until a search vessel arrives next year."

The wind dropped, and it was almost warm.

"It is over, then." Adams' head throbbed. His shoulders were raw from the track rope. He knew he should mourn Franklin and his men but instead felt cheated of a prize. Shame weighed upon him like chain mail. "I thought God had chosen me."

Robinson's response was terse. "If you must pity anyone, pity them, not yourself."

"But we shall never find them now." Adams' chin dropped to his chest. He imagined the flat, empty land around them as the surface of a vast ocean, gently undulating and featureless. He floated upon it now, adrift and aimless, wishing the current to take him and cast him up on some distant shore far from this place.

Billings chewed his meat noisily. "Are we going home now?"

Robinson puffed on his pipe. He took a small bite from a strip of meat. "Do you think it likely there are records aboard *Erebus* and *Terror*?"

Adams raised his head, frowning. "What records?"

"Journals, diaries. Messages like the one we found here. Surely there is more. What if Crozier abandoned the ships not because they were about to sink but only because they were stuck fast? He would have left a log or journal in case the ships were found before he was. If they were frozen in for two years, I have no doubt he would have written a full account."

Adams stared at him. So Robinson had not abandoned the pursuit.

"But we do not know where the ships are."

"We know where they *were* a year ago. They were five leagues north-northwest of this very spot. Crozier said so, right here." Robinson brandished the message from the cairn.

"They would have drifted with the ice, or sunk," said Adams. "Or perhaps Crozier got the coordinates wrong. Other parts of his message are little more than babble. Why trust that part?"

He sucked on a strip of reindeer flesh, afraid he would soon be spitting teeth into his palm if he did not soften the dried meat first. He tested an unsteady molar with his tongue, then guided the strip of meat to the opposite side of his mouth, where the teeth felt sturdier.

Robinson leaned forward, bringing his pallid face close to Adams'. The red mist of broken blood vessels behind pale-blue irises lent his gaze a hypnotic allure.

"The ships were stuck fast for two years, and Crozier thought they would not move. That is precisely why he abandoned them." Robinson pointed to the northwest. "That pack ice is being driven south by the currents and winds." He slapped the map with his hand. "The coast of King William Land trends southwest from here. If the pack has carried the ships south, they might still be sitting in the ice near the western edge of King William Land. We may be able to see them."

Adams felt an unexpected admiration for the man. Robinson seemed to know no self-reproach, felt no contrition for his failures. He was no sooner thwarted than mulling his next gambit. If he could replicate a single aspect of Robinson's character, it would be this.

Robinson appeared to take Adams' silence as reticence. He pressed him further, as if pushing on a door he felt was sure to swing open.

"It would take but a day or two to walk out four or five leagues. If we see nothing, we shall turn back to Cape Felix and return to Fury Beach. Would you agree to that?"

The sky overhead was low and falling, like the ceiling of a vast cavern.

Adams gripped his Bible and held it to his forehead. "Is it brave to go further? Or foolish?"

Robinson sat back. He swigged from his canteen. "I consider myself neither."

"I would follow this path, see it through, but . . ."

"God is testing your resolve? I have always understood one should expect that of Him."

Adams once thought of his faith as heavy and immovable, like a ship's anchor. Today he imagined it more as the trunk of a sapling bent over in a screaming gale. Stripped of leaves, groaning and creaking, roots ready to tear from the soil at one more gust.

"Captain Bird told me not all men are suited to Arctic service," said Adams.

"No man is suited to this."

"Jimmy." Adams looked at Billings. The young seaman stared back with a frightened expression. "Can you go a little further?"

Billings bit his lip. "I miss my ma. She said I had to come home. The cholera took my brothers, see?"

Adams whispered to Robinson. "We pay out more and more rope but are yet to hang ourselves. We are like mice following a chunk of cheese on a string. At some point, a bootheel will crash down upon our heads."

"Is it so odd to imagine your fate was never to rescue Sir John at all, but to carry the news of his fate back to the Admiralty?"

"Ma said I had to come home," said Billings, "or else she'd be in the workhouse."

Adams' mouth was dry. He regarded Robinson with something approaching awe. "How is it you have no doubts?"

Robinson shrugged. "If we run out of food and cannot find more, we will die. There is no ambiguity in it."

"The bear . . . ," said Adams. "The one I shot."

The memory of it, never far from his mind, was in his head again now: the massive white head with its small black eyes, the huge teeth, the broad taloned paws.

"What of it?"

"I shot nothing larger than a grouse before that."

———

The sky took on the colour of slate, and the clouds knotted and heaved like creatures in a sack. The ice pack rumbled in the west. The clouds burst open, and a screaming wind reigned unimpeded across the flatland. The tentpole blew down, and they wore every piece of clothing they had, huddled together and freezing. The collapsed tent cocooned them as the gale roared for two days. The deafening wind circled the planet, thunder a ceaseless cannonade in the heavens. The earth shook as if likely to split apart. Adams stuffed cotton into his ears but could hear pieces of ice rolling along the beach in the wind. He lay curled up, his entire body clenched, his fingers gripping his arms, his eyes staring at the sailcloth inches from his nose.

———

Adams woke to find his blanket bag sodden; water had seeped through the floorcloth. He could not hear the wind, and there was no sound from the sea ice. He pulled on his boots and stood to insert the tentpole. Robinson and Billings lay asleep in their blankets.

Adams ate a small piece of biscuit. He could dry the wet bedding if he could find enough driftwood to make a fire. He checked his gun, collected his ammunition bag and telescope, and stepped out of the tent. The sky was overcast and the day warm. He removed the thick sweater beneath his coat, then took his blanket bag from the tent and laid it over some stones to dry.

All along the shore, the gale had tossed chunks of ice up out of the sea. Pieces of driftwood lay strewn across the shingle like the corpses of drowned sailors. The water to the west between the shore and the pack gleamed in the post-storm stillness. He scanned the beach for bears and looked skyward for birds. A white haze obscured the horizon. He took out his pipe, then turned. He felt the blood drain from his face, an itchy sensation like ants running down his neck. His hand went to his mouth.

An enormous cross, twice the height of a man and the colour of bone, stood at the water's edge one hundred yards down the beach. It loomed over the shore, erupting from the earth, its long shadow stretched across the stones. Shorter than the left, the right crossbar pointed at the ocean so that the object appeared to face in his direction.

Unable to tear his gaze from the cross, Adams stumbled toward it, tripping over whale bones and pieces of ice and driftwood. The tree trunk was perhaps two feet in diameter, bleached by years riding the floes. The crossbars were truncated branches, misshapen and scarred. The tree's base was embedded in the shingle, driven deep into the earth by the gale like a giant spear. A large chunk of ice buttressed the base of the trunk on the ocean side, holding it upright.

He searched the vicinity for debris from the missing vessels but saw nothing. He removed his glove. The surface of the wood was cool and smooth beneath his fingers. He recognised this tree. It was the storm-buffeted sapling of his imagination, stripped of leaves and riven now with fissures, but even after the previous day's gale, the cross stood tall and straight. He had been heard. It was a message.

Adams dropped to his knees before the cross. Tears were hot on his cheeks. He put his shotgun on the ground beside him, then closed his eyes and clasped his hands together.

Merciful Lord and Saviour, I pray for Your guidance and Your love.

———

Robinson approached the kneeling Adams, his boots crunching on the stones. He stopped behind him and studied the trunk. *My God,* he thought, *we are fortunate something this large did not land on our tent.*

"Remarkable," he said. "The storm must have thrown it up." He approached the trunk and touched it. "It must have been in the pack for years."

"It is a sign of His presence," said Adams. "To appear here, now, while we are here."

"It is spruce, I think."

"It is affirmation."

"Of what?"

"Of our sacred mission."

Robinson regarded him with a mixture of amusement and contempt. Adams had recovered his courage by kneeling to a dead tree. So be it. He needed him strong. If his renewed fervour lent him vigour, Robinson was unconcerned whence it came.

"It is a blessing," said Adams. "The Lord urges us on. He is telling us not to have doubts."

"I would rather He blessed us with a fat duck or a reindeer."

Adams reached up and gripped Robinson's wrist, his eyes wide. "You are correct about the ships, I am sure of it. If we look in the ice, we *will* find them." He pointed at the giant cross. "This is the proof we require."

Robinson felt a prick of envy. He marvelled at the ability of the pious to discern the presence of the divine in the merely peculiar. Elizabeth's illness would be easier to accept if he believed it to be simply the will of the Almighty. Nobody to blame, no retribution possible. It would make for a simpler world.

Adams knelt again and prayed silently. Robinson collected driftwood and made a fire near the tent. Smoke from the fire rose and twisted in the air, then was swept on the wind and whisked away across the lifeless expanse to the east. Billings emerged from the tent and wandered down the beach toward them. When he noticed the tree, he stopped and stared, slack-jawed.

Adams sat beside Robinson. "God has shown us the way. My faith was being tested. But I know now He will protect me. He will lift me."

"It is quite the chalice he passes to you." Robinson stoked the fire and laid some strips of meat out on the stones near the flames. Not for the first time he wondered if he should think better of the man. He was deluded by his fervour, perhaps, but that delusion lent him a resilience Robinson admired. Never extinguished, Adams' devotion smouldered like a low fire, embers glowing on the coldest night. He needed only a prayer or hymn to fan his zeal into flame whenever misery or exhaustion threatened to snuff it out. It seemed so easy for him. *But in my own weaker moments,* he thought, *my resolve leaves me. The coals of my own fire grow cold and black. Rekindling it sometimes requires more strength than I think I can summon. In those moments there is no one to help me. At least he has God.*

"Very good," he said. "We shall go and look for the ships. We shall find out what happened."

Adams nodded. "Through great hardship does man know himself. Thus, he knows God. The Bible tells us this. We must share in the sufferings of our Lord Jesus Christ."

Robinson rocked forward and held his hands near the flames. "Then I suspect we could be in no better place."

———

They walked west over the sea ice. King William Land sank into the whiteness behind them. A dark object on the ice raised its bullet head to look at them, then flicked its tail and disappeared into a hole. Robinson scanned the icy crags around them, his shotgun at the ready. He blew on his fingertips and ran them over the nipples and examined the barrel for moisture. Where there were seals, there would be bears.

The ice was corrugated with ridges and hummocks, great chunks rising like the broken columns and crumbling walls of an ancient city of white, long abandoned. Walking on numb feet, they bent into a relentless wind. The drift stung their faces. The three men crawled and slid over the hummocks and stepped around meltwater pools, pulling the sledge behind them. The runners hissed over the thin snow coating the ice. The murky sky was low overhead, but Robinson's eyes smarted from the glare.

Every hour he dropped his knapsack in the lee of a tall hummock and climbed an ice ridge to scan the horizon with the telescope. He bruised his knees on outcrops and stepped in puddles of freezing water collected in depressions in the ice. Adams and Billings walked in circles below, stamping their feet and slapping each other's shoulders to stay warm. Early in the morning, they encountered a wall of ice twenty feet high and a hundred feet across. A row of hummocks had fused, rearing up like a long wave frozen the instant before crashing on a beach. Robinson propped his shotgun against the hummock.

"Wait for me. I will try again here."

He approached the ice wall and began hacking footholds in the ice with his shovel. The sky above was empty of birds. When he reached the top, his heart galloped against the freezing wall of the hummock. He lifted the telescope like a sentry atop a rampart and swept the horizon. With the sun in his eyes, he could not gauge the distance. He raised a gloved hand to block the sun and held the telescope, trembling, in the other. Far away in the pack, a tiny black stick protruded above a craggy white mass.

He squeezed his eyes shut, took a deep breath, exhaled, and shook his head to clear it. He knew not to trust his eyes in the Arctic. Many a mirage had appeared on the voyage north through Davis Strait: inverted icebergs, ships sailing through the air, mountain ranges on the open sea—all witnessed by dozens of officers and seamen. The light could deceive tired, hungry, hopeless men.

Adams' thin bearded face and Billings' wide eyes looked up at him from below. He raised the telescope and looked again. The mast was still there, swimming in his vision. He leaned forward and touched his forehead to the ice wall. His breath came in sharp, uneven bursts, oddly unsynchronised with the ragged rhythm of his heart.

"A mast!" Robinson called down. "I see a mast!" His voice seemed far away. He climbed backward down the wall, sliding down the last slope of the hummock on his backside. He passed Adams the telescope. "Take this and tell me I am mistaken." He doubled over, trying to catch his breath. "Over to the southwest. I could only see one of them. It has drifted south, just as we thought. But the topmast is up."

Robinson threaded a path through the hummocks. Adams and Billings followed, pulling the sledge. Their view obscured by the icy hillocks, they twice lost their way and scaled ice ridges to confirm their position. Particles of drift sparkled and danced in the cold air, and the wind whined over the ice. Each time Robinson's view of the distant mast was blocked as they picked their way through the pack, he expected it to have disappeared when they emerged into the open again. They rounded a hummock and halted on a flat area of ice. One ship sat half a mile from the other, unnatural black silhouettes against a curtain of white. They were like great shackled creatures, their heads hanging, spirits broken.

Terror listed heavily to starboard, its spars nearly touching the floe. Its one-hundred-foot keel lay exposed to the iron sky. Pieces of loose oakum protruded between weathered timbers streaked with dirt and sleet. Enormous banks of hard-packed snow were pushed against the hull. The topmasts were all missing, giving the ship an incomplete look. A huge awning had been pulled over a pair of spars lashed end to end between the amputated foremast and mizzenmasts twenty feet above the deck. One side of the awning had pulled loose from the gunwale and sagged against the masts like the wall of a collapsed tent. Three-foot icicles as thick as a man's wrist hung from the scuppers on the portside. The bowsprit protruded twenty feet over the ice, as stiff as a dead limb.

It was *Erebus* whose mast they had seen; the ship sat upright. The trio approached and halted beside the vessel. Robinson removed his glove and touched the cold black timbers of the hull as if feeling for a pulse. Broken pieces of wood and glass were scattered around them. A coil of rope lay half-buried in the snow.

Billings' face was ashen. "Where are the people, Mister Adams?"

It was close to midnight, and the sun was a bronze coin glowing on the horizon. All three of *Erebus*' masts were capped with their topmasts, each casting a long shadow across the ice. Articles of clothing hung out to dry on the ratlines were rigid from cold, banging against the rigging like empty suits of armour.

Adams pointed up at the ship. "The winter awning over the upper deck has been removed. There must have been someone here as recently as the spring."

"They abandoned *Terror*. Evacuated her and retreated to *Erebus*." Robinson gestured at the topmast. "They were surveying the ice, looking for the thaw." He collected himself, then cupped his mittened hands around his mouth. "Hallo!" he called. "Hallo on deck!"

He unslung his shotgun and checked the priming. He hoisted it to his shoulder and fired into the air. The great boom of the gun reverberated off the ship's hull and was plucked away by the breeze. Shivering, they waited. No heads appeared at the gunwale above them. No shouts rose from the ship. The wind picked up, whistling across the ice behind them. The sound of a floe cracking some distance to the north was like a pistol shot.

Robinson glanced at Adams and jerked his head at the ship. "Let us get inside." He gestured at a snow ramp built beside the hull, leading from the ice up to the gunwale ten feet above. "At least we shall be out of the wind."

They stepped over the gunwale onto the upper deck. The ship rang hollow beneath their boots. The boats were missing, the davits standing poised like unsheathed claws. The upper deck was bare but for three large wooden casks beside the mainmast. Robinson tugged off a mitten and rapped on the side of each one with his knuckles. All were empty. Unease stirred in him as he looked up at the masts. Not even the prison hulks at Plymouth were as lifeless and still as this. *Erebus* was now the corpse of something that had once been a ship, the masts and spars like the limbs of a dead man frozen in rigour.

Robinson heard a soft, rhythmic grunt and turned to see Billings with a knuckle thrust in his mouth. His eyes rolled in fear as he tried not to weep. For the first time, Robinson felt compassion for the man-child. He touched him on the shoulder.

"Fear not, Billings. Have courage, now."

Aft and starboard of the mainmast, an iron chimney—an exhaust tube from the locomotive engine in the ship's hold—jutted several feet above the deck. Adams held his bare hand close to the surface of the metal, then looked across at Robinson and shook his head.

The capstan was located on the deck between the mainmast and mizzenmast, the empty sockets of the drumhead like the gaps in a mouth lacking half its teeth. They looked down through the dirty windows of the skylight. No glimmer of light was visible in the gun room below. A belaying pin lay on the deck. Aft of the mizzenmast, the spokes of the double-wheeled helm protruded like skeletal fingers, the twelve-foot tiller a bone stripped of flesh.

They moved to the gunwales, Adams to port and Robinson to starboard, and walked forward to the bow. Shadowing Adams, Billings averted his eyes from the coats and trousers dangling from the hoary ratlines like the corpses of hanged criminals. Robinson knelt and wiped away dirt and ice from the small round windows in the deck timbers. The cabins below were dark.

Adams stopped and pointed. "Mister Robinson."

The main hatchway was open.

The two men went to the hatchway and looked down. Nothing was visible in the blackness below. Robinson knelt by the hatchway and placed his face in the opening.

"Hallo!"

The murk below swallowed his voice. Both men cocked their heads and listened. Silence. The hairs on Robinson's forearms rose. He swung his legs out over the hatchway and descended the companion ladder. The rungs were slippery in his hands, and he paused on each crosspiece so as not to fall. Adams climbed down the ladder after him. Billings knelt at the hatchway and looked down but made no move to follow them.

At the bottom of the ladder, the sound of the wind was far away above Robinson's head. He and Adams stood listening, allowing their eyes to adjust to the gloom. Light fell in a shaft from the main hatch. No candles or lamps. The odour of mildew and woodsmoke. Behind them a timber creaked.

Robinson turned.

A tall figure stood before them at the edge of the shaft of light, a resurrected cadaver stepping from a tomb. Motes of dust swirled around him. His face was gaunt and drawn, the whites of his red-rimmed eyes bright against the grimy, wrinkled skin. His hair was ragged and filthy, his beard a tangled nest of brown and grey below sharp cheekbones. He wore a stained sweater beneath a long coat hanging loosely from his shoulders. Robinson winced at the stench of excrement.

The man's mouth hung open. He stared with wide eyes, his lips trembling. He held out both his hands, groping like a blind man. Robinson was dazed, speechless, shivering with disgust as the man's fingertips caressed his beard.

When the man's voice came, it was something old and unused, a faint rasp like fingernails across sandpaper.

"Are you here?" he whispered. "Are you real?"

The man gripped Robinson's hand and ran the other hand up to his shoulder, squeezing it. His touch was as light as a bird's. A tear described his ravaged cheek.

Finally, Robinson could speak. "We are here," he said. "Lieutenant Robinson and Assistant Surgeon Adams from HMS *Investigator*. Captain Bird is at Port Leopold."

The man's eyes rolled up, and his knees buckled. Robinson caught him before he fell. Despite the man's height, his body was like a child's.

CHAPTER TWELVE

"Slowly," Adams told Robinson. "Give it to him slowly."

The man sat propped on the couch in the gun room, his back supported by cushions. Robinson knelt beside him with a bowl of weak broth Adams had made from some of their reindeer meat. The man's head lolled back, his eyes closed behind a curtain of greasy hair. His hands trembled in his lap. Adams had wiped the shit from the man's box cloth trousers, but the faint smell of it mingled in the still air with the odour of urine and mould.

Stripped of its furnishings, the gun room was a gloomy cell. The table at which the ship's officers had once dined was missing. Splinters of wood stood out from the wall where cupboards and sideboards had been wrenched away. Dark stains marked the floor timbers.

Robinson tipped a spoonful of soup into the man's mouth. The patient gagged and toppled sideways, heaving most of the liquid onto the floor. Adams recognised the syrupy-sweet odour on his breath as the smell of a man starving to death. The man sat back, eyes clenched shut, coughing until there was blood on his lips and he could barely draw breath. Adams touched Robinson's back and took the spoon from him.

"Let me."

Adams crouched beside the invalid and swept the hair from his face. He dribbled a few drops of soup onto his tongue. The man tasted the broth and licked his lips. He opened his eyes and blinked at Adams.

"Who are you?" asked Adams.

The man fixed him with a tired gaze. He cleared his throat as though unsure his voice would come.

"Fitzjames." His voice was a sepulchral whisper. "Captain. HMS *Erebus*."

"We are from Fury Beach," said Robinson. "Captain Ross is looking for you too."

"What . . . ?" Fitzjames tried to raise his head. "What is the date, please?"

"It is the third of July."

"July." Fitzjames' shoulders shook. "My God." He began to sob, each breath a struggle. His long hair fell back over his face.

"Sir James Ross is on North Somerset," said Robinson. "His men are searching Barrow Strait and Prince Regent Inlet."

Tears etched tracks down Fitzjames' grimy cheeks.

"Captain Fitzjames," Adams asked gently, "can you tell us what happened? Where is Sir John Franklin?"

Fitzjames looked at him, screwing up his eyes like a man staring into a bright light. He swallowed, his Adam's apple a mountainous peak in his wasted throat. Adams tried again. He lay a hand gently on Fitzjames' shoulder.

"Captain, we found your note at Victory Point. Is it true Sir John has passed?"

Fitzjames sighed. He looked at them and wrinkled his brow as he tried to form the words. His lips trembled.

"Victory Point?"

"Yes." Adams carefully spooned more broth into Fitzjames' mouth. The captain coughed and swallowed.

"You were frozen in," Adams said. "Do you remember?"

Fitzjames did not answer. He looked around for the spoon in Adams' hand.

Adams continued. "You were frozen in, so you went across the ice to Victory Point. Is Sir John buried there?"

Fitzjames' head bowed in thought, then snapped erect. He stared hard at Robinson, panic on his face. He blinked rapidly and looked around the room before turning back to the two men.

"Who are you?" He shrank back against the sofa, his hands raised as if to ward off blows. "Please," he said, "do not hurt me. I have no food to give you."

Adams took Fitzjames' hand. He was shocked at its wasted condition, like a bundle of sticks wrapped in parchment. He had seen many a dead man in a better state.

"Calm yourself, Captain," he murmured. "You are safe here."

Adams lifted the spoon and tipped more broth into Fitzjames' mouth. The man erupted in another coughing fit, rocking forward on the couch, hugging his ribs. Adams sat him upright, patted his back until the spasm passed, and gently lowered him back to the cushions. He sat, shaking, spittle and soup trickling from the corners of his mouth.

"More," Fitzjames said between gasps. "Please."

"Slowly. Just a little," said Adams. "Your stomach cannot take much." He had treated patients with cholera, scurvy, and bullet wounds, but how was he to feed a man whose body could take no nourishment?

Tears coursed down Fitzjames' nose and dripped onto his hands. Adams lifted his canteen to the man's lips.

Fitzjames looked up. "What is the date, please? Can you tell me?"

"It is the third of July."

"Third of July." Fitzjames' head nodded and drooped. "Third of July."

"Captain, what happened to Sir John?" Adams asked again. "What happened at Victory Point?"

Fitzjames' head swayed. "I am so sorry." Fresh tears rolled down his nose. "We had to eat—"

"What?" Adams felt a sense of disquiet. Fitzjames wore the haunted expression of a man recalling something horrific. Adams pressed him. "What did you eat?"

Fitzjames' voice was faint. "Jacko."

"You ate Jacko?"

Fitzjames nodded, closing his eyes. "Yes. Sir John was very fond of him."

Adams exhaled. So that was it. "I see." He stood, took Robinson by the arm, and guided him to the far corner of the room.

"What is he saying?" Robinson whispered.

"The monkey. Jacko was the ship's monkey."

Robinson frowned. "My God."

Adams went back to the sofa and knelt beside Fitzjames.

"Do not blame yourself," he said. "You had no choice."

"No choice," Fitzjames whispered.

Robinson's tone was impatient. "You remember Sir John, Captain? What became of him? And where is Captain Crozier?"

Fitzjames seemed to grow stronger at this, as if given an elixir. He sat up straight, his eyes clearer.

"Sir John said for our theatrical we shall do *The Rivals* this year," he said. "I will play Sir Lucius. Or Bob Acres." His tone was assured. He was a man giving orders now. "But not Mrs Malaprop or Lydia."

Adams had seen this before, in the naval hospital at Haslar. Dying men would rally, their strength ebbing and resurging, delirious one moment and coherent the next. Robinson glanced across at him with a raised eyebrow. Adams met his gaze and gave a barely perceptible shrug.

Fitzjames' brow furrowed. "The younger officers do not mind the female roles," he said. "They say it makes the men laugh. But I do not care for it. It is undignified for an officer, even in jest. The carpenter will knock together some sets. A few of the men are handy with a needle and thread. They shall make the costumes."

Adams nodded. "Sir Lucius it is, then," he said.

Mollified, Fitzjames relaxed and nodded. "Well, then."

Robinson again drew Adams aside and spoke in a whisper. "He is delusional. We will learn nothing from him."

"Starvation brings on delirium. Paranoia too. The broth may restore him a little if he can keep it down," said Adams. "I will feed him a little more; then we should let him sleep. He may have more to say later."

Behind them, Fitzjames muttered to himself. "We did *High Life Below Stairs* last winter." Then he stared at Adams for a long moment, smiling. He seemed to recall an old memory. "Good old Sir John. He was . . . in a story I once read."

Adams frowned. "I beg your pardon?" He leaned forward and put his hand on Fitzjames' shoulder.

"Once upon a time," Fitzjames whispered. He stared at the back of his hands, then turned them over and examined the palms as if seeing them for the first time. "Once upon a time, there was a brave naval captain. He had to eat his boots." He gazed at Adams with rheumy eyes of faded blue. He swallowed, and again the great lump in his throat rose and fell. "Do you have anything to eat?" His eyes closed, and his head lolled against the sofa. Then he sat erect again. "The date. What is the date, please?"

———

Robinson left Billings on the deck to keep watch. With Fitzjames asleep on the gun room couch, he and Adams entered the great cabin. The odour of coal dust and old charcoal. The captain's table stood in the centre of the room. The chairs were gone. The two men opened the storage lockers. Empty bottles that once held wine, gin, and brandy stood in rows.

Adams stared at the bare shelves. "Where are the books? Franklin had a thousand volumes."

Robinson peered out through the smoke-stained windows. He ran his fingers over the shelves. They came away thick with dust.

"They burned them," he said. He stood looking around the cabin. "They burned whatever they could to keep warm. The last of the coal would have been gone years ago."

Robinson went to the corner of the cabin and opened the narrow door to the captain's private quarters. The small chamber reeked of unwashed blankets and rotting rope. Filthy linen lay crumpled on the stained mattress. The desk was bare. Once heated in the stove to warm the cabin, a cannonball dangled in chains from a hook in the ceiling like a tool of torture in a dungeon. Bone fragments lay scattered on the floor. He picked one up and sniffed it warily. It was a pork bone, gnawed upon and licked so much, it was smooth and shiny. He threw it back on the floor, then retrieved two crumpled pieces of paper and peered at them in the gloom.

Adams looked in through the door of the cabin. "What do you have there?"

Robinson examined the papers. Both pieces were ripped along the side, torn from whatever volume once held them. He shook his head. "Pages from the chronometer journal. A list of variations in the ship's timepieces." He pointed at one. "This one is dated April '46."

"I found a few pages from the mess book in the captain's cabin," said Adams. "They were dated July '45."

"They were still in Baffin Bay then."

Adams sighed. "No ship's log. No personal journals."

Robinson looked around. Had they burned every page? The pieces of a chess set stood on the floor in the corner, the two opposing armies arranged in the starting position. He searched the drawers and shelves but found no chessboard.

Robinson left the cabin and walked the passageway running down the ship's portside. Adams explored the corridor on the starboard side. The timbers under their boots creaked in the silence. The air was heavy with the smell of creosote and wet oak.

Robinson slid open the door of each cabin and looked inside. Seven feet in length and less in width, each cubicle contained a bunk with a horsehair mattress stripped of blankets. The odour of lamp oil and stale wool was thick in the back of his throat. A washstand stood in the corner, an inch of water frozen in the basin. The shelves above the bunks were bare. The drawers beneath had been wrenched out, leaving gaping holes in the woodwork. Dirty, tattered clothing lay in untidy heaps on the floor. In one cabin, an overcoat hung from a hook on the wall. In another, the small folding table screwed to the wall had been lifted to the upright position, a collection of rodent bones neatly arranged upon it. Bleary fingers of grey light reached through the six-inch glass illuminators in the ceiling. A solid puddle of tallow, once a candle, sat in a saucer. Robinson searched beneath mattresses for journals or letters. He found nothing.

At the end of the passage, he slid the last door open and recoiled as if struck. The contents of his stomach twisted and rose at the cold, greasy smell of decay that slunk from the cabin and wiped its wet palm on his cheek. He coughed and spat, but the odour was in his hair, his mouth. He unwound his scarf and wrapped it around his face until only his eyes were uncovered. The stench seemed to seep in through his eyeballs.

A dead man lay on the bunk, his hands crossed over a well-thumbed pocket Bible. Robinson could not guess his age. The man was thin, with half-open eyes and deep wrinkles in his face where the grey flesh beneath had sagged. A red beard curled on his chest. He was dressed in a heavy coat and sweater. Were it not for the smell, Robinson would have thought the man had just stepped off the ice, but as he ventured closer, he saw the bare feet, the mottled skin.

Robinson tried to imagine the last man to have stood here, someone content to take a dead man's boots and stockings but too ill or weak or callous to haul him up the ladder to the upper deck and bury him in the ice. Someone who thought *Erebus* would soon sink and become the man's tomb, or a man simply in a hurry to get away from the ship? Holding his breath, he searched the man's coat pockets but found no evidence of rank or identity. Robinson gently touched the man's cold folded hands. The skin shifted under his fingertips, the flesh almost ready to slough from the bones. He closed his eyes in a brief prayer, then backed into the corridor and quietly slid the door closed. The scarf still over his face, he walked three paces before he knew it was hopeless. He bent over and retched on the floor of the passageway.

———

Robinson moved forward toward the seamen's mess. Far from the shaft of light at the main hatch, the lower deck was an assembly of shadows and indistinct shapes.

He reached the seamen's mess and looked up, expecting to see the mess tables lashed overhead. All were missing. A seaman's chest was open on the floor. He found toy boats whittled from wood and a pair of inexpertly darned socks. On another chest lay a fiddle, its strings broken and curled. A huge pile of empty food canisters, dull red in the low light, had been stacked against the great black galley stove. The smell of ancient pork fat and mildew hung in the air.

Robinson peered into the gloom. A dozen large cigar-like shapes hung suspended in the darkness, like bundles trapped in a spider's web. He moved closer. They were hammocks strung up across the mess. A peculiar shape protruded from one hammock. He reached out to touch it, then quickly withdrew his hand. The object was a human hand, the fingers curled and motionless. He held his breath, his pulse throbbing in his ear. The man in the hammock appeared to be asleep. He extended his hand again but pulled it back abruptly as a soft rustling sound in the blackness made him start.

"Who's there?" Robinson called out. "Show yourself! We are Royal Navy officers."

Adams emerged from the passageway behind him and stood at Robinson's shoulder. Together they squinted into the murk. Something moved in the darkness. A small, ghostly figure appeared from behind the galley stove and tottered slowly toward them. A gaunt man, young and clean-shaven, stood hunched and trembling. His face was the colour of old bone long buried. He wore a dirty sweater with holes in the sleeves and carried a cup of water and a small canvas bag over his shoulder.

"Who are you?" Robinson asked.

The man hurriedly knuckled his forehead. He spoke in a whisper.

"Richard Aylmore, sir. Gun room steward." He looked around and gestured at the hammocks. "I—I must see to them, sir."

"See to them?"

"Feed them, sir. Fetch them water. Wash them. I hear confessions too." He suddenly took on the worried look of a man caught in a transgression. "I know I am not ordained, of course, sir. But it makes them feel better."

Robinson felt a rush of hope. If these men were ambulatory, he and Adams might yet lead them back to Fury Beach. His gamble may yet pay off. He may yet be the great saviour.

"What happened to Sir John Franklin?" Robinson asked. "Can you tell us?"

Aylmore looked at the floor and shuffled his feet. "Sir John is gone, sir. A long time ago now."

Robinson grasped the young man's thin wrists and pulled him close with more vigour than he had intended. "Yes, but how? How did he pass? What happened?"

Aylmore cried out and squirmed. He tried to pull away but could not break Robinson's grip. With both arms pinned, he turned his face into his shoulder. "I do not know, sir." He began to cry. "I am but a steward. Please, sir."

"What did the surgeon say about it?" Robinson demanded.

"Dr Stanley, sir? He is dead, sir."

Robinson gritted his teeth. "But was he not alive when Sir John passed?"

"Sir, I do not remember, sir." Aylmore's eyes brimmed with tears.

Robinson's nails cut into the flesh of the man's arms. How could this boy notice nothing when his shipmates were dying around him? "Where is Sir John buried? Is he on King William Land? Did he leave any papers?"

Aylmore moaned and shuddered and twisted in Robinson's grip. "I don't know, sir. I don't know."

Robinson dragged Aylmore closer until their noses almost touched. He could see the grime in the man's pores and the black holes in his mouth where several teeth had gone. The steward's fetid breath was a cudgel in his face.

"Think, man! Where does Captain Fitzjames keep his papers? Take a guess, for God's sake."

Aylmore's body went limp, and his head fell back, the white of his throat flashing in the gloom.

"Enough!" Adams stepped forward and touched Robinson's arm. "Let him go. You have frightened him."

Robinson sighed. He released the young man and stepped back. Shaking, the steward stood, rubbing his wrists. He stared at the floor, teardrops bursting darkly on his boots.

Robinson felt a twinge of remorse. He had allowed his excitement to get the better of him. The young steward had suffered more than he could know. Eliciting the information he needed would require a patient hand. "I am sorry," he said. "You must return with us." He waved a hand at the hammocks. "All of you. How many can walk?"

Aylmore raised his eyes quickly, panicked. "Return with you?" His wet, shiny eyes were huge in the dark. "Where to, sir?"

"First back to King William Land," said Robinson. "Then to Fury Beach and Port Leopold."

Aylmore took a step backward. "No." He shook his head and waved both hands. "No, I will not go there."

Robinson frowned. Did the lad not understand? "Boy, if you stay here, you will die."

The steward took another step backward. "You'll find them!" Aylmore's face was suddenly goblin-like, snarling and malevolent. He bared his teeth and screamed—a long, high-pitched keening that filled the darkness of the lower deck, echoing off the bulkheads. Adams and Robinson were pushed back on their heels, wincing. As Robinson opened his eyes, the top of Aylmore's head connected with his belly and shoved him backward. He collided with Adams and knocked him off his feet. The pair collapsed on the dusty timbers. Robinson heard Aylmore's boots scrabbling on the floor and turned to see him melting into the darkness like a subterranean creature retreating into its burrow.

"Wait, man!" Adams shouted.

He stood and stepped forward in the direction the steward had disappeared, then paused and peered into the darkness. Winded, Robinson lay gasping, his hand on his solar plexus. Adams went to him, sat him up, and patted him on the back.

"Are you injured?"

Robinson shook his head and got to his feet, sucking in the damp, heavy air until finally he could breathe. The two men stood in the dark, listening. A soft thump came from beneath their boots. Robinson held a finger to his lips.

"He's down on the orlop deck," he breathed. "Or in the hold."

"We must fetch him."

"Not now," said Robinson. "Without a candle, it will be black down there. He knows every nook. We do not. And he may have a weapon, perhaps even a blade. If he is dangerous, he is best left until we can retrieve him safely." He pointed at the men in the hammocks. "Examine these fellows first. Find out how many we can take with us. We'll get one of them to talk to the boy."

Robinson sat on a seamen's chest and took out his pipe. He needed to plan their retreat. Their encounter with Aylmore and his shipmates on the lower deck required some recalculation. He would need the young steward's help to take inventory of *Erebus'* remaining provisions. They might need to build more sledges.

He watched Adams walk between the hammocks, stopping at each one to whisper to the occupant. Every man was emaciated and heavily bearded, clad in dirty, tattered clothes. Adams patted their hands and felt for their pulses, examining bruises and sores on their wrists and throats. Robinson reminded himself to have Adams inspect the ship's medicine chest before their departure.

He stood and went to join Adams, who lingered beside a hammock occupied by a man with a thick red beard and eyes of the lightest, clearest blue. His eyelashes were so fair, they appeared white even in the gloom of the lower deck.

Adams rubbed his face, despair etched in his features. "We will learn nothing here," he said. "I think Mister Aylmore is utterly out of his head."

Robinson frowned. "What do you mean? The lad seems lucid. Frightened and sick, perhaps."

Adams shook his head. "You do not understand. There is no one else we can ask."

Robinson gestured at the hammocks suspended in the gloom. "Do none of them have a word to say about Franklin?"

"They are dead." Adams wiped his hands on his coat. "Every single one of them is dead. Our Mister Aylmore has been tending to corpses."

CHAPTER THIRTEEN

Robinson climbed the ladder to the upper deck and stood in the cold breeze. Adams followed him, and together they watched the ice pack turn from white to grey in sunlight leaking through fissures in the ashen clouds. A bank of fog approached from the north.

"We should tell Captain Fitzjames his men are dead," Adams said. "That he has a madman ministering to his dead fellows belowdecks."

Robinson huddled into his coat. "It would serve no purpose to tell him. He may not even understand."

He thought of Fitzjames with a mixture of envy and admiration. The man had what Robinson desired most: the rank of captain. Fitzjames had left the Thames a commander, but Crozier would have promoted him in the field upon Franklin's death. Robinson felt a welling of pride in the man. Even when starving, hallucinating, half out of his head, Fitzjames could correctly state his rank. He knew he was a captain. And he would more than likely die a captain.

"Those empty preserved-meat canisters in the galley—" Robinson checked himself, then continued. "The vendor's name on the label was Goldner—the same vendor who supplied the preserved meats to our ships."

Adams looked puzzled. "What of it?"

"There is something you should know. Last summer, when we were still in Davis Strait, the cook brought a canister of boiled beef to

Captain Bird." Robinson turned to face Adams. "The contents were utterly rancid."

Adams frowned. "Rancid? How could that be?"

"Captain Bird summoned the senior officers to witness it. The contents of the can were green, revolting. I will not soon forget the stench."

Adams pressed him. "Are you sure it was not damaged earlier, during the gale off Cape Farewell? Perhaps it sustained a blow and was perforated."

Robinson shook his head. "The cook opened it with his bayonet only ten minutes before. He swore to it."

"So it was rotten when first placed in the can?"

"It would seem so." Robinson shrugged. "Sometimes they do not force out all the air before they solder them shut. Or they do not cook them long enough. The cook later found two other putrid boiled-beef canisters, but the mutton and veal were perfectly edible. The preserved soups were tolerable too."

"Why was I not informed?"

"Captain Bird's orders. He did not wish it to get about, did not want the crew to know. There were also at least two cans of beef containing nothing but offal. Intestines, a bit of liver. One was filled largely with tallow. And quite a few unopened cans were unnaturally light in the hand, well short of the stated weight. The contents of one eight-pound can I examined could not have weighed more than four pounds."

Adams digested this. "Sir John's men would have been issued preserved meats every other day, twelve ounces per man. So when he thought he was provisioned for three years—"

"—he would have assumed his preserved meats were unspoiled," said Robinson. The bank of fog was much closer now, draining the world of colour. "If some of his meats were also putrid or underweight, they would have run out of food. Probably quite some time ago, I should think."

Adams and Robinson went looking for the steward, Aylmore.

Billings shied like a nervous pony from the black maw of the hatch-way leading from the lower deck down to the hold. The whites of his eyes glistened in the gloom. His breath came in short gasps. Adams had wrapped the decaying corpse from the cabin in a blanket and had Billings carry it up the companion ladder to the deck and down to the ice, but the stench still hung in the air, coating their throats, adhering to their cheeks and fingers.

Robinson snapped at him. "Move, Billings! You've been in *Investigator*'s hold a hundred times, have you not?"

Billings looked on the verge of tears. He glanced toward the corpses in the hammocks.

"It weren't like this. Smells like death."

"You have smelled worse, I'm sure," said Robinson. "The streets of Manchester are hardly any more sweet-smelling."

Adams put a hand on the seaman's shoulder. "Go up top, will you, Jimmy?" he said softly. "We need a man to keep watch."

The big man looked relieved to have a task for which he could use his talents. "I can see real good."

"Shout if you see a bear. There's a good man," said Adams. "We shall want some meat from him."

Adams and Robinson descended the ladder to *Terror*'s hold. With only a stub of tallow candle from his pocket to light the way, Adams felt he was exploring a cave. The hold was bare, the coal once stored there consumed years before. Two feet of bilge water had frozen solid. The smell of sewage and rotten bacon rose around them. A dead rat hung suspended in the frozen muck beneath his boots, its claws extended and mouth open in a silent scream.

Shadows thrown by Adams' candle shuddered on the reinforced oak beams. The two men stepped carefully across the slippery surface in search of hull breaches but could see little in the darkness. Adams imag-ined himself walking through the empty rib cage of some enormous dead creature. The huge locomotive engine was silent, slung sideways across the hold like a fossilised heart. An ice axe stood propped against the wall of the hull. Adams hefted it in one hand.

"Mister Aylmore!" he called. "Come out! We will not hurt you!" The darkness swallowed his voice. He and Robinson stopped and listened. A slow drip plinked somewhere in the dark.

They climbed one level to the orlop deck. Once crammed with provisions, it, too, had been stripped. Flour spilled on the floor of the Bread Room by careless hands had frozen into a filthy rock-hard residue. Finger tracks were visible in the grey muck. Adams opened two tin cases of ship's biscuit but found them both empty. The Slop Room was empty, every coat and boot gone. The lock that had once secured the Spirit Room lay in rusty pieces on the floor. Not a cask or barrel or bottle remained. Several rusty nails and a saw with a broken handle lay on the floor. All the spare canvas was missing from the Sail Room. Half a dozen empty food canisters lay scattered on the floor.

Adams looked in the Carpenter's Store. A long shape stretched from the ceiling almost to the floor. Richard Aylmore hung from a rope looped around an overhead beam. An upturned seaman's chest lay near his dangling heels.

"Here!" Adams shouted.

He ran forward and lifted the young man around the waist. Robinson rushed in behind him and reached up to cut the rope with his knife. Aylmore's body slumped over Adams' shoulder, but the muscles were already stiff. He laid the thin body on the floor. Adams felt for a pulse, then put his ear to Aylmore's mouth. He gazed down at the man's face, the eyes half-open, the skin grey and slack. Adams had seen dead men. If he had known them, he mourned. He felt regret and frustration for sick men he had failed to treat, sympathy for the mortally maimed. Now he knew only bewilderment. He looked up at Robinson, uncomprehending.

"But we were going to take him with us."

"We buried him in the ice," said Fitzjames.

He lay stretched out on the gun room couch. The tiny flame of Adams' candle stood motionless in the still air from a saucer on the floor. Shadows flitted on the walls. Adams thought the creases in Fitzjames' skin deeper even than a few hours earlier. More of the man had leaked away. A cluster of purple bruises nestled in the notch of his throat. Adams feared his head might topple from his neck if it trembled much more. He knelt beside Fitzjames with a bowl of soup and a spoon, feeding him tiny sips.

"The surgeon said it was apoplexy," Fitzjames said. His expression was doleful. "Sir John lingered for a day, but it was not . . . a good death."

Adams' throat tightened, and his eyelids grew hot. He could see how it must have been, Fitzjames and Crozier standing over their dying commander, waiting for the final breath of the man they had expected to lead them through the Passage. He imagined the carpenter hammering the coffin, the men taking turns at the long saw to cut a hole in the ice, then standing with caps in hand as Franklin was lowered into the black water.

"I saw you." Fitzjames stared at him. "You were here before. With me."

"Yes," said Adams gently. He lifted the spoon to Fitzjames' lips and waited for him to swallow.

"My mind is foggy," Fitzjames whispered, "like I am . . . groping around in a sack. But my head is a little clearer today. The soup is very good." His hands quivered in his lap. He turned them over, first examining the palms, then curling the fingers of one hand around the thin, corded wrist of the other.

"Captain," said Adams, "why did you not bury Sir John on King William Land?"

"I would have." Fitzjames shrugged. "But he insisted, before he was ever ill. When we were still in the Thames, he said if it ever came to it, he would want to be buried at sea. He laughed about it. None of us thought . . ." He stopped. "We thought the ice would melt within weeks and we would sail on. By the time we sought a safe harbour for the winter, we were trapped. Only later did we realise we would never get out." Fitzjames gazed down at the candle flame quivering on the floor. "We blasted holes in the ice with gunpowder," he said, "but they froze over in minutes. We hoped the ice might break up this summer. *Terror* is lost, I think, but *Erebus* may yet be seaworthy." He sighed. "But we are not strong enough to man the ship now. I had the topmast sent up in the spring to survey the state of the ice, but none of us can climb it."

"Where is Sir John's journal?" asked Robinson. "The ship's log?"

"Captain Crozier has them. He went hunting. With some men who were still strong enough. He said they would return with meat for us."

"The note at Victory Point said you went south to Back's Fish River," said Adams.

Fitzjames shook his head sadly. "Too many were sick. I returned to *Erebus* with the invalids."

"Did they leave you with nothing?"

Fitzjames' head fell back on the cushions. He stared up at the ceiling and watched the shadows of the three men. "Crozier left us what he could—some canned provisions, mostly. But I think there was a sickness in them. We threw many of the cans overboard. Our hunters shot the odd bird or fox, but there is so little game. I ordered the hunters to bring back all meat to share with the others. But they ate whatever they shot before they returned to the ship. I saw them licking the blood off their mittens."

Adams lifted the spoon again, but Fitzjames turned his face away. The ship's hull creaked under the pressure of the pack. The candle sputtered, the wick nearly consumed. A slender coil of soot spiralled upward. The room darkened. When Fitzjames spoke again, his voice was faint.

"We made soup from scraps of leather and hide and sealskin. I let the men stay in their hammocks now. It is all I can do to keep them warm. We all feel the cold terribly."

Adams took his hand. "We shall lead you back to Fury Beach. From there we can bring provisions from Port Leopold on the steam launch."

Fitzjames shook his head. "Too far. The men are ill. Scurvy. Dysentery. The dreadful melancholy is the worst." He stopped, his chest heaving. Tears shone on his cheeks. He closed his eyes, and his chin fell to his chest. Adams thought he had fallen asleep when Fitzjames sighed and opened his eyes.

"Forgive me," he said. "I am very tired."

"Return with us," Adams said. "There is nothing more you can do here."

"You are mistaken." Fitzjames looked at Adams with a kind expression. "I can stay with my men. We have been together four years, and our mission is at an end. I will see it through. I made that decision some time ago and will not retreat from it. The Lord will keep me."

"We may yet find some of your men on King William Land," said Robinson.

"They are not my men anymore." Fitzjames would not meet Adams' gaze. "You shall leave me here. I do not think I can stand any longer. My heart bothers me. There is nothing to be done. I have made my peace with it."

Adams bowed his head and took Fitzjames' hand. "I am sorry," he said, his voice cracking. "I had the finest words rehearsed. For Sir John, for you."

Fitzjames patted Adams' hand. "I am grateful for my good fortune. I am glad to be going out with the staunchest of fellows. Such are the curious merits of a slow death. A musket ball through the heart and it would all be over in an instant, before one even knew it. Before one had a chance to reflect. Instead, I have been able to remember people who were kind to me."

Robinson stood. "Would you have us carry any letters?"

Fitzjames took a deep breath and exhaled slowly. He gestured at a letter lying on the table. "I wrote this sometime ago. It is for my parents."

"Is there nothing for the Admiralty? Your journal?"

"Someone stole it. Burned it, I expect." Fitzjames turned his head away. "But you can tell them."

"We know so little," said Adams.

"Tell them we became stuck in the ice and could not escape."

"They will want to know more."

"Tell them we went out bravely, like Royal Navy men. Tell them the conduct of the men was exemplary when Providence was unkind. That they accepted their fate with dignity and did nothing to bring shame upon their families." He relaxed against the cushions. "Give some thought to the story. Knead it and bake it into something palatable. Thus, heroes are born of men."

Fitzjames' gaze was fixed on Adams' face, his voice barely audible. Adams leaned in and put his ear near Fitzjames' lips. The candle flame flared once and died, and the room was black. Robinson fished a nub of candle from his pocket and struck his flint and steel but could not ignite the denuded wick.

"You know," Fitzjames whispered in the darkness, "you would think a man is most likely to freeze to death here. I think it more accurate to say he *erodes*. The cold hardens a man's spirit; then it becomes brittle and is burned off by the glare and ground down by the wind and whittled away by hunger until his will to live is snuffed out. Some of the men laid down on their bunks and hoped never again to wake. They just close their eyes and die. But do you know"—he stopped, then spoke in wonder, as if relating a great discovery—"the more one desires it, the more difficult it becomes."

The wick of Robinson's candle finally ignited. A yellow light bloomed. He held it close to the stricken man's face. Fitzjames' lips trembled. Adams leaned in until he could feel his breath on his ear.

"Perhaps I shall manage it today."

Robinson had found the Passage. He could prove it now.

He rolled up his map and leaned on the captain's table with both hands. He had hoped to bring Franklin home, but the location of the Passage was worth far more. He could show Franklin's ships had sailed down the uncharted waterway west of Boothia before becoming ice-bound. Franklin was heading to Point Turnagain and, from there, west to Behrings Strait. The Admiralty would mourn Franklin and his men, yes, but they would soon see them as martyrs in the acquisition of the greater prize. He was eager to be on his way.

He and Adams wrapped Fitzjames in blankets taken from the corpses on the lower deck and laid him in his bunk. Fitzjames watched them, saying nothing, then closed his eyes. Adams and Robinson returned to the captain's cabin.

"How long, do you think?" Robinson asked him.

"Not long. Hours."

"But it could be longer?"

Adams sighed and rubbed his matted hair. "Perhaps as long as a day or two. I cannot be certain."

"We must leave now," said Robinson. "We have so little food left. There is no time."

"No." Adams' tone was flat. "We stay. It is our duty."

"He is beyond help. If we cannot get back, it will all have been for nothing."

Adams turned and stared into Robinson's eyes. "He deserves a burial. It is the decent thing."

The decent thing. Robinson found the notion amusing. What was the decent thing when confronted with demented and starving men, dwindling provisions, and an advancing summer? In England, the meaning of the term would have been clear to him, but here it was indeterminate, something never quite within reach, like a fluttering moth you grasp at over and over but cannot seize.

It seemed to him that he and Adams orbited each other, separated by their polarities yet captured and held by the gravity of their mission. Each unable to break free of the other but destined never to intersect.

———

"You have no more detours to propose?" Adams meant it as a quip but was suddenly seized with a fear Robinson would change his mind and declare they must march a farther two hundred miles to Back's River in search of Crozier.

Robinson grunted, tried to smile, and failed. He shook his head. "No more. We have but pieces of a story, many chapters missing. It will have to do. Only Crozier knows the rest, but we have missed him now."

Adams called Billings down from the upper deck, gave him and Robinson two strips of dried meat and a piece of biscuit each, and took the same for himself. He sat on the table in the captain's cabin and stitched a hole in his stocking. Robinson sharpened his knife on a leather strap he had found on the orlop deck. Billings played soldiers with the chess pieces they had discovered in the captain's private quarters. The two officers cleaned their shotguns and went hunting out on the ice. Half a day later they returned, having seen no sign of life. Fitzjames lay lifeless in his bunk. Adams looked down at his waxen features: eyes half-open but dull and empty, long greasy hair, cracked and pale lips parted just enough to see the yellow teeth beneath.

"Another prayer, then?" Robinson asked.

Adams shook his head. He felt something heavy slipping from his heart and thought it might be the notion that he ever had any power to help these men. He pulled the blanket over the dead man's face.

"He was more prepared to meet the Lord than any man I have known."

Robinson turned on his heel and made for the door of the cabin. "Then it is time to leave."

———

Robinson climbed the ladder to the upper deck and looked out at the snow dissolving into freezing mush. Rivulets of water ran down *Erebus'* hull. Above his head, drops of water rained from stalactites in the rigging. Tiny pockets of turquoise gleamed where the sunlight struck the icy outcrops. Adams and Billings followed him up the ladder. Together they stepped over the gunwale and carefully climbed down the snow ramp to the ice below. When they planted their boots on the surface of the snow, they sank to their ankles.

They walked away through the hummocks of ice toward King William Land. The wind came at them out of the sun and ran them through with freezing blades. It lifted clouds of drift off the snow and bore them forward like malevolent spirits. Dark clouds descended and smothered the sun. In the half-light, the ice took on a metallic sheen.

Robinson turned for a last glimpse of the two ships, *Erebus'* masts a trio of dead trees in a desert of white. When the end came for the ships, it would be swift. When they finally lost their battle against the floes, they would be crushed and sucked into the black water below. The masts would shudder as they dropped into the swirling ice, the thick doubled-planked timbers popping and snapping like twigs, the frozen bodies of Fitzjames' men squashed flat in their bunks and hammocks. The ice would close over the holes in the floe within minutes. Nothing would remain, nothing to say Franklin's men were ever here.

———

The three men walked blind for two days but did not find the land. Adams craned his neck and sought the sun in vain. Clouds and banks of mist combined to form a whiteness that rose and dissolved the world. He stumbled through icy pools and slipped on patches of smooth ice. The sledge snagged on ice outcrops, recalcitrant like an exhausted child, forcing Billings to retrace his steps and ease it free. His boots filled with freezing water, and he lost all sensation in his fingers and toes.

Adams checked their provisions. He guessed their remaining food at twelve pounds of biscuit and fifteen pounds of meat. Enough for a week, perhaps, if they marched on reduced rations. A loose tooth wobbled at the touch of his tongue. His legs ached, his bones afire. Billings hobbled beside him, favouring his right hip. The toe of his boot dragged on the ice. Adams reached into his tobacco pouch and filled his pipe, and the smoke streamed out behind him.

Adams' hands shook. His shotgun was a cannon across his shoulders. He looked skyward for ducks or geese but could see nothing in the mist. Clambering over the ridges of ice left them all doubled over, panting for breath. His mind began to wander. In their confused state, he worried they would walk in circles on the floes. Only a few feet above sea level, the low stony shore of King William Land concealed itself somewhere ahead, offering no mountains or glaciers by which to navigate. They chewed on frozen pieces of meat and filled their canteens from puddles in the ice.

Robinson's blurry shape moved ahead of Adams in the wind. Occasionally, the lieutenant bent over his compass, shook it, and turned it in his hand, peering into the blank sky. They had already walked for half a day longer than on their journey out from King William Land to *Erebus*. Adams thought to ask Robinson if he was sure of their direction, but with no better idea of their position, he held his tongue and followed him through the fog. Were they heading south? King William Land was somewhere to the east, but its coastline south of Victory Point was uncharted. If the shoreline turned east, they might walk forever over the sea ice and not reach land.

The snow became heavier, whipped around them by the wind. Adams pulled his bandanna high on his nose. Every few minutes, he reached out with his gloved hands to scrape away the snow caked around Billings' eyelids. They stopped to sleep in the morning. Adams lay shivering in his blanket and held his frozen fingers gingerly to his chest as if cupping a tiny bird. Any movement and the pain in his legs and bowels would wrap him in its coils and squeeze the breath from him. He thought of the men dead in their hammocks on *Erebus* and understood how they had done it. When he rolled himself in his blanket, he imagined himself crawling into a dark hole, his only respite from the light and wind.

Three days out from *Erebus*, Robinson saw the low coast of King William Land appear before them like the brown hump of a whale rising in a white sea. He walked ashore, stepping over banks of shattered limestone pushed onto the land by ancient glaciers and left to freeze and crack into flat shards. Robinson dropped the sledge rope. He fell to all fours and touched his forehead to the shingle. Adams put his hands on his knees. Billings stood dazed and blinking. A thin layer of fresh snow covered much of the ground above the tidemark. Small reddish-brown boulders were visible through the slush, like pustules bubbling to the surface.

Robinson produced his compass and sextant and knelt on the gravel, his map unrolled. "We have landed too far south," he said. He gestured to the northeast, where fog shrouded the coastline. "Victory Point is that way."

"How far?"

Robinson hesitated. "Forty miles, I think." He paused. "Perhaps more." He led the other two men to the higher ground above the beach. The land stretched into the grey distance as though a great force had swept across it, scraping away not only all animal life and vegetation but also every undulation and blemish in the earth until all was utterly flat and lifeless. The wind died away, and the only sound was the clack of the stones under their boots. The sun climbed in the sky to the northwest, painting a glittering orange stripe on the ice that led almost to their feet. The only shadows were their own, unfamiliar shapes rippling across the dead land.

Suddenly there was only the sound of two pairs of boots on the gravel. Robinson stopped and turned. Billings stood twenty yards behind them, gazing into the distance with vacant eyes.

"Billings," said Robinson, "are you unwell? We must push on. Stopping here will delay us. We can rest this evening."

Billings did not reply.

Adams went to him and placed a gloved hand on his shoulder. "Jimmy, can you go on?"

"'Keep an eye out,' you said." Billings' voice was quiet. He lifted a hand and pointed. "Something moves there."

CHAPTER FOURTEEN

Robinson approached and stood beside Billings. Far ahead, an object shifted on the shingle.

Robinson's breathing was loud in his head. He raised the telescope to his eye. More than one object, he decided. They were too small to be musk ox and exhibited none of the lope and nod of reindeer.

"People," he said at last. "At least two."

They walked faster, limping and rolling on sore feet. Billings and Adams drew the sledge, holding the track rope in their hands to spare their bleeding shoulders. An adult Esquimaux couple and a child of no more than ten watched them approach. Their faces were dark with sun and smudged with soot. All were clad in reindeer-skin parkas and trousers. Beside them, a pack of dogs stood hitched to a sledge.

"Hello!" Robinson called out, his hand raised in greeting.

The man and woman stared warily. The man held a bow and arrow in one hand. He raised the other and responded with a shout. He did not smile. Adams and Robinson placed their shotguns on the gravel and raised their hands. Billings stood behind them. The Esquimaux couple watched in silence.

"They are not afraid like the other fellow we met," said Adams.

"They have seen white men before." Robinson kept his voice calm.

The man had not discarded his bow and arrow. There was no bon-homie in his manner. The boy sat on the sledge, his ruddy face ringed by a halo of caribou fur. His lips were a lustrous red, and the brown skin of his cheek was smooth and unblemished. A rectangular metal box sat on his lap, its hinged lid open. Robinson felt something flutter in his stomach.

"What is that? What does he have there?"

From his position closer to the boy, Adams tried to peer into the box.

"A journal or logbook of some kind. Leather-bound, I think."

The child picked a piece of paper from the box and held it above his head. Robinson's mouth was dry. "No. Please, do not—"

Before he could say more, the child tore the piece of paper in two, the dry slashing sound incongruous in the barren landscape. He flung both scraps into the air. The breeze snatched them away in an instant, flapping and tumbling like tiny birds in a gale. His eyes round with fascination, the child twisted his torso and watched until the paper was out of sight. Robinson thrust out both his hands.

"Stop!" he shouted. "For God's sake, stop!"

The boy froze. He stared at the two white men, the box still open on his lap. The woman scowled and stepped in front of the child. The man shouted angrily at Robinson in words he did not understand. Robinson cursed his own impatience.

"I am sorry!" He bowed his head and backed away, waving his hands in what he hoped was a conciliatory gesture. "I will not hurt the boy." He attempted a smile. The parents glared at him. Robinson reached into his backpack and brought out his last packet of needles. He held it out to the woman. The suspicion melted from her face, which was instantly blank. She inspected the contents of his hand. Unsmiling, she reached out and took the needles. Robinson pointed again at the box.

"Where did you get this? Were there white men there? *Kabloona?*"

The woman spoke to her husband, then looked back at Robinson. He heard the word *kabloona* but understood nothing else. The woman pointed to the northeast and spoke again. Her gibberish stirred irritation in Robinson. How could these throaty grunts and clicks constitute a language? He glanced sideways at Adams.

"You try," he said quietly.

"Please," Adams said to the boy, affecting a soft, lilting tone. He pointed at the box. "May we see that?" Smiling broadly, he approached slowly, his hands spread wide. He pointed again at the box. "Please may we see your box?" He slapped one hand with the other and pointed two fingers of one hand at his eyes, then pointed at the box. "I will not take it. Will not touch it."

The man and the woman stood motionless, their eyes fixed on Adams. The boy tore another piece of paper from inside the box and tossed it into the air. It bucked and flew away on the wind. Again the boy swivelled to watch the paper until it disappeared. Robinson wanted to scream.

The Esquimaux couple glared at him again, their nostrils flared and their jaws set. The woman muttered something in her throat. Her fingers closed around the handle of a small knife. She took two steps forward. Robinson caught the odours of oil and sweat and fish. *If I had my cutlass,* he thought, *I would run you through, you witch.* He attempted an apologetic smile but could feel his blood hot in his face. "I am sorry. Sorry." He pointed at the box, then spread his hands in an interrogative gesture. "This box. Where did you find it?"

Her eyes were black. She bared her teeth at him and snarled, the sound of a knife blade across bone. Robinson felt his fists clenching. His throat tightened. The situation was slipping from him. His patience snapped like a thread pulled on once too often. These savages had something he needed. He no longer cared whether they understood.

"Enough!" he exclaimed. "We shall have that box. It is Royal Navy property." He pointed at the boy and said, "Billings, retrieve it this instant. That is an order."

Billings strode forward. The boy stared at him, round-eyed. Billings' shadow fell across him. Alarm flashed on the woman's face. She raised her knife, hissing. The man nocked an arrow and raised his bow in one fluid movement.

"No!" Adams shouted, both hands in front of him, fingers splayed. For an instant the man hesitated.

Robinson was on his knees. He swept up the shotgun and fired in a single motion, the weapon only inches above the earth. The recoil spun the gun from his grasp. The barrel sprang back, striking him above the eyebrow. A hot pain shot through his hand. The ball took the Esquimaux man in the chest and kicked him backward. The woman shrieked—a long, high-pitched wail that continued for longer than Robinson knew a human could exhale. The smell of gun smoke and blood settled like a cloak. The man lay motionless, one leg bent under the other. He stared upward, his fingers curled around the bow.

Robinson put his uninjured hand to his brow, astonished when it came away bloody. The woman stopped screaming, the sudden silence louder than any sound he had ever heard. She seized the reins of the sledge and made a noise in her throat. The dogs ran, bounding off quickly to the south. The boy sat like a stone idol on the sledge, expressionless, the round hood of his fur parka shrinking as it pulled away. Within a minute they were black specks far out on the stony shore.

The three men stood in silence. Each avoided the others' gaze. Billings' face was ashen, both his hands clapped over his mouth. He turned his back and stared out at the pack. Adams went to the fallen man. The wound in his chest welled with glistening blood. He turned to Robinson, pale and shaking.

"Did you have to press them like that?"

Blood dripped into Robinson's eyes from the gash on his brow. He touched the burn on his hand. "It could have been Crozier's log," he said. "It could have told us everything." He wanted to explain to Adams the alacrity with which the passion overtook him, how he was helpless against it. He wanted Adams to understand that he had needed a moment of authority, just one thing over which he had control, but even as he rehearsed them in his mind, the words sounded frail and hollow. They would not carry the weight he needed them to bear.

Adams' eyes were wet. "You frightened them! What parents would not defend their child?"

"I never meant—"

"We could have traded something."

"We have nothing left."

Adams' glare denounced him now. A vein throbbed in his neck. "Are you blind?" He waved a hand at the dead man and shouted, "You saw he was armed!"

Robinson could summon no more words to explain himself. "It . . . it was Royal Navy property."

"Here is your navy property." Adams lifted the volume the boy had dropped and held it out to Robinson. "We were already too late. That was the last page. The boy tore them all out."

He fingered the eviscerated spine, then hurled the book at Robinson. Too heavy to be carried off by the wind, it dropped like a bird felled by a bullet. Robinson stared dully at it, as if it might spring magically to life. Adams stood glaring, his chest heaving. Judging him.

Robinson felt a sudden fury rise in him. He had indulged Adams thus far, but the man's callowness was a source of mounting exasperation. His tolerance was waning like a wick burning down to its end. Why could Adams not understand? The man believed that whatever he desired should be his merely because he bowed his head and carried a Bible. He had set out to find Franklin because he thought himself anointed by some celestial magician. Robinson had never considered himself entitled to anything. He had always known that whatever he wanted, he would have to earn. Whatever he could not earn, he would take. Sanctimonious windbags and obstreperous savages be damned.

They left large stones on the shallow grave in case she returned for her man.

Adams said nothing more to Robinson, wretched by the Esquimaux's death, wretched now that he could do nothing but bury the man in this emptiness. Wretched that when it was time to make their report, he would say it had all been an accident, the result of a misunderstanding. An act of self-defence. If the Esquimaux woman were ever to report the incident, her word would not be taken over that of a Royal Navy officer. He was appalled at the finality of it, that a man could die so needlessly and there would be so little to say about it. To further reproach Robinson demanded a strength he no longer possessed. Pity for the dead man was futile. He could make no more sense of it than that, and it left him sick with guilt. There was no keeping men alive here.

The plain to the east was veined with meltwater streams snaking to the sea. Swathed in grey haze, the sun guttered like an old lamp. A single yellow poppy nodded in the dirt. Adams worried for Billings. The young seaman walked with his head down, far behind Adams, making no attempt to close the distance. He had not spoken a word since the man was killed. Adams wondered how to explain it all to him. His words seemed to reassure the simple lad less and less.

Robinson had rendered his own verdict. Already he had begun to weave his own story, contrition fading into exculpation. "There was nothing to be done," he said. He walked alongside Adams, hands in his pockets. His expression was grave. "They are not known to be so hostile. It is their way to discard their weapons and greet travellers unarmed on the ice. We did our part when we dropped our guns. I can only think they had met white men who had mistreated them."

Adams sighed. It was someone else's fault, then? Perhaps Robinson's attempts at extenuation were not entirely without merit. Could Crozier have so enraged the Esquimaux?

They trekked north along the beach toward Victory Point. Ahead, the horizon gleamed, white like hot metal. After two days' clambering over icy hummocks, they found progress easier on the long, flat stretches of shingle. The wind was a hollow hum, the scraping of the sledge runners like an axe on a whetstone. The three men marched in step, their boots rising and falling in unison. Adams watched the ice for seals and the skies for geese.

After they had walked for half a day, an object appeared on the shingle ahead, above the tidemark. A ship's boat, thirty feet in length, sat on a long wooden sledge. Lacking a mast, rudder, and sail, it seemed oddly bare. Then Adams realised.

"They removed all the iron fittings."

"To make her lighter," said Robinson. "They were dragging her."

"On this?" Adams kicked the wooden sledge with the toe of his boot. "It looks like mahogany. It must be at least as heavy as the boat—six, seven hundred pounds. They were planning to haul this all the way to Back's River?"

Adams thought of the davits standing empty on the deck of *Erebus*. He imagined Franklin's exhausted and hungry men dragging the boats from the stricken ships over the broken ice pack to shore, pushing them up twenty-foot hummocks and lowering them down the other side. They stood at the gunwale of the boat and looked inside. The body of a large man lay across the stern, swathed in pieces of a bearskin and the remnants of a blanket. The corpse's bare head lay under a thwart. Some portion of the scalp remained, patches of grey hair adhering to the skull.

Adams' chest tingled. Upon leaving *Erebus* he had not expected to find any trace of Crozier or his papers, but hope remained his intractable companion, returning to him even when unexpected.

"Is it him? Is it Crozier?"

Robinson leaned over to inspect the corpse. "I think not," he said. "Crozier was not this tall."

Birds had taken the eyes. Blotchy yellow-white skin was tight across the cheekbones below the empty sockets. Thin whiskers sprouted from the shrivelled skin of the chin. The man's jaw hung open, teeth bared. He reclined as on a throne, each arm positioned on a large pile of discarded clothing stacked on either side. He wore mittens on his hands and stockings on his booted feet. Sections of the limbs were exposed, the thin flesh yellow and shrunken over the bones. Adams explored the corpse gently with the tip of his knife.

"The torso has suffered trauma, but of what origin, I cannot say. I think foxes have been in there and consumed the soft parts."

"And bears, perhaps."

Robinson pointed to the bow of the boat, and Adams noticed a second body, a collection of bones scattered across the floor of the boat beneath the foremost thwarts. There was no sign of the dead man's clothing. No flesh or skin remained on the bones. Adams picked up a jawbone but could not find the skull.

"I am not even certain this man's entire body is here." Adams examined the other bones. "I see only a single femur."

Robinson examined two double-barrelled shotguns standing in the stern, their barrels pointed at the sky. One barrel of each gun was loaded. Bags of powder and shot and brass percussion caps were stacked in the stern. A cobbler's awl, its sharp steel point sheathed in a cork, lay near an empty pemmican canister amid empty cans, pieces of silver cutlery, and pairs of steel scissors. Robinson collected a pocketknife and tested the blade carefully with his thumb before placing it in his knapsack. They searched the piles of clothing and equipment for messages. Adams retrieved a book and peered at the cover.

"*The Vicar of Wakefield.* And there is a Bible here too."

Robinson pulled off his cap and scratched his head. He picked up a pair of spectacles, examined them, then tossed them back into the boat. A small packet of tobacco lay there. He held it to his nose. Satisfied, he put it in his pocket.

"Do you think these two went with Crozier?"

"If so, they must have turned around. If one were dragging the boat south, would not the bow be pointing that way? But look." He pointed to the northeast. "It is pointing that way. Toward the ships."

"They were ill, or too weak to hunt with Crozier. They were going back to join Fitzjames."

Robinson grimaced. He scanned the empty land. "Or else there is something they were trying to get away from here."

They finished their pipes crouched in the boat's lee to escape the wind. Stretching endlessly to the east, the raw earth was like an enormous pan of ash in the evening light. A mile along the beach, they discovered a tent ring on a low rise. Neatly positioned in a circle, the stones were free of moss and lichen. Robinson filled his pipe with the tobacco he had salvaged from the boat. He held out the packet to Adams, who accepted it with a nod. Billings knelt, his arm buried to the elbow in a lemming burrow.

They approached the abandoned campsite and scanned the earth. Scraps of navy-blue cloth and slivers of wood were scattered around the ring of stones. A broken axe handle stuck out of the ground, the shaft splintered like a jagged piece of bone. Long pieces of white lay scattered on the ground. Adams counted a dozen bones. Two others protruded from the ground at odd angles. He wondered if they had been tugged from the icy gravel by foxes or wolves.

"Reindeer bones," he called to Robinson. "Perhaps there is game here."

He stepped among the scattered remains, then stopped. At his feet lay a longer bone. He picked it up and turned it over in his hands. It was a human femur. He looked back at the bones on the ground. Human ribs. He pushed his goggles up to his forehead and peered at the head of the femur. He threw his mitten off and ran his bare fingertips over the bone. Then all strength left his hands, and the bone clattered on the gravel. Ten feet away, Robinson looked up and turned to him.

"What is it?"

Adams did not answer. At his feet was a human skull. Its jawbone was missing. He knelt to examine it. He turned the skull over carefully. In the side of the skull was a round hole about the size of a sixpence.

CHAPTER FIFTEEN

"Look, Mister Adams!" Billings stood fifty feet away, his arms raised in triumph. He held a squirming lemming in each hand. Adams tried to smile at him but could not. His jaw was clamped, the muscles of his cheek twitching.

Robinson took the skull from him. "You are the surgeon, not I. Look here," he said, his fingertip resting on the edge of the hole in the bone.

Adams looked away. "So? Perhaps the poor fellow hit his head on a rock. Or an animal may have gnawed on it. A fox or a wolf. Perhaps a wandering bear disturbed the body and its tooth punctured the bone."

"And left no other marks? A bear or wolf would have crushed the skull completely."

"No Christian would do such a thing," said Adams. "'Whoever sheds the blood of man, by man shall his blood be shed—'"

"Spare me the scripture!" Robinson's face was dark, the veins stark in his neck. "You expect too much of starving men. You may not forgive them their frailties, but you may at least attempt to comprehend them."

"Men eating men?" This was it, the sense of unease that had dogged him for days, a shadowy assailant tracking him across the dead land. He had suspected it but would not turn and confront it. He closed his eyes, toes curling. "To even imply it is a gross insult to every man who serves."

Robinson sighed. "I imply nothing," he said. "Surely you see it. That"—he touched the hole in the skull—"represents a fatal wound.

Probably a lead ball, possibly a boarding pike." He shrugged, his voice trailing off to a murmur. "But perhaps they were merely trying to get at the brain of a man already dead."

"The Esquimaux. They could have done it, could they not? If they attacked en masse, they could have overpowered a small group of Franklin's men."

Robinson gaped at him. "For what reason?"

"A gesture misconstrued, a greeting mispronounced? Have we not seen it ourselves? You know how quickly such things can lead to violence." The taunt was intended to wound.

A look of sadness crossed Robinson's face. He spoke in a whisper. "I suppose it is possible." He bent down to retrieve the femur, pulled off his left mitten with his teeth, and rested a dirty fingernail on a mark close to one end. Adams leaned in, peering.

"Do you see that?" Robinson asked.

"That scratch?"

"Not a scratch. A cut mark. Done by a blade."

Adams took the bone from Robinson and lifted it for closer inspection.

"A surgeon might amputate a frost-bitten digit or even a hand or foot," Robinson said patiently. "But you can see as well as I, this bone was removed at the hip."

Adams fell silent and hung his head in the cold, still air. He felt bruised, dizzy. His long-held convictions were collapsing, falling away like old masonry. The afternoon sunlight cast a greasy sheen on the ice pack offshore.

"Sir John was dead before they did this," said Robinson. "Your man is unsullied. Content yourself with that."

Adams walked away. He sat down on the stones and hugged his knees, rocking to keep warm. *This changes a man,* he thought. *I am changed. Stripped bare. Hollowed out. I look no different, but I am tougher, stringier. My teeth are loose, my gums sore, my frozen limbs in a permanent state of pain.* He looked at the sky. Bars of sunlight pierced the clouds like knives and made him think of blades on flesh, of bright blood. He thought of yellow teeth, bloodshot eyes, and filthy, wasted, bearded faces. He imagined the smell of meat in the cookpot, of men crowding around, holding out their bowls.

———

Billings lay on his stomach in his blanket bag, whittling a piece of driftwood with a small knife.

"Mister Adams, do you think they still remember us back home?"

"Yes, Jimmy, of course. We have only been away a year."

Billings' face was in shadow. "I'm afraid my ma will forget me."

"She will not," Adams said. "Mothers do not forget their children."

A lone gull cried out somewhere far above the tent.

"I've forgotten our pa," Billings said quietly. "He died."

"Was it a long time ago?"

Billings nodded. "When I was a lad. I was a scavenger in the cotton mill. Used to clean up under the spinning mules. I came home and ma said they found him in the cesspit. Drowned, she said. On account o' the drink, she said."

Adams drew on his pipe, exhaled blue smoke. "It takes a long time to forget someone, Jimmy."

"How long?"

"Much longer than a year. But we shall do something great. Then they shall all remember us."

Billings propped himself on one elbow and looked eagerly at Adams. "What will we do, Mister Adams?"

Relieved to see the young man had recovered his cheer, Adams smiled. "We shall discover what happened to poor Sir John. People still think of Sir John, do they not?"

Billings digested this. "Why do people think of Sir John, Mister Adams?"

Adams was suddenly unsure what to tell him. Because Franklin served at Trafalgar? Because he sailed around the Australian continent? Because he had been governor of Van Diemen's Land? Billings would neither understand nor care about such things. Why are some men remembered and not others?

Robinson spoke. "It is because he is the one who didn't return. They will want to know why."

Adams ignored him. "It is because he does God's work," he told Billings.

Billings' expression cleared, and he smiled. "I remember now. You told us. Sir John ate his boots."

"Yes, he ate his boots on the way back from Point Turnagain. Twenty-seven years ago, before you were even born. People still remember that, don't they?"

"Yes." Billings nodded emphatically. Then he suddenly looked alarmed. "Will we eat our boots too?"

"No, we shall wear them home, Jimmy."

Billings smiled again. "Then we'll tell them all what happened."

At this, Robinson sat upright. His teeth were clenched on the stem of his pipe. He jabbed a finger at Billings. "Listen to me. You shall tell them nothing." His eyes were narrow slits. "God knows what you'll say, but you're sure to get it wrong. You shall leave the telling to me, is that clear?"

———

Adams told Billings to wait with the sledge as he and Robinson hunted along the shore. The sun turned the surface of the meltwater pools to mercury. To the east, King William Land was flat and stony. Shallow rocky pools dotted swampy plains of yellow grass. Sunlight spattered on the gravel. The summer colours were leaking from the landscape, each day more a pencil sketch than a watercolour.

Thin slices of limestone cracked beneath their heels. They stepped carefully over pools of water and tufts of pale grass. Thick mud rimmed their boots. Strips of grey cloud were like the furrows in a man's brow. They walked with their guns at the ready but saw nothing living. The landscape undulated gently, low gravel hillocks punctuated by shallow depressions still filled with snow. The sun was a watery disc behind a bank of clouds.

Adams heard the flap of wings. A ptarmigan alighted on a small outcrop twenty feet in front of him. The bird had begun to shed its winter plumage for the speckled brown feathers of the summer. Its brown head was like a helmet atop its rotund white body. The bird regarded him curiously for a moment, then lowered its head to peck at a small shrub jutting from the stony soil. Adams raised his shotgun and aimed. The ptarmigan's head jerked up. The bird stared boldly at him. When he pulled the trigger, the wind took the sound of the blast, and the volley of shot blew the bird backward onto the gravel.

Adams signalled to Robinson, who was hunting one hundred yards away. He knelt to collect the bird. As he looked down, his eye went to the stone where the ptarmigan had perched. He reached down and flicked dirt away from it with his glove. Two semicircular shapes jutted an inch above the soil, an inch apart. Adams frowned. Each object was yellow, like a seashell, with a smooth edge. He pulled off his glove and ran his fingertip over one, then pulled his hand away.

He was looking at a pair of toenails.

Robinson approached and stood behind Adams as he knelt. The grave was barely eighteen inches deep and covered with several large, flat stones. He watched as Adams slowly removed each of them from atop the corpse, then gently chiselled away the frozen soil with the tip of his knife. The wind was light and the day warm. Robinson sweated into his flannel undershirt.

Robinson wondered why this corpse had been buried. The others they had found were abandoned in hammocks or boats, or scattered as unburied bones. He knew from experience the effort required to get down more than a foot in this frozen ground. Was this an officer?

A knuckle protruded from the ground. Scraps of dark-blue cloth. Adams scratched at the soil with his knife, revealing more of the fabric. Robinson looked around and found a flat stone. He knelt beside Adams, and together they scraped more earth from the top of the grave. When they had removed two inches of soil, most of the shroud was exposed. Robinson raised his pocketknife and slit the cloth upward from the corpse's feet to the throat. He sat back, panting.

He peeled the cloth back. There was no odour of decay. The shroud was stiff with frost and unmarked. He saw a pair of thin, bare feet. The two big toes were bound together with twine. He raised the shroud. The knees were also bound. The blue-white flesh was like porcelain, the skin stretched tightly over ropelike tendons. The corpse wore only a pair of linen trousers and a thin shirt.

When Robinson exposed the face, he stopped. The dead man's eyes were intact and slightly open. Tousled blond hair was plastered to his scalp. The lips were drawn back, exposing yellow teeth within a scraggly brown beard. Robinson half expected the eyes to swivel in their sockets and look at him.

"Too young to be an officer," Robinson said. "Can't be more than twenty."

The left forearm was entirely stripped of flesh between the wrist and elbow, exposing the radius and ulna. A slit ran down the front of one trouser leg. Robinson gently separated the two edges of the fabric. Chunks of flesh had been clumsily hacked from the thigh and calf, leaving jagged dark-red holes an inch across. The bones of the leg were exposed in three places. The face of the corpse was at peace.

"Perhaps," Robinson said, "this was one of the first. They were still practicing with him. When the idea was still new."

"He was scorbutic," said Adams. "They buried him, then returned to him later."

Robinson's innards curled. "Like visiting some ghastly larder."

They had buried him to keep him fresh. Or to hide him from bears. He pictured a visitor kneeling over the grave in silence, his face wrapped in a filthy scarf. Unaccustomed to such surgery, the butcher would have worked quickly, with a blunt knife grasped in a trembling hand.

Robinson wiped his hand across his face. "The body has not been here long."

Adams stood and scanned the empty expanse. The stony plain stretched out in every direction, unbroken and endless. "This poor fellow deserves a prayer. I doubt he received one."

Robinson thought of the men who had left their shipmate here. "They did not finish with him. They may be back."

Adams hesitated, then said softly, "God is a source of strength. He helps me with my burden."

"I would not know what to ask Him."

"God hears the prayer of the righteous. So it says in the Bible."

"Am I more righteous than he?" Robinson jerked his chin at the grave. "Are you?" On the grey sky, a thin black line was scribbled vertically to the northeast. He unstrapped the telescope from across his back and put it to his eye. It was a column of smoke rising in the distance. He followed it upward to where the breeze picked at the smoke, shredding it like strands of black yarn pulled apart.

Billings came running across the gravel. "Mister Adams!"

"I see it, Jimmy."

The three men stood staring up at the smoke.

Robinson nodded at the body in the earth. "Say your prayer, but do not delay. We would be wise to avoid them."

"They are starving. They may need our assistance."

Robinson scoffed. "What assistance would you offer them? What will you do for them when there is nothing left to eat?"

"You cannot know they mean us harm," said Adams.

"Indeed I cannot, any more than you can be certain they do not."

"You always assume the worst in men."

Robinson's ire rose again. "And you insist upon assuming the best. This is at the heart of what separates us." He gestured at the body in the earth. "Ask him. Do you imagine men who did this will sit and listen to you read the Bible?" Robinson pointed at the smoke column. "Fury Beach is that way, beyond the smoke. We cannot go back. We must try and go around them." He unshouldered his shotgun. "Check your weapon. Wipe it down. Have it ready."

CHAPTER SIXTEEN

The ice pack blocked the way north. They could do nothing but hurry their pace along the stony beach. The distance between them and the smoke column closed. Toward morning, Robinson lifted the telescope. Two distant silhouettes were framed on the skyline to the east. They readied their shotguns and waited. The men shuffled toward them, stopping to rest every few minutes. When Robinson saw they were not armed, he and Adams lowered their weapons.

The two men limped forward and halted. In torn and dirty Guernsey frocks and sealskin trousers, they had a furtive look, like escaped felons. Their faces were thin, eyes sunk deep in their skulls, bearded faces mottled with filth. One leaned on a makeshift crutch fashioned from an oar. The other leaned on a staff cut from a tentpole. A grimy bandage bound his left hand, three fingers of which appeared missing. They stared silently at Robinson and Adams, then looked at Billings, blinking.

Robinson spoke. "Identify yourselves."

The man with the missing fingers crumpled to his knees, sliding down the length of his staff. He put his face in his ruined hand and squeezed his eyes shut. He began to laugh, a dry, desperate hack.

The other man stumbled forward, coughing. A long red scar ran down his pocked cheek and curled under the sparse red and grey whiskers along his jaw. His upper lip curled inward where teeth should have been. He reached out a trembling hand. Robinson grasped it. The hand was emaciated, knuckles unnaturally swollen, dark veins shrunken beneath dry, papery skin.

If I did not see this man standing here moving and breathing, Robinson thought, *I would think this a corpse's hand.*

"You're not from *Erebus*," the man said, a thick lisp twisting each syllable. "We thought you was from *Erebus*."

"Lieutenant Frederick Robinson, Assistant Surgeon Edward Adams," said Robinson. "We are from HMS *Investigator* under Captain Bird. HMS *Enterprise* is with her, under Sir James Ross."

The man sank to the earth and hugged Robinson's knees.

"Thank God," the man said. "Thank God."

Robinson's nose wrinkled at the sharp odour of dried sweat and urine.

"Who are you?" he demanded. "Is Captain Crozier here?"

The man looked up, his eyes still streaming. "Do you have any food, sir?"

"Some. On your feet, now." He prised the man's hands from around his knees and lifted him.

"Wh-where is your ship?" the man asked.

"She is frozen in at Port Leopold. Where is Captain Crozier?"

The scarred man's face was blank for a moment; then his jaw dropped. Robinson caught a glimpse of purple-black gums. The man's eyes widened, and his lips quivered. "Port Leopold?" His voice fell to a whisper. His face crumpled into itself, creases appearing like a piece of paper crushed in a fist. Fresh tears welled in his bloodshot eyes. He stared back at the man kneeling on the ground behind him.

"Sam, he says their ship is at Port Leopold! How far is that? Are they not here to save us?" A spasm of coughing overtook him, and he bent over and spat bloody phlegm.

"The ice stopped our ships," said Robinson. "Sir James Ross has taken a sledge party and is searching North Somerset for you." He put his hand on the scarred man's shoulder. It felt light and fragile under his fingers, the bones hollow and the muscles wasted. He thought it might shatter if he squeezed.

"We shall lead you there. There are provisions at Fury Beach."

The man called Sam hauled himself to his feet and stepped forward. He unwound the filthy bandage from his maimed hand and rewrapped the fabric tightly, pinning it to his palm with his thumb. "Three hundred miles, innit? To Port Leopold?"

"Who are you?" Robinson asked. "Are you part of Captain Crozier's party?"

"We're our own party."

"What is your rank?"

"Ain't got one no more." The man shrugged. "Things drop off here and go missing. Fingers, toes, noses. Names and ranks too. You don't notice them go most of the time." He drew a long breath, seemingly exhausted by the need to explain further. "I am Petty Officer Samuel Honey. I was the blacksmith on *Terror*. That there's Able Seaman John Handford."

"Where are the officers?" Adams asked.

"Dead. Or gone."

"Gone where? Where is Captain Crozier?"

Honey shrugged again. "People get lost out here."

The scarred man, Handford, pushed forward to interrupt Honey. "Their ships are not here? Sam, why are their ships not here?"

"Now, Johnny, buck up." Honey's gaze remained fixed on Robinson's face as he spoke soothingly to his man. "Three hundred miles ain't so far. The Rosses covered more ground in '32, and with more men too." Honey stepped closer to Robinson and Adams and whispered urgently to them. "But others from your vessel are comin'?"

"No," said Robinson.

"But they might, yes?" His tone was hopeful, pleading for a treat he might keep from his comrade, a treasure for himself alone. "They might come lookin' for you?"

"No one is looking for us."

Adams pitched the tent to shelter the two new arrivals from the wind. They sat with blank, wooden faces, exhibiting none of the animation of men. Their jaws worked slowly on shreds of reindeer meat Adams had sliced and pounded into small fragments. Billings loitered outside the tent, peering in. He beckoned to Adams.

"Are they really Sir John's men, Mister Adams?"

"Yes, Jimmy."

For the first time, Billings seemed to doubt him. He eyed the men suspiciously, as if he had encountered an exotic creature for the first time, only to discover it did not resemble a picture he had seen in a book.

"They don't look right."

"They have suffered, Jimmy."

"That ain't what I mean." He frowned, groping for the words. "Their eyes."

"No." Adams sighed. He glanced through the tent opening at the two men's broken, wasted bodies and sullen faces. "No, they do not look right."

"Did they do something to that man we found in the ground?" Billings' face had a wary, unforgiving cast.

Adams patted him on the shoulder. "I would relish some fresh fowl, Jimmy. Go and look along the beach. Tell Lieutenant Robinson if you see any ducks."

Billings' gaze lingered on the tent. "I don't understand," he said, shaking his head. "You said we'd find Sir John, but we didn't. You said his men were brave." He gestured helplessly. "But they're . . . like this." He dropped his gaze and moved off.

Adams watched him go, ashamed. There were no promises to be kept here, no certainties to rely upon. Only disappointment and resentment. He had run out of assurances for Billings.

He returned to the tent. Eating appeared to have sapped the two survivors' strength. Honey lay on the floorcloth, a shirtsleeve across his eyes. Handford sat, staring out through the opening.

"We saw the smoke from your fire," Adams said. "But there is no fuel here. No driftwood."

Handford's head lolled, too heavy to stay upright. "We burned the boat, bit by bit."

"But how would you return to the ships if you needed to?"

"We'd walk. Weren't goin' to need the boat. Ice ain't never goin' to melt." He sat back and grinned, his lips stretched across a black cavern of a mouth with three brown teeth. "Captain Crozier and his men took a whaleboat with them. Said they might haul it to Back's River and use the boat to go upriver." He shook his head. "Bloody madness, if you ask me. The bloody thing's too heavy to drag even on flat ground. Dunno how they expect to haul it over rapids. Can I have more meat, sir?"

Adams shook his head. "Your stomach is withered. It would make you ill to have so much at once."

"More meat, damn you!" A snarl contorted the man's face. His sunken yellow eyes flashed like gems in mud.

Adams maintained a patient tone. "You must eat only a little, and slowly. If your belly can accept it, I will give you more."

Handford was immediately obsequious, bobbing his head. "Yes, sir. Yes. Pardon my language, sir. Terribly rude of me, sir." His body shook. Tears coursed down his face.

"We found human bones," said Adams.

The man gaped at Adams with an expression the assistant surgeon could not read.

"On the beach, a few miles from here. They had injuries. Unnatural injuries," Adams said. "What do you know of it?"

The man craned his neck, trying to see the knapsack on Adams' back. "Is it in there? The meat?"

Adams' gaze fell upon the man's boots. His bare toes were visible through a large hole in the left boot. He wore no stockings. Shiny and black, the toes were misshapen and curled like overripe fruit. Adams caught the odour of rotten meat.

"How long has your foot been like this?"

The man's eyelids flickered. He said nothing.

"Not one of us still has all his fingers and toes," said Honey. He pulled the shirtsleeve from his eyes and raised his hand with its missing fingers. "The frostbite has touched us all."

Adams lowered his voice, addressing Honey. "I cannot leave his toes like this. There is a risk of gangrene. I must remove them."

"Do it."

Adams hesitated. Handford appeared to have entered a trance. He sat staring at nothing, drool hanging in a string from his lip. Adams whispered to Honey. "Does he understand what I propose to do?"

Honey shrugged. "Do it. I already told you—things fall away here. We are used to it."

Adams sharpened his knife on a stone, then wiped it on his sleeve. He removed Handford's boot and placed the stone beneath the man's foot. Placing the knife blade on one of the man's toes, he picked up another stone the size of his fist. Handford seemed to regain his senses. He swung his head around and inspected Adams' efforts with a disinterested air. When Adams brought the stone down, there was a sound like a dart striking a board. The toe rolled in the dirt. There was no blood, and the expression on Handford's face was unchanged. He continued to stare into the air and did not speak. Adams removed two more toes and threw them away across the gravel. When it was done, Handford put his hand on Adams' sleeve.

"The reindeer meat. Where is the meat, sir?"

Adams did not answer him. He leaned in to peer at something. "Is this a bite mark, Mister Honey?" With a strip of cloth, he bound a crescent-shaped wound on Honey's pale forearm and tied it off. Pinkish fluid oozed through the fabric. "How did you get it?"

Honey shrugged. "Don't remember. Never heals."

Adams opened the tent flap. Sunlight streamed in, bathing the tent's interior in a yellow glow. He lifted Honey's shirt and drew a sharp breath at the raised ridges of the man's ribs and the scattering of bruises on his skin. The clavicles protruded like two great handles. What remained of the flesh of his torso was thin, steamed away in some awful vat. Folds of skin bunched tightly across his concave belly. Adams smelled the oddly putrid odour of dried sweat on Honey's clothes. The stink of scurvy.

"After we came ashore last spring," Honey said, "Captain Crozier said we'd spend the summer huntin'. We shot a few reindeer, a few foxes and geese, but it weren't enough. There were maybe sixty alive after the winter. The sick stayed aboard *Erebus* with Fitzjames; the rest camped on the land. Crozier wanted to go south to find the reindeer, said if we could find enough fresh meat, we would fetch through. He wanted to place caches of meat along the coast of King William Land, then draw on 'em when he evacuated the invalids from the ships."

Adams frowned. "An arduous task to complete in a few short weeks before the winter."

Honey grunted his assent. "He thought some men might return to the ships before winter with meat for the sick. He hoped to meet some Esquimaux and spend the winter with them, then make for Repulse Bay or the fur-trading post on Great Slave Lake. Told him we'd stay behind and hunt until we'd shot enough game to build up our strength. But that's not why we stayed. There'd have been too many to feed."

"Why did the ship's provisions not last?"

Honey sighed. The conversation appeared to bore him. "They lasted well enough. For a time, at least. We still had canned meat, some soup. A fair amount of biscuit. The more men died, the more provisions remained for the rest of us. That was the problem."

"What do you mean?"

"None of it stopped the scurvy." He stopped and stared into space. "Last winter was the worst. We housed the ship over in November when the sun went down. It was so cold, we couldn't sleep for the ship's timbers cracking. Sounded like gunshots in the dark. Fifty below, some nights. The sick got sicker. Teeth fell out, limbs swelled up. Men bled from old scars. The lemon juice was all gone months before. So much debility." He sighed again. "I remember the day we lost all hope."

"When rations were reduced?"

"No." He wore a sad expression. "When the grog ran out. We mixed it weaker and weaker with water, could barely taste it by the end. When it was gone, I've never seen more men in tears at any funeral."

"You said you thought we were from *Erebus*," said Adams.

"Aye, we wasn't expecting to see you. We'd stopped hopin' someone would come. We thought it'd be better to team up with someone from the ship."

"Better than what? Were the two of you not out here alone?"

"Not alone. We were with Mister Gregory and his men. He used to be engineer on *Erebus*. But there weren't enough straws left."

Adams frowned. "What do you mean?"

"Last time, we drew straws to see which of us would go and cut up the dead fellas. But there weren't many straws left. We didn't want to wait and find out what happened when they ran out."

A serpent wound itself in cold coils in Adams' gut. "How many men does Gregory have?"

"There's three. Walker, Orren, and Caulker's Mate Frank Dunn."

"Are they armed?"

"Three shotguns between the four of 'em."

"Ammunition?"

"Enough."

Robinson appeared at the door of the tent. "The column of smoke has disappeared."

Honey nodded. "Then they'll be comin'."

———

"We must leave them," said Robinson.

He glanced back over his shoulder at the tent two hundred yards behind them, where Honey and Handford lay sleeping. "We have found them too late. They are too weak, too sick."

He and Adams walked in a circle. Billings stood watch on the plain a mile away.

"We cannot abandon them," said Adams.

There was only the cold and the smell of the ocean. The skyline in the west was a jagged line of white. A flat pan of shingle and scattered lakes lay to the east.

"Think of the mission," said Robinson.

Adams rubbed his temples. "Remind me—what is the mission now?"

"We fail if we do not report back to the Admiralty. All will have been for naught. I would escort them if it were possible, truly I would. But we cannot feed them, and soon we shall have to drag them." It was enough for Robinson that his words were sincere; he did not need to say the rest: without Franklin's two men to muddy the waters, it would be he that the Admiralty turned to for the entire story. When they spoke of the discovery of the Passage, it would be his name on everyone's lips.

"God may yet smile upon us," said Adams.

Robinson's laugh was mirthless. "I have not seen so much as a twitch of His lip thus far."

"You wish these men dead?" Adams challenged him.

"I do not. But if their comrades pursue us, we shall be outnumbered. Do you think these two"—he gestured at the tent—"will hesitate to rejoin their old shipmates against us?"

Adams' voice was empty of passion, his features as blank as a stone wall. "If we do not take them," he said, "you must shoot me now, for I shall not go further with you."

Robinson had never heard an utterance more earnest and unfeigned. The finality in Adams' tone was absolute, the words standing like battlements between them in the cold air. No wind would take them, no tremor would knock them down.

You must shoot me now.

The image was in Robinson's head for only the briefest instant before he pushed it away. It flashed and vanished like the beam of a lighthouse on a dark night: the gun in his hands, the recoil, the smell of gunpowder, the sight of Adams dead on the earth and Robinson standing alone. Robinson, the lauded lone discoverer of the North-West Passage, greeting his rescuers at Fury Beach. The story his alone to tell, with no one to contradict him. He saw Adams' eyes and knew the man had imagined it too. He marvelled at how a brief fancy could be shared wordlessly with a glance. In that instant, both men knew the other's mind with the utmost clarity; then each dismissed it a heartbeat later as a product of their weary, fevered brains. As something that could never and would never be.

Robinson coughed and looked down at the earth. He had never fought a true battle but knew when to withdraw from a skirmish. "Very well. But you must not promise Billings we will get these two men home. You build up his hopes unfairly."

"They frighten him. He will not go near them unless I am present."

"He is simple. You might as well ask a circus acrobat to argue the law, or a coal miner to converse in Greek. What if he tells them we could have brought them home safely when it was never possible? It will not reflect well on either of us. He need only say the wrong thing and everything we say will be questioned."

"Everything *you* say will be questioned."

Robinson sighed and turned his back. To argue with the man was like rubbing a sore. "We must leave this evening," he said. "We must put some distance between us and them."

In the distance, great masses of cloud along the horizon were like smoke from a fire consuming the earth.

Robinson scanned the eastern horizon with his telescope but saw no one in pursuit. He stood before the men of his party and pointed to the north.

"Victory Point is twenty miles in that direction. We shall salvage whatever we can carry, then follow the coast north to Cape Felix, cross back to Boothia over the ice, and go north to Fury Beach."

Robinson led them north across the dead terrain of King William Land, his telescope in hand. Billings hauled the sledge carrying their bedding, tent, stove, and food. Adams strapped his gun across his back. Honey and Handford shambled along behind them like condemned prisoners.

Five thin, exhausted men shivered in the wind and watched their shadows ripple across the crushed earth. Around midnight, the wind dropped. Sea smoke rose from the tips of the small bergs grounded in the shallow water, like dead souls departing the earth.

After each mile, Robinson stopped and looked back. He saw nothing moving.

CHAPTER SEVENTEEN

"What sort of man is Gregory?" Adams asked Honey as they sat in the tent.

"An evil bastard. That's what sort."

"We would have taken him back with us. Taken all of you."

"He'd never go with you. He said if someone saw the bones on the beach, they'd know what we was eatin' and we'd hang. He wanted to go back to *Erebus* and sail her out once Captain Fitzjames was dead and nobody could stop him. He said no one would understand what we did."

Then he was not wrong about everything, Adams thought.

Honey would not look at him. "You found the boat on the beach?"

"Two bodies."

Honey nodded. "They was goin' back to *Erebus*. Gregory told us they were goin' to tell Fitzjames what we'd been up to. Said we had to kill 'em; said the others would come for us when we ran out of food. Once you start believin' lies, it's easy to keep doin' it. The others ran. Probably went south, chasing Crozier. We left the boat there. Gregory said we might need it if the ice melted before we could walk back to *Erebus*."

"The bodies had been disturbed," said Adams. "Scattered by animals."

"Animals?" Honey cocked his head, a puzzled look on his face. "Not likely. No animals around here. I reckon that was probably Billy Orren did that. I never did ask him about it, though."

The words were out of Adams' mouth before he realised he had spoken. "You feel no shame? At what you did?"

Honey studied him from under heavy lids, his expression bored. "Shame? Dunno what that means anymore. It went along with everything else. Peels away like, I dunno . . . dead skin or somethin'." His voice was nonchalant, empty of regret.

"I cannot fathom it."

"At first, when you're starvin', you try to ignore the pain in your gut. I used to pretend it was because someone had punched me, not 'cos I was hungry. Then I tried biting me thumb, tried to make something else hurt to take me mind off it. Then one of me teeth came away."

Honey paused. It seemed to Adams that the man might have been discussing the weather.

"Once you do it," Honey went on in a weary monotone, "it ain't so strange. You don't think about it. Some questions a man has no answer for. Do you wait for the thaw or try and walk out over the ice? Do you leave the invalids behind or take them with you?" He looked Adams directly in the face. "Do you starve to death or do you eat a man?"

The question was like an arrow Adams could not evade. He answered too quickly. "I would rather starve to death," he said. "I have no doubt."

Honey smiled for the first time, his few teeth yellow in his thick beard. He gave a wheezy chuckle.

"You're so sure, ain'tcha? I've known a few like you."

———

The limestone shingle clicked under Robinson's boots. The temperature rose to thirty-five degrees, but his wasted body trembled with every gust of wind. When the fog thickened, they halted, shivering, and waited for the mist to lift enough to reveal a glimpse of the sea ice to the west. The wind whistled across the ice. Streaks of drift reached out like fingers. Tufts of grass crunched underfoot, hard as wire. Ptarmigan whizzed past them, their wing tips touching the stones, but he and Adams were so weak, the birds were out of range before they could raise their guns.

Robinson mulled over Honey's tale, imagining scores of dismembered, partially consumed corpses laying in shallow depressions inches beneath the rocky soil of King William Land. He thought back to *Investigator*'s arrival at Upernavik the year before. The northernmost outpost on the western coast of Greenland, huddled on a bony slope overlooking a small bay, seemed like the loneliest place a man could die. A group of Esquimaux and a pack of dogs milled on the shore. He made out a small graveyard high on the hill through his telescope. Standing over the bones of unfortunate whalers and stubborn Danish colonists was a row of crosses silhouetted against the ashen sky. But even in that wilderness, the dead were gathered together, properly buried and remembered, their presence noted with headstones. They were torn apart and eaten here on King William Land, the pieces scattered across a desolate land, lost and forgotten.

In the morning, after a night of walking, he and Adams sat the two invalids on the gravel and searched for game while Billings pitched the tent. Honey and Handford leaned against each other, back-to-back like stone carvings, their mouths agape, their hands in their laps. Robinson looked at the two men sitting silently on the ground. If the three of them walked away and left them, would the two stricken men move? Would they even make a sound?

Robinson left the others in the tent and retraced their steps for two miles, his shotgun ready. He stood listening. The pungent, muddy odour of the thawing earth hung in the air.

A noise reached him from far off in the haze, and he knelt, waiting.

Snow fell in thick flakes but vanished as it hit the ground. The stony earth steamed. The distant noise came again, distorted by wind and mist and cold. He knew it was the pack moving, but it resembled something else each time. One moment it was like an axe on a tree stump, the next the crump of a firework. He went back to the tent and woke Adams.

"Get them up."

———

The sun tired a little more each evening on the northern horizon at midnight.

Billings leaned forward in the sledge harness, knees bent like pistons, his back parallel to the earth. He stumbled on broken rocks, ripping holes in his trousers.

Adams worried for him. As he sensed impatience and frustration building in Robinson, he saw the opposite in Billings: a gradual capitulation, like an untended flame slowing dying out. At the crest of each rise, Robinson turned back and swept the horizon with the telescope. Adams knew they would need to find game soon. Within a few days, they would have nothing left. He gave Billings a full ration of reindeer meat and fed Honey and Handford more than he kept for himself, but Franklin's two crewmen grew ever weaker.

Several times a day, the two men fell. He and Robinson lifted them to their feet and walked with their arms around their shoulders. The pair moved, bent over like rusted dolls. Their hair and beards were long and wild, their faces taut and dark with grime. When Adams examined them in the evening, they stared straight ahead, as patient as horses. Their mouths were black, their pelvic bones protruding like china plates under the skin. Kneecaps like stones atop brittle branches.

Adams inspected Handford's feet. Only two toes remained on each foot, but the amputations he had conducted had not led to any infection.

"You said you will go back to Sunderland, Mister Handford?"

"What?" Handford blinked as if waking from a dream. "What?"

"Sunderland. Who do you go back to there?"

Handford swallowed. "There's no one now. My mam died of the typhus in '31."

"You said you wanted to go back to the shipyards."

Handford nodded. "I liked the smell there."

"Which smell is that?"

Handford was silent for a moment, appearing to recall a life he had not thought of for a long time. "I was a rigger on the Wear." He smiled. "Hot tar. Fresh-cut timber. New rope. Wet paint. Even the fresh water in the new barrels smells fine, before it goes green and slimy." His face took on a dreamy expression. "It all smelled like . . . I dunno, somethin' being born, y'know? Somethin' not spoiled yet. Out here, everything just goes to shit. Timber rots, food goes bad, metal rusts, caulking falls out. Men go mad. They stink, and bits fall off. Then they die." He paused, imagining it. "If I can get a whiff o' that nice new smell, I reckon I'll fare well enough."

———

The scurvy was advancing. Adams' feet were like lumps of wood, swollen and numb to the touch. He felt nothing when he ran the tip of his knife over his heel. When he changed into his dry bed socks and lay down to sleep, shooting pains lit up the veins in his legs.

Only when Adams saw Robinson's mitten red with blood did the lieutenant notice that an old injury to his elbow had opened. Billings' neck was speckled with bruises, as though he had been throttled. Red and blue spots had appeared on the big man's legs, and his gums were the colour of rotting plums.

They found a small beluga, recently dead, rolling in the shallows. While Adams and Billings watched for prowling bears, Robinson hacked through the reeking blubber and brought out a few pounds of evil-smelling meat. Honey and Handford thrust handfuls into their mouths. Within minutes they both vomited it back up and lay gasping and moaning on the ground.

They watched the sun sink through the long evening until it skimmed the northern skyline at midnight, then lifted itself into the cold sky again. Shallow lakes glimmered in the east. Their layers of wool and linen were as thin as cotton when the wind howled out of the north. Clouds bunched and elongated, great celestial caterpillars changing colour above their heads.

They traversed the grey land like wounded survivors of a war. They walked with a dull, mechanical tread, clothes stiffened by frost and dried mud, throats sore, cheeks wind-blasted, bellies hollow. As the snow melted, the surface of the earth dissolved into freezing slush. The sledge runners sank into green clay.

Bodies of water frozen for months split open underfoot. Snow upon the surface of lakes was in places only an inch thick, hardening to a thin crust in the cold twilight. A row of thick white clouds along the horizon was like surf upon a beach. Distant cracking sounds, like shotguns discharging, carried to them from the ice pack far to the west as the floes fractured on the tide. Large patches of olive moss and orange lichen were like splashes of paint on the brown stones.

When the mosquitoes arrived, Adams thought it would finish them. The insects fell upon them in black clouds, burrowing into their ears, stabbing at their faces, reducing them to tears. The brush of a glove or the shake of a head did nothing to deter them. Weeping at the absence of vegetation, Adams yearned for a campfire piled with green branches, desperate for the choking smoke just to be free of the insects for a few moments. Nearby, the other four men performed an absurd dance, stamping their feet and waving their gloved hands at the winged monsters. They rolled themselves in their blankets until they could not breathe. The mosquitoes lanced through the strips of linen they wrapped around their faces.

Anguish settled on Adams like mortar hardening. He wanted to bellow his rage at Franklin, scream into the emptiness, anything to raise him from his grave. *O Lord,* he thought, *forgive me. Pray do not turn away from us.*

—

Adams imagined himself aboard *Erebus* in the winter before Crozier brought them ashore on King William Land. The shooting parties returned in the long twilight with nothing. Before long, the sun was gone, and it was too dark and cold to venture out to hunt. The surviving officers rationed slimy three-year-old salt pork and canned provisions that were putrid when opened. The men consumed it all without comment, their sore jaws crunching on the weevils in the biscuit. They swept the decks and wiped the condensation from the walls of the lower deck. Huddling in their blankets, they wished for the rum and coal that ran out two years earlier. In the crushing melancholy of the long, black, freezing night, a dozen pairs of eyes watched the last tallow candles wink out. Adams finally knew grief then, with the tiny flame mourned more than any dead shipmates they had tipped through the hole in the ice or buried in the hard ground. He treated bruises that blackened and spread across thin bodies and wasted limbs. He watched men falling dead and going mad and starving to death in their hammocks, and when the drift was deep around the gunwales of the ship, he went on deck in his heavy coat and Welsh wig, where a man could scream forever and never be heard.

When he woke, he thought only of food. Rotten salt junk. Weevil-infested biscuit. Any kind of meat.

CHAPTER EIGHTEEN

The knife shook in Adams' hands as he crouched and scraped lichen from the rocks. When he had a small pile, he scooped water from a meltwater pool and concocted a thin soup with fragments of dried reindeer meat. His heartbeat quickened at the exertion. Pain pulsed in his bowels. He sat back on his heels. Something moved on the eastern horizon.

"What is that?" Adams pointed. "There is something there. Jimmy, can you see it?"

Billings stared but said nothing. Adams held his gloved hands around his face, willing his eyes to focus. A small group of black dots moved slowly northward.

"Is it men?"

Robinson unstrapped his telescope and held it to his eye. "Reindeer," he said. "Three of them."

He jerked his chin at Billings. "You stay with the sledge. Look after these two."

Slack-jawed, Honey and Handford sat in silence on the ground. Billings grasped Adams' arm, misery in his face. "Mister Adams, let me come."

Robinson barked at him. "You will stay!" He swung his shotgun from across his back and checked his ammunition bag. To Adams, he said, "We shall have to chase them." He pointed to the north. "You get around in front of them. I will approach from their eastern flank. We will trap them on the shore."

Billings tugged harder on Adams' sleeve, his eyes glistening. "Please, sir, don't leave me alone with them two."

Adams wiped his gun barrel and spoke in a soothing tone. "Jimmy, the deer will see you from miles off, and we shall never get a shot at them. You must stay. Don't worry, they will not hurt you. I will be back soon."

Billings hung his head, beaten. Adams left him gnawing on his knuckle. Robinson walked off across the stones. Adams hefted his shot bag and set off to the north.

They shadowed the deer most of the evening, shepherding them west toward the shore. A pattern of grey clouds stretched across the blue sky was like a fleece flung high into the heavens. A strong breeze blew out of the north, numbing Adams' cheekbones. He stumbled over the stones, often losing sight of Robinson. When the distance between himself and the deer began to close, he saw the lieutenant far out on the plain to the northeast.

Adams looked around for cover. He dropped into a shallow depression in the earth and lay on his stomach, peering over the lip of the hole. Propped on his elbows, he looked along the trembling shotgun barrel. The soil smelled of decay. He eased off his right mitten with his teeth and blew on his fingers. The clouds thickened and darkened, spreading across the sky like ink spilling across a canvas.

Lying prone, he had lost all sense of distance. Were the reindeer in range of his gun? He removed his snow goggles for a clearer view. Immediately his eyes teared in the wind. His entire body shook. Hunger was a fist under his ribs. It began to rain. Countless tiny projectiles slammed into his back and struck the earth around him.

He heard a shout. Robinson had begun his charge. How far away was he—half a mile? The lieutenant shuffled across the stony earth on scurvy-stiffened legs, yelling and waving his arms. The three reindeer tossed their heads and wheeled away from Robinson. The distance between them and Adams began to close.

He squinted through the rain, taking aim at the three brown shadows. He exhaled slowly and squeezed the trigger. The barrel of the shotgun bucked. He listened for the soft slap of the ball striking flesh but heard nothing. All three reindeer peeled off and galloped away across the empty expanse. Still stretched out on the ground, Adams lowered his head and let his tears run down on the stock of his shotgun.

Robinson approached, his face dark. He kicked at the stones and spat on the ground.

"You had three to aim at," he said between clenched teeth. "We only needed one."

Stretched on the ground, Adams was possessed of the notion that Franklin and his men had pushed the spirits of this land too far. Parry, Ross, Back—they had all lost men. Perhaps the spirits were issuing a warning that was ignored. *Persist no more with this folly,* they were saying. Then with Franklin, their patience ran out, and they said, *You have not heeded us. Very well. This time we shall have the lot of you.*

"Something's dead there." Billings stopped and pointed. His voice was soft and toneless.

A body lay on a thin bed of snow. Robinson took it for a pile of blankets or buffalo robes as they approached. The breeze flicked at the tips of the shaggy brown hair covering the carcass of a partially eaten reindeer. Nubs of bone protruded through dark-crimson patches of meat rent by deep striations. At one end of the carcass was a helmet of bone, antlers thrusting like talons raking the air. Robinson examined the remains, lifting flaps of skin with the tip of his shotgun barrel.

"There is some meat left here," said Robinson.

"We shall have some marrow for our soup tonight," said Adams.

Robinson scanned the area. "The bear that killed this beast may return. God knows how far they can smell blood."

Honey stared at something to the east. Three wolves paced back and forth on the stony ground a mile off, eyes fixed on the men. To Robinson they seemed like spies, not bold enough to mount an assault but slinking harbingers of some larger and darker menace.

Adams had Billings retrieve the cookpot from the sledge. Together they lifted it as high as they could and slammed it down on the spine of the deer carcass. The bone snapped, and with his knife, Adams scraped out fragments of red marrow from the broken sockets. Honey and Handford sat on the ground, watching him drop tiny shreds of marrow and flesh into the pot.

Robinson held his shotgun across his chest. He walked out toward the wolves as they watched with yellow eyes, their heads low. He approached them until he was almost within range, then held the shotgun up and fired a single shot into the air. The wolves peeled off and loped away over a low rise. Robinson stood watching the empty skyline for a long time.

From somewhere far away came a faint sound. Robinson cocked his head and closed his eyes, waiting. The sun settled into a bank of grey clouds stretched across the horizon. The wolves did not return. He walked back to the tent, twisting his fingers in his beard. He sent Billings to stand watch and sat with Adams on the floorcloth next to the two sleeping invalids. A wind rose. The tent wall shook.

"I have lost much flesh," Robinson said.

He gripped his left forearm with his right hand, then ran both hands down his thighs to his knees. Would there be enough of him to finish this? He looked at the two sleeping men. For some time now, he had wondered how a man like him became a man like them. It no longer seemed such a mystery.

"I think a man's resolve crumbles in stages," he said. "Like a castle in the sand washed away by the incoming tide. Once swept away, it loses all cohesion and cannot be reconstituted." His head ached. He closed his eyes and pinched the bridge of his nose between his thumb and forefinger.

"I used to be comforted that Franklin had so many men with him," Adams whispered. He sat staring at his hands. "I thought if one must be lost in the wilderness, it would be better at least to have companions than to be alone. I thought it would not be so frightening." Adams' gaunt, white face was stark against the shadowy canvas in the tent's gloom, like a marble bust on a shelf.

"Be sure not to leave the muzzle of your shotgun on the ground," Robinson said. "Water in the barrel will result in a wet charge."

Outside the tent, the sound of the wind was like countless voices gasping.

———

Adams sifted through the items discarded on the shore at Victory Point. Honey and Handford sat on the sledge. The gravel plain to the east was tinged with the first tendrils of summer green. A pair of sandpipers flitted over the stones, then rose in the air and vanished into the sky. The salty smell of the ocean was light on the air. Robinson kicked a cooking stove with his boot.

"What is this, sir?" Billings stared at an object on the ground that appeared to be a large square knapsack.

Robinson stood over the object, staring down. "I think it is a Halkett boat," he said.

"A boat?" asked Billings.

"An airboat." Robinson knelt to examine it. "It inflates like a balloon, then floats. There is a bellows here, and oars. You row it like a raft. It might help us to cross the ice from King William Land to Boothia. Three weeks ago the ice was still intact, but it may not be so now. There could be open water between Cape Felix and Boothia. Even if the floes have not broken up, the meltwater pools could be waist deep."

Billings took their wet socks and laid them out on a large flat stone to dry, then sat on the ground to darn the holes in his trousers. Inside the tent, the two Franklin survivors sat like a pair of ascetics over a thin soup made with fragments of meat from the deer carcass. They stared into their bowls but could not seem to lift their spoons.

Robinson saw Adams watching them. "Very soon you shall have to decide," he said.

"Are we being pursued?"

Robinson's expression was pensive. "I hear sounds in the mist."

"Wolves?"

"Not wolves. They might be gunshots. Or just the ice. But we must hurry just the same. We are making barely eight miles a day. At this rate we will not get back to Port Leopold before Captain Ross sails."

Adams nodded at Honey and Handford. "They cannot go faster," he said. "Not without meat and rest. They are too weak."

"Neither will see Port Leopold," Robinson said. "Pretending otherwise dooms all three of us."

Adams dropped his voice to a whisper. "We will drag them," he said. "On the sledge."

Robinson frowned. "Splendid. Except not even Billings has the strength to haul them. Do we then leave them, or stay and die with them, like Fitzjames?"

Adams hissed through clenched teeth, "You would shoot them both like horses?"

Robinson shrugged. "You are a man of faith. When a patient is badly stricken, do you pray for him?"

"Of course."

"And if there is no hope?"

"I pray for the Lord to take him quickly and without pain."

Robinson nodded. "Then pray now. For if He does not take them soon, He will take us all."

The same hint of menace in Robinson's tone was there again. It was stronger now, portentous, like a tremor deep in the earth. Days earlier he had dared Robinson to shoot him when he refused to leave the invalids. He had seen the instant of vacillation then in the lieutenant's eyes. Could he bluff him a second time? The man would accept no counsel, tolerate no dissent. Leave them and live. Take them and die. Robinson had made his decision, but for Adams it was a dilemma with no solution, a boulder he pushed against but could not move. He explored Robinson's face, then shook a finger at him.

"There will be questions to answer. If not from the Admiralty, then from Fleet Street."

"I shall inform Their Lordships and the editor of the *Times* that we have seen the North-West Passage. I shall assure them it is glorious and strongly recommend they come and see it for themselves."

Adams frowned. "But they would never do such a thing."

Robinson nodded wearily. "Precisely." His was the expression of a man winning an argument. "Finally you understand."

Adams and Robinson set out again in the evening in a light fog. Billings dragged the sledge. The gaunt figures of Honey and Handford stumbled alongside. The sky brightened as though a lamp was suddenly hung overhead. Golden bars of sunlight reached through the grey clouds, steaming away the mist.

The first ball took Handford behind the right shoulder. He spun around, jerking like a fish on a line. The sound of the gunshot followed an instant later. A second ball struck him in the chest, twirling him in a grotesque jig. He pitched to the earth, crumpling in his overcoat in a heap so small, Adams could hardly believe there was a man within. The assailants had approached under cover of the mist, forced into their attack by the emergence of the sun. They walked three abreast like infantry with weapons levelled, their shadows rippling darkly on the ground.

"Spread out!" Robinson ducked his head and ran, bent at the waist.

Adams ran in the opposite direction. Honey dropped to the ground beside the sledge. Frozen, Billings stared down at Handford's body, mouth agape. The three attackers stood together in the open. They did not seek cover, for there was none. The man who had killed John Handford was reloading with twitching hands. The second man swung the barrel of his gun toward Adams as he ran across the open ground. The man's body jerked with the recoil. A ball whined past Adams' head. The man fired again, but Adams saw he had rushed the shot. The ball pinged off the stones behind him.

Adams stopped and raised his shotgun. His first ball struck the man in the chest. He went down, the back of his head bouncing on the gravel. Adams looked across and saw Billings still standing by the sledge. Honey lay face down, his hands over his head.

"Jimmy! Get down!"

Billings turned his gaze on Adams. A beam of sunlight fell across him. His eyes were yellow lamps in his head. The third man had his shotgun levelled. Robinson had dropped to one knee, his weapon at his shoulder. Both fired simultaneously, the two gunshots resounding as one colossal blast. Neither man fell, but Billings folded and dropped, nerveless, as if beaten on the back of the knees with a baton. He crashed face-first to the earth, limbs splayed. Adams swung the barrel of his gun around and shot Robinson's attacker. The man's head snapped back in a bloody spray. His body arched and struck the earth.

The distant sun boiled in the cold air. As rays of light streamed across the stones, Adams wondered if the assailants' errant shots had somehow pierced the clouds. The remaining attacker abandoned his attempt to reload and flung his weapon to the earth. He stood unmoving, hands by his sides. Only now did Adams see an unarmed fourth man stumbling in from the east. The melting snow created a patchwork of shallow lakes and rivulets on the flat terrain. Ripples rose on the surface of the water. The stink of gunpowder hung in the air, too heavy for the wind to disperse.

Robinson approached the two survivors with his gun raised. Adams went to Billings, heavy-footed. His face was hot, the rest of his body freezing. The wind ruffled Billings' hair, and for the briefest moment, Adams thought he might be moving. But then he saw the wound in his throat and the blood on the ground. He knelt, dizzy and dry-mouthed.

The man who had thrown down his gun watched Robinson and Adams approach, his expression doleful. He hung his head, his great brown beard on his chest, and sighed.

"Well, that didn't work out so well." He looked at Robinson's shotgun. "Go on, then. Get on with it."

"Which one are you?" Robinson asked. "Are you Gregory?"

"I am James Walker, able seaman." He gave a casual salute, then pointed at the unarmed man who had walked in from the plain and now stood behind him with terror in his eyes. "That there's Francis Dunn." He gestured at the body of the man Adams had shot through the heart, who now lay on his back with his arms flung wide. "That's Gregory there." Walker looked at the body of the second man. "And that's Billy Orren." He winced. "Oh, Jesus, you made a right mess of his face."

Adams' heavy ball had taken much of Orren's tongue and jaw. Shards of bone flashed white in the sunlight. Blood pooled around his head. He was still moving, his eyes rolled back to yellow moons, eyelids flickering. Fingers curling and grasping at nothing. His head fell to the side. A great gob of blood fountained onto the gravel, and he died. Walker looked past Adams and Robinson at the two bodies lying behind them. He sighed.

"Ah, bugger. I got Johnny Handford. Didn't mean to do that. My eyes ain't much good no more. I went for the one in the middle. Thought he was one of you."

"Gregory had you do this?" asked Robinson.

"We was gonna come when you slept. Then the fog lifted, and we got caught out."

"You could not refuse him?"

Walker sneered. "You know what makes one man follow another?"

Robinson kept his gun trained on the man's chest. "Explain it to me."

Walker regarded him with indifference. "You know what to tell a man who's starvin'? When he's just a death's head upon a mopstick?"

Robinson said nothing.

"When he's so hungry, he'll boil down his shoes and his belt and his wolfskin and the bones of a lemming that's dead for a week? When he'll pull a knife on another man over a bit of meat the size of your fingernail?"

"There is no excuse for—"

"Have you ever seen a man so hungry, he will shoot his messmate dead and eat him? Have you seen that?"

Robinson met the man's gaze. "I have not seen that."

Walker looked tired. "Well, then, you're hardly likely to understand."

"What happened to you?"

Walker shrugged. "A war."

"A war?"

Walker gestured at the man standing behind him and spread his arms wide. "Behold the victors."

"No. The losers." Robinson took a step toward him and raised his shotgun at Walker's head.

The man stared back at him, satisfaction in his eyes.

Adams put a hand on Robinson's arm. "No," he whispered.

Robinson stiffened, disbelief in his voice. "Good God, man, he has just killed your best lad!"

Adams had no appetite for an argument. "I am tired. Are you not tired? I know only melancholy."

Robinson did not look at him. He held the shotgun high, staring down the barrel at Walker. Adams saw his finger twitch on the trigger.

"Three dead men," said Adams. "What good will two more be?"

Robinson bristled. "They will hang, in any case. There will be quite the crowd at Newgate."

"Show them mercy," said Adams.

"How am I not merciful?" Robinson turned to face Adams now, his expression incredulous. His chest rose and fell in great heaves. "It is precisely why I would shoot them both now. As the senior officer, I have the authority. I will have you acknowledge that."

"Consider what they have endured—"

"Step back, sir. We can hardly take them back. We have no shackles. They shall be on us as soon as we turn our backs." Robinson's eyes were wild and shining. Adams saw his expression and, for the first time, feared him. He could not fight this. Something had fractured in the man, and the air between them was changed forever.

"For God's sake, hurry and be done with it," said Walker, his tone bored.

High against Robinson's shoulder, the shotgun no longer trembled in his grip.

Adams looked past him at the vast landscape. A meltwater pool glittered with an encrusted film of ice, and he thought it more exquisite than any jewel. He fought off a wave of nausea and lost all sense of time passing, of distance traversed, of the number of men dead.

Robinson lowered the shotgun. "My powder and ball is precious," he said. "I shall not waste it." His gaze was locked on Walker's face, but his words were directed at Adams. "You should know it is more than they would have done for us."

"I do not thank you," said Walker, taunting him. "You do us no favours."

"Go back the way you came," Robinson said. "Try for Repulse Bay. Or the Red River Colony. Maybe west to the Columbia District. Tell them your story there."

Walker scoffed. "Jesus, man, d'ye think we'd speak of this? We'll hang if we do. Once you've done what we've done, there is nowhere you can go. We might as well have tattoos on our faces."

"You will not walk with us and slit our throats in the night."

"You send us to our deaths."

"You would just as soon send us to ours."

Walker stared back at him. He appeared to be readying another plea. His gaze went to Billings' body. A quizzical expression creased his features. "Y'know, I didn't see Billy Orren aiming for that big fella. We could see he wasn't armed. I reckon that was an accident." Then he shrugged and spat, resigned to the futility of apologies. "Give us a gun and a shot bag, at least. You can't deny us something to hunt with."

"I'll deny you whatever I damn well please," said Robinson, but appeared to mull over the man's request. He looked at the second survivor, Dunn, and pointed at Gregory's body. "You. Take his ammunition bag and walk over that way, two hundred paces." To Walker: "You wait over there, apart from him. Stay that distance from each other and walk until I cannot see you."

"So it's to be lemmings and hares for us, then?"

"Look for the reindeer."

"Reindeer." Walker chuckled and shook his head ruefully. "More likely to find a bloody unicorn. Captain Crozier told us there were herds of reindeer and musk oxen at Back's River, but we knew they wouldn't migrate this far north, not in the winter. We lost two men who went shooting in the snow and never came back."

Robinson said nothing more. He still held his shotgun across his chest. Walker studied him, then sighed.

"So be it. But I must say a last farewell to Mister Gregory. We were together four years. If you don't like it, shoot me if you can spare the ball."

He strode toward Robinson and stood before him, touching an index finger to the point between his eyes. "Only make sure you do it right here—there's a good fella."

Robinson did not move.

Walker waited.

Adams held his breath.

Walker gave a derisive grunt. He turned away and went to Gregory's body, then pulled out a knife. "You may not wish to watch this, but we need provisions for our journey, and there is nothin' else. Understand it, or do not."

Walker knelt next to Gregory's corpse and began cutting. He called to Dunn.

"Frankie, bring me a canvas bag, will you, mate?" He grunted with the effort as he sawed and stabbed. "I need something to carry this in."

CHAPTER NINETEEN

Robinson helped Adams use the sledge to fetch four large stones to place on Billings' and Handford's graves. Together they sang a hymn for the two men. Adams remained by the graves with his Bible. Clouds streaked a mustard sky.

Robinson took the first watch when Adams returned to the tent to sit with Honey. He sat facing south with his shotgun across his knees. Walker and Dunn did not reappear on the horizon. Had he erred in releasing them? Things would go easier for him with Adams' cooperation, but it was important the man not underestimate his determination.

An accident. Walker was a brazen bastard, saying Billings' death was an accident. He rehearsed the story he would tell. The Admiralty should know as little as possible. He and Adams had met a dying crewman who revealed the location of the ships, and thus he, Lieutenant Frederick Robinson, had determined the location of the Passage. Franklin dead a year before they left the Thames, Fitzjames starving to death, Crozier disappearing to the south, bones on the beach, half-eaten corpses, gun battles with murderous seamen—none of that need be known. It would be enough for the Admiralty to reward the officer who had risked his life to bring back the truth. He was unsure he could remember which parts to omit, so he would need to leave it all out. He sighed. *Ambition writhes like an eel in a bucket,* he thought. *It will not be grasped, then turns and bites your hand, just when you think you have it.*

He went to the cairn. In his hand was the message they had found two weeks earlier, telling of Franklin's death and the departure of the survivors for Back's Fish River. He tapped the metal cylinder on his palm, then reached up and began removing stones from the top of the cairn. When he had opened a hole in the pile, he slid the message cylinder into the centre of the cairn and began replacing the stones.

Adams' voice cracked from behind him. "What in God's name are you doing?"

"My duty."

"You must report your findings to the Admiralty."

"And I shall, but the Admiralty will need the story to be cleaner. There are too many parts they will not want to hear." Robinson turned to face him. "The newspapers enjoy tales of suffering and hardship, but only if Englishmen triumph. Both ships are lost. Franklin and his officers are dead. The survivors were eating the flesh of their shipmates and would have done the same to us. Who will reward us for delivering such news?"

The indignation faded from Adams' face. His voice was that of a small child. "But . . . we must tell them what happened."

"Must we? I also used to think so." Robinson shook his head. "Think of what they will do to us. They will call us liars, tear us down. They will deny it could be true. Will you be the one who tells Lady Jane her husband blundered into the pack and died twitching in his bunk? Do you think she will clasp your hand, weep with joy, and say, 'Thank you, good sir, for the truth. I am so glad to know it, for now I shall rest easy'?"

Adams looked at the cairn. "Somebody else will find the cylinder. They will ask why we did not report seeing it."

"Perhaps. But I shall be a captain by then." Robinson shrugged. "We shall say we did not get this far. That we got only as far south as Cape Felix before our supplies ran out. Or that we did not see the cairn in the fog."

"You are a coward." Adams' words were like mortars thudding into the earth between them.

Robinson coughed wetly. "Yes, quite possibly." He shrugged. "But you know, I used to think myself as courageous as the next man. I will say this: the prospect of reporting the truth of Franklin's fate frightens me. It should frighten you. We are complicit now in a great crime."

The wind dropped, and the air was cold and still.

"We have done nothing wrong," said Adams.

"No. It has touched us, like some ghastly miasma. We must shield ourselves if we are to resist it."

Light drained from the sky but did not entirely leave it. Clumps of poppies dotted the slopes above the tent, their yellow heads dipping and bowing in the light rain. A pair of hares, their white winter fur replaced now by the dark grey of summer, darted away between the rocks. Adams picked up his shotgun and followed them.

Robinson watched him go. He thought of Elizabeth in her sickbed, coughing blood into her pristine white handkerchief. He imagined her sitting in her wicker chair on the veranda when the weather was warm, watching the shadows in the garden change shape. Waiting for him. Waiting for the end. He thought the worst kind of death was that which affords one altogether too much time to contemplate it. He thought Fitzjames was wrong when he said it was best to die slowly. *Give me the ball in the heart.*

Adams returned with a hare on his belt. He tore the skin from the carcass and threw the innards on the ground. They ate the dark-red flesh raw. The sound of meltwater streams trickling down through the boulders above them was like music.

Robinson was quiet for a time. "We can tell them the Esquimaux did it. They attacked and raided Franklin's ships."

"No." Adams shook his head slowly and gazed at a moon collared in mist. "It does not sit well with me. It would be a monstrous lie."

Robinson nodded. "Utterly monstrous. But I remember you telling stories to the men aboard *Investigator*. You had a flair for it. Were it not for you, I would not know Frobisher went looking for the Passage in a vessel barely fifty feet long. Or that he took an Esquimaux arrow in the arse."

"Those stories were true," Adams said.

Robinson sat up, his teeth red and shining with the hare's blood. "True, you say? How do you know? We only know Henry Hudson was set adrift in a boat because those who did it said so. Who is to say the mutineers did not cut his throat and eat him?" Clouds masked the sun. The ocean to the west was the colour of charcoal. "Perhaps," he continued, "you and I are victims of an elaborate conspiracy. Those other fellows—Frobisher, Davis—I think they were ashamed to go back and say they had found nothing but ice, so they invented tales about this place. They knew their sponsors would not sail to the Arctic and see for themselves, and they knew their wealthy patrons would keep shelling out for a good story. Why return and admit the whole venture was folly?"

Adams traced shapes in the dirt with his knife.

Robinson was sombre. "I thought I knew what needed saying," he said, "but now I am unsure. People were amused when Franklin ate his boots. They will not be so amused to hear what his men ate this time. Our story will require a little judicious censorship." He patted Adams' knee. "Do not look so melancholy. How often do you get to stitch your own history? Parry did it. James Ross did it. Even George Back did it, and he got a river named after him. Look on the map—is there a peninsula or mountain that takes your fancy? I have one marked out for myself. Stake your claim. The boldest lies always receive the least scrutiny."

———

Adams scanned the skies as he walked, his shotgun at the ready. No birds appeared. He trod carefully, like a dancer; if he missed a step, he would stumble on a stone or plunge into a puddle. An injury here to an ankle or knee could be as fatal as a knife to the heart. Nothing remained of the meat they had carved from the deer carcass. The bones had been boiled and pounded and consumed. They walked over mile after flat mile of shattered stones and gravel and wiry olive grass, but saw no game. Lightning flashed like artillery fire on the horizon. At midnight, the sun was a sullen orange. When they stopped in the morning, Adams counted out the rations. Three pairs of eyes remained fixed on his hands as he divided the last few broken pieces of stale biscuit.

They huddled in the gloom of the tent, kneading their frozen limbs. Adams lay down in his blanket, the stones beneath him sharp in his back. He felt as if the flesh beneath his skin had melted away, leaving only his bare skeleton stretched out on the rocky earth. Once stout and rigid within him, his bones felt like the ancient whale bones they often found on the shingle; one stout blow and they might crumble to powder. In the darkness of the tent gloom, Robinson lay asleep.

"Boiled pork and pease pudding," said Honey.

Adams whispered so as not to wake the lieutenant. "Something else, please," he said. "I have had my fill of pork."

"A joint of beef, then," Honey said.

Adams grunted. "Not with these unsteady teeth. I want a Manchester pudding. Our housekeeper would put brandy in it."

"Pigeon pie."

"Yes, very good. And kedgeree. And roast pheasant." Adams groaned at the thought. He closed his eyes and thought of large fat birds hanging for a week in the autumn.

"We caught foxes that first winter on Beechey Island," said Honey. He coughed, the phlegm bubbling thick in his throat. "They're good roasted. Better than salt pork."

"Much better."

"When it got too cold to hunt, we'd trap 'em. Got an empty cask, put a flap on the top made from an old iron grate. Then we'd put a bit of old pork in there and leave it on the ice." Honey's expression was distant, his voice hushed. "You have to be careful gettin' 'em out. Vicious little buggers, give you a nasty bite. Once we got one, saw blood all over the inside of the barrel. I remember it was all wet and shiny." He paused, remembering.

Adams frowned. "Had it bitten you?"

Honey shook his head slowly. When he spoke again, his voice was a croak. "I saw something stuck to the iron grate. Like a bit of meat. It was his tongue."

"His tongue?"

A tear gleamed on Honey's cheek.

"He'd licked the iron grate, see? To see if it was food. It was so cold, his tongue stuck to the metal. He must've pulled and pulled and torn it out from the roots." He sobbed in thick, gusty breaths, his mouth twisted and his cheeks wet. He squeezed his eyes shut. "Poor little bugger."

———

Elizabeth's white nightdress billowed in the breeze as she walked alongside Robinson. Her face was ruddy in the cold air, her breath sweet. A hint of her jasmine scent carried across the air between them.

"Billings is dead because of me," he said. "He wanted his mother and a pie. He was a good man, but I did not tell him that."

"It was not your fault," said Elizabeth.

"It is difficult for me to speak plainly with the men."

"Nobody needs know of it. You shall be a captain."

"Mister Adams knows," he said.

"It was Mister Adams who insisted he travel with you. Do not blame yourself."

"Elizabeth, he had a man's body and a child's mind. He would have done anything Adams asked of him." His voice dropped to a whisper. "I would like someone to look to me like that."

"I do. Come home to me, and we shall have a child. A son. He shall look to you as I do."

He allowed himself a moment to think of it, to imagine the boy. His eyes dark like hers. His hair shining like hers, his hand clasped in hers. He saw nothing of himself in the lad and was glad of it, for he would wish better for the boy.

"You were right not to let Humphreys have the rum," she said.

"He did not think so. Nor did Adams. I would protect them, but they do not understand."

"Fitzjames and Aylmore would not have lived. You knew it."

"Adams thinks me wicked for wanting to leave them. But I would save both his life and mine, even if I could not save theirs. And he thinks I wished Walker and Dunn dead."

"You would not shoot a man for being hungry."

He sighed. "I could not let four men die if two could be saved. There was not enough food for all."

"But to take a man's life for it? You would not have done that."

"Would I not?" He shook his head, uncertain. He took out his pipe and put the stem in his mouth. His tobacco was used up long ago, but the flavour was a pleasant memory. "I do not know."

She brushed her dark hair from her eyes and smiled at him, like she had when they stood beneath the elm at the bottom of her father's garden, waiting for the rain to stop. As on that day, her hair was beaded with mist.

"Mister Adams does not see things as clearly as you. He does not understand. You cannot trust him to tell Their Lordships all that you have learned. It may . . . colour their opinions."

And then she convulsed, coughing. Her churchyard cough. A sound too deep and hollow for such a thin, frail frame, like that of a trapped creature thrashing in an empty barrel. Specks of blood appeared on the front of her nightdress. She fell behind. Soon he heard only the sound of his boots on the ice.

"A man is dead because of me," he said.

He turned to see if she followed him, but she was not there.

——

Adams stepped out of the tent, shivering in a wet breeze. The mercury read thirty-five degrees. Grey clouds were strung out in a jagged line overhead. The smell of wet soil rose as if the earth were rotting beneath his feet. Far out to sea, ice hummocks rose under the pressure of floes pushed down from the north. He helped Robinson pack the tent. They pulled Honey to his feet and began walking. The last of the spring snow was melting. The white slush on the surface of the frozen earth drew back to reveal jagged rocks poking through like broken bones, ripping and slashing at their stumbling boots. It was three weeks after the summer solstice. Each day the sun sank lower, its reflection turning pools of water into puddles of blood. After midnight, their shadows stretched far across the ground. A line of ducks flew north, far out of range of their guns.

Honey's knees folded beneath him, and he fell without a sound. Adams went to him and lifted the man to his feet, but before he could take another step, Honey toppled again. Adams propped him into a sitting position on the ground. He sat, sagging and limp, his eyes dull.

Adams and Robinson placed Honey on the sledge and secured him with ropes. They hitched the sledge ropes over their shoulders and made three miles. The earth sloped almost imperceptibly upward, and though Honey weighed barely one hundred pounds, they sank to their knees, exhausted. Robinson threw down the sledge rope. He and Adams lifted Honey from the sledge and placed him on the ground, then erected the tent. Wrapped in his blanket bag, Honey turned his head to one side and spat a tooth and a bloody pool of spittle onto the floorcloth. His gums were black and oozing. He lay with his eyes closed. Adams helped him drink from his canteen and rolled the man in his blanket, where he lay shaking.

"Dreams . . ." Honey's voice was a croak. "Me dreams are . . . round the wrong way."

"What do you mean?" Adams asked.

Honey lay with his eyes closed. He was quiet for a time, gathering the strength to speak. "When you have a nightmare, you wake up and the bad dream is gone, right? It were just a dream, it weren't real. Right?"

"Yes. Not real."

"But when I dream, I see me old life—me wife, me little ones, all the good stuff I miss. Then I open me eyes and it's . . . all this shite. Cold. Pain. Hunger. All the bad stuff that should be in the nightmare is what's real now. Me good life is only in me dreams. It's supposed to be t'other way round. You know what I mean?"

"I know what you mean."

Honey grunted. "I reckon that's what drives men bonkers." He lay in silence for a time. Then he spoke in a whisper. "Did you see young Billings fall?"

"I saw him."

"Walker said Billy Orren shot him by mistake."

"Yes."

"It ain't what I saw," said Honey.

Adams leaned over him. "What did you see?"

Honey's eyes remained closed. He frowned, straining to speak. "Orren was a better shot than most." He opened his eyes and regarded Adams through slitted lids. "If he was aiming at Lieutenant Robinson, he wouldn't have hit the Billings boy."

———

Adams and Robinson surveyed the ice pack. Three dark cylinders lay on the ice, two hundred yards from the beach. One lifted its head and rolled over, lazily lifting a flipper. Adams checked his shotgun. Leaving Robinson with the sleeping invalid, he walked in a crouch out over the shore ice.

He sank to his hands and knees one hundred yards from the sleeping seals. He pinned the stock of the shotgun in his armpit and held the barrel up with one hand to keep it out of the shallow puddles that dotted the surface of the ice. Inching forward, he raised his head occasionally to check the position of the seals. Icy water soaked the heavy wool of his trousers and penetrated his linen drawers, leaving his knees raw and freezing. His hands were wet and cold in his gloves. He crawled on, clenching his jaws to keep his teeth from chattering. When he had approached to within thirty yards of the seals, one raised its head. Adams hauled himself to his knees and levelled his shotgun. As he aimed, all three seals flicked their tails and vanished into unseen holes in the ice before his finger could even twitch on the trigger.

He stomped back over the ice, his boots full of icy water. Tears blurred his vision. He pulled off his boots, stripped off his sodden stockings, and threw them on the ground. He imagined the pungent taste of the seal's red flesh in his mouth, felt his hand warming over the flame rising from a kettle of its oil, and thought, *Never have I wished this much to kill something.*

———

Outside the tent, Robinson paced. The sun fell toward the northern horizon, painting a golden streak across the meltwater pools on the shore ice. Still a bright white at noon in the southern sky, the sun was a weary orange in the late evening. Nearly an hour after midnight, it touched the horizon and remained poised there for half a minute. It glowed a fiery red and daubed crimson along the skyline, then began its ascent again. There was a languor in its movement, as though rising into the heavens consumed all its remaining strength. As if the end was not far.

Had Franklin named the waterway he had sailed down west of Boothia? He wondered if it might be possible to claim it. True, such honours were usually the privilege of lords and patrons, but perhaps it could be done with a spot of lobbying by his father, using his extensive connections in a way he would not object to. Robinson Sound. He imagined the words inscribed on a map of the Arctic as he showed it to his son.

In his few truncated minutes of sleep, he dreamed he was looking down at his boots, trudging forward over the ice and gravel. When he looked up, he found himself walking along a narrow path snaking along the top of a snow-covered mountain ridge. On both sides the hill dropped away steeply into a blue abyss. As he balanced there on the spine of rock, trembling in the cold air, he felt his head cracking. He pressed both palms to his temples, because if he dropped his hands, his head would split open, and he would not be able to stop screaming.

———

Adams sat beside Honey and listened to the sick man's shallow wheezing. Honey's pallor was grey beneath the dirt, and his fingers were curled into his palms. The clouds blackened like a new bruise. The drizzle turned to heavy rain, hammering the cold earth around them. Robinson sat staring at his hands. When the rain stopped, the mercury rose to forty-five degrees.

Adams went hunting. He returned four hours later with a dozen dovekies taken with two blasts of shot. The seven-inch birds spilled from his knapsack onto the stones at Robinson's feet. Their black and white feathers were damp and lustreless. He hacked at the small bony carcasses with a blunt knife, scraping an ounce of dark-red meat from each bird. He added it to the cooking pot with a handful of grey-green leaves he withdrew from his bag.

"Iceland moss." He pointed to the south. "There are patches of it growing about a mile down that way. It is bitter, but if it's boiled, we can eat it."

The soup was sour and tasted of spoiled fish. Adams and Robinson consumed it without comment. Adams propped Honey against the tentpole and carefully spooned soup into his mouth. The man could no longer chew. Adams picked out all but the tiniest fragments of meat and lifted the man's chin so the soup would run down his throat. Ten minutes later, Honey turned his head to the side and vomited the soup onto the shingle. He toppled over and lay coughing on the stones. Adams propped him back up as Robinson left the tent to stand watch.

Honey licked his lips and swallowed, trying to speak. Adams leaned in to hear him.

"How much further?"

Adams put an arm around his shoulder. "Not far now." He watched Honey's chest rise and fall and took his hand. "We have some reindeer meat cached ahead," he said. "I shall make you a fine soup."

"I can't see you."

"I am here." He squeezed Honey's hand.

"I'm not hungry."

"You are merely tired."

"I should be hungry. Tommy weren't hungry either. At the end."

"Tommy?"

"My brother. He was a carpenter on *Terror*."

"I'm sorry."

Honey was quiet for a time. Then, in the softest of murmurs, he spoke only to himself. "It's what happens. I seen it."

"What have you seen?"

"None of 'em were hungry at the end."

"You will feel better once you sleep."

"You oughta watch out for 'im."

"Lieutenant Robinson?"

"I seen men go down like that. Angry. Scared. He'll use that gun on you before long."

CHAPTER TWENTY

Adams lay awake in his blanket bag. His feet and legs throbbed. Sharp pains lanced through his stomach. The air in the tent was heavy upon him. He concentrated on forcing his sternum up, felt the cold air seep into a body that, in spite of everything, remained impossibly warm. Honey was now too weak to lift a hand. Adams examined him. He brought his hand to his mouth as his gut tightened. *God,* he thought, *when I thought I had seen all the ways a man can suffer, You show me more.*

The man was dying in colours. Yellow teeth, purple flaking lips, crimson oozing from sores on his elbows and legs, the blood dripping from his wrists. His legs were swollen like great ghastly sausages. At forty degrees, it was warm, but he shivered uncontrollably in his blanket bag. There were bare patches on his head where clumps of hair had detached, the skull all jutting ledges of bone and sunken crevices. Adams cut a strip of reindeer skin into tiny pieces. He hoped to make a broth and searched for driftwood to make a fire but found none. Gasping between each word, Honey asked Robinson and Adams not to exert themselves further on his behalf.

"Bury me in the ice, will you?" His voice was a scratchy whisper, like fingernails on a ship's timbers. "I do not fancy being chewed on by a bear."

Adams and Robinson swallowed some lichen the assistant surgeon had scraped from the stones. When he offered it to Honey, the man turned his head away.

"Enough," he whispered. "I've had enough."

———

Adams stood on the shore, southeast of Cape Felix, and looked out at the ice pack toward Cape Adelaide. The sun settled into a bank of grey clouds stretched along the horizon. Robinson unpacked the Halkett boat and placed its bellows and paddles on the ground. Adams watched the rectangular canvas bundle expand into an oval-shaped object nine feet long and four feet across.

Honey could not stand. Adams and Robinson dragged him into the boat. He lay with eyes closed and head lolling. They placed their tent and bedding beside him and hitched the sledge on the side. They departed at nine in the evening. The ice was firm underfoot but dotted with meltwater pools. Adams and Robinson pulled on the canvas shoulder straps, and where the ice was flat, the airboat glided easily over the ponds. Honey rested, unmoving, his head on the side of the boat. Adams attempted to engage him in conversation, but the stricken man could no longer speak. At midnight the wind abated, and the clouds disappeared. A thin crust of ice formed late at night when the sun dipped below the horizon. By morning it was gone.

Far out on the ice, a bear stood staring at them atop a small, twisted hummock. They held the animal in their sights and waited, hoping it might approach them to investigate. The bear tossed its head and went behind the hummock, and they did not see it again.

A storm grumbled on the horizon to the south. Veins of lightning crackled against darkly stained clouds, dead white trees holding up the sky. Channels of water blocked their path, and they walked hundreds of yards around to find a floe strong enough to bear their weight. After ten miles they reached an islet, a windswept mound of rubble-strewn limestone rising through the ice. Leaving Honey and the airboat on the shingle, they climbed to the top of the crag, gasping and coughing with the effort. Two larger islets lay to the north. The coast of Boothia was visible through the haze, a thin grey silhouette twenty-five miles to the east.

Adams' throat was raw and painful when he swallowed. His fingers were red and cramped with cold. The sky darkened, and when the rain arrived, it blew sideways, needles on his cheeks. He joined Robinson to erect the tent on the tiny shingle beach, and they sat looking out at the rain.

Honey lay unconscious in his blankets. His breath rattled in his throat, its sickly, fruity odour filling the tent. A groan of thunder made Adams turn his gaze skyward. A moment later, the rumble came again. It seemed to emanate from beneath their feet.

"The ice pack," said Robinson. "It is breaking up."

Adams lay down in his blanket, a bitter taste in his mouth and a dull pain in his stomach. The long dark cylinder of Robinson's shotgun barrel protruded from his blanket. He seemed to keep his weapon closer than before. Bears remained a constant threat, and both men needed to keep watch for game, but Adams had not seen the gun leave Robinson's hand since the confrontation with Walker and Dunn.

I seen men go down like that, Honey had said. *You oughta watch out for 'im.*

Adams tried to sleep. His mind simmered with suspicion. Robinson had not spoken of Billings' death. Honey had said Orren was a good shot. He may have mistakenly shot Billings down while targeting Robinson, but if he did not, the fatal ball could only have originated from the weapon of one other. It may have been an accident. Robinson was a poor shot. Perhaps his shot at Orren had gone wide. But Robinson seemed to harbour an enmity for Billings that bordered on loathing.

You shall tell them nothing, he had said. *God knows what you'll say.*

He wished he knew how to speak to the man. There was a wall around him; he was a city of one, and the gates never swung open. If he were to sleep soundly, he would need to hide the lieutenant's shot bag on the sledge tonight.

———

Robinson heard Honey die at four o'clock in the afternoon.

Lying next to Robinson in the gloom of the tent, Honey inhaled deeply, then let out a long, slow wheeze. Robinson waited for the sound of his next breath, but none followed. He sat up, leaned over him, and took Honey's curled, palsied hand in his own. The man's face was the colour of old putty. His cheeks were sunken pits in his skull. Robinson turned his face from the scorbutic stink of the man. He pulled the blanket from Honey's body, then rolled the corpse onto its side so it faced away from him. He looked across at Adams. Lying in his blanket, the assistant surgeon observed him in silence. Robinson rolled himself in the dead man's blanket and was instantly asleep.

———

Adams wrapped Samuel Honey's body in a piece of canvas cut from the tent. He stood looking dully at it. He wondered if they had somehow erred in their confusion, parcelling up a block of timber or a collection of tentpoles by mistake. Shrouded in canvas, the corpse looked too small to be that of even a hundred-pound man. Shrunken and anonymous, merely an object to be hauled and buried.

They set out from the islet toward Boothia. The hard ice bruised the soles of their feet through their stockings and cork-soled boots. The water pooled in depressions on the surface was only an inch deep, so they deflated the airboat and looped the track ropes over their shoulders, hauling the sledge carrying Honey's body. Adams felt the strength seeping from his body at each step. He could not remember what it was to be free of pain, to possess the vigour to climb a ladder or mount a horse. He and Robinson had eaten only lichen and reindeer skin since the soup of dovekies and Iceland moss. With no means of making a fire on the floes, they could not singe the hair from the hide. Adams used his knife to scrape as much hair from the skin as he could, leaving the pair to suck on it until it was soft enough to chew. He worried that the aches in his belly were less frequent now. The pangs abated every few hours, leaving him with no feeling of hunger. Even the thought of prayer left him empty of emotion and bereft of solace. After a day walking over the ice pack, Robinson stopped and dropped his head. Panting, he raised both hands to Adams in surrender.

"We must leave him."

Adams stared at the corpse on the sledge, thinking it might rise and render its own verdict. Benumbed by fatigue, he opened his mouth to speak, but no words emerged.

"I thought we would find a hole in the ice, at least a seal's breathing hole," said Robinson, "but look at it." He limped to the sledge and removed the shovel. He leaned on it for a moment, gathering himself, then jabbed at the ice with the blade. It clanged with the sound of a sword swung on a boulder. "This is old ice," he said. "Not this season's. It was carried here from the north by the current. Harder than stone. There is no getting through it."

Adams fought to catch his breath. "If we leave him here on the ice, a bear might get him."

Robinson fixed him with a bleary gaze. There was no guile in his expression. "I am spent."

"But he did not want this." Adams crumpled to his knees. Freezing water soaked through the fabric of his trousers. Hot tears were in his beard.

Robinson squinted into the glare at the coastline of Cape Adelaide. It was close, no more than five miles away. "You remember where we left the reindeer meat, yes? The oddly shaped boulder. Near that small peninsula." His voice sounded hollow now, a deep echo in his chest.

Adams stood. "I remember." He had thought of little else for days. He coughed and spat, gasping in long, ragged gusts. Relief and guilt warred within him. As wicked as he found the thought of abandoning the body of Sir John Franklin's last man, the prospect of hauling it another mile made him tremble with dread. This was a man who had joined his shipmates in eating the flesh of his fellows. A man whose dreams were back to front and who wept at the torment of a maimed fox. "We should be ashamed, leaving him unburied."

"We should," said Robinson.

"Promises to dying men should be fulfilled." Adams bowed his head to conceal the insincerity he feared was all too obvious on his face.

Robinson nodded. "There was a time I would not have broken such an oath."

"He liked pigeon pie."

Robinson knelt and untied the shrouded corpse. It slid off the sledge, rigid as a log, and came to rest against the foot of a snowy hummock. He straightened and regarded Adams in silence.

It is a challenge, Adams decided. *He waits for me to protest. If I acquiesce, it will be easier for us both—if I concede this thing on the ice is not Samuel Honey anymore. Just something stiff and old to be discarded, a heavy weight to be thrown off. Something to flee and forget.*

He gazed at rows of grey clouds dragged out across the heavens, so low that if they kept walking, the land and sky must surely be stitched together along a seam somewhere, and they would be unable to go farther. Patches of old ice clung to the shore, crusty and permanent. Up in the hills above Cape Adelaide, more ice hugged depressions and holes in the ground like dough pressed by huge wet fingers. He blinked away the frost in his eyelashes.

"God's work exacts a toll, does it not?" Robinson asked. "More, perhaps, than you thought it might require you to pay. But do not doubt Franklin and his men will be remembered." The lieutenant's tone was contemplative. "Time changes a man. I do not mean how it whitens the hair and wrinkles the skin. Time goes on changing a man after he is dead. A man dies and becomes a hero, or a villain. Likely he becomes less than he was when alive. Sometimes, but rarely, he becomes more."

Adams thought he might only now be comprehending a great truth about the Passage. "I think," he said, "that man is the hound chasing the carriage, barking and howling, wanting this strange and exotic thing.

We lust after it. Die for it. But we have not the slightest notion of what we shall do with it when we catch it." He went to the sledge and put a hand on the rolled-up tent. "Let us decide what to do with him once we have rested. Perhaps then we will be strong enough to bury him."

Robinson fixed him with a doubtful gaze. "There is nothing to eat here. It would not be wise to tarry."

"Just a few hours."

Robinson shrugged. He appeared too exhausted to argue. Together they pitched the tent and slept. The dead man lay on the ice outside.

Adams woke. His mouth was parched, and his limbs felt like they were made of iron. Hunger was once again a dull ache in his belly, as if he had swallowed a large stone. He glanced at Robinson. The lieutenant lay in his blanket, his breathing slow and regular. Adams grimaced as he flexed the fingers of one hand and massaged them with his other. Frozen and thawed countless times, his fingertips had almost wholly lost feeling, and he felt that same insensitivity extending to his mind. It was becoming numb. He could see something horrific but feel nothing. He was either in agony or experienced no sensation at all.

He drank from his canteen. He took a square of reindeer skin from his bag and put it between his teeth. These past days, he had taken to deceiving himself that he was eating. The scrap of hide had no flavour, but as he bit down, his mouth ran with saliva, and for a few moments he could imagine it was meat. He pulled on his stockings and boots and left the tent. Ten yards away, Honey's swathed corpse lay at the foot of the hummock where they had left it. He stood transfixed, staring at the wrapped bundle.

He thought he must still be in his blanket, dreaming. Something within him bent and fractured and fell away, and he was different. A pair of hands moved before him, and boots walked on the ground below but were not his. He could not picture his father's face or hear Frances' voice. He could not recall the shape of the tower at the parish church in Great Barton or the colour of the River Lark's waters near the ruins of the abbey in Bury St Edmunds. Time stretched out, each intake of his breath loud in the silence. He was a creature shedding its carapace, emerging as something new and unrecognisable. The pain in his belly was a throb. He folded his hands over his stomach and remembered what Honey had said.

It ain't so strange.

Nor was it. He understood that now. He knelt next to the corpse, peeled back the canvas, and sat gazing at the dead man within. Honey's face was composed, his skin pale and lined. The glimmer of life that had flickered beneath was gone, as when a candle is withdrawn from beneath a sheet of vellum. He lifted Honey's shroud and pulled up his linen undershirt. The flesh of his chest had withered and sunk, and the bruises had expanded across the yellow skin. Each of the ribs protruded so much, he imagined tearing them out with his fingertips and gnawing on the bone. The knife was light in his hand. He ran his thumb down the blade, then laid it flat across Honey's chest. He remembered the ragged holes in the leg of the corpse they had found buried on King William Land.

No need to be so graceless. He would have more respect, make a neater incision. Then it would be acceptable. Honey would not begrudge him. Honey had known how it would be. He had seen into Adams' soul and had told him so.

I've known a few like you.

Adams imagined his face as in a looking glass, the vacant expression in his eyes and the slackness in his jaw, and thought, *This is what I am now.* This was not his doing; it could only be what the Lord commanded. *Everything is as God wills it,* he thought. *He wills that I eat.* God wanted Franklin dead from apoplexy, Fitzjames starving to death in his bunk, Billings with a bullet in his throat. God would have him do this because it could not be only Lieutenant Robinson who returned to report to Captain Ross at Port Leopold. It was nothing less than his duty. Robinson would becloud the tale, conceal the truth. He would deny renown to brave men. Without Adams, Fitzjames' message honouring his men would never be delivered. It had to be this way. Nothing had ever made more sense.

Adams leaned over the dead man and placed a hand on his leg. He took a deep breath and squeezed his eyes shut. His body shook. He reversed his grip so he could stab downward with the knife and touched the tip of the blade to the corpse.

Some questions are too hard to answer.

His knuckles were white on the handle of the knife. He pressed down gently, his eyes welling.

You don't think about it.

He worked quickly to combat the trembling in his hands. He was mechanical, spiritless. The act was in motion, and he could not stop now. He brought the knife down again and again. He closed his eyes and bowed his head. Tears dripped from his chin.

CHAPTER
TWENTY-ONE

Robinson had made his decision. "We shall leave him."

He stood beside Honey's shrouded corpse, studying Adams' face for any sign of dissent. The man would not meet his gaze, and that, he decided, was enough. He stood with his back turned, staring up into a glaucous sky.

Robinson had awakened the evening before at the sound of Adams' knife scraping Honey's bones. He looked out from the tent to see Adams crouched by the corpse. He felt only yawning detachment where there might once have been shock or disgust. What had the seaman Walker said? *Understand it, or do not.* Robinson thought if he held his hand over a flame or plunged a knife into his flesh, he would feel nothing.

But he needed to protect himself. A man who would eat the flesh of one man might eat the flesh of another. He decided he would not allow Adams to walk behind him. He would keep the nipple of his gun clean and dry, the percussion cap fresh. The lead balls in his shot bag were a comforting weight in his hand. He sharpened his knife on a stone, ensuring that Adams saw him do it. Once they reached the cache of deer meat, they would both be safe, and there would be no need to speak of it. His spirits rose. Surely he could convince Adams to leave *this* part of the tale out of his report. Then it would be easier to persuade him to omit others. He waited, giving Adams a final opportunity to object.

Finally, Robinson pulled the sledge out to a clear patch of ice and slid one of the track ropes over his shoulder. Adams picked up the other. Neither glanced at the swathed corpse on the ice.

They walked away and did not look back.

———

Harnessed with Robinson, Adams walked more urgently than he had in days. He found himself several strides ahead of the lieutenant. The track rope stretched uncomfortably, forcing him to slow his pace.

Now that it was done, he sought only to flee the scene of his disgrace. He tried not to think of it, but as the ache in his belly subsided and his strength returned, the shame rose within him like a monster emerging from a cave. It had been lurking unseen, driven into the shadows by his need, but it snarled at him now. An act that hours earlier seemed not only permissible but essential, he saw now as the most egregious of sins. He still felt the knife in his hand, imagined the blade in the corpse's leg, the strips of red. He glanced across at Robinson, hating him for not waking to take the knife from his hand, for not hauling him back from the precipice. He touched the Bible in his pocket. It felt puny and impotent against the enormity of his crime—a weapon so paltry, it could only bounce off the thick hide of his remorse.

He was most frightened by the notion that nothing he knew of the world would help him here. Not law. Not God. He looked at a burnished blue sky and saw no clouds. Naught to obscure him or protect him.

How can Thou not see me, Lord? I am here.

———

"Good Lord, why are there no wars anymore?" Robinson's father puffed on a cigar as he strolled along beside him. He wore a patterned velvet waistcoat over a white linen shirt. "The navy does no fighting!

Chastising slavers and pirates, chaperoning British merchantmen—it is all the navy can find to do."

"I shall soon be a captain," said Robinson. "You shall see how wrong you were." Only out here, walking over dead land and dead sailors, could he say things to his father he would never say to his face.

"So what will your story be, lad? Make it a good one." His father's coattails flapped like a pair of blackbirds in the wind. "I would have placed a wager on you to find the Passage, but in truth the odds were always too long to tempt me. I am investing in railways now, you know. The returns are entirely satisfactory."

"I might not only be the man to *find* the Passage," said Robinson, "I may yet be the first to sail *through* it if the Admiralty gives me command of the next expedition." His mind raced, considering the possibilities. "If we can get across the North Water early enough in the summer, there will be time enough to leave a depot at Barrow Strait and more caches at locations along the west coast of Boothia."

His father lifted an eyebrow and stroked his whiskers. "Perhaps I should go into shipping. Surely, as the father of the man who found the Passage, I shall receive some dispensation. Perhaps the Crown will give me preferential access to the Passage."

"No doubt Mother will be pleased," said Robinson. "She enjoys living in a manor with a large court and walled gardens built four hundred years ago by a knight whose name she cannot remember."

"Ah, well. We are from money. It is what she knows."

From money? Robinson frowned. His father's father was a farmer and potter, barely a generation removed from costermongers. "If there is one thing I have taken from you, it is that a man can make history with ink, a quill, and a penchant for mendacity."

"Then I have at least achieved something. You know, do you not, that celebrity cannot be shared, it can only be diluted? Your reputation would be greatly enhanced if your companion is not there to contradict your version of events. Their Lordships of the Admiralty have a short span of attention, and men have short memories. They can only remember one name. It must be yours, not his. There can only be one hero here."

"He is brave."

His father tapped ash from his cigar and watched it fall like snow. "I knew you would not amount to much. There is no room for sentimentality."

"That is your other lesson, then, is it?"

His father sighed. "Frederick, why could you not have had a head for business?"

"I thought it akin to gambling. And too much time spent with dishonourable men."

"Dishonourable men?" His father let out a blue cloud of cigar smoke. "Your comrade ate a fellow. I question your standards, boy."

———

Adams looked up at the sun, pinned high in the heavens like a brooch on a gown. The sky was a blue shell. A light breeze blew. They left the ice and stepped ashore on the coast of Boothia. The stony beach stretched away to the north. They left the sledge on the shingle and clambered up a low bluff to survey the landscape. The climb left them breathless and shivering, their hearts hammering in their chests.

Robinson lifted his telescope and swept the western ice pack below them for a long time. He lowered it, wiped the lens with a cloth, and held it to his eye again.

"Are we pursued?" Adams asked.

Robinson hesitated. "I thought I saw movement. Perhaps a bear." He lowered the telescope. "We have no time to return and chase it." He pointed to the north. "The cache is close. Two days' walk, I should say."

Adams coughed. He grimaced at a pain in his hip that he had not noticed before. "How far is Fury Beach?"

"No more than two hundred miles."

No more than that? Robinson's casual tone brought a smile to Adams' lips. Two hundred miles. Once he might have comprehended such a distance. "Through great trial does man know himself. And thus does he know God. The Bible tells us this."

"Two weeks." There was a hardness in Robinson's eyes. "We will manage it in two weeks."

Adams prayed silently. Consuming Honey's flesh had left his body stronger but placed a great weight upon his spirit. He remembered the texture of it in his mouth, the click of his jaws and the wet sensation of the meat between his teeth. Most of all, he remembered the taste of the man's flesh. It was forever in his mouth now, a glowing-hot sensation blistering the surface of his tongue but no longer offering nourishment. He hawked and spit on the ground and rinsed his mouth with freezing meltwater, but the taste remained.

They descended to the beach. Small flocks of ducks flew low over the sea. They checked their guns, concealed themselves among the rocks above the waterline, and lay down to wait. Minutes later, another flock appeared. Both men lifted their weapons and fired. A single bird tumbled from the air and splashed into the water a dozen yards from the beach. It lay in a few inches of water, its feathers ruffled by the wind. Adams removed his stockings and boots and danced out into the freezing shallows to retrieve it.

When he returned to the pebbled beach, he knelt at a patch of moss between the stones and pried it up with the tip of his knife as Robinson cleaned the bird. Adams struck his flint and steel against the clump of moss and blew on it until it caught. Smoke from the cooking fire billowed around them, cloaking them in a choking fog. The duck was only half-cooked when the two starving men could wait no longer. They tore the bird to pieces. The sun climbed. They rolled out their floorcloth, pulled the tent canvas over them like a cocoon, and slept like creatures hibernating in the earth.

Light rain fell. Adams put the tent, floorcloth, and blanket bags on the sledge. He knelt and began to roll up the deflated airboat.

"Leave it here," said Robinson. "The lighter our load, the sooner we shall get to the meat."

Adams hesitated. Weeks earlier they had walked across frozen bays and inlets that might now be free of ice. Was it worth hauling the extra weight to save walking around bodies of water?

Robinson sensed his misgivings. "We have no time to waste."

They both looked up as more ducks passed overhead, outside the range of their guns. Robinson collected a handful of feathers from the fire-blackened stones and tossed them into the breeze.

"We were lucky to get this duck. We may not soon encounter more. We must have the deer meat."

Adams remembered butchering the reindeer carcass, the scrape of his knife on the bones and the snap of the spine. The misted dead eyes of the animal, the red flesh and the white fat. The misted dead eyes of Samuel Honey. The sallow skin and the yellow fat.

They must have the meat. Once they had the meat, they could make Fury Beach. He dropped the airboat on the shingle, and they set out in a gloomy twilight. The sea to the west was the colour of lead. Adams' beard was wet with rain.

On their best day, they made seventeen miles when the ground was firm.

They skirted a small bay fringed with green lichen and limped over the muddy earth, through a place where nothing lived or grew and where all was slush and gravel and clay and rock scraped flat by the ice for millennia. More than once they came upon a bay or headland that Adams could have sworn they had already traversed, as if a great cosmic hand had swept up the land in their wake and set it down in their path to make them endure it again. At dawn, they pitched the tent on the stony ground. Each watched the other check and clean his shotgun. They crawled beneath their blankets with the weapons tight in their grasp.

Adams listened to the wind. He thought of nothing but the squelching of boots in the mud and the scrape of sledge runners on the gravel. In a dream his hand hovered over Honey's corpse with a sharp knife that pricked the waxy skin. Steam rose from the meat, and clear pink fluid gushed from the limb like the juice from a turkey. The image was still vivid when he woke, the tart taste of Honey's flesh lingering on his tongue. For the hundredth time he thought, *I have damned myself. There is no forgiveness to be had for this.*

The next day he shot a hare. They ate the last scraps of the creature and sucked the bones, then pounded them into powder and swilled them down with water. In a shallow depression in the earth, a collection of large flat stones stood atop one another like broken teeth. Moss grew on the stones. Bones lay scattered on the ground. They searched the area for meat cached by passing Esquimaux but found nothing and walked on.

Adams was so weak, the thin flesh on his bones was itself a tremendous burden, like a suit of armour growing heavier with each step. His bones clicked and scraped. He shuffled to a stop and gripped his wrist to feel his galloping pulse. His foot was a club on the end of his leg. His hip ached, and his gums were sore and swollen, teeth unsteady in his head.

Robinson limped along a dozen yards from him. He muttered to himself, sometimes angrily, other times in a gentle murmur. He cast sidelong glances at Adams, looking away quickly if Adams returned his gaze. He no longer strapped his shotgun across his back but carried it ready in his hands. In the morning they rested. Adams lay awake and watched Robinson until the lieutenant fell asleep with his gloved hand on the stock of his gun.

Clouds massed overhead. Fog blanketed the shore. A freezing northerly breeze numbed Adams' face. They hunched into their coats and listened to the ice disintegrate in the channel to the west.

Robinson pointed. "We are close!" he said, grinning. His mood had lightened. The excitement in his voice was boyish, unfamiliar. "Do you remember that hill? The boulders were at the foot of it."

Adams watched him, jaw agape, exhausted. Which Robinson was this? The brave and resourceful officer? The sullen and selfish bully, the coward? The killer? Adams did not know which man he followed along the stony beach on aching feet. Above the tidemark, two hundred yards away, a cluster of large boulders emerged from the fog at the foot of a slope.

Robinson slipped his shoulder out of the harness and unslung his shotgun, dropping it on the sledge. He broke into a shuffle. His left leg moved unnaturally, the knee barely bending. His telescope wobbled on his back.

Adams halted, swaying with fatigue. His eyes streamed in the wind. Overcome by dizziness, he sat down on the sledge and tried to force air into lungs that felt half their normal size. When he looked up, Robinson had reached the boulders. The lieutenant was kneeling, his chin on his chest, obeisant to the rocks before him. He crawled forward on all fours and began scraping at the earth at the base of one boulder with his hands. As Adams watched, the strength seemed to depart Robinson's body, and his forehead sank to the earth. Then he reared, shouting at the boulder before him. With the breeze rasping across his ears, Adams could not make out his words.

And then, with a jolt, he understood.

The meat was not there.

His empty belly dropped out from under him, and he thought he might topple. *No,* he thought, *Robinson must be mistaken. He must have dug in the wrong place.*

Adams staggered along the beach toward him. The stones beneath his boots glowed green with copper ore. The lieutenant sat on the ground, staring vacantly at his muddy hands. Nothing remained of the meat they had buried. The stones they had placed over the hole at the foot of the boulder lay six feet away, flung aside by powerful claws. Robinson rose to his feet, his face twisted in fury. He retrieved his shotgun from the sledge and spun to face Adams.

"Damn you! We might have meat if you had not missed your shot at Victory Point!"

Adams' ire flashed instantly, standing and roaring like a flame in dry grass. He rose to his feet, shaking. "Do you think I missed on purpose? You put the message back in the cairn and say we must tell them nothing, so it is all for naught!"

Adams saw that Robinson had been straining to keep something within him in check, something that now crumbled. Robinson raised a balled fist and screamed into the cold air—a long, drawn-out howl of anguish.

"And the seals! Three to aim at, but you could not fire a shot! Why?" He planted his feet, grasping his shotgun across his chest, and stared at Adams with eyes red from pain and glare. With his unkempt whiskers and his jacket stained and torn, he resembled the first of Franklin's men that Adams and Billings had encountered weeks earlier. "Is it that you covet a different kind of meat?"

"What?" Adams' mouth was dry.

"You say you will tell them everything. What will you tell them about Honey?"

Adams held Robinson's gaze. He fought to suppress the tremor in his voice. "That he died of starvation and scurvy."

"I know what you did," said Robinson. The shotgun was massive in his hands. "Your special calling is nothing but a conceit. But your sin? That is undeniable."

"I do not deny it." Exhaustion sapped him of all desire to argue. "Condemn me. It is no more than I deserve."

His acquiescence seemed only to inflame Robinson further. He clenched his teeth. "What will you tell them about Billings?" His fingers opened and closed on the stock of the shotgun.

Adams was afraid now. He cleared his throat. "That it was an accident," he said quietly. He felt he was staring down a wild beast of the forest.

Robinson's rage boiled and broke now, like floodwaters through a dam wall. Flecks of spittle spotted his beard. The pitch of his voice rose. "Liar! You will blame me. Never once did you intend to support my claim. And now we have naught to eat."

He raised the shotgun and trained it upon Adams' face. Inches from his eyes, the mouths of the barrels were oddly round and symmetrical, alien shapes in a landscape of jagged, broken edges.

"I see how fragile are the shackles we place upon our true natures," Adams whispered, "and how readily they shatter and fall away." He closed his eyes. A sense of relief washed upon him. This was how he would atone for his sin. Gratitude and pity for Robinson swirled within him. He would not condemn a man boiled down by circumstance to his most urgent of instincts, no more than one could blame a sick man raging and twisting with fever. Surely the man was God's instrument. He was no longer hungry. The pain in his limbs was gone. Salt air fresh on his tongue.

The wind changed, a warmer breeze blowing from the south. Robinson's boots crunched on the gravel. A second may have passed, or a minute. Adams opened his eyes. Thick mist swirled around him, but the sky directly overhead was a deep navy blue, empty of stars.

Robinson faced away from him, staring into the fog. He held the shotgun down by his side. When he looked back at Adams, he had changed again. The rage and pain were gone from his face, replaced with an expression of puzzlement.

Adams opened his mouth to speak. Robinson shook his head and put a gloved finger to his lips. He pointed at the curtain of mist. Adams held his breath. Both men stood and listened. With a raised palm, Robinson instructed Adams to remain where he stood. He trod silently over the earth on the balls of his feet, taking care not to kick any pebbles. Adams peered into the fog but saw nothing. Robinson halted.

With a languid, unhurried motion, he lifted his shotgun to his shoulder and pointed it into the mist.

Three huge shapes appeared at the edge of the fog. Their long brown hair hung almost to the earth. They seemed to float above the ground in the mist; then Adams made out the creatures' hooves beneath. Huge bony helmets, each with horns that curved outward, rested atop shoulders six feet above the ground. The animals raised their heads from the stunted grass and stood motionless, watching the two men.

The largest of the three musk oxen stood in front of the other two. The tips of the bull's shaggy hair flickered in the breeze, hanging down around its hindquarters like a skirt flecked with mud and snow. Adams guessed the animal's weight at six hundred pounds.

Robinson looked back at Adams and pointed at the assistant surgeon's gun. With a sweep of his arm, he instructed Adams to circle away at an angle to Robinson's position. Adams nodded, understanding that Robinson sought to catch the oxen in a cross fire. He slowly walked sideways. A wind began to rise. His heart knocked against the thin wall of his chest.

The ox watched Robinson approach. Adams swung around to the creature's left flank. The ox took a step in Robinson's direction, then another. When it stood fifteen yards away, it stopped and swung its head from side to side. The fog began to melt away.

Robinson and the ox stared at each other.

The ox dropped its head and charged.

The lieutenant aimed and fired. Adams heard a sound like a stone striking a rock as the ball ricocheted off the ox's bony helmet. The animal halted and shook its head. Robinson pulled the trigger again, and Adams saw the creature's long hair flicked by the heavy ball that slammed into its shoulder. Snorting, the bull wheeled away and ran.

The cow and calf broke into a run, shadowing the bull. Adams fired at the fleeing cow but missed. He knelt and steadied himself, then exhaled and fired again. The second ball struck the calf behind the shoulder, and the animal dropped, its face crashing into the dirt. The two larger oxen disappeared into the fog.

A new sound made Adams wheel around—an urgent, angry grunt.

Then he saw the bear.

CHAPTER
TWENTY-TWO

The bear appeared from the thinning fog between Adams and Robinson. It swung its head to study one man, then the other. Adams knew that Robinson, standing with his back turned, had neither seen nor heard the animal. He opened his mouth to shout a warning, but his breath was trapped in his chest. His shotgun was too heavy to lift.

For a moment, he hoped the bear might retreat at the presence of a human threat on each flank. Then it raised its head and sniffed the breeze. The long white snout was crosshatched with scars. It had smelled the calf's blood. Still oblivious to the bear, Robinson stared into the fog where the fleeing oxen had vanished. He knelt beside the fallen calf and laid his shotgun on the gravel. He drew his knife, his fit of rage forgotten.

"Fine shooting, Mister Adams! We shall have meat after all!"

Fingers of sunlight stroked the earth through the remnants of the mist. The bear tossed its head and broke into a lumbering trot toward Robinson and the dead ox. Adams' breath returned. He forced air into his lungs and cried out, a wordless shout. The bear's shadow fell across the gravel in front of Robinson. The lieutenant whirled around. The bear stood on its hind legs a few paces from him, its head five feet above his own. Adams' feet would not move. He watched, helpless, his stomach a cold pit, knuckles skeletal-white on the stock of his shotgun.

Robinson raised his arms above his head, his knife in one hand. He bellowed at the bear, a drawn-out shout of anger. The animal dropped to all fours and lunged forward like an enormous cat. Robinson's shout was cut off abruptly as the bear's paw knocked him off his feet. He tried to scramble backward, but it was on him. He flung both arms up to protect his face, and the bear raked him again with his paw. Blood sprayed. The bear seized Robinson's shoulder in its jaws and shook him. Robinson's body convulsed in the animal's grip, fluttering like a rag in a dog's mouth.

Adams' blood was hot in his fingertips and cheeks. He aimed his shotgun, squinting down the quivering barrel, and fired. At the boom of the gun, the bear released Robinson. Its snout was red with his blood. Adams heard the heavy ball from his gun strike the gravel somewhere out in the mist. Robinson lay motionless beside the ox carcass.

Adams screamed at the bear. It tossed and shook its head at him. Adams' limbs began to function, and he shuffled toward the creature. Guessing his distance at just over thirty yards, he stopped and dropped to one knee, took aim, and fired. The ball struck the bear on the flank. It wheeled around and roared. Blood streaked its fur. It swung its gaze back to the prone Robinson.

"No!" Adams shouted. "Here, damn you! Here!"

The bear turned its head back and stared at Adams. Without making a sound, it began snapping its jaws, its massive incisors flashing. His shotgun was empty. Adams reached for the shot bag slung over his shoulder but found it unnaturally light. His ammunition was gone. His fingers found only a tattered canvas edge where the bag had torn, spilling the heavy lead balls onto the ground in the miles behind him. He wheeled around and scanned the gravel. His eyes were wet and his vision blurry. He could see none of the balls among the broken stones. The bear stood still, staring at him. It lowered its head like a bull preparing to charge.

Adams locked eyes with the bear and knew it would come at him. He seized his powder bag and poured a measure down the barrel of his shotgun. He could see the bear approaching across the gravel from the corner of his eye. He detached the ramrod, shoved it down the barrel as far as he could, then placed a fresh percussion cap on the nipple. In a single motion, he threw the shotgun to his shoulder and swung the barrel around. The bear was on him, its enormous ivory mass filling his vision. He caught a glimpse of the yawning jaws, smelled the stench of its breath. His bladder released, and hot liquid gushed in his groin. He pulled the trigger, and the shotgun bucked and boomed, snatching away all sound. The bear collided with him, knocking him backward, forcing the breath from his lungs. The back of his head struck the stones, and the shotgun spun from his grasp.

His only thought was: *It is done now.*

———

He opened his eyes and held his breath. Through holes in the fog above, wispy clouds swirled in a blue sky. His head throbbed from the shotgun blast. The bear's head was heavy on his chest. A massive paw lay across his leg. He smelled blood and piss and the odour of algae on the bear's fur. He lay still, playing dead. His lungs screamed for air, desperate for more than silent, shallow breaths through clenched teeth. Fractured slabs of limestone dug into his cheek.

When the bear woke, it would rake him with its claws and clamp him in its jaws. He listened for the sound of its breathing but heard only the hiss of the breeze over the empty ground.

A minute passed, then another. He had no choice but to try to steal away. Moving as slowly as he could, he extracted himself from under the bear. The animal's massive head dropped limp to the gravel. An enormous paw lay outstretched and reaching. The huge white body lay motionless. One black eye stared at Adams. Twelve inches of Adams' ramrod protruded from the other. The remainder was buried in the bear's brain.

He ran to where Robinson lay. The pool of crimson on the stones was so bright, it sucked away all other colour, turning even the light grey. Robinson's eyes were closed, his teeth clenched. His complexion was waxy, his breathing rapid and shallow. His shoulder and left arm were a bloody mess of torn flesh and fabric. The bear's claws had shredded the sleeve of his coat, sweater, and the linen shirt beneath, ripping the flesh between the shoulder and elbow. Shards of bone were visible in the tattered, bloody mess. Adams knew the arm was shattered in multiple places. Blood splashed onto the stones and ran down Robinson's arm, staining his mitten red. There were more striations across the front of his coat, and blood seeped from deep gashes in his chest.

Adams ran back to the sledge and retrieved a linen shirt. He tore it into strips and bound Robinson's arm and shoulder as tightly as he could. The cloth was instantly soaked through with blood. Robinson's eyes flickered open, red with pain and shock. He tried to speak but could only grunt.

"Lay still," said Adams.

Adams wrapped Robinson in a blanket bag. He cradled the injured man's jaw in a trembling hand, placing a knapsack under his head. Robinson's skin was clammy, his pulse weak. His breathing slowed, and then he fainted. Adams could do nothing to stop the bleeding. He breathed into his cupped hands to warm his bloody fingers. Mist rose from the land, and colours changed in the sky.

He dragged the unconscious Robinson behind a boulder to shield him from the wind. He fashioned a crude lean-to from the remains of the tent canvas and the handle of the shovel, then hauled pieces of driftwood from the shore below and built a fire next to their shelter. While the injured man slept, he walked to a stream in a nearby ravine. He washed the lieutenant's blood from his hands and refilled both their canteens. He stumbled to the carcass of the musk ox calf and pressed his mouth against the creature's wound. Its blood warmed his cracked lips. Then he sat back on his haunches in the twilight. He hacked and tore at the carcass with his blunt knife, pausing every minute to catch his breath, until he brought forth a chunk of bloody meat. A drop of blood fell from the tip of his knife and splattered on the toe of his boot. Breathing heavily, he wiped the blade on his trousers. He knelt again, sawed away the hide, and cut the meat into small pieces. He sat on the stones and chewed slowly before sitting back. Blood ran down his face.

——

When he returned to the lean-to, Robinson's eyes were open and glassy. The evening light cupped his cheek in a yellow hand. A mask of pain, his bloodless face had aged a century. The edge of his whiskered jaw seemed to thrust through the skin, casting shadows along his withered throat.

"Do not move," Adams told him. He held a canteen to the lieutenant's lips and waited while the injured man sipped. "You have lost much blood."

Robinson coughed and winced. "My arm."

"I have bound it," said Adams.

"How bad is it?"

"Lay still."

Robinson attempted to look down at his injury, but his eyes rolled back with the pain. "Must it come off?"

Adams would have removed the shattered arm already if he had a suitable saw. And if Robinson had not lost so much blood. He looked down at his blunt and filthy knife, still red with the blood of the ox calf. The prospect of performing surgery with it filled him with dread.

"We shall see," he said. "For now, you must eat." He forced a nonchalant tone. "We have rather a lot of meat—your choice of musk ox or bear."

Robinson coughed once, turned his head, and spat. "You told me once you felt compelled to sail to the Arctic, to find Franklin. You said it was a calling."

"I did."

"Did it never occur to you this might be a punishment? For a lie you told, a person you once maligned?"

"Do not talk anymore," Adams said softly.

"A penance," Robinson whispered. "It feels like that to me. Water."

Adams held his canteen to Robinson's lips, and he drank.

"In my knapsack," Robinson said, "you will find two diaries. One is for Captain Ross. It is a bland thing: observations on the terrain, the weather. It's what he expects. The other diary I would ask that you keep hidden. Give it to my wife if she still lives."

"I will." The promise came easily. *If we were friends,* Adams thought, *I would feign horror. No, buck up! Give it to her yourself. We will fetch through.* But without bandages and splints and sutures, all he had to salve Robinson's pain was assurances he may not live to keep.

Robinson lay unmoving for so long, Adams thought he had lost consciousness. Then he spoke again, his voice a faint croak.

"Do you hear God's voice?" he asked.

"When I pray. In here." Adams tapped the side of his head.

"I used to listen. When I was a boy. I never heard it."

"He listens to you."

"What does He sound like?"

Adams lifted the canteen to Robinson's lips. "I hear my father's voice," he said. "He is with God now. To you, He will sound different."

Robinson coughed weakly. "What was your father's sin? It must have been great."

Adams hesitated. "He drowned. He was . . . affected by melancholy."

Robinson digested this in silence. Finally, he asked, "Would you forgive him that sin?"

"Of course."

"Then why do you imagine God would not? Why must you appease Him with a bauble like the Passage?"

Adams' tears ran into his whiskers and dripped onto his gloves. "Because my father's death was my doing," he whispered. "He chose to be with God because I was not enough to keep him in this world. If I found Franklin or helped him find the Passage, my father would know I had honoured him. And God would forgive him his sin."

"You have been punishing yourself, then."

Adams hung his head.

"Edward."

Adams looked up at Robinson's use of his first name. The lieutenant fixed him with a gentle gaze.

"Understand this: your faith is your greatest strength. I envy the courage it lends you." Robinson coughed and winced. "But you said yourself, all is as God wills it. I doubt He will smile upon you merely because you find a lost captain or a waterway through the ice. I suggest you cease trying to bend Him to *your* will. It smacks of hubris."

Adams could only nod, ashamed.

"You seek to atone for the sin of another," said Robinson. "It is like taking on another man's debt merely because you think it noble. You would make a poor banker. Best atone for your sin and leave others to settle their own accounts."

At this, he groaned and slumped back. Adams sat up in alarm. Blood dripped from the bandage around Robinson's shoulder and pooled in tiny depressions in the gravel.

His eyes closed, Robinson grunted, "I see it now."

"What is it you see?"

"Both our fathers have much to answer for."

Adams looked down on the gravel beach as the sun fell from sight. The midnight sky along the horizon was a flaming orange lit by subterranean fires that charred the clouds above. He saw contorted pieces of melting ice reaching from the water near the shore like damned souls in torment.

Robinson whispered in tones barely audible. "I think the Arctic is like an abyss," he said. "A man ventures into it, and it draws more of his kind in his wake. The Passage is no great undertaking, no path to salvation. Purgatory is not a place of purifying fire; it is a place of ice and cold, a kingdom of wind and bones and monsters and dead things."

—

Adams woke in a blue-grey light. Beside him, Robinson's eyes were open, unfocused. His breathing was shallow, his pallor whiter than the chunks of ice scattered on the beach below. His starved visage was skeletal. The flesh sank into the hollow of his throat, and his eyes were deep in their sockets, his legs as thin as a child's. Blood seeped again from his wound, saturating the makeshift bandage and soaking into the earth beneath the injured man's elbow. Adams ripped another piece of linen from the shirt and bound the wound again. Robinson lay limp and unflinching.

"Elizabeth." Robinson spoke softly. His right hand stirred on his chest, as if he sought to raise it to her cheek.

Adams held his breath.

"Elizabeth!" Robinson's voice was an urgent rasp.

"Yes, my dear," Adams said softly. If all he could do was pretend to be her, he would do that.

"Father was not pleased," said Robinson.

Adams held his canteen to Robinson's lips. "Drink some water."

The injured man appeared not to see the canteen. He made no move to drink. "'What will you do to move up, Frederick!' he would say. 'Eight years a lieutenant! What will you do?'"

Adams placed the palm of his hand on Robinson's forehead. It was hot with fever.

"I embarrassed him. What a sin that was," said Robinson. "What a crime."

Adams spoke softly. "Do not talk."

"I shall not let him have the boy, Elizabeth."

Adams saturated a piece of linen with water from his canteen, held it above Robinson's parched lips, and dripped water into his mouth. The injured man's tongue touched his teeth. He coughed twice and swallowed, his Adam's apple huge, like a stone trapped in his throat.

Robinson's voice dropped to a whisper. "I could never go against him."

"My dear, you must rest."

"He never even let me speak. He just raised his hand to me, cut me off. 'I will see to it,' he said. 'I know people.'"

Adams placed the cold, wet cloth on his forehead. Robinson did not seem to feel it.

Then Robinson whispered again. "I do not know people. I am not like that. And those who know me do not regard me highly."

———

Adams sat in the lean-to with Robinson, watching the soft light of the long twilight polish the sea. He lay next to the injured man for warmth, pressing against him from shoulder to ankle, a blanket over them both. Meteors flashed across the sky, scarring its dark-blue canvas. Later, when the sun rose higher, the clouds gleamed and the icebergs were so white, they seemed to glow from within. Adams stood and picked up his shotgun. He left Robinson sleeping and circled the camp to check for bears. Far to the east, a flock of eider ducks floated like toys on a shallow pond. He returned to the lean-to. Robinson's eyes were open, gazing at the ice.

"Elizabeth," he whispered, "a man once told me he saw beauty where I saw none."

"There is beauty all around us."

"Yes, yes, I see it now," he said. "I once saw a pretty girl, Elizabeth. When she turned her head, when the light fell upon her a certain way, I could see how her face would age, how it would one day be . . . less. The colour in her cheeks would fade, the lines in her face would deepen. Her beauty would go, never to be re-created. That is when I understood— beauty's temporary nature is what makes it exquisite. We desire it so, for we know it will not last."

"I think you have struck at the very heart of the matter," Adams whispered.

Robinson swallowed. "Elizabeth," he gasped. His eyes were wide.

"Yes?" He took Robinson's hand gently in his own and leaned closer.

"It is marvellous, Elizabeth."

"Yes, marvellous."

Adams gripped his hand. Robinson's chest rose and fell with agonising slowness. Shadows cast by the rocks crawled over the earth as the sun moved across the sky. Still holding Robinson's hand, he leaned back and rested on his knapsack. Outside the lean-to, the tips of the wiry grass shivered in the breeze. Robinson's chest deflated slowly, like a punctured bellows.

Adams lay with Robinson's cold fingers curled in his own. Water tinkled in the nearby ravine. The smell of rain was on the air. He thought of Fitzjames slipping quietly away, Billings shot down, and mad young Aylmore at the end of a noose. *Lord,* he thought, *if there is a lesson here, I have learned nothing.*

———

Adams opened Robinson's knapsack and took out his flint and steel, pipe, and notebook. He put them into his knapsack and was about to throw the empty bag to one side when he noticed a flat rectangular object at the bottom. It was a letter. He raised the tent flap and opened it in the grey light.

Captain Sir James Clark Ross, HMS *Enterprise*

Captain Edward Bird, HMS *Investigator*

21 July 1849

Dear Sirs,

It is with the greatest regret that I report my failure to discover the whereabouts of Sir John Franklin and his men. The decision to continue our search south of Fury Beach was mine alone, with Assistant Surgeon Edward Adams and Able Seaman James Billings accompanying me only at my direct order.

I must also regretfully report that Seaman Billings, who displayed great energy and enduring pluck, lost his life in the performance of his duty. I request that all appropriate remuneration be made to his family.

Assistant Surgeon Adams has proved himself a courageous and capable officer in the most difficult of circumstances. I ask that the record reflect his exemplary conduct.

Frederick Robinson

Lieutenant

HMS *Investigator*

Adams folded the letter and sat with it in his lap. Partially melted slabs of ice, thick like gigantic chunks of sugar, sat dissolving in the shallows. The fog had lifted, and the air was clear. A solid mass of cloud stretched almost to the horizon, a grey rug pulled halfway across the pale-pink sky.

He thought of all Franklin's men: skeletons in the soil of King William Land, rotting in the floating mausoleum that was *Erebus*, fed on by bears on the ice off Cape Felix. Bubbling in the cookpots of Gregory's men. Robinson had told him to spend his life another way, to atone for no man's sins but his own. He spit on the ground again, but the acrid taste of Honey's flesh on his tongue persisted. God was telling him how he might absolve himself. Recover the dead, and he might yet sluice the bitter taste from his mouth and the stain from his soul. He had stood over so many graves full of bones he wished to see buried in consecrated ground. If God returned him safely to England, he would return for them. If He did not, he would know that no atonement was possible. For the first time, it was clear.

He was unsure of the date. Captains Ross and Bird would leave Port Leopold any day. He was so very tired.

CHAPTER
TWENTY-THREE

The drizzle persisted for hours. In the afternoon it turned to snow that fell throughout the night. Adams dreamed of snow piling up in ten-foot drifts that buried him without a trace, but in the morning there was only a thin layer of grey slush on the earth. A film of ice had formed on Robinson's eyelashes. Adams brushed it off and pulled the blanket over the blue-white face.

He took Robinson's shot bag and stood over the carcass of the bear, shivering in the cold. With the toe of his boot, he kicked the ramrod protruding from the bear's eye, then bent down and gripped it with his gloved hand. It would not budge. He aimed his shotgun point-blank at the bear's skull and held it there, shaking, for a full minute, but did not pull the trigger.

The sky was a leaden grey, the clouds full of shadows. He walked across the grass to the edge of the ridge and studied the sea. A thin layer of young ice had formed on the water during the night. When the wind rose again, long cracks appeared in the floes to the west, and the icy veneer on the water disappeared. Adams returned to the campsite and began digging the grave. He paused between swings of the shovel to chew on slivers of ox meat and glance into the low hills, searching the gullies for movement. So much blood had been spilled—the ox calf, the bear, Robinson—it would not be long before more bears appeared.

When he had reached a depth of four feet, the blade of the shovel fell off the handle. He stood back, panting. Sweat ran down his face and trickled through his beard.

He crossed Robinson's hands over his chest and wrapped his body in a piece of canvas cut from the tent. It would not leave him with enough canvas to make a tent for himself on the last leg of his journey, but if he could hobble ten miles a day, he guessed he could reach Fury Beach in eight days. If the weather held, if God no longer scowled at him, he could sleep in the open with just his blanket and a torn fragment of canvas. He dragged Robinson's body into the grave and stood over it. He opened his Bible. The text swam in his vision. What would Robinson wish him to say? He shook his head, closed the Bible, and turned his face to the heavens.

"Father," he said aloud, "a man of courage has laid down his life in a noble cause. During his life, he sought but could not find Thee. Now I know he walks with Thee."

Adams put Robinson's pipe and silver pencil case in the dead man's coat pocket. He filled in the grave and stamped down on the earth. He looked around for a landmark he would remember when he returned for Robinson's remains. There was nothing. The surrounding land was bare and flat—all mud, gravel, clay, and rock scraped flat for millennia by the ice. He scanned the ground for stones to build a cairn, but there were none. The land had already swallowed him.

He stood the lieutenant's shotgun vertically in the grave, its muzzle pointing downward. The gunstock would be Robinson's grave marker. He would see the artificial shape protruding from the earth if the weather was clear, but he would need to return within a year to find this site again. Any longer and the grave would fill with rainwater that would freeze and thaw and freeze again. The gun would topple to the earth, or a passing Esquimaux, astonished by his find, would pluck the gun from the soil, and then there would be no recovering him. Adams stood at the grave until he began to shiver, then turned away. He folded chunks of ox meat into strips of dirty canvas and placed them in his knapsack. He left the stove and the broken shovel on the ground and strapped Robinson's telescope across his back. The sledge held little more than his blanket bag and floorcloth now. He gripped his shotgun and walked north with his unlit pipe in his teeth.

———

Meltwater falls emptied over two-hundred-foot cliffs. A strip of grey mist hovered over the water to the west like a cloud plucked from the heavens and laid out like a blanket on the sea. Two hours before midnight, the moon rose in a purple sky. Adams approached a stretch of moraine and picked his way gingerly over boulders the size of pumpkins. He chewed on pieces of ox meat as he walked and splashed across a flat, pebbly riverbed before reaching a field of Arctic cotton. Droplets of water hung trembling like glass lamps from the woolly white heads of each tiny plant.

From a hilltop he saw an enormous glacier filling the mouth of a valley to the north. The mile-wide river of ice stretched inland, a gigantic stream of molten glass covering the plain. As he approached, he saw the face of the glacier was riven with cracks. Teased out by the approaching summer, water gushed from beneath the glacier like arterial blood. The urgent force of the torrent had carved trenches twenty feet wide through the sharp rocks below the ice shelf, the grey water jumping and seething.

Shotgun at the ready, he followed bear tracks that descended through a series of narrow ravines, each separated by a ridge that rose like the spine of some buried monster. Purple saxifrage was an angry rash across the gravel. In the evening, a curtain of shadow rose over sheer granite cliffs above him, and it was very cold. A pair of hares bounded across the sand in front of him. He shot one and stood over the ruined carcass, looking down at the creature's dead eye. He left the animal untouched on the ground and walked on.

———

The thought of finding Port Leopold deserted filled him with terror. Could he live for two years on the provisions Captain Ross would leave there for Franklin's men? He knew he would not survive that long.

But if he did? He imagined them finding him there, stick-thin and toothless, filthy and mad, tripping on his long beard. They would take him back, put him in a sideshow, and charge a penny a time. *Look, good people! Come and see what the Arctic does to a man!*

Then he was seized by a different fear. Perhaps they already knew what he and Robinson had discovered, what they had done. Perhaps Captain Ross' team had reached King William Land, found the campsite at Victory Point, and returned to Port Leopold before him. They would have seen the grave of the half-eaten man, the bones on the ground. They may have crossed the ice and found Honey's shrouded corpse with its unnatural wounds. Walker and Dunn may have spun their own tale, with Adams as the villain. Surely *Investigator* and *Enterprise* would sail away and leave him to his fate. What sort of decent Royal Navy captain would not?

A sound like a rifle shot made him whirl around. A large ice floe, two hundred yards long, had broken off the main pack and moved lazily on the tide. The floe fouled itself in the shallows and broke into four smaller pieces. Adams watched the chunks spin in the water. Then something far away on the southern skyline caught his eye. He had known only the straight, flat lines of treeless horizons for weeks. A distant, unfamiliar shape now snagged his attention like a garment on a nail. Before he raised the telescope, he knew what he had seen.

He tried to guess the distance. Ten miles? Perhaps more. The hollow sensation in his stomach was not hunger. The tremor in his hand was not fatigue.

He saw a man.

Summer was near its end, but the seasons seemed to change in reverse as Adams fled north. He crossed regions still mired in winter, with streams frozen and stretches of iron-hard ground dusted with snow. He sought the colder, harder ground that was easiest to walk upon, detouring hundreds of yards to avoid swamps of knee-deep mud.

An enormous mesa rose from the surrounding land, shrouded by a thin band of white clouds. A colony of guillemots stood guard on the two-hundred-foot cliffs. They squawked and cackled with a jarring nonchalance, like a crowd jostling and gossiping at a market on an unremarkable day. He thought to stop for eggs, but the nests were too far above his head, the bluff too sheer to climb. The birds jeered at him as he headed north.

He slept in depressions in the earth and the lee of boulders, his shotgun primed and cradled in his arms. His hands and feet were numb with cold. He had lost his flint and steel and could find no driftwood for a fire. He placed his knapsack of ox meat beneath him and pulled his mutilated canvas cape over himself. His entire body felt swollen. Pain in his stomach, his back, his feet. Bears stalked his dreams, their massive jaws wide. He tried to recall the sensation of heat upon his skin, but no such memory would come to him. When he woke, a hard shell of frost crackled on his blanket and cap.

He arrived at a ravine thirty feet across and fifty feet deep. The chasm was an enormous crack in the earth, pried apart by some great creature with gigantic claws, extending to the ocean in the west and east as far as he could see. He explored the edge of the narrow gorge on the ocean side until he found a section of the steep, rocky slope he was strong enough to descend.

Tossing his knapsack to the ravine floor, he climbed gingerly down the cliff wall. He used the harness to lower the sledge, feeling for hand-holds as he went. He rested to suck on some ox meat at the bottom of the chasm. Tiny pools of water glistened in a line of huge paw prints strung out across a patch of mud.

He proceeded up the opposite wall with his knapsack on his back and the sledge dangling from the rope tied around his waist. Each time he found a handhold, he paused to haul the sledge up and balance it on an outcrop before climbing higher. After two hours, he crawled over the ravine's edge and lay gasping, staring at the sky.

"There you are."

Adams jumped to his feet. Walker stood on the opposite side of the ravine. His face was streaked with filth, and his brown beard was shot through with grey, but he looked strong and nourished. He stared down into the chasm, then regarded Adams with admiration.

"Looks like that took some work to get across." He dropped his bedroll and sat on the ground, canteen in hand. "I don't fancy rushing it. Think I'll rest for a bit first. Took a bit out of me, catching you up." He took a swig from his canteen. "Nearly lost you comin' over the ice," he said.

Adams did not reply.

"I found an ox carcass," said Walker. "Was that you? A bear had been at it, but there was a bit left for me." He toasted Adams with his canteen. "I thank thee for that."

Adams found his voice. "Where is Dunn?"

"Where is the lieutenant?" Walker shot back. He winked. "Didn't do anything rash, did you?"

"A bear," he said, then swore inwardly at himself. He owed this man no explanation.

Walker's expression was sympathetic. "Ah. Poor chap. Unlucky." He took another drink. "Frankie was unlucky too."

Adams swallowed. "Are you saying Dunn met a bear as well?"

Walker shrugged. "Something like that."

"What is your intention?"

Walker looked surprised. "My intention? Thought you knew that. I'm goin' home. I don't know the way, so I'm followin' you."

"And when we get back?"

Walker smiled, revealing gaps between broken yellow teeth. "I'm sure we can reach an understandin'. *Brave officer rescues Franklin's last man,* somethin' like that. You'll get to meet the bloody queen."

"I shall report only the truth."

Walker's eyes narrowed. "Oh, you don't want to do that. You wouldn't want Sir John's last man to hang, would you? How would that look?"

"The magistrate will decide."

Walker clucked. "And there I was thinkin' you were a reasonable fella. Might as well have let the lieutenant shoot me." He let out a sigh and looked almost wistful. "I was ready for it then. I was. I'd had enough. I wanted 'im to do it." Then his reverie was broken, and his expression was stony. "I don't feel that way now, though. I've come this far. I rather fancy gettin' home."

Adams seized his shotgun and knapsack and ran.

———

He hurried north. A row of tall boulders stooped over the shingle like taciturn idols. He stumbled up a steep slope and along the top of a cliff, seeking a view to the south. He swept the horizon with his telescope but did not see Walker. He chewed his lip, waiting for his breathing to slow. The undulating coastline was pocked with small bays and cliffs. Any one of them could conceal an army. He rechecked his shotgun and limped on through a grassy field. Two butterflies with brown-and-orange wings fluttered past his head. He reached another cliff, whose edge was not sheer but a scree slope slanting down to a point twenty feet below. Beyond that was a hundred-foot drop.

He mulled tactics. Should he conceal himself behind a boulder and ambush Walker as he followed? Should he just run? A flock of ducks flew overhead and vanished into the russet sky. His boots had walked on ten thousand stones, but this one rolled under his boot, wet and slippery like a small piece of the earth come alive. He stumbled, and his boot slid out. His leg twisted. Something in his ankle tore, and a boiling liquid shot up through his leg. His back arched in agony, and the sound of a wild creature escaped his lips. The world tilted and crashed. His cheek struck the earth hard, and the telescope and his knapsack of ox meat slid from his back. Dazed, he watched them gather speed as they slid down the scree to the cliff edge. The knapsack struck a large rock, flipped into the air, and disappeared into the chasm below. The telescope slid and stopped at the precipice before it spun twice like the hands of a clock. It stood for an instant in a final salute and was gone.

He lay with his teeth clenched and his eyes screwed shut at the pain in his ankle. When he could sit up, he bent over the injured leg. He tugged his mittens off with his teeth. The skin around his ankle was intact but already blackening. Even with fingertips seared and deadened by the cold, he could feel the ankle swelling. He feared he would not get his boot back on his swollen foot if he removed it. He sat sucking air through his teeth until the pain eased from a blaze to a throb.

He still had his shotgun, and his shot bag was slung across his chest. He rolled up his blanket bag as tightly as possible, then made a crude harness from the track rope and put the rolled-up blanket on his back. The final piece of tent canvas, now barely five feet long, became a raincoat tied around his shoulders. There was no sign of Walker on the cliff behind him. Was Walker as weary as he? Was he hurt? He abandoned the sledge and hobbled north like a beggar with his bedroll on his back.

The thaw had altered the shape and colour of the country since he and Robinson had gone south seven weeks earlier. He scanned the surrounding area for landmarks but recognised nothing. The melt had made a rushing river of what had been a shallow brook running an inch deep over stones. He sat on the rocky bank and rolled down his stocking. The flesh around his ankle was fat and black, but he did not think the bone was broken. He hobbled upstream for two hours until he found a shallow place to ford the river. He removed his boot and numbed his swollen ankle in the freezing water, then bound it with a length of flannel torn from his shirt.

A duck's nest lay at his feet. He dropped to his knees and pulled aside the down and grass lining of the nest. Five pale-green eggs. He tipped his head back, swallowed the eggs' contents, and tossed the shells on the ground. A short silent prayer on his lips, he rose to his feet using the shotgun as a crutch and limped on, cursing his slow pace. Every minute, he stopped to look over his shoulder, ready to drop with fatigue. His head slumped, and he saw only the gravel three feet ahead.

When he had not slept for a day, a tall shadow rose before him, and he cried out in fear. The sun was in his eyes. His injured ankle gave way, and he fell backward. He pulled the trigger of the shotgun and heard the ball strike stone. The sound of the blast receded. He squinted up at the shape looming over him. Silhouetted against the sun was the cairn of stones he and Robinson had built seven weeks earlier to alert Franklin's men to the provisions left for them at Port Leopold. He stared at the structure and thought of Robinson returning Crozier's message cylinder to the cairn at Victory Point, two hundred miles and half a dozen men's lives ago.

Who will reward us for delivering such news? Robinson had asked. *They will call us liars.*

Would Robinson have had him tear this cairn down too? Perhaps he would have urged Adams to leave no trace of their passage along this shore. There would be so many questions. He hung his head and tried to think. To the west, the ice pack was streaked with wide cracks. Small chunks of ice bobbed in the shallows. A waning gibbous moon was like a broken button on the sky. The scurvy left his mind feeling dull, like an overused blade. He remembered Samuel Honey's words: *Some questions a man has no answer for.*

He groaned and rose to his feet.

Walker had not shown himself for hours, but Adams' pace had flagged since his injury, and he knew the man must be close. He would have heard the shot.

———

Adams thought he might die here.

He stood at the top of a rocky bluff, staring down at a mile-wide channel of boiling black water he had no means of crossing. He dropped to his knees and put his face in his hands, a gnarled claw in his gut. *The thread of my life has unravelled and brought me farther than I ever imagined,* he thought, *but I think no more remains on the spool.*

He was very tired. He could not remember crossing such a wide channel on his journey south with Robinson. How could they have missed it? Then he thought of the pack he had seen splinter in the ocean to the west and understood. A month earlier, the shore ice had extended west into the waters of the sound, allowing them to travel quickly down the coast. They had unknowingly crossed the mouth of a frozen strait, thinking it merely the floor of another snow-covered valley.

How was he to cross a mile of open water? He cursed himself for agreeing to abandon the airboat on the shores of Boothia after crossing the ice pack from King William Land. Had it been a week since then? A hundred miles? Too far to go back and retrieve it. He thought of the whaleboat abandoned by Crozier's men on King William Land. Sitting on a sledge dragged across miles of gravel, it had seemed so absurd. But Crozier had known open water lay ahead.

He would have to find a place to cross. A mile to the east, a bank of mist hovered over the strait. With the arrival of summer, much of the snow had melted from the surrounding ridges, revealing featureless brown hills. He stumbled down a gravel slope before making his way eastward for two miles along the shore of the strait. An enormous bank of grey clouds billowed in the northern sky, poised like a beast's claws about to strike. A powerful wind buffeted his face. He smelled rain.

The width of the channel narrowed as he progressed, until it was no more than half a mile. Confined in the sheltered part of the channel, a section of ice remained intact where the two sides of the strait were closest, forming a bridge two hundred yards wide.

He would cross here.

Light rain began to fall. The sky darkened. Downstream from the rigid section of ice, loose pieces of the floe rose and fell on the strong current. The wind freshened. A large fragment of ice bucked on the swell, detached itself from the pack's western edge, and began moving away on the tide toward the mouth of the strait. He realised the ice bridge to the far shore was breaking up. If he did not traverse it now and reach the opposite shore, the ice would disintegrate, and he would never get across.

Soon I shall encounter Charon, waiting on his skiff, he thought, *but I have no money to pay him, so I must wander these shores for a hundred years.*

He sensed movement behind him and turned.

Walker stood no more than a hundred yards away.

The seaman shouted to be heard over the wind. "What is your name?"

Adams stared back at him.

Walker called again. "You never told me your name!"

Adams levelled his shotgun and fired. Walker flinched at the sound of the blast, dropping into a crouch. When he saw he was not struck, he straightened, blinking. His own shotgun was at his shoulder as he approached. Adams aimed and pulled the trigger again. He heard the click, but no explosion followed.

Walker grinned. "They will do that. 'Specially when they get wet." He crossed the distance between them and stopped three feet from Adams with the barrel of his gun pointed at his face.

"I have a confession," he said. He threw the shotgun to the ground. "I've had no ball or shot left this past week. But it's good for show. Helped me get close to you, didn't it?" He reached a hand under his coat and brought out a knife. "This still works, though."

Adams bent over in surrender. He lowered his shotgun.

Walker smiled.

Adams went for him then.

Expecting Adams to recoil from the knife, Walker's eyes widened as Adams brought the shotgun around, gripped in both hands like an axe. Walker threw his arms up to protect his face, but Adams had gone for the leg. The shotgun barrel struck Walker on the side of the knee. Something cracked. Walker screamed. The force of the blow swept both his legs out from under him and he went down.

Adams ran.

CHAPTER
TWENTY-FOUR

Adams hunched his shoulders into the wind. The rain came at him in freezing bullets out of the north. He stepped off the shingle and ran out onto the frozen strait, where the gravel shore met the unbroken section of ice spanning the channel. The floe under his feet was intact, but ahead he could see cracks where the shore ice met the pack. Behind him, Walker followed down the slope, knife in hand, his knapsack and bedroll shouldered. He hopped desperately on his left leg, the injured right leg flailing. He crumpled and fell but was almost immediately on his feet again, using his shotgun as a crutch.

Adams turned away and hobbled forward over the ice. The heavens were the colour of old steel. The hills on the far shore rose in the dim light. He pulled his heavy coat tight around himself and dropped his head into the face of the gale. A crash of thunder shook the air. His body convulsed in the cold. He splashed through shallow pools, his injured ankle numb in its boot. Slung around his shoulders, the remnants of the tent canvas flapped against his legs.

Pieces broke off the pack and floated away, bobbing in the violent current. The width bridging the strait had narrowed to only a hundred yards. Squinting through the gale, he could feel the ice bucking under his feet, wanting to burst. Far to his left, the floe split open as cleanly as skin parting under a scalpel blade. A chunk the size of a carriage floated free of the pack. Black water fountained through the widening gap like blood from an artery.

He looked back. Walker remained in pursuit. The seaman had reached the edge of the icebound strait and set out across it with his shotgun crutch, slipping and scrambling like some demented three-legged insect. He waved an arm, held a hand to his mouth as if shouting, but Adams heard nothing over the storm.

Adams was halfway across the strait when he slipped and fell on his face, his chin ploughing the ice. A hot smear of pain licked his jaw, and bright blood trickled in his beard. He scrambled to his feet and kept moving, blood pumping in his throat, muscles twisting like cords. Three hundred yards ahead of him, three indistinct grey shadows moved on the ice. A bear and two half-grown cubs stood between him and the far shore of the strait. They moved with a languid indifference to the gale. The adult sow padded patiently over the ice, her head swinging back and forth. The two cubs trailed in her wake, their coats slick with rain.

Adams dropped to his knees, blinking through the teeming water. The sow wandered across to his left and out of his path, her attention focused on the floe's edge. Behind her, the two cubs stopped and sat on the ice. One nuzzled the other, which raised its snout and yawned and lazily batted its sibling with a paw. He looked over his shoulder. Walker was four hundred yards behind him, dragging his bad leg in a crab-like scuttle, something between a crawl and a stagger.

Adams gripped his wet and useless shotgun. Beyond the bears he could see the ice cracking, pounded by the dual onslaught of wind and current. The span to the far side was now barely fifty yards wide. The sow raised her head and seemed to gaze directly at him through the wall of rain. He did not move. His knees and hips were afire, the wind like a scourger's cat on his neck. The bear stood unmoving, her snout in the air. Blood dripped from his lacerated chin onto his hands. He held his breath.

The bear swung its head to look back at its offspring. The cubs moved toward her, their padded feet sliding over the ice. The three animals ambled away. As he watched, the ice they rode broke up, and they slid casually into the black water. Their heads moved away in the current.

Lord, keep me and make me strong.

Adams wiped the rain from his eyes, then rose to his feet and ran in his hobbling, broken gait. A violent gust caught the saturated blanket on his back and threw him sideways. For an instant he mistook a crack of thunder for a shotgun blast, thinking Walker had somehow kept his weapon dry and opened fire. He did not look back.

He ran on. The ice bridge ahead of him was almost gone. Chunks separated from the edge every few moments, ripped away by the current. Water spouted up through the ice as it cracked and split around him.

He was yards from shore when a fissure opened in the ice beneath his boots. He raised the shotgun, heavy as an iron bar, and threw it with both hands. It fell on the rocky shore and slid to a halt inches from the water's edge. The ice below him parted, and he sank waist deep in the freezing water. The pain took all his breath, tearing at him as though some great jawed beast had seized him around the midsection. He took the last few steps up the slope onto the shingle and sat, shaking and gasping. The rain eased to a drizzle, and the wind abated.

Walker stood on a small, jagged floe thirty feet across, two hundred yards away in the strait. The ice between him and the shore was gone. He glanced down at the cracks in the ice at his feet, then looked up and stared across at Adams. The little floe fractured and burst, and Walker dropped straight down into the black water.

When the sun emerged, Adams laid out his blanket to dry on the stones and cleaned his gun, then walked inland through the silence. Winter stalked him across the waste, drawing a blanket of cold and darkness across the land. When the sun slept, either side of midnight, he moved through a cold, murky twilight until it reappeared minutes later, weary and old. Heavy rain churned the earth's surface, and he was black to the waist. During the brief night, ice had formed on the surface of the mud. He stumbled for twenty miles around the shore of an enormous shallow lake spread across the land like a mirror.

The soles of his boots were holed in half a dozen places, and sharp stones cut into his feet. The pain of his swollen ankle was merely one of many now; fires blazed in his joints, limbs, and bowels. His head throbbed, and his legs swelled with edema. The evening sun dripped molten iron through a gash in a bank of grey clouds. Two days after leaving the coast, his knees buckled, and he could not rise. He scanned his surroundings for a boulder to crawl behind, yet there was nothing but an endless stretch of flat, stony gravel. Green stubble coated a row of hills in the distance.

Perhaps the bears would stay close to the coast to hunt seals and not concern him here. He drew his blanket and canvas over himself, clutched his shotgun to his chest, and slept on the open ground. He dreamed of his own mutilated body in the stony earth, thawing and refreezing with the cycles of the seasons. Dead eyes filmed over, staring into a midnight-blue shroud an inch from his nose, men visiting to cut at his flesh.

He woke in a puddle, shivering with fever. His breath came fast and sharp. An unfamiliar knocking in his ear was the sound of his teeth chattering. He curled into a ball and lay on the stony ground as the sun sank and ignited the horizon in fiery hues.

Lord, I had once hoped for Paradise, but Thou hath sent me to another place entirely.

Something moved over the stones nearby. He pulled the blanket from his face and rolled over, his shotgun cold and heavy in his hands. Twenty yards away, a fox stared back at him. He shot it and crawled over the gravel to where the creature lay. He pulled out his knife and skinned it, ripping the fur from the still-steaming flesh. The blood ran in his whiskers as he ate the fox raw.

The empty land stretched away in all directions. The blue sky pushed down upon him. He sat shivering on the cold ground, his white breath on the air, and wept for a long time. Without knowing he could, he stood and walked.

A shrivelled, skeletal Sir John Franklin walked beside him, his uniform hanging off him in tatters.

"Sir John, it was all lies," Adams said. "The Arctic has an ocean, but not one a ship can sail across. It has a sun that burns the skin and the eyes but offers no warmth. It has wild beasts that will eat a man but provide precious little food. It has so many dead men but so few graves."

"It is not such a prize, is it?" Franklin said. "I wonder what made us want it so. Once uttered, a lie can harden and become as durable as clay fired in a kiln. A man need only laugh and spin a yarn for a falsehood to become fact. It takes so little effort to make it true."

The fingers of night stole out a little farther each day. The sun sank at ten in the evening and rose again at two in the morning. He had lost over an hour of daylight in the past week alone. He limped around a headland and was confronted by another wide river. Yellow poppies grew under his feet. He stopped and leaned on his shotgun. For the first time in weeks, the blue-grey ocean was visible to the east: Prince Regent Inlet.

He drank from his canteen and hobbled on over the gravel. His ankles and hips and knees screamed, and his heart thrashed in his chest. His boot fell apart and lay in pieces on the ground, the sodden leather soft and rotten like old skin. Swaddling his heel and ankle with strips of flannel, he tied the last patches of canvas around his leg and limped on. A hidden sun suffused the clouds with a pink blush, then emerged like the eye of an omnipotent being lifting a heavy blanket to peer down at the forlorn creature shuffling along beneath.

—

Adams stared out across Prince Regent Inlet from the hills above Fury Beach.

The ice that had covered the sea weeks earlier had thinned, but he could see the waters near the shore rotating and thickening like honey. The ocean would soon freeze again. Leads in the ice were like veins across white skin. A blurry silhouette flickered behind a curtain of wind. Shaking with fever, he stumbled toward it. The wind blew harder. The source was a tremendous taloned beast with three faces, standing in the ice, trapped, beating its wings to drive all warmth from the world. The figures of men, lost souls, hung suspended under the ice. The beast held a corpse in each of its three sets of jaws, pawing at him, raking him with its claws. Adams staggered back, cried out, threw up his hands. The men began climbing up the beast's legs from beneath the ice, grabbing handfuls of its hair and clutching at him. Franklin's men, toothless and toeless and fingerless, with their eyes still filmed over from their time in their shrouds, stabbed him with bony fingers. Others pressed him with suppurating sores and bared their teeth to show fragments of rotten flesh. Adams heard them imploring him over the roar of the wind.

This is what awaits you if you abandon us.

Hands gripped Adams' shoulders, pawed at his arms.

"Edward!"

Adams screamed. He tore himself from the men's grasp, but they followed him. He wheeled away and fell, sprawling on the stones. Their shadows fell across over him, blocking the light. His pursuers reached down to him. He covered his face with his hands and thought, *I am damned.*

"Edward? Is that you?"

Adams opened his eyes and peered through his fingers. Five men stood over him. He lowered his hands and stared into the face of his friend, John Barnard, second lieutenant on *Investigator*. His own ship. Next to Barnard, he recognised Thomas Osbourne, *Investigator*'s boatswain. Adams stared at the smooth faces and trimmed whiskers in wonder.

Barnard's face went slack in shock. "Edward, can you stand?"

The men started talking in a rush. Adams could not make out their words. Their faces were clean, their backs straight. They were giants, as strong as oxen. Barnard helped him to his feet. Adams looked around and saw the weathered timber bones of Somerset House. He had been here before. With Robinson. With Billings and Humphreys, looking for Sir John. It was the ruined hut built at Fury Beach by John Ross a quarter century earlier, now more imposing, more breathtaking than the grandest mansion. So long ago now.

A large boat, fifty feet long, was drawn high up on the stony beach. A steam engine sat in the boat just forward of the centre, its exhaust tube rising ten feet above the gunwale. For a moment, Adams could only stare at it. Then he understood what he saw. Captain Bird had sent *Investigator*'s steam launch. *Twelve miles an hour,* he thought. *If the water was calm and there is little ice, it can do twelve miles an hour.*

"Edward, where is Lieutenant Robinson?" Barnard's hand gripped his shoulder. "Is he following behind?"

Adams dropped his shotgun and blanket. Barnard caught him as he fell.

———

Later he would have no memory of it, but Barnard told him the journey back to Port Leopold from Fury Beach took nine hours.

"We were fortunate," Barnard said. "Captains Ross and Bird have had us cutting a canal in the harbour ice to get the ships out. The ice will break up soon. And then we shall leave." He put an arm around Adams' shoulders. "I think perhaps Sir John and Captain Crozier will be there on the dock at Woolwich when we get back. I can only think we have missed them somehow."

Adams woke to the smell of unwashed bodies and pork fat. Mission commander Captain Sir James Clark Ross gazed down at him. Captain Edward Bird, his face impassive, appeared behind Ross and gently closed the door to the tiny room. Adams recognised the timbers and shelves around him—he was in *Investigator*'s sick bay.

Ross' face was pale and deeply lined, as if somebody had gone to work on him with a knife, sculpting him crudely from a lump of his own flesh. For a moment, Adams thought Ross was frowning at him, but the grimace on his face told him the man was in considerable pain. Leaning on a cane, Ross carefully lowered himself onto a stool beside Adams' bunk, grunting with the effort.

"Well, Mister Adams," Ross said, "I am glad to see you back with us. We had thought you were lost. All the other sledge teams have been back for weeks. Most of the men are terribly fatigued. I understand you have endured much hardship. My own sledge journey was not easy either. You must get well. We have need of your services—there is much sickness aboard. Debility, scurvy, and more. We shall discuss that. But first things first."

The captain leaned forward, placing his weight on his cane, until his face was inches from Adams' own. Ross' breath stank of brandy. Adams turned away.

"Tell me, did you find anything?" Ross asked. "How far south did you go? Was there any sign of him?"

If his body was stronger, his mind clearer, he may have tried to soften the edges of the tale. He might have stitched together a narrative from facts, half-truths, and outright lies to satisfy Ross and Adams' own conscience. But when he began, the words gushed from him and would not stop. He omitted no detail, embellished nothing. Ross remained silent for most of it. He interrupted only occasionally to ask short, pointed questions. Ross shifted in his chair to relieve the stiffness in his limbs. His face bore a guarded, pained expression. Standing behind Ross, Bird remained impassive, his face gradually draining of colour. When Adams had finished, Ross stared at the blank wall and chewed his lip. Adams waited for an outburst, a reprimand, but Ross looked thoughtful, his expression no longer one of shock but of indecision. His gaze returned to Adams.

"You are not to breathe a word of this to anyone."

Without waiting for an answer, Ross stood abruptly and left the room. Bird glanced down at Adams with a look of the purest wonder, then followed Ross out and slid the door closed.

CHAPTER
TWENTY-FIVE

Barnard visited Adams in his sick bunk.

"My sledge team reached the north shore of Barrow Strait," he said, "but we could go no further. It was only forty miles to Cape Hurd, but my men were completely spent. I have never seen such ice. Hummocks thirty feet high. I dearly wished to proceed further to Wellington Channel, but I could not in good conscience risk the lives of my men."

Adams studied his friend. The junior lieutenant was thinner than he remembered, not the giant he had imagined when rescued at Fury Beach. Grey hairs sprouted in the young man's brown whiskers.

"We are cutting our way out of the harbour ice," Barnard went on. "Two hundred feet per day. But it has been so cold, Edward. There is little meltwater on the ice, and it is still several feet thick. Captain Ross has every available man at the saws. We are scattering gravel on the ice to melt it, but it is hard work, and so many of the men are unwell. If we do not get out of here, I worry we will be trapped for another winter."

Adams lay back and closed his eyes.

"Captain Ross says we are to continue the search," Barnard said. "Once we are out of the harbour, we are to head for the north shore of Barrow Strait and then to Wellington Channel. I believe he wants to try for Melville Island. It seems we can go neither forward nor back." He leaned forward to whisper. "Edward, there is much sickness aboard.

Most of those who went on the sledge missions remain ill. Dr Robertson himself nearly died of scurvy over the summer, and we lost poor Mister Matthias while you were away. They say he had consumption before he even left England. Two dozen men are in their sick bunks. The preserved provisions are of such poor quality, and we cannot shoot enough fowl for everybody. If we try to sail west to Melville Island, I fear for us all. Captain Ross has left a depot of provisions and built a hut for Franklin's men from the spare spars. He has even left them *Investigator's* steam launch. Do you think they will find it?"

Adams opened his eyes and studied the ceiling. "I don't know, John."

"I could not see it before," Barnard whispered. He seemed anxious to divulge a great secret.

Adams patted his hand. "What is it you see, John?"

"I could never understand how one hundred and twenty-nine men and two of Her Majesty's ships could become trapped. I was sure that if the ice blocked Sir John and his men, they would merely turn around. I think now of my conviction, and I feel foolish."

"Man is a creature of great hubris, John. I find myself thinking this a great deal."

Barnard nodded dully. "Why do we think ourselves in control of what only God can determine?"

Adams gripped his hand. He sat up and gazed into Barnard's eyes. "Yes, John. That is it precisely. Someone I knew once told me God does not enter into transactions. One cannot buy a ticket to His grace."

"Will you write an account of your journey, Edward? The newspapers would pay well for your tale."

"I do not wish to speak of it." *I shall write no letters,* he thought. *Not to Frances, not to Lieutenant Robinson's wife. I shall make no entries in my journal.*

His story was a monster trapped in his head. He would not wish it into existence and see it wreak havoc only to discover he could not banish it to whence it came. He would keep it shackled and unseen in a black hole.

Adams gazed at two-hundred-foot icebergs that emerged and then disappeared again in swirling fog banks. His scurvy symptoms had eased in the two weeks since he arose from the sick bunk to which he had been confined for a month. *Investigator's* shooting parties had brought in fresh fowl and eggs, but his weight remained twenty-five pounds less than before the sledge mission. The swelling in his ankle had subsided, but he could not arrest the tremor in his hands.

The ice that had imprisoned the two ships was breaking up. Leaving Port Leopold a month before, Ross had ordered the ships to steer north across Barrow Strait, hoping to make for Wellington Channel. Instead, *Enterprise* and *Investigator* were swept 250 miles eastward, cemented in the heart of a 200-square-mile floe. Helpless, the two vessels were like toys on an enormous white platter, borne along on the current into Baffin Bay.

Captain Ross decided not to sail back into the ice with a sick crew. When he gave the order to turn for home, the crews of both vessels wept with joy. They ran around the upper deck, whooping with excitement. Men forgot their enmities and abandoned grudges born of prolonged proximity. They embraced and slapped each other on the back.

Adams stood at the gunwale, watching snow flurries turn to fog. Minutes later, the mist lifted to reveal blue skies scraped bare of cloud by the sun. The sea changed its cloak hourly, clear of ice one moment, then cluttered with bergs that glowed from within. Countless tiny pieces the size of a man's hand bobbed in the water, as if a berg had detonated somewhere, belching fragments of itself out across the sea. As the sun set, the ocean turned the colour of ink, and the three masts of HMS *Enterprise* were stencilled like charred trees on the blazing western sky.

———

Captain Sir James Clark Ross went ashore at Scarborough and sum-moned Adams to a small tavern near the waterfront. As he made his way from the dock, Adams caught the odour of horse manure and open drains. A light drizzle was cold on his face. He pulled his cap down and turned up his collar. Carriage wheels and horses' hooves clattered on the cobbles. He scraped the manure from his boots on a stone and stepped through the tavern door.

Ross awaited him in a small, gloomy room at the rear of the build-ing. The walls were bare, the plaster cracked and stained. The window looked out on a narrow alley. Adams glanced through dirt-streaked glass at bricks slimy with moss. A blackened fireplace in the wall was empty and cold. A pair of candles and a bottle of brandy stood in the middle of a long table. The brandy was the colour of honey in the candlelight.

Ross ushered him into the room and closed the door. He was unsteady on his feet. Most of the sledge-team members had begun to recover in the weeks since the ships left Port Leopold, but the mission commander remained unwell. He shuffled away from the door, his cane tapping on the timbers. He walked slowly across the room to a straight-backed chair next to the table. His lined and pouchy face, red-rimmed eyes, and thick white hair made him seem far older than his forty-nine years. The captain sank into the chair with a grunt. He bent forward and placed both elbows on the table before him, bowing his head and lacing his fingers like a penitent sinner. He glanced at Adams, then looked away again.

"You are looking better, I see."

"Yes, sir."

Ross nodded distractedly. "Good."

He examined the table's surface, then poured some brandy into a glass and swilled it around. Adams noticed something unfamiliar in Ross' manner. The aloof, soldierly demeanour of the navy's greatest polar explorer was absent, replaced with the insouciance of a man exhausted after setting down a heavy load. And then he understood.

Ross was drunk.

The commander frowned at him. "Oh, at ease, man! Our mission is ended. I am weary of formalities."

"Thank you, sir."

"Sit."

Ross pointed to a chair. He poured Adams a brandy, pushed the glass across the table at him, then sat back in his chair and rubbed his eyes. The two men drank. Voices carried faintly through the door from the tavern. A shoeblack called out for trade in the street outside. Adams heard the fluttering of pigeons. Ross sat back in his chair and eyed him.

"Mister Adams, we are to be conspirators, you and I. Guardians of a secret. Oh yes, Captain Bird, too, of course. But he will say nothing. Drink."

Adams sipped from his glass and felt the brandy burn his throat. Warmth spread through his veins.

"I am to take the carriage from here straight to Whitehall," said Ross, "and there I shall deliver my report to the Admiralty. So . . ." He drained his glass, set it back on the table, and poured himself another. "This is what I shall tell them: I shall say we found no trace of Sir John. I shall recommend that no further search expeditions enter Lancaster Sound from the east. I shall tell them the ice in Barrow Strait is too heavy to penetrate and not worth more lives. All this, I happen to believe most sincerely." He stood and turned and stared into the dead fireplace. "At least I can begin with the truth, but I cannot end with it. Lieutenant Robinson was entirely correct about one thing: I cannot possibly repeat the remainder of your tale to Whitehall. The Admiralty would not accept it, even from me. I would receive a better reception if I walked in and dumped a rotting corpse on their mahogany table."

Adams drank. He felt lightheaded. An image of Honey's corpse lingered in his head, sprawled across a polished wooden table, buzzing with flies. Their Lordships were sitting back and examining it sagely through their pince-nez, port and cigars in their hands. Ross turned back to face Adams across the table.

"And yet we cannot leave them out there. I have known Sir John and Frank Crozier for thirty years. Even if they are gone, I must ensure they are buried at home. And as many of the others as we can find." He reached out one hand and held it close to the candle flame, turning it, watching the yellow light curl and bounce on his fingertips. "I will tell Whitehall to continue the search from the west through Behrings Strait, to follow the northern coast of the mainland, past the mouth of the Mackenzie south of Wollaston Land and past Point Turnagain. I don't suppose they shall get there before the summer of '51."

Adams blinked. The brandy sang in his chest and his fingertips.

"I never guessed they went as far south as they did," said Ross softly, as if talking to himself. "My God, King William Land. Even now I cannot imagine how he managed it through so much ice." He was silent for a moment, then poured himself another drink. "It was supposed to be me, you know, in '45. Lord Haddington wanted me to go after I returned from Antarctica. Instead, I recommended he appoint Sir John."

"You promised your wife you would not go to the Arctic again." The brandy had loosened Adams' tongue.

"You know about that?" Ross laughed. "Well, I suppose it is no secret. Of all your promises, make sure you keep the ones you make to your wife. She loved Frank Crozier as much as I did, though, so she let me go and look for my friend. But now I am finished. I cannot be the one to go next time."

The blood in Adams' veins was all brandy now, rich and hot. He nodded, his head heavy, wobbling on his neck. "Promises must be kept," he intoned.

Ross regarded him with a kind expression. "Were you and Lieutenant Robinson friends?"

Adams cupped his glass with both hands and stared into its caramel depths. He thought of Robinson's silence in the wake of Samuel Honey's death, and then the lieutenant's blood pooling in the gravel and his fingers going cold in Adams' hand.

"I would not know how to describe it, sir." He took another drink. Tears were on his cheeks. "I would need to invent a new language entirely."

"The Arctic is full of Sirens, calling one back," said Ross. "Nine winters I've spent in the ice. I would not survive another. But I would like you to go. Find the graves. Just do not mention that business on King William Land."

"I will atone for my sins," said Adams. The stinging burn of Honey's flesh on his tongue was there again, reminding him. No quantity of brandy could scour it away.

"We all must," said Ross. "I have spent my life searching for things. Sometimes we do not find them. But our friends are never truly lost. They are always somewhere."

Adams understood that the truth of Franklin's fate was not a secret but a disease he now shared with Ross. It was a sickness afflicting those who returned alive. It could turn a man's hair white and line his face and leave him crippled with guilt. It was like a can of putrid meat from the ship's stores. One caught a whiff of something unpleasant if one stood close to it. If opened and passed around, the stench would be overwhelming.

———

Adams stood on the wharf and looked out over the Woolwich dockyard stretching half a mile along the south bank of the Thames. *Enterprise* and *Investigator* stood like workhorses in the docks. He heard the faint clang of metal against metal from the smith's shop. Teams of men with crates and sacks on their shoulders trudged to the wharf from the timber shed and storehouses. A succession of lighters brought barrels and crates down the fat ribbon of the river from Deptford. The air was heavy with the smell of rope and tar.

He looked out over the slipways, dry docks, and mast pond to the clockhouse tower. At the western end of the yard, a redbrick chimney rose 180 feet into the air above the steam engine factory. Shouts rang across the wharf and from the masts above. A handful of men clambered over *Enterprise*'s spars, replacing the rigging. Others hung from the gunwale in harnesses, sanding, painting, and caulking the hull.

"They are going out again, Edward!"

John Barnard rushed up to Adams, almost colliding with him as his boots slipped on the timbers. "*Enterprise* and *Investigator*—the Admiralty is sending them around to Behrings Strait to go in from the west!"

Adams smiled. "Yes, John, I know."

Barnard placed a hand on his shoulder.

"Captain Ross has declared Franklin could only have gone west from Melville Island or north through Wellington Channel. Lady Jane and Fleet Street will not let the matter rest."

Adams and Barnard looked out at the two ships in the dock. They watched a group of men disappear into the ships' hatchways with casks and crates on their shoulders.

"Remarkable," Barnard said. "Only three weeks since our return, but wipe them down and copper their hulls, replace a few spars and a bit of oakum, and they are almost ready again. Did you get a letter?"

Adams withdrew an envelope from his inside pocket and held it up. "I did."

"Which ship, Edward?" Barnard asked urgently. "I am to be second lieutenant on *Enterprise*."

Adams smiled at him. Barnard's neatly trimmed whiskers were incongruous against a face roughened by the Arctic air.

"They have also asked me to serve aboard *Enterprise*."

"Then we shall be together again! We are to go around via Valparaiso and the Sandwich Islands. I wonder who will be in command. They say

Captain Ross will not go; he is too old. We shall find them this time. They must be stuck in the west, poor fellows."

"We might do well to temper our expectations, John." Adams hunched his shoulders against the breeze rising off the river. "This is their fifth winter. We lost eight men in just one."

Barnard was solemn. "Indeed, Edward. But I am seized by the sense of a task unfinished."

"As am I." Adams nodded. "We must fetch them home."

"Then will you go?"

He gripped Barnard's hand. "I will go."

"Splendid! Come now, and dine with me."

"I hope you will excuse me," Adams said. "I may have eaten something that disagreed with me. Perhaps I will feel better soon."

"Of course." Barnard clapped his left hand on Adams' shoulder. "God bless you, Edward."

Adams smiled. "I can only hope He will."

After Barnard left him, Adams watched the work continue at the dock until the sun descended and the shadows lengthened on the river. A bell tolled. The men in the rigging and dangling from ropes along the hull took their tools and disappeared toward the taverns and brothels. Silence fell upon the wharf. Lamps flared on the barges in the river. The silhouette of the two ships' masts grew fainter as the sky darkened.

Stars glimmered in the dusky sky. He realised now how much he had missed them during the long Arctic summer. Invisible through months of relentless sunlight, they remained hidden behind a sky of blue or grey or primrose, but never black. *Curious that some things are revealed only in darkness,* he thought. Leaving for Fury Beach under the midnight sun, he had believed his path was clear. It occurred to him now that the ceaseless glare had obscured the truth that Franklin's fate had never been his to know. Robinson had seen it, accusing him of hubris, of demanding a bargain with the Almighty for which he, Adams, could set his own terms. Only when the hours of darkness lengthened and men began to die did it dawn on him that his journey had a wholly different objective. Robinson had told him his faith was a strength. He now suspected it sustained and blinded him in equal measure.

The white moon rippled in the glassy black surface of the river. The lights of the city to the west blurred in the fog drifting on the water. He decided he would no longer presume to know his fate. The need to atone for his father's sin had left him. The Passage, too, had lost its allure. Frances had been right. No navigable route existed through the ice. This was more hubris, of which both he and the Admiralty were guilty, a shared hysteria. That much he would admit to her when she arrived on the train from Ipswich with her father.

He felt not cheated of a prize but chastened, redirected to a path from which he had strayed. A lightness of spirit came upon him, a clarity of purpose. By serving man he would serve God, and this time he would ask for nothing for himself. When *Enterprise* reached Wollaston Land, he would volunteer to lead a sledge team east to King William Land. He would bring home as many as he could. He thought of Robinson in his grave on a lonely beach far away. Of Billings and Handford laid to rest beneath the stones. *Captain Ross was right,* he thought. *Our friends are never lost. They are always somewhere.*

The breeze died away, and he wrinkled his nose at the smell of human waste rising from the river. Below him, a dim figure in a lighter pulled on his oar in the darkness. Sure of his direction, the man required no lamp.

Ross had said he and Adams were to be conspirators. Untroubled and guiltless at the lies of omission that would entail, Adams felt no anguish at such a pact. The notion of truth required such malleability. Robinson would have had him conceal Fitzjames' fate and the discovery of the survivors on King William Land to protect his own reputation, but he and Ross would do it for theirs. What was it Fitzjames had said? Knead your tale into something appetising. Thus, heroes are born of men.

AUTHOR'S NOTE

Bitter Passage is a work of fiction. It features characters who share the names of historical figures but who have been fictionalised for the purpose of storytelling. While inspired by real individuals, the portrayal of these characters in this work is entirely a product of my imagination. I acknowledge the use of creative liberties in the development of these characters and their actions within the narrative.

Theories about the fate of Franklin and his men abound, and there is little about the mystery that is completely undisputed. This much, however, is true: after *Erebus* and *Terror* were last seen in Baffin Bay in 1845, no information about their ultimate fate was discovered for nine years. For much of this period, it was hoped in England that at least some of Franklin's men might be found alive. Captain Sir James Clark Ross in *Enterprise* and Captain Edward Bird in *Investigator* spent one winter of 1848–49 at Port Leopold and dispatched several sledge teams to search for Franklin in the early summer of 1849. Second Lieutenant Frederick Robinson led one sledge team south from Port Leopold to Fury Beach, but he returned having found no trace of Franklin. In his brief report to the Admiralty upon his return, Captain Ross wrote only that Robinson "extended his examination of the coast for several miles to the southward of Fury Beach."

Here is the point at which *Bitter Passage* takes a turn to the fictional. Assistant Surgeon Edward Adams did indeed serve aboard *Investigator*, although my depiction of him as a member of Robinson's sledge team is fictional, as is the pair's journey south from Fury Beach and their experiences thereafter.

Back once more to the facts: Edward Adams and Lieutenant John Barnard joined the crew of *Enterprise* under Captain Richard Collinson, who searched unsuccessfully for Franklin from Bering Strait between 1850 and 1855.

In 1851, searchers from Captain Horatio Austin's four-vessel expedition discovered three graves and assorted debris on Beechey Island, where Franklin and his men appeared to have spent their first winter (1845–46). No written record was discovered to reveal the direction in which Franklin sailed thereafter.

In 1854—nine years after *Erebus* and *Terror* vanished—Dr John Rae, an Orcadian explorer and frontiersman, was in the process of charting the last unexplored portion of the west coast of Boothia when he encountered an Inuit man wearing a gold cap-band near Pelly Bay. The man told Rae that "a party of "Kabloonans" had died of starvation, a long distance to the west of where we then were, and beyond a large River;—He stated that, he did not know the exact place; that he had never been there; and that he could not accompany us so far."[1]

Subsequent interviews by Rae with other Inuit at Repulse Bay revealed that four winters earlier (ostensibly in 1850, although the exact year was unclear), some Inuit families had met a group of perhaps forty white men dragging a boat southward on King William Island. They also told Rae they had discovered about thirty bodies on the mainland south of King William Island, and five more on an island even farther south, possibly Montreal Island in Chantrey Inlet. "From the mutilated state of many of the bodies," Rae wrote, "and the contents of the kettles, it is evident that our wretched countrymen had been driven to the last dread alternative as a means of sustaining life."[2]

---

1   John Rae, *John Rae's Arctic Correspondence, 1844–1855* (Victoria, BC: TouchWood Editions, Classics West Collection, 2014), 341. Kindle.

2   Ibid., 342.

The response in England to the conclusions of Rae's report was one of outrage and disbelief, due less to doubt over Rae's claims than to his temerity to have gone public with them. None other than Charles Dickens—acting at the behest of Franklin's widow, Lady Jane—dismissed the notion that "Franklin's gallant band" could be capable of cannibalism and referred to the Esquimaux as "loose and unreliable savages" whose word should not be believed.

In 1859, Captain Leopold McClintock was hired by Lady Jane Franklin to lead a search mission to King William Island, where his second in command, Lieutenant William Hobson, discovered the abandoned campsites at Cape Felix and Victory Point. At the latter he retrieved the note left by Crozier and Fitzjames in April 1848, after they'd abandoned *Erebus* and *Terror*.

Bones believed to be those of Franklin's men have been discovered in many locations on the western and southern shores of King William Island. Of the 129 men of the Franklin expedition, only the remains of the three men buried at Beechey Island have been conclusively identified, although speculation lingers over the identity of at least three other sets of remains found on King William Island.

In 2014, a search mission led by Parks Canada located the sunken wreck of HMS *Erebus* in Queen Maud Gulf. It is possible the vessel drifted south from the western coast of King William Island, but it may have been sailed to that location; Inuit oral history tells of a handful of survivors who came ashore on Adelaide Peninsula.

The sunken wreck of HMS *Terror* was discovered in Terror Bay, off the southwestern coast of King William Island, in 2016.

Several geographical points significant to Royal Navy explorers on discovery service before 1850 are no longer featured on many of today's maps. Such locations featured in this story include Possession Bay (on what is now known as Bylot Island), Port Leopold, Cape Walker, and Cape Adelaide (on Boothia Peninsula).

The names of certain other places have changed over the past century and a half. What the Royal Navy knew as North Somerset in 1848 became known as Somerset Island after the discovery in 1852 of the waterway—Bellot Strait—which separates it from Boothia Peninsula (previously known as Boothia Felix) to the south.

The waterway down which *Erebus* and *Terror* are thought to have sailed in 1846 (that is, immediately west of North Somerset) is today known as Peel Sound. However, in 1848, no Royal Navy explorer had named it and lived to tell the tale, so it remains unnamed in this story.

King William Island is referred to as King William Land, as it was not determined by Europeans to be an island until 1854. Royal Navy officers of the era generally used the term *North-West Passage* or *North-west Passage* rather than the *Northwest Passage* that is typically used today.

Port Leopold is the small harbour at the northeastern tip of North Somerset where HMS *Investigator* and HMS *Enterprise* spent the winter of 1848–49. It is located approximately eight miles south of Prince Leopold Island, which was named by William Parry (as "Prince Leopold's Isles") on his way westward to Melville Island in 1819. Although the Hudson Bay Company erected a short-lived trading post at Port Leopold in the 1920s, the harbour has not featured a permanent human settlement in modern times and usually does not appear on today's maps.

What is today known as the Bering Strait was referred to by Royal Navy personnel of the day as either "Behring's Straits" or "Behrings Strait." I have chosen to use the latter, although several variations were used in the mid-nineteenth century.

This work of historical fiction features certain words, terms, and attitudes which, based on my own research, are provided for historical context and seek to accurately reflect the cultural and social conditions of the period as I understand them. It is important to note, however, that some such phrases and descriptions may be considered offensive or insensitive by modern standards. The use of such terms is not intended to disrespect or offend any individual or group of people, does not necessarily reflect my own attitudes, and may be inappropriate in a contemporary story.

FURTHER READING

Those interested in knowing more about the Franklin Expedition and the quest for the Northwest Passage may wish to begin with the following texts:

- Beattie, O., and J. Geiger. *Frozen in Time: The Fate of the Franklin Expedition.* London: Bloomsbury, 2004.
- Berton, P. *The Arctic Grail: The Quest for the North West Passage and the North Pole, 1818–1909.* Guilford, CT: Lyons Press, 2000.
- Fleming, F. *Barrow's Boys.* New York: Grove Press, 1998.
- M'Clintock, F. L. *The Voyage of the "Fox" in the Arctic Seas; A Narrative of the Discovery of the Fate of Sir John Franklin and His Companions.* London: J. Murray, 1860.
- Potter, R. A. *Finding Franklin: The Untold Story of a 165-Year Search.* Montreal: McGill-Queen's University Press, 2016.
- Woodman, D. C. *Unravelling the Franklin Mystery: Inuit Testimony.* Montreal: McGill-Queen's University Press, 1991.

A complete list of the sources consulted in my research for *Bitter Passage* can be viewed on my website, www.colinmills.com.au. Any inaccuracies or misrepresentations of historical detail are entirely my responsibility.

ACKNOWLEDGMENTS

I am forever grateful to Dr Stuart Glover for helping me get started, and to Dr Patrick Holland for his insightful comments and suggestions on the manuscript. I would also like to thank Robert Mills, John Hunter, and Kali Napier for their helpful comments on early drafts. I am indebted to my agent, Alec Shane of Writers House, for his boundless enthusiasm and support, and to Chantelle Aimée Osman, Jason Kirk, and the team at Lake Union Publishing for their invaluable editorial assistance.

Finally, to Annelie: thank you for sticking with me through the development of the manuscript and all that followed, and for never losing faith. To my daughters, Sky and Ainsley, thank you for never wavering in your belief in your dad. It matters more than I can say.

ABOUT THE AUTHOR

Photo © 2023 Annelie Tria-Mills

Colin Mills graduated from the University of Queensland in 1987 with a BA in arts, majoring in Japanese language and literature. He spent most of the next eighteen years in Japan, where, after a brief career as a wire service reporter, he spent ten years in investment banking in Tokyo and a further decade in the portfolio management industry. He left the financial services industry in 2008 and is currently pursuing a PhD in creative writing at the Queensland University of Technology. Colin lives in Brisbane with his wife and two daughters. For more information, visit www.colinmills.com.au.